Praise for the Patrick Melrose novels

'From the very first lines I was completely hooked . . . By turns witty, moving and an intense social comedy, I wept at the end but wouldn't dream of giving away the totally unexpected reason'
Antonia Fraser, *Sunday Telegraph*

'St Aubyn conveys the chaos of emotion, the confusion of heightened sensation, and the daunting contradictions of intellectual endeavour with a force and subtlety that have an exhilarating, almost therapeutic effect'
Francis Wyndham, *New York Review of Books*

'Wonderful caustic wit . . . Perhaps the very sprightliness of the prose – its lapidary concision and moral certitude – represents the cure for which the characters yearn. So much good writing is in itself a form of health'
Edmund White, *Guardian*

'Vicious and hilarious, with a steely integrity. St Aubyn is unbelievably good at describing the way one talks in the privacy of one's own head'
Mark Haddon, *The Times*

'The act of investigative self-repair has all along been the underlying project of these extraordinary novels. It is the source of their urgent emotional intensity, and the determining principle of their construction . . . A terrifying, spectacularly entertaining saga'
James Lasdun, *Guardian*

'Humour, pathos, razor-sharp judgement, pain, joy and everything in between. The Melrose novels are a masterwork for the twenty-first century'
Alice Sebold

'A humane meditation on lives blighted by the sins of the previous generation. St Aubyn remains among the cream of British novelists'
[illegible] *Times*

'The Patrick Melrose novels can be read as the navigational charts of a mariner desperate not to end up in the wretched harbor from which he embarked on a voyage that has led in and out of heroin addiction, alcoholism, marital infidelity and a range of behaviors for which the term "self-destructive" is the mildest of euphemisms. Some of the most perceptive, elegantly written and hilarious novels of our era . . . Remarkable'

Francine Prose, *New York Times*

'The main joy of a St Aubyn novel is the exquisite clarity of his prose, the almost uncanny sense he gives that, in language as in mathematical formulae, precision and beauty invariably point to truth . . . Characters in St Aubyn novels are hyper-articulate, and the witty dialogue is here, as ever, one of the chief joys'

Suzi Feay, *Financial Times*

'The Melrose sequence is now clearly one of the major achievements of contemporary British fiction' *Evening Standard*

'The darkest possible comedy about the cruelty of the old to the young, vicious and excruciatingly honest. It opened my eyes to a whole realm of experience I have never seen written about. That's the mark of a masterpiece' *The Times*

'Edward St Aubyn, like Proust, has created a world in which no one in their right mind would like to live but which feels real and vivid and hilariously and dangerously vacuous. Who better than he to turn to if your faith in the future of literary fiction is wavering' Alan Taylor, *Herald*

'The bravura quality of St Aubyn's performance is irresistible. Brilliant' *Sunday Telegraph*

'St Aubyn's Melrose novels now deserve to be thought of as an important roman-fleuve'
Henry Hitchings, *Times Literary Supplement*

'St Aubyn's Melrose series slices and dices morality with prose so chiselled and a narrative so intense that the hairs on the back of your neck stand up' Geordie Greig, *Evening Standard*

'Blackly comic, superbly written fiction . . . His style is crisp and light; his similes exhilarating in their accuracy . . . St Aubyn writes with luminous tenderness of Patrick's love for his sons'
Caroline Moore, *Sunday Telegraph*

'His prose has an easy charm that masks a ferocious, searching intellect. As a sketcher of character, his wit – whether turned against pointless members of the aristocracy or hopeless crack dealers – is ticklingly wicked. As an analyser of broken minds and tired hearts he is as energetic, careful and creative as the perfect shrink. And when it comes to spinning a good yarn, whether over the grand scale or within a single page of anecdote, he has a natural talent for keeping you on the edge of your seat' Melissa Katsoulis, *The Times*

'A masterpiece. Edward St Aubyn is a writer of immense gifts'
Patrick McGrath

'Irony courses through these pages like adrenaline . . . Patrick's intelligence processes his predicaments into elegant, lucid, dispassionate, near-aphoristic formulations . . . Brimming with witty flair, sardonic perceptiveness and literary finesse'
Peter Kemp, *Sunday Times*

PATRICK MELROSE VOLUME 2

EDWARD ST AUBYN was born in London in 1960. His superbly acclaimed Melrose novels are *Never Mind*, *Bad News*, *Some Hope*, *Mother's Milk* (shortlisted for the Man Booker Prize 2006) and *At Last*. He is also the author of the novels *A Clue to the Exit*, *On the Edge*, *Lost for Words* and *Dunbar*.

Also in this series

PATRICK MELROSE VOLUME 1

Never Mind, Bad News, Some Hope

Also by Edward St Aubyn in Picador

ON THE EDGE

A CLUE TO THE EXIT

LOST FOR WORDS

EDWARD ST AUBYN

PATRICK MELROSE
VOLUME 2

MOTHER'S MILK AT LAST

PICADOR

First published 2018 by Picador
an imprint of Pan Macmillan
20 New Wharf Road, London N1 9RR
Associated companies throughout the world
www.panmacmillan.com

ISBN 978-1-5098-9770-4

Mother's Milk first published by Picador 2006. First published in paperback 2006 by Picador.
At Last first published by Picador 2011. First published in paperback 2012 by Picador.

1 3 5 7 9 8 6 4 2

A CIP catalogue record for this book is available from the British Library.

Typeset by Ellipsis Digital Limited, Glasgow
Printed and bound by CPI Group (UK) Ltd, Croydon, CR0 4YY

Contents

MOTHER'S MILK

For Lucian

AUGUST 2000

1

Why had they pretended to kill him when he was born? Keeping him awake for days, banging his head again and again against a closed cervix; twisting the cord around his throat and throttling him; chomping through his mother's abdomen with cold shears; clamping his head and wrenching his neck from side to side; dragging him out of his home and hitting him; shining lights in his eyes and doing experiments; taking him away from his mother while she lay on the table, half-dead. Maybe the idea was to destroy his nostalgia for the old world. First the confinement to make him hungry for space, then pretending to kill him so that he would be grateful for the space when he got it, even this loud desert, with only the bandages of his mother's arms to wrap around him, never the whole thing again, the whole warm thing all around him, being everything.

The curtains were breathing light into their hospital room. Swelling from the hot afternoon, and then flopping back against the French windows, easing the glare outside.

Someone opened the door and the curtains leapt up and rippled their edges; loose paper rustled, the room whitened, and the shudder of the roadworks grew a little louder. Then the door clunked and the curtains sighed and the room dimmed.

'Oh, no, not more flowers,' said his mother.

He could see everything through the transparent walls of

his fish-tank cot. He was looked over by the sticky eye of a splayed lily. Sometimes the breeze blew the peppery smell of freesias over him and he wanted to sneeze it away. On his mother's nightgown spots of blood mingled with streaks of dark orange pollen.

'It's so nice of people . . .' She was laughing from weakness and frustration. 'I mean, is there any room in the bath?'

'Not really, you've got the roses in there already and the other things.'

'Oh, God, I can't bear it. Hundreds of flowers have been cut down and squeezed into these white vases, just to make us happy.' She couldn't stop laughing. There were tears running down her face. 'They should have been left where they were, in a garden somewhere.'

The nurse looked at the chart.

'It's time for you to take your Voltarol,' she said. 'You've got to control the pain before it takes over.'

Then the nurse looked at Robert and he locked on to her blue eyes in the heaving dimness.

'He's very alert. He's really checking me out.'

'He is going to be all right, isn't he?' said his mother, suddenly terrified.

Suddenly Robert was terrified too. They were not together in the way they used to be, but they still had their helplessness in common. They had been washed up on a wild shore. Too tired to crawl up the beach, they could only loll in the roar and the dazzle of being there. He had to face facts, though: they had been separated. He understood now that his mother had already been on the outside. For her this wild shore was a new role, for him it was a new world.

The strange thing was that he felt as if he had been there before. He had known there was an outside all along. He used to think it was a muffled watery world out there and that he lived at the heart of things. Now the walls had tumbled down and he could see what a muddle he had been in. How could he avoid getting in a new muddle in this hammeringly bright place? How could he kick and spin like he used to in this heavy atmosphere where the air stung his skin?

Yesterday he had thought he was dying. Perhaps he was right and this was what happened. Everything was open to question, except the fact that he was separated from his mother. Now that he realized there was a difference between them, he loved his mother with a new sharpness. He used to be close to her. Now he longed to be close to her. The first taste of longing was the saddest thing in the world.

'Oh, dear, what's wrong?' said the nurse. 'Are we hungry, or do we just want a cuddle?'

The nurse lifted him out of the fish-tank cot, over the crevasse that separated it from the bed and delivered him into his mother's bruised arms.

'Try giving him a little time on the breast and then try to get some rest. You've both been through a lot in the last couple of days.'

He was an inconsolable wreck. He couldn't live with so much doubt and so much intensity. He vomited colostrum over his mother and then in the hazy moment of emptiness that followed, he caught sight of the curtains bulging with light. They held his attention. That's how it worked here. They fascinated you with things to make you forget about the separation.

Still, he didn't want to exaggerate his decline. Things had been getting cramped in the old world. Towards the end he was desperate to get out, but he had imagined himself expanding back into the boundless ocean of his youth, not exiled in this harsh land. Perhaps he could revisit the ocean in his dreams, if it weren't for the veil of violence that hung between him and the past.

He was drifting into the syrupy borders of sleep, not knowing whether it would take him into the floating world or back to the butchery of the birth room.

'Poor Baba, he was probably having a bad dream,' said his mother, stroking him. His crying started to break up and fade.

She kissed him on the forehead and he realized that although they didn't share a body any more, they still had the same thoughts and the same feelings. He shuddered with relief and stared at the curtains, watching the light flow.

He must have been asleep for a while, because his father had arrived and was already locked on to something. He couldn't stop talking.

'I looked at some more flats today and I can tell you, it's really depressing. London property is completely out of control. I'm leaning back towards plan C.'

'What's plan C? I've forgotten.'

'Stay where we are and squeeze another bedroom out of the kitchen. If we divide it in half, the broom cupboard becomes his toy cupboard and the bed goes where the fridge is.'

'Where do the brooms go?'

'I don't know – somewhere.'

'And the fridge?'

'It could go in the cupboard next to the washing machine.'

'It won't fit.'

'How do you know?'

'I just know.'

'Anyway . . . we'll work it out. I'm just trying to be practical. Everything changes when you have a baby.'

His father leant closer, whispering, 'There's always Scotland.'

He had come to be practical. He knew that his wife and son were drowning in a puddle of confusion and sensitivity and he was going to save them. Robert could feel what he was feeling.

'God, his hands are so tiny,' said his father. 'Just as well, really.'

He raised Robert's hand with his little finger and kissed it. 'Can I hold him?'

She lifted him towards his father. 'Watch out for his neck, it's very floppy. You have to support it.'

They all felt nervous.

'Like this?' His father's hand edged up his spine, took over from his mother, and slipped under Robert's head. Robert tried to keep calm. He didn't want his parents to get upset.

'Sort of. I don't really know either.'

'Ahh . . . how come we're allowed to do this without a licence? You can't have a dog or a television without a licence. Maybe we can learn from the maternity nurse – what's her name?'

'Margaret.'

'By the way, where is Margaret going to sleep on the night before we go to my mother's?'

'She says she's perfectly happy on the sofa.'

'I wonder if the sofa feels the same way.'

'Don't be mean, she's on a "chemical diet".'

'How exciting. I hadn't seen her in that light.'

'She's had a lot of experience.'

'Haven't we all?'

'With babies.'

'Oh, babies.' His father scraped Robert's cheek with his stubble and made a kissing sound in his ear.

'But we adore him,' said his mother, her eyes swimming with tears. 'Isn't that enough?'

'Being adored by two trainee parents with inadequate housing? Thank goodness he's got the backup of one grandmother who's on permanent holiday, and another who's too busy saving the planet to be entirely pleased by this additional strain on its resources. My mother's house is already too full of shamanic rattles and "power animals" and "inner children" to accommodate anything as grown-up as a child.'

'We'll be all right,' said his mother. 'We're not children any more, we're parents.'

'We're both,' said his father, 'that's the trouble. Do you know what my mother told me the other day? A child born in a developed nation will consume two hundred and forty times the resources consumed by a child born in Bangladesh. If we'd had the self-restraint to have two hundred and thirty-nine Bangladeshi children, she would have given us a warmer welcome, but this gargantuan Westerner, who is going to take up acres of landfill with his disposable nappies, and will soon be clamouring for a personal computer powerful enough to launch a Mars flight while playing tic-tac-toe with a virtual buddy in Dubrovnik, is not likely to win her approval.' His father paused. 'Are you all right?' he asked.

'I've never been happier,' said his mother, wiping her glistening cheeks with the back of her hand. 'I just feel so empty.'

She guided the baby's head towards her nipple and he started to suck. A thin stream from his old home flooded his mouth and they were together again. He could sense her heartbeat. Peace shrouded them like a new womb. Perhaps this was a good place to be after all, just difficult to get into.

That was about all that Robert could remember from the first few days of his life. The memories had come back to him last month when his brother was born. He couldn't be sure that some of the things hadn't been said last month, but even if they had been, they reminded him of when he was in hospital; so the memories really belonged to him.

Robert was obsessed with his past. He was five years old now. Five years old, not a baby like Thomas. He could feel his infancy disintegrating, and among the bellows of congratulation that accompanied each little step towards full citizenship he heard the whisper of loss. Something had started to happen as he became dominated by talk. His early memories were breaking off, like slabs from those orange cliffs behind him, and crashing into an all-consuming sea which only glared back at him when he tried to look into it. His infancy was being obliterated by his childhood. He wanted it back, otherwise Thomas would have the whole thing.

Robert had left his parents, his little brother and Margaret behind, and he was wobbling his way across the rocks towards the clattering stones of the lower beach, holding in one of his outstretched hands a scuffed plastic bucket decorated with vaulting dolphins. Brilliant pebbles, fading as he ran back to show them off, no longer tricked him. What he was looking for now were those jelly beans of blunted glass buried under the fine rush of black and gold gravel on the shore. Even when they were dry they had a bruised glow. His father told him that glass was made of sand, so they were halfway back to where they came from.

Robert had arrived at the shoreline now. He left his bucket on a high rock and started the hunt for wave-licked glass. The water foamed around his ankles and as it rushed down the beach he scanned the bubbling sand. To his astonishment he could see something under the first wave, not one of the pale green or cloudy white beads, but a rare yellow gem. He pulled it out of the sand, washed the grit from it with the next wave and held it up to the light, a little amber kidney between his finger and thumb. He looked up the beach to share his excitement, but his parents were huddled around the baby, while Margaret rummaged in a bag.

He could remember Margaret very well now that she was back. She had looked after him when he was a baby. It was different then because he had been his mother's only child. Margaret liked to say that she was a 'general chatterbox' but in fact her only subject was herself. His father said that she was an expert on 'the theory of dieting'. He was not sure what that was but it seemed to have made her very fat. To save money his parents weren't going to have a maternity nurse this time but they had changed their minds just before coming to France. They almost changed them back when the agency said that Margaret was the only one available at such short notice. 'I suppose she'll be an extra pair of hands,' his mother had said. 'If only they didn't come with the extra mouth,' said his father.

Robert had first met Margaret when he came back from the hospital after being born. He woke up in his parents' kitchen, jiggling up and down in her arms.

'I've changed His Majesty's nappy so he'll have a nice dry botty,' she said.

'Oh,' said his mother, 'thank you.'

He immediately felt that Margaret was different from his mother. Words drained out of her like an unplugged bath. His mother didn't really like talking but when she did talk it was like being held.

'Does he like his little cot?' said Margaret.

'I don't really know, he was with us in the bed last night.'

A quiet growl came out of Margaret. 'Hmmm,' she said, 'bad habits.'

'He wouldn't settle in his cot.'

'They never will if you take them into the bed.'

'"Never" is a long time. He was inside me until Wednesday evening; my instinct is to have him next to me for a while – do things gradually.'

'Well, I don't like to question your instincts, dear,' said Margaret, spitting the word out the moment it formed in her mouth, 'but in my forty years of *experience* I've had mothers thank me again and again for putting the baby down and leaving it in the cot. I had one mother, she's an Arab lady, actually, nice enough, rang me only the other day in Botley and said, "I wish I'd listened to you, Margaret, and not taken Yasmin into the bed with me. I can't do anything with her now." She wanted me back, but I said, "I'm sorry, dear, but I'm starting a new job next week, and I shall be going to the south of France for July to stay with the baby's grandmother."'

Margaret tossed her head and strutted about the kitchen, a downpour of crumbs tickling Robert's face. His mother said nothing, but Margaret rumbled on.

'I don't think it's fair on the baby, apart from anything else – they like to have their own little cot. Of course, I'm used to having sole charge. It's usually *me* has them during the night.'

His father came into the room and kissed Robert on the forehead.

'Good morning, Margaret,' he said. 'I hope you got some sleep, because none of the rest of us did.'

'Yes, thank you, your sofa's quite comfortable, actually; not that I shall be complaining when I have a room of my own at your mother's.'

'I should hope not,' said his father. 'Are you all packed and ready to go? Our taxi is coming any minute now.'

'Well, I haven't exactly had time to *un*pack, have I? Except for my sun hat. I got that out in case it's blazing at the other end.'

'It's always blazing at the other end. My mother wouldn't stand for anything less than catastrophic global warming.'

'Hmmm, we could do with a bit of global warming in Botley.'

'I wouldn't make that sort of remark if you want a good room at the Foundation.'

'What's that, dear?'

'Oh, my mother's made a "Transpersonal Foundation".'

'Is the house not going to be yours, then?'

'No.'

'Do you hear that?' said Margaret, her waxen pallor looming over Robert and spraying shortbread in his face with renewed vigour.

Robert could sense his father's irritation.

'He's far too cool to be worried about all that,' said his mother.

Everyone started to move about at the same time. Margaret, wearing her sun hat, took the lead, Robert's parents struggling behind with the luggage. They were taking him outside, where the light came from. He was amazed. The world was a birth room screaming with ambitious life. Branches climbing, leaves flickering, cumulonimbus mountains drifting, their melting edges curling in the light-flooded sky. He could feel his mother's thoughts, he could feel his father's thoughts, he could feel Margaret's thoughts.

'He loves the clouds,' said his mother.

'He can't see the clouds, dear,' said Margaret. 'They can't focus at his age.'

'He might still be looking at them without seeing them as we do,' said his father.

Margaret grunted as she got into the humming taxi.

He was lying still in his mother's lap, but the land and sky were slipping by outside the window. If he got involved in the moving scene he thought he was moving too. Light flashed on the windowpanes of passing houses, vibrations washed over him from all directions, and then the canyon of buildings broke open and a wedge of sunlight drifted across his face, turning his eyelids orange-pink.

They were on their way to his grandmother's house, the same house they were staying in now, a week after his brother's birth.

2

Robert was sitting in the window sill of his bedroom, playing with the beads he had collected on the beach. He had been arranging them in every possible combination. Beyond his mosquito net (with its bandaged cut) was a mass of ripe leaves belonging to the big plane tree on the terrace. When the wind moved through the leaves it made a sound like lips smacking. If a fire broke out, he could climb out of the window and down those convenient branches. On the other hand, a kidnapper could climb up them. He never used to think about the other hand; now he thought about it all the time. His mother had told him that when he was a baby he loved lying under that plane tree in his cot. Thomas was lying there now, bracketed by his parents.

Margaret was leaving the next day – thank God, as his father said. His parents had given her an extra day off, but she was already back from the village, bearing down on them with a deadly bulletin. Robert waddled across the room pretending to be Margaret and circled back to the window. Everyone said he did amazing imitations; his headmaster went further and said that it was a 'thoroughly sinister talent which I hope he will learn to channel constructively.' It was true that once he was intrigued by a situation, as he was by Margaret being back with his family, he could absorb everything he wanted. He pressed against the mosquito net to get a better view.

'Ooh, it's that hot,' said Margaret, fanning herself with a knitting magazine. 'I couldn't find any of the cottage cheese in Bandol. They didn't speak a word of English in the supermarket. "Cottage cheese," I said, pointing to the house on the other side of the street, "cottage, you know, as in house, only smaller," but they still couldn't make head or tail of what I was saying.'

'They sound incredibly stupid,' said his father, 'with so many helpful clues.'

'Hmmm. I had to get some of the French cheeses in the end,' said Margaret, sitting down on the low wall with a sigh. 'How's the baby?'

'He seems very tired,' said his mother.

'I'm not surprised in this heat,' said Margaret. 'I think I must have got sunstroke on that boat, frankly. I'm done to a crisp. Give him plenty of water, dear. It's the only way to cool them down. They can't sweat at that age.'

'Another amazing oversight,' said his father. 'Can't sweat, can't walk, can't talk, can't read, can't drive, can't sign a cheque. Foals are standing a few hours after they're born. If horses went in for banking, they'd have a credit line by the end of the week.'

'Horses don't have any use for banking,' said Margaret.

'No,' said his father, exhausted.

In a moment of ecstatic song the cicadas drowned out Margaret's voice, and Robert felt he could remember exactly what it was like being in that cot, lying under the plane trees in a cool green shade, listening to the wall of cicada song collapse to a solitary call and escalate again to a dry frenzy. He let things rest where they fell, the sounds, the sights, the impressions. Things resolved themselves in that cool green shade, not because he knew how they worked, but because he knew his own thoughts and feelings without needing to explain them. And if he wanted to play with his thoughts, nobody could stop him. Just lying there in his cot, they couldn't tell whether he was doing anything dangerous. Sometimes he imagined he was the thing he was looking at, sometimes he imagined he was in the space in between, but the best was when he was just looking, without being anyone in particular or looking at anything in particular, and then he floated in the looking, like the breeze blowing without needing cheeks to blow or having anywhere particular to go.

His brother was probably floating right now in Robert's old cot. The grown-ups didn't know what to make of floating. That was the trouble with grown-ups: they always wanted to be the centre of attention, with their battering rams of food, and their sleep routines and their obsession with making you learn what they knew and forget what they had forgotten. Robert dreaded sleep. He might miss something: a beach of yellow beads, or grasshopper wings like sparks flying from his feet as he crunched through the dry grass.

He loved it down here at his grandmother's house. His family only came once a year, but they had been every year since he was born. Her house was a Transpersonal Foundation. He didn't really know what that was, and nobody else seemed to know either, even Seamus Dourke, who ran it.

'Your grandmother is a wonderful woman,' he had told Robert, looking at him with his dim twinkly eyes. 'She's helped a lot of people to connect.'

'With what?' asked Robert.

'With the other reality.'

Sometimes he didn't ask grown-ups what they meant because he thought it would make him seem stupid; sometimes it was because he knew they were being stupid. This time it was both. He thought about what Seamus had said and he didn't see how there could be more than one reality. There could only be different states of mind with reality housing all of them. That's what he had told his mother, and she said, 'You're so brilliant, darling,' but she wasn't really paying attention to his theories like she used to. She was always too busy now. What they didn't understand was that he really wanted to know the answer.

Back under the plane tree, his brother had started screaming. Robert wished someone would make him stop. He could feel his brother's infancy exploding like a depth charge in his memory. Thomas's screams reminded Robert of his own helplessness: the ache of his toothless gums, the involuntary twitching of his limbs, the softness of the fontanelle, only a thumb's thrust away from his growing brain. He felt that he could remember objects without names and names without objects pelting down on him all day long, but there was something he could only dimly sense: a world before the wild banality of childhood, before he had to be the first to rush out and spoil the snow, before he had even assembled himself into a viewer gazing at the white landscape through a bedroom window, when his mind had been level with the fields of silent crystal, still waiting for the dent of a fallen berry.

He had seen Thomas's eyes expressing states of mind which he couldn't have invented for himself. They reared up from the scrawny desert of his experience like brief pyramids. Where did they come from? Sometimes he was a snuffling little animal and then, seconds later, he was radiating an ancient calm, at ease with everything. Robert felt that he was definitely not making up these complex states of mind, and neither was Thomas. It was just that Thomas wouldn't know what he knew until he started to tell himself a story about what was happening to him. The trouble was that he was a baby, and he didn't have the attention span to tell himself a story yet. Robert was just going to have to do it for him. What was an older brother for? Robert was already caught in a narrative loop, so he might as well take his little brother along with him. After all, in his way, Thomas was helping Robert to piece his own story together.

Outside, he could hear Margaret again, taking on the cicadas and getting the upper hand.

'With the breast-feeding you've got to build yourself up,' she started out reasonably enough. 'Have you not got any Digestive biscuits? Or Rich Tea? We could have a few of those right away, actually. And then you want to have a nice big lunch, with lots of carbohydrates. Not too many vegetables, they'll give him wind. Nice bit of roast beef and Yorkshire pudding is good, with some roast potatoes, and then a slice or two of sponge cake at tea time.'

'Good God, I don't think I can manage all that. In my book it says grilled fish and grilled vegetables,' said his tired, thin, elegant mother.

'*Some* vegetables are all right,' grumbled Margaret. 'Not onions or garlic, though, or anything too spicy. I had one mother had a curry on my day off! The baby was howling its head off when I got back. "Save me, Margaret! Mummy's set my little digestive system on fire!" Personally, I always say, "I'll have the meat and two veg, but don't worry too much about the veg."'

Robert had stuffed a cushion under his T-shirt and was tottering around the room pretending to be Margaret. Once his head was jammed full of someone's words he had to get them out. He was so involved in his performance that he didn't notice his father coming into the room.

'What are you doing?' asked his father, half knowing already.

'I was just being Margaret.'

'That's all we need – another Margaret. Come down and have some tea.'

'I'm that stuffed already,' said Robert, patting his cushion. 'Daddy, when Margaret leaves, I'll still be here to give Mummy bad advice about how to look after babies. And I won't charge you anything.'

'Things are looking up,' said his father, holding out his hand to pull Robert up. Robert groaned and staggered across the floor and the two of them headed downstairs, sharing their secret joke.

After tea Robert refused to join the others outside. All they did was talk about his brother and speculate about his state of mind. Walking up the stairs, his decision grew heavier with each step, and by the time he reached the landing he was in two minds. Eventually, he sank to the floor and looked down through the banisters, wondering if his parents would notice his sad and wounded departure.

In the hall, angular blocks of evening light slanted across the floor and stretched up the walls. One piece of light, reflected in the mirror, had broken away and trembled on the ceiling. Thomas was trying to comment. His mother, who understood his thoughts, took him over to the mirror and showed him where the light bounced off the glass.

His father came into the hall and handed a bright red drink to Margaret.

'Ooh, thank you very much,' said Margaret. 'I shouldn't really get tipsy on top of my sunstroke. Frankly, this is more of a holiday for me than a job, with you being so involved and that. Oh, look, Baby's admiring himself in the mirror.' She leant the pink shine of her face towards Thomas.

'You can't tell whether you're over here or over there, can you?'

'I think he knows that he's in his body rather than stuck to a piece of glass,' said Robert's father. 'He hasn't read Lacan's essay on the mirror stage yet, that's when the real confusion sets in.'

'Ooh, well, you'd better stick to Peter Rabbit, then,' chuckled Margaret, taking a gulp of the red liquid.

'Much as I'd love to join you outside,' said his father, 'I have a million important letters to answer.'

'Ooh, Daddy's going to be answering his important letters,' said Margaret, breathing the red smell into Thomas's face. 'You'll just have to content yourself with Margaret and Mummy.'

She swung her way towards the front door. The lozenge of light disappeared from the ceiling and then flickered back. Robert's parents stared at each other silently.

As they stepped outside, he imagined his brother feeling the vast space around him.

He stole halfway down the stairs and looked through the doorway. A golden light was claiming the tops of the pines and the bone-white stones of the olive grove. His mother, still barefoot, walked over the grass and sat under their favourite pepper tree. Crossing her legs and raising her knees slightly, she placed his brother in the hammock formed by her skirt, still holding him with one hand and stroking his side with the other. Her face was dappled by the shadow of the small bright leaves that dangled around them.

Robert wandered hesitantly outside, not sure where he belonged. Nobody called him and so he turned round the corner of the house as if he had always meant to go down to the second pond and look at the goldfish. Glancing back, he saw the stick with sparkly wheels that Margaret had bought his brother at the little carousel in Lacoste. The stub of the stick had been planted in the ground near the pepper tree. The wheels spun in the wind, gold and pink and blue and green. 'It's the colour and the movement,' said Margaret when she bought it, 'they love that.' He had snatched it from the corner of his brother's pram and run around the carousel, making the wheels turn. When he was swishing it through the air he somehow broke the stick and everyone got upset on his brother's behalf because he never really got the chance to enjoy his sparkly windmill before it was broken. Robert's father had asked him a lot of questions, or rather the same question in a lot of different ways, as if it would do him good to admit that he had broken it on purpose. Do you think you're jealous? Do you think you're angry that he's getting all the attention and the new toys? Do you? Do you? Do you? Well, he had just said it was an accident and wouldn't budge. And it really was an accident, but it so happened that he did hate his brother, and he wished that he didn't. Couldn't his parents remember what it was like when it was just the three of them? They loved each other so much that it hurt when one of them left the room. What had been wrong with having just him on his own? Wasn't he enough? Wasn't he good enough? They used to sit on the lawn, where his brother was now, and throw each other the red ball (he had hidden it; Thomas wasn't going to get that as well) and whether he caught it or dropped it, they had all laughed and everything was perfect. How could they want to spoil that?

Maybe he was too old. Maybe babies were better. Babies were impressed by pretty well anything. Take the fish pond he was throwing pebbles into. He had seen his mother carrying Thomas to the edge of the pond and pointing to the fish, saying, 'Fish.' It was no use trying that sort of thing with Robert. What he couldn't help wondering was how his brother was supposed to know whether she meant the pond, the water, the weeds, the clouds reflected on the water, or the fish, if he could see them. How did he even know that 'Fish' was a thing rather than a colour or something that you do? Sometimes, come to think of it, it was something to do.

Once you got words you thought the world was everything that could be described, but it was also what couldn't be described. In a way things were more perfect when you couldn't describe anything. Having a brother made Robert wonder what it had been like when he only had his own thoughts to guide him. Once you locked into language, all you could do was shuffle the greasy pack of a few thousand words that millions of people had used before. There might be little moments of freshness, not because the life of the world has been successfully translated but because a new life has been made out of this thought stuff. But before the thoughts got mixed up with words, it wasn't as if the dazzle of the world hadn't been exploding in the sky of his attention.

Suddenly, he heard his mother scream.

'What have you done to him?' she shouted.

He sprinted round the corner of the terrace and met his father running out of the front door. Margaret was lying on the lawn, holding Thomas sprawled on her bosom.

'It's all right, dear, it's all right,' said Margaret. 'Look, he's even stopped crying. I took the fall, you see, on my bottom. It's my training. I think I may have broken my finger, but there's no need to worry about silly old Margaret as long as no harm has come to the baby.'

'That's the first sensible thing I've ever heard you say,' said his mother, who never said anything unkind. She lifted Thomas out of Margaret's arms and kissed his head again and again. She was taut with anger, but as she kissed him tenderness started to drown it out.

'Is he all right?' asked Robert.

'I think so,' said his mother.

'I don't want him to be hurt,' Robert said, and they walked back into the house together, leaving Margaret talking on the ground.

The next morning, they were all hiding from Margaret in his parents' bedroom. Robert's father had to drive Margaret to the airport that afternoon.

'I suppose we ought to go down,' said his mother, closing the poppers of Thomas's jumpsuit, and lifting him into her arms.

'No,' howled his father, throwing himself onto the bed.

'Don't be such a baby.'

'Having a baby makes you more childish, haven't you noticed?'

'I haven't got time to be more childish, that's a privilege reserved for fathers.'

'You would have time if you were getting any competent help.'

'Come on,' said Robert's mother, reaching out to his father with her spare hand.

He clasped it lightly but didn't move.

'I can't decide which is worse,' he said, 'talking to Margaret, or listening to her.'

'Listening to her,' Robert voted. 'That's why I'm going to do my Margaret imitation all the time after she's gone.'

'Thanks a lot,' said his mother. 'Look, even Thomas is smiling at such a mad idea.'

'That's not smiling, dear,' grumbled Robert, 'that's wind tormenting his little insides.'

They all started laughing and then his mother said, 'Shhh, she might hear us,' but it was too late, Robert was determined to entertain them. Swinging his body sideways to lubricate the forward motion, he rocked over to his mother's side.

'It's no use trying to blind me with science, dear,' he said, 'I can tell he doesn't like that formula you're giving him, even if it is made by organic goats. When I was in Saudi Arabia – she was a princess, actually – I said to them, "I can't work with this formula, I have to have the Cow and Gate Gold Standard," and they said to me, "With all your experience, Margaret, we trust you completely," and they had some flown out from England in their private jet.'

'How do you remember all this?' asked his mother. 'It's terrifying. I told her that we didn't have a private jet.'

'Oh, money was no object to them,' Robert went on, with a proud little toss of his head. 'One day I remarked, you know, quite *casually*, on how nice the Princess's slippers were, and the next thing I knew there was a pair waiting for me in my bedroom. The same thing happened with the Prince's camera. It was quite embarrassing, actually. Every time I did it, I'd say to myself, "Margaret, you must learn to keep your mouth shut."'

Robert wagged his finger in the air, and then sat down on the bed next to his father and carried on with a sad sigh.

'But then it would just pop out, you know: "Ooh, that's a lovely shawl, dear; lovely soft fabric," and sure enough I'd find one spread out on my bed that evening. I had to get a new suitcase in the end.'

His parents were trying not to make too much noise but they had hopeless giggles. As long as he was performing they hardly paid any attention to Thomas at all.

'Now it's even harder for us to go down,' said his mother, joining them on the bed.

'It's impossible,' said his father, 'there's a force field around the door.'

Robert ran up to the door and pretended to bounce back. 'Ah,' he shouted, 'it's the Margaret field. There's no way through, Captain.'

He rolled around on the floor for a while and then climbed back onto the bed with his parents.

'We're like the dinner guests in *The Exterminating Angel*,' said his father. 'We might be here for days. We might have to be rescued by the army.'

'We've got to pull ourselves together,' said his mother. 'We must try to end her visit on a kind note.'

None of them moved.

'Why do you think it's so hard for us to leave?' asked his father. 'Do you think we're using Margaret as a scapegoat? We feel guilty that we can't protect Thomas from the basic suffering of life, so we pretend that Margaret is the cause – something like that.'

'Let's not complicate it, darling,' said his mother. 'She's the most boring person we've ever met and she's no good at looking after Thomas. That's why we don't want to see her.'

Silence. Thomas had fallen asleep, and so there was a general agreement to keep quiet. They all settled comfortably on the bed. Robert stretched out and rested his head on his folded hands, scanning the beams of the ceiling. Familiar patterns of stains and knots emerged from the woodwork. At first he could take or leave the profile of the man with the pointed nose and the helmet, but soon the figure refused to be dissolved back into the grain, acquiring wild eyes and hollow cheeks. He knew the ceiling well, because he used to lie underneath it when it was his grandmother's bedroom. His parents had moved in after his grandmother was taken to the nursing home. He still remembered the old silver-framed photograph that used to be on her desk. He had been curious about it because it was taken when his grandmother had been only a few days old. The baby in the picture was smothered in pelts and satin and lace, her head bound in a beaded turban. Her eyes had a fanatical intensity that looked to him like panic at being buried in the immensity of her mother's shopping.

'I keep it here,' his grandmother had told him, 'to remind me of when I had just come into the world and I was closer to the source.'

'What source?' he asked.

'Closer to God,' she said shyly.

'But you don't look very happy,' he said.

'I think I look as if I haven't forgotten yet. But in a way you're right, I don't think I've ever really got used to being on the material plane.'

'What material plane?'

'The Earth,' she said.

'Would you rather live on the moon?' he had asked.

She smiled and stroked his cheek and said, 'You'll understand one day.'

Instead of the photograph, there was a changing mat on the desk now, with a stack of nappies next to it and a bowl of water.

He still loved his grandmother, even if she was not leaving them the house. Her face was a cobweb of creases earned from trying so hard to be good, from worrying about really huge things like the planet, or the universe, or the millions of suffering people she had never met, or God's opinion of what she should do next. He knew his father didn't think she was good, and discounted how badly she wanted to be. He kept telling Robert that they must love his grandmother 'despite everything'. That was how Robert knew that his father didn't love her any more.

'Will he remember that fall for the rest of his life?' Robert asked, staring at the ceiling.

'Of course not,' said his father. 'You can't remember what happened to you when you were a few weeks old.'

'Yes I can,' said Robert.

'We must all reassure him,' said his mother, changing the subject as if she didn't want to point out that Robert was lying. But he wasn't lying.

'He doesn't need reassuring,' said his father. 'He wasn't actually hurt, and so he can't tell that he shouldn't be bouncing off Margaret's floundering body. We're the ones who are freaked out, because we know how dangerous it was.'

'That's why he needs reassuring,' said his mother, 'because he can tell that we're upset.'

'Yes, at that level,' his father agreed, 'but in general babies live in a democracy of strangeness. Things happen for the first time all the time – what's surprising is things happening again.'

Babies are great, thought Robert. You can invent more or less anything about them because they never answer back.

'It's twelve o'clock,' his father sighed.

They all struggled with their reluctance, but the effort to escape seemed to drag them deeper into the quicksand of the mattress. He wanted to delay his parents just a little longer.

'Sometimes,' he began dreamily in his Margaret voice, 'when I'm stopped at home for a couple of weeks between jobs, I get itchy fingers. I'm that keen to lay my hands on another baby.' He grabbed hold of Thomas's feet and made a devouring sound.

'Gently,' said Robert's mother.

'He's right, though,' said his father, 'she's got a baby habit. She needs them more than they need her. Babies are allowed to be unconscious and greedy, so she uses them for camouflage.'

After all the moral effort they had put in to conceding another hour of their lives to Margaret, they felt cheated when they found that she wasn't waiting for them downstairs. His mother went off to the kitchen and he sat with his father on the sofa with Thomas between them. Thomas fell silent and became absorbed in staring at the picture on the wall immediately above the sofa. Robert moved his head down beside Thomas's and as he looked up he could tell from the angle that Thomas couldn't see the picture itself, because of the glass that protected it. He remembered being fascinated by the same thing when he was a baby. As he looked at the image reflected in the glass, it drew him deeper into the space behind him. In the reflection was the doorway, a brilliant and perfect miniature, and through the doorway the still smaller, but in fact larger, oleander bush outside, its flowers tiny pink lights on the surface of the glass. His attention was funnelled towards the vanishing point of sky between the oleander branches, and then his imagination expanded into the real sky beyond it, so that his mind was like two cones tip to tip. He was there with Thomas, or rather, Thomas was there with him, riding to infinity on that little patch of light. Then he noticed that the flowers had disappeared and a new image filled the doorway.

'Margaret's here,' he said.

His father turned around while Robert watched her plaintive bulk roll towards them. She came to a halt a few feet away from them.

'No harm done,' she said, half asking.

'He seems OK,' said his father.

'This won't affect my reference, will it?'

'What reference?' asked his father.

'Oh, I see,' said Margaret, half wounded, half angry, all dignified.

'Shall we have lunch?' said his father.

'I shan't be needing any lunch, thank you very much,' said Margaret.

She turned towards the staircase and began her laborious climb.

Suddenly, Robert couldn't bear it any longer. 'Poor Margaret,' he said.

'Poor Margaret,' said his father. 'What will we do without her?'

3

Robert was watching an ant disappear behind the sweating bottle of white wine on the stone table. The condensation suddenly streaked down the side of the bottle, smoothing the beaded surface in its wake. The ant reappeared, magnified through the pale green glass, its legs knitting frantically as it sampled a glittering grain of sugar spilt by Julia when she had sweetened her coffee after lunch. The sound of the cicadas billowed around them in and out of time with the limp flapping of the canvas awning over their heads. His mother was having a siesta with Thomas, and Lucy was watching a video, but he had stayed behind, despite Julia almost forcing him to join Lucy.

'Most people wait for their parents to die with a mixture of tremendous sadness and plans for a new swimming pool,' his father was saying to Julia. 'Since I'm going to have to renounce the swimming pool, I thought I might ditch the sadness as well.'

'But couldn't you pretend to be a shaman and keep this place?' said Julia.

'Alas, I'm one of the few people on the planet with absolutely no healing powers. I know that everyone else has just discovered their inner shaman, but I remain trapped in my materialistic conception of the universe.'

'There's such a thing as hypocrisy, you know,' said Julia.

'There's a shop round the corner from me called the Rainbow Path, I could get you a drum and some feathers.'

'I can already feel the power surging into my fingertips,' said his father, yawning. 'I, too, have a special gift to offer the tribe. I didn't realize until now that I have incredible psychic powers.'

'There you go,' said Julia encouragingly, 'you'll be running the place in no time.'

'I have enough trouble looking after my family without saving the world.'

'Looking after children can be a subtle way of giving up,' said Julia, smiling at Robert sternly. 'They become the whole ones, the well ones, the postponement of happiness, the ones who won't drink too much, give up, get divorced, become mentally ill. The part of oneself that's fighting against decay and depression is transferred to guarding them from decay and depression. In the meantime one decays and gets depressed.'

'I disagree,' said his father, 'when you're just fighting for yourself it's defensive and grim.'

'Very useful qualities,' Julia interrupted him. 'That's why it's important not to treat children too well – they won't be able to compete in the real world. If you want your children to become television producers, for instance, or chief executives, it's no use filling their little heads with ideas of trust and truth-telling and reliability. They'll just end up being somebody's secretary.'

Robert decided to ask his mother whether this was true, or whether Julia was being – well, like Julia. She came to stay every year with Lucy, her quite stuck-up daughter a year older than Robert. He knew his mother wasn't wild about Julia, because she was an old girlfriend of his father's. She felt a little bit jealous of her, but also a little bit bored. Julia didn't know how to stop wanting people to think she was clever. 'Really clever people are just thinking aloud,' his mother had told him, 'Julia is thinking about what she sounds like.'

Julia was always trying to throw Robert and Lucy together. The day before, Lucy had tried to kiss him. That was why he didn't want to watch a video with her. He doubted that his front teeth would survive another collision like that. The theory that it was good for him to spend time with children of his own age, even if he didn't like them, ground on. Would his father ask a woman to tea just because she was forty-two?

Julia was playing with the sugar again, spooning it back and forth in the bowl.

'Since divorcing Richard,' she said, 'I get these horrible moments of vertigo. I suddenly feel as if I don't exist.'

'I get that!' said Robert, excited that they had chosen a subject he knew something about.

'At your age,' said Julia, 'I think that's very pretentious. Are you sure you haven't just heard grown-ups talking about it?'

'No,' he said, in his dazed by injustice voice, 'I get it all on my own.'

'I think you're being unfair,' said his father to Julia. 'Robert has always had a capacity for horror well beyond his years. It doesn't interfere with his being a happy child.'

'Well, it does, actually,' he corrected his father, 'when it's going on.'

'Ah, when it's going on,' his father conceded with a gentle smile.

'I see,' said Julia, resting her hand on Robert's. 'In that case, welcome to the club, darling.'

He didn't want to be a member of Julia's club. He felt prickly all over his body because he wanted to take his hand away but didn't want to be rude.

'I always thought children were simpler than us,' said Julia, removing her hand and placing it on his father's forearm. 'We're like ice-breakers crashing our way towards the next object of desire.'

'What could be simpler than crashing one's way towards the next object of desire?' asked his father.

'*Not* crashing one's way towards it.'

'That's renunciation – not as simple as it looks.'

'It's only renunciation if you have the desire in the first place,' said Julia.

'Children have plenty of desire in the first place,' said his father, 'but I think you're right, it's essentially one desire: to be close to the people they love.'

'The normal ones want to watch *Raiders of the Lost Ark* as well,' said Julia.

'We're more easily distracted,' said his father, ignoring her last remark, 'more used to a culture of substitution, more easily confused about exactly who we do love.'

'Are we?' said Julia, smiling. 'That's nice.'

'Up to a point,' said his father.

He didn't really know what they were talking about now, but Julia seemed to have cheered up. Substitution must be something pretty wonderful. Before he got the chance to ask what it meant, a voice, a caring Irish voice, called out.

'Hello? Hello?'

'Oh, Christ,' muttered his father, 'it's the boss.'

'Patrick!' said Seamus warmly, walking towards them in a shirt covered in palm trees and rainbows. 'Robert,' he greeted him, ruffling his hair vigorously. 'Pleased to meet you,' he said to Julia, fixing her with his candid blue eyes and his firm handshake. Nobody could accuse him of not being friendly.

'Oh, it's a lovely spot here,' he said, 'lovely. We often sit out here after a session, with everyone laughing or crying, or just being with themselves, you know. This is definitely a power point, a place of tremendous release. That's right,' he sighed, as if agreeing with someone else's wise insight, 'I've seen people let go of a lot of stuff here.'

'Talking of "letting go of a lot of stuff",' his father handed the phrase back to Seamus, held by the corner like someone else's used handkerchief, 'when I opened the drawer of my bedside table I found it so full of "Healing Drum" brochures that there was no room for my passport. There are also several hundred copies of *The Way of the Shaman* in my wardrobe which are getting in the way of the shoes.'

'The Way of the Shoes,' said Seamus, letting out a great roar of healthy laughter, 'now that would be a good title for a book about, you know, staying grounded.'

'Do you think that these signs of institutional life,' continued his father coldly, rapidly, 'could be removed before we come down here on holiday? After all, my mother does want the house to return each August to its incarnation as a family home.'

'Of course, of course,' said Seamus. 'I apologize, Patrick. That'll be Kevin and Anette. They were going through a very powerful personal process, you know, before going back to Ireland on holiday, and they obviously weren't thorough enough in getting things ready for you.'

'Are you also going back to Ireland?' his father asked.

'No, I'll be in the cottage through August,' said Seamus. 'The Pegasus Press have asked me to write a short book about the shamanic work.'

'Oh, really,' said Julia, 'how fascinating. Are you a shaman yourself?'

'I had a look at the book that was in the way of my shoes,' said his father, 'and some obvious questions spring to mind. Have you spent twenty years being the disciple of a Siberian witch doctor? Have you gathered rare plants under the full moon during the brief summer? Have you been buried alive and died to the world? Have your eyes watered in the smoke of campfires while you muttered prayers to the spirits who might help you to save a dying man? Have you drunk the urine of caribou who have grazed on outcrops of *Amanita muscaria* and journeyed into other worlds to solve the mystery of a difficult diagnosis? Or did you study in Brazil with the *ayahuascaras* of the Amazon basin?'

'Well,' said Seamus, 'I trained as a nurse with the Irish National Health.'

'I'm sure that was an adequate substitute for being buried alive,' said his father.

'I worked in a nursing home for many years, doing the basics, you know: washing patients who were covered in their own faeces and urine; spoon-feeding old people who couldn't feed themselves any more.'

'Please,' said Julia, 'we've only just finished our lunch.'

'That was my reality at the time,' said Seamus. 'I sometimes wondered why I hadn't gone on to university and got the medical qualifications, but looking back I'm grateful for those years in the nursing home – they've helped to keep me grounded. When I discovered the Holotropic Breathwork and went to California to study with Stan Grof, I met some pretty out-there people, you know. I remember one particular lady, wearing a sunset-coloured dress, and she stood up and said, "I am Tamara from the Vega system, and I have come to the Earth to heal and to teach." Well, at that point, I thought about the old people in the home in Ireland and I was grateful to them for keeping my feet firmly planted on the ground.'

'Is holo . . . whatever you called it, a shamanic thing?' asked Julia.

'No, not really. That's what I was doing before I got into the shamanic work, but it all ties in, you know. It gets people in touch with that something beyond, that other dimension. When people touch that, it can trigger a radical change in their lives.'

'But I don't understand why this counts as a charity. People pay to come here, don't they?' said Julia.

'They do, they do,' said Seamus, 'but we recycle the profits, you see, so as to give scholarships to students like Kevin and Anette who are learning the shamanic work. And they've started to bring groups of inner-city kids from the estates in Dublin. We let them attend the courses for free, you know, and it's a wonderful thing to see the transformations. They love the trance music and the drumming. They come up to me and say, "Seamus, this is incredible, it's like tripping without the drugs," and they take that message back to the inner city and start up shamanic groups of their own.'

'Do we need a charity for tripping?' asked his father. 'Of all the ills in the world, the fact that there are a few people who are not tripping seems a wild hole to plug. Besides, if people want to trip, why not give them a strong dose of acid, instead of messing about with drums?'

'You can tell he's a barrister,' said Seamus amiably.

'I'm all for people having hobbies,' said his father. 'I just think they should explore them in the comfort of their own homes.'

'Sadly, Patrick,' said Seamus, 'some homes are not that comfortable.'

'I know the feeling,' said his father. 'Which reminds me, do you think we could clear out some of those books, advertisements, brochures, bric-a-brac.'

'Surely,' said Seamus, 'surely.'

His father and Seamus got up to leave and Robert realized that he was going to be left alone with Julia.

'I'll help,' he said, following them round the terrace.

His father led the way into the hall and stopped almost immediately.

'These fluttering leaflets,' he said, 'advertising other centres, other institutes, healing circles, advanced drumming courses – they're really wasted on us. In fact, this whole noticeboard,' he continued, unhooking it from the wall, 'despite its attractive cork surface and its multicoloured drawing pins, might as well not be here.'

'No problem,' said Seamus, embracing the noticeboard.

Although his father's manner remained supremely controlled, Robert could feel that he was intoxicated with rage and contempt. Seamus clouded over when Robert tried to make out what he was feeling, but eventually he groped his way to the terrible conclusion that Seamus pitied his father. Knowing that he was in charge, Seamus could afford to indulge the fury of a betrayed child. His repulsive pity saved him from feeling the impact of Patrick's fury, but Robert found himself caught between the punchbag and the punch and, feeling frightened and useless, he slipped out of the front door, while his father marched Seamus on to the next offence.

Outside, the shadow of the house was spreading to the flower beds on the edge of the terrace, indicating to some effortless part of his mind that the middle of the afternoon had arrived. The cicadas scratched on. He could see without looking, hear without listening; he was aware that he was not thinking. His attention, which usually bounced from one thing to another, was still. He pushed to test its resistance but he didn't push too hard, knowing that he could probably make himself pinball around again if he tried. His mind was glazed over, like a pond drowsily repeating the pattern of the sky.

The funny thing was that by imagining a pond he had started disturbing the trance it was being compared to. Now he wanted to go to the pond at the top of the steps, a stone semicircle of water at the end of the drive, where the goldfish would be hiding under a shield of reflection. That was right; he didn't want to go round the house with his father and Seamus, he wanted to scatter bread on the water to see if he could make that slippery Catherine wheel of orange fish break the surface. He ran into the kitchen and grabbed a piece of old bread before sprinting up the steps to the pond.

His father had told him that in winter the source gushed out of the pipe and thundered down among the darting fish; it overflowed into the lower ponds and eventually into the stream that ran along the crease of the valley. He wished he could see that one day. By August the pond was only half full. The algae-bearded pipe dripped into greenish water. Wasps and hornets and dragonflies crowded its warm dusty surface, resting on the water-lily pads for a safer drink. The goldfish were invisible unless tempted by food. The best method was to rub two pieces of stale bread together until they disintegrated into fine dry crumbs. Pellets of bread just sank, but the crumbs were held on the surface like dust. The most beautiful fish, the one he really wanted to see, had red and white patches on its skin. The others were all shades of orange, apart from a few small black ones which must either turn orange later on, or die out, because there were no big black ones.

He broke the bread and grated the two halves, watching a rain of light crumbs land on the water and spread out. Nothing happened.

The truth was that he had only seen the swirling frenzy of fish once, and since then either nothing had happened or a solitary fish fed lazily under the wobbling sinking crumbs.

'Fish! Fish! Fish! Come on! Fish! Fish! Fish!'

'Are you calling to your power animal?' said a voice behind him.

He stopped abruptly and swung round. Seamus was

standing there, smiling at him benevolently, his tropical shirt blazing in the sun.

'Fish! Fish! Fish!' Seamus called.

'I was just feeding them,' mumbled Robert.

'Do you feel you have a special connection with fish?' Seamus asked him, leaning in closer. 'That's what a power animal is, you know. It helps you on your journey through life.'

'I just like them being fish,' said Robert. 'They don't have to do anything for me.'

'Now fish, for instance, bring us messages from the depths, from under the surface of things.' Seamus wriggled his hand through the air. 'Ah, it's a magical land here,' said Seamus, pushing his elbows back and twisting his neck from side to side with his eyes closed. 'My own personal power point, you know, is up there in the little wood, by the bird bath. Do you know the spot? It was your grandmother first pointed it out to me, it was a special place for her too. The first time I did a journey here, that's where I connected with the non-ordinary reality.'

Robert suddenly realized, and as he realized it he also saw its inevitability, that he loathed Seamus.

Seamus cupped his hands around his mouth and howled, 'Fish! Fish! Fish!'

Robert wanted to kill him. If he had a car he would run him over. If he had an axe he would cut him down.

He heard the upper door of the house being opened, and then the mosquito door squeaking open as well and out came his mother, holding Thomas in her arms.

'Oh, it's you. Hello, Seamus,' said his mother politely. 'We were half asleep, and I couldn't work out why a travelling fishmonger was bellowing outside the window.'

'We were, you know, invoking the fish,' said Seamus.

Robert ran over to his mother. She sat down with him on

the low wall around the edge of the pond, away from where Seamus was standing, and tilted Thomas so he could see the water. Robert really hoped the fish didn't come to the surface now, or Seamus would probably think he had made it happen with his special powers. Poor Thomas, he might never see the orange swirl, he might never see the big fish with red and white patches. Seamus was taking away the pond and the wood and the bird bath and the whole landscape from him. In fact, when you thought about it, Thomas had been attacked by his own grandmother from the moment he was born. She wasn't a grandmother at all; more like a stepmother in a fairy tale, cursing him in his cot. How could she have shown Seamus the bird bath in the wood? He patted Thomas's head protectively. Thomas started to laugh, his surprisingly deep gurgling laugh, and Robert realized that his brother didn't really know about these things that were driving Robert crazy, and that he needn't know, unless Robert told him.

4

Josh Packer was a boy in Robert's class at school. He had decided (all on his own) that they were best friends. Nobody else could understand why they were inseparable, least of all Robert. If he could have broken away from Josh for long enough he would definitely have made another best friend, but Josh followed Robert round the playground, copied out his spelling tests, and dragged him back to his house for tea. All Josh did outside school was watch television. He had sixty-five channels, whereas Robert only had the free ones. Josh's parents were very rich, so he often had amazing new toys before anyone else had even heard of them. For his last birthday he had been given a real electric jeep, with a DVD player and a miniature television. He drove it round the garden, squashing the flowers and trying to run over Arnie, his dog. Eventually, he crashed into a bush and he and Robert sat in the rain watching the miniature television. When he came round to Robert's flat he said how pathetic the toys were and complained that he was bored. Robert tried to make up games with him but he didn't know how to make things up. He just pretended to be a television character for about three seconds, and then fell over and shouted, 'I'm dead.'

Jilly, Josh's mother, had telephoned the day before to say that she and Jim had rented a fabulous house in Saint-Tropez for the whole of August, and why didn't Robert's family come over for a day of fun and games. His parents said it would be good for him to spend a day with someone of his own age. They said it would be an adventure for them as well, because they had only met Josh's parents once, at the school sports day. Even then Jim and Jilly were too busy making rival movies of Josh's races to talk much. Jilly showed them how her videocam could make the whole thing go in slow motion, which wasn't really necessary as Josh came in last anyway.

Now that they were actually on their way, Robert's father was ranting at the wheel of the car. He seemed to be much grumpier since Julia had left. He couldn't believe that they were spending a day of their precious holiday in a traffic jam, in a heatwave, crawling into this 'world-famous joke of a town'.

Robert was sitting next to Thomas, who was in his old baby chair facing the wrong way, with only the stained fabric of the back seat to entertain him. Robert made barking noises as he climbed Thomas's leg with a small toy dog. Thomas couldn't have been less interested. Why should he be? thought Robert. He hasn't seen a real dog yet. Mind you, if he was only curious about things he'd seen before, he'd still be trapped in a whirlpool of birth-room lights.

When they finally found the right street, Robert was the one who spotted the tilted script of '*Les Mimosas*' scrawled across a rustic tile. They thrummed down the ribbed concrete to a parking lot already congested with Jim's private motor show: a black Range Rover, a red Ferrari and an old cream convertible with cracked leather seats and bulbous chrome fenders. His father found a space for their Peugeot next to a giant cactus, its serrated tongues sticking out in every direction.

'A neo-Roman villa decorated by a disciple of Gauguin's syphilitic twilight,' said his father. 'What more could one ask?' He slipped into his golden advertising voice, 'Situated in St Tro-pay's most prestigious gated community, only six hours' drive from Brigitte Bardot's legendary pet cemetery—'

'Sweetheart,' interrupted his mother.

There was a tap on the window.

'Jim!' said his father warmly, as he wound down the window.

'We're just off to buy some inflatables for the pool,' said Jim, lowering the videocam with which he'd been filming their arrival. 'Does Robert want to come along?'

Robert glanced at Josh slumped in the back of the Range Rover. He could tell that he was playing with his GameBoy.

'No, thanks,' he said. 'I'll help unpack the car.'

'You've got him well trained, haven't you?' said Jim. 'Jilly's poolside, catching some rays. Just follow the garden path.'

They walked through a whitewashed colonnade daubed with Pacific murals, and down a spongy lawn towards the pool, perfectly concealed under a flotilla of inflatable giraffes, fire engines, footballs, racing cars, hamburgers, Mickeys, Minnies and Goofys, his father lopsided by the baby chair in which Thomas still slept, and his mother like a mule, her sides bulging with bags. Jilly lay stunned on a white and yellow sunbed, flanked by two glistening strangers, all three of them in wigs of Walkman and mobile-phone wires. His father's shadow roused Jilly as it fell across her baking face.

'Hi, there!' she said, unhooking her headphones. 'I'm sorry, I was in a world of my own.'

She got up to greet her guests, but was soon staggering backwards, staring at Thomas, a hand sprawled over her heart.

'Oh, my God,' she gasped, 'your new one is beautiful. I'm sorry, Robert,' she dug her long shiny nails into his shoulders to help steady him, 'I don't want to fan the flames of sibling rivalry, but your little brother is something really special. Aren't you a special one?' she said, swooping down towards Thomas. 'He's going to make you dead jealous,' she warned his mother, 'with all the girls throwing themselves at his feet. Look at those eyelashes! Are you going to have another one? If mine looked like that, I'd have at least six. I sound greedy, don't I? But I can't help it, he's so love-ly. He's made me forget myself, I haven't introduced you to Christine and Roger yet. As if they cared. Look at them, they're in a world of their own. Go on, wake up!' She pretended to kick Roger. 'Roger's a business partner of Jim's,' she filled them in, 'and Christine's from Australia. She's four months pregnant.'

She shook Christine awake.

'Oh, hi,' said Christine, 'have they arrived?'

Jilly introduced everybody.

'I was just telling them about the pregnancy,' she explained to Christine.

'Oh, yeah. Actually, I think we're in major denial about it,' said Christine. 'I just feel a little heavier, that's all, as if I'd drunk four litres of Evian, or something. I mean, I don't even feel sick in the mornings. The other day Roger said, "Do you wanna go skiing in January? I've got to be in Switzerland on business anyway," and I said, "Sure, why not?" We'd both forgotten that that's the week I'm supposed to be giving birth!'

Jilly hooted with laughter and rolled her eyes skywards.

'I mean, is that absent-minded, or what?' said Christine. 'Mind you, pregnancy really does your brain in.'

'Look at them,' said Jilly, pointing to Robert's mother and father, 'they're absolutely gobsmacked – they're loving parents.'

'So are we,' protested Christine. 'You know how we are with Megan. Megan's our two-year-old,' she explained to the guests. 'We've left her with Roger's mother. She's just discovered rage – you know the way they discover emotions and then work them for all they're worth, until they get on to the next one.'

'How interesting,' said Robert's father, 'so you don't think emotions have anything to do with how a child is feeling – they're just layers in an archaeological dig. When do they discover joy?'

'When you take them to Legoland,' said Christine.

Roger woke up groggily, clasping his earpiece.

'Oh, hi. Sorry, I've got a call.'

He got up and started to pace the lawn.

'Have you brought your nanny?' asked Jilly.

'We haven't got one,' said Robert's mother.

'That's brave,' said Jilly. 'I don't know what I'd do without Jo. She's only been with us a week and she's already part of the family. You can dump your lot on her, she's marvellous.'

'We quite like looking after them ourselves,' said his mother.

'Jo!' shouted Jilly. 'Jo-o-euh!'

'Tell them it's a mixed leisure portfolio,' said Roger. 'Don't give them any more details at this stage.'

'Jo!' Jilly called again. 'Lazy bitch. She spends the whole day gawping at *Hello!* magazine and eating Ben & Jerry's ice cream. A bit like her employer, you might say, hem-hem, but it's costing me a fortune, whereas *she's* getting paid.'

'I don't care what they told Nigel,' said Roger, 'it's none of their bloody business. They can keep their noses out of it.'

Jim came striding down the lawn, glowing with successful shopping. Tubby Josh followed behind, a tangle of dragging feet. Jim got out a foot-pump and unfolded the plastic skin of another inflatable on the flagstones next to the pool.

'What did you get him?' asked Jilly, staring furiously at the house.

'You know he had his heart set on the ice-cream cone,'

said Jim, pumping up a strawberry Cornetto. 'And I got him the Lion King.'

'And the machine gun,' said Josh pedantically.

'Inland Revenue,' said Jim to Robert's father, jerking his chin towards Roger, 'breathing down his neck. He may want some legal advice over lunch.'

'I don't work when I'm on holiday,' said his father.

'You don't work much when you're not on holiday,' said Robert's mother.

'Oh dear, do I detect marital conflict?' said Jim, filming the strawberry Cornetto as it unwrinkled on the ground.

'Jo!' screamed Jilly.

'I'm here,' called a big freckly girl in khaki shorts emerging from the house. The words 'Up For It' danced on the front of her T-shirt as she bobbed down the lawn.

Thomas woke up screaming. Who could blame him? The last thing he knew he had been in the car with his lovely family, and now he was surrounded by shouting strangers with blacked-out eyes; a nervous herd of monsters jostling brightly in the chlorinated air, another one swelling at his feet. Robert couldn't stand it either.

'Who's a hungry young man?' said Jo, leaning in on Thomas. 'Oh, he's beautiful, isn't he?' she said to Robert's mother. 'He's an old soul, you can tell.'

'Get these two parked in front of a video,' said Jilly, 'so we can have a bit of peace and quiet. And send Gaston down with a bottle of rosé. You'll love Gaston,' she told Robert's mother. 'He's a genius. A real old-fashioned French chef. I've put on about three stone since we arrived, and that was only a week ago. Never mind. We've got Heinrich coming to the rescue this afternoon – he's the personal trainer, great big German hunk, gives you a proper old workout. You should join me, help to get your figure back after the pregnancy. Not that you don't look great.'

'Is that what you want,' his mother asked Robert, 'to watch a video?'

'Yeah, sure,' he said, desperate to get away.

'It's difficult to see how he could swim,' admitted his father, 'with all the inflatable food in the pool.'

'Come on!' said Jo, sticking a hand out on each side. She seemed to think that Josh and Robert were going to take a hand each and skip up the hill with her.

'Isn't anybody going to hold my hand?' howled Jo, in a fit of mock blubbing.

Josh joined his pudgy palm with hers, but Robert managed to stay free, following at a little distance, fascinated by Jo's pouting khaki bottom.

'We're entering the video cave,' said Jo, making spooky noises. 'Right! What are you two going to watch? And I don't want any fighting.'

'*The Adventures of Sinbad*,' shouted Josh.

'Again! Crikey!' said Jo, and Robert couldn't help agreeing with her. He liked to watch a good video five or six times, but when he knew all the dialogue by heart and each shot was like a drawer full of identical socks, he started to feel a twinge of reluctance. Josh was different. He started out with a sort of sullen greed for a new video and only developed real enthusiasm somewhere around the twentieth viewing. Love, an emotion he didn't throw around lightly, was reserved for *The Adventures of Sinbad,* now seen over a hundred times, far too many of them with Robert. Videos were Josh's daydreams, Robert's daydream was solitude. How could he escape from the video cave? When you're a child nobody leaves you alone. If he ran away now, they would send out a search party, round him up and entertain him to death. Maybe he could just lie there and think while Josh's borrowed imagination flickered on the wall. The whine of the rewind was slowing down and Josh had collapsed back into the dent already made by his breakfast viewing and resumed munching the bright orange cheese puffs scattered on the table next to him. Jo started the tape, switched off the light and left discreetly. Josh was no fast-forward vandal: the warning about video piracy, the previews of films he had already seen, the plugs for merchandised toys he had already discarded and the message from the Video Standards Authority were not allowed to rush past like so many ugly suburbs before a train breaks out into the bovine melancholy of true countryside; they were appreciated in their own right, granted their own dignity, which suited Robert fine, since the rubbish now pouring from the screen was too familiar to make any impact on his attention at all.

He closed his eyes and let the pool-side inferno dissipate. After a few hours of other people, he had to get the pile-up of impressions out of him one way or another; by doing impersonations, or working out how things worked, or just trying to empty his mind. Otherwise the impressions built up to a critical density and he felt as if he was going to explode.

Sometimes, when he was lying in bed, a single word like 'fear' or 'infinity' flicked the roof off the house and sucked him into the night, past the stars that had been bent into bears and ploughs, and into a pure darkness where everything was annihilated except the feeling of annihilation. As the little capsule of his intelligence disintegrated, he went on feeling its burning edges, its fragmenting hull, and when the capsule flew apart he was the bits flying apart, and when the bits turned into atoms he was the flying apart itself, growing stronger instead of fading, like an evil energy defying the running out of everything and feeding on waste, and soon enough the whole of space was a waste-fuelled rush and there was no place in it for a human mind; but there he was, still feeling.

He would reel down the corridor to his parents' bedroom, choking. He would do anything to make it stop, sign any contract, take any vow, but he knew it was useless, he knew that he had seen something true, that he couldn't change it, only ignore it for a while, cry in his mother's arms, and let her put the roof back on and introduce him to some kinder words.

It was not that he was unhappy. It was just that he had seen something and sometimes it was truer than anything else. He first saw it when his grandmother had a stroke. He hadn't wanted to abandon her but she could hardly speak and so he had spent a lot of time imagining what she was feeling. Everybody said you had to be loyal, so he stuck at it. He held her hand for a long time and she gripped his. He didn't like it but he didn't let go. He could tell that she was frightened. Her eyes were dimmed. Part of her was relieved: she had always had trouble communicating, now nobody expected her to make the effort. Part of her was already gone, back to the source, perhaps, or at least far from the material plane about which she had such chronic doubts. What he could get close to was the part of her that was left behind wondering, now that she couldn't help keeping them, if she wanted all those secrets after all. Illness had blown her apart like a dandelion clock. He had wondered if he would end up like that, a few seeds sticking to a broken stem.

'This is my favourite bit,' said Josh, love-struck. Pirates were boarding Sinbad's ship. The ship's parrot flew in the face of the meanest-looking pirate. He staggered around disoriented and was effortlessly tipped overboard by Sinbad's men. Shot of pleased parrot squawking.

'Hmm,' said Robert. 'Listen, I'll be back in a minute.'

Josh paid no attention to his departure. Robert scanned the corridor for Jo, but she was not there. He retraced the route they had come in by, and when he got to the garden door, saw that the grown-ups were no longer around the pool. He slipped outside and hooked round to the back of the house. The tailored lawn petered out to a carpet of pine needles and a couple of big dustbins. He sat down and leant back against the ridged bark of the pine, unsupervised.

He wondered who was wasting the most time by spending a day with the Packers, not counting the Packers themselves who were always wasting more time than anybody, and usually had a film to prove it. Thomas was only sixty days old, so it was the biggest waste of time for him, because one day was one-sixtieth of his life, whereas his father, who was forty-two, was wasting the smallest proportion of his life. Robert tried to work out what proportion of their lives a day was for each of them. The calculations were hard to hold in his mind, so he imagined different sizes of wheels in a clock. Then he wondered how to include the opposite facts: that Thomas had his whole life ahead of him, whereas his parents had quite a lot of theirs behind them, so that one day was less wasteful for Thomas because he had more days left. That created a new set of wheels – red instead of silver – his father's spinning round and Thomas's turning with a stately infrequent click. He still had to include the different qualities of suffering and the different benefits for each of them, but that made his machine fantastically complicated and so, in one salutary sweep, he decided that they were all suffering equally, and that none of them had got anything out of it at all, making the value of the day a nice fat zero. Hugely relieved, he got back to visualizing the rods connecting the two sets of wheels. It all looked quite like the big steam engine in the Science Museum, except that paper came out at one end with a figure for the units of waste. It turned out, when he read the figures, that he was wasting more time than anyone else. He was horrified by this result, but at the same time quite pleased. Then he heard Jo's dreadful voice calling his name.

For a moment he froze with indecision. The trouble was that hiding only made the search party more frantic and furious. He decided to act casual and amble round the corner just in time to hear Jo bawling his name for the second time.

'Hi,' he said.

'Where have you been? I've been looking for you everywhere.'

'You can't have been, or you would have found me,' he said.

'Don't get smart with me, young man,' said Jo. 'Have you been fighting with Josh?'

'No,' he said. 'How could anyone fight with Josh? He's just a blob.'

'He's not a blob, he's your best friend,' said Jo.

'No he isn't,' he said.

'You *have* been fighting,' said Jo.

'We haven't,' he insisted.

'Well, anyway, you can't just go off like that.'

'Why not?'

'Because we all worry about you.'

'I worry about my parents when they go away, but that doesn't stop them,' he remarked. 'Nor should it.'

He was definitely winning this argument. In an emergency, his father could send Robert to court on his behalf. He imagined himself in a wig, bringing the jury round to his way of seeing things, but then Jo squatted down in front of him and looked searchingly into his eyes.

'Do your parents go away a lot?' she asked.

'Not really,' he said, but before he could tell her that they had never both been out of the house for more than about three hours, he found himself swept into her arms and crushed against the words 'Up For It', without fully understanding what they meant. He had to tuck his shirt in again after she had pulled it out of his trousers with her consoling back rub.

'What does "Up For It" mean?' he asked when he got his breath back.

'Never you mind,' she said, round-eyed. 'Come on! Lunch time!'

She marched him into the house. He couldn't exactly refuse to hold her hand now that they were practically lovers.

A man in an apron was standing beside the lunch table.

'Gaston, you're spoiling us rotten,' said Jilly reproachfully. 'I'm putting on a stone just looking at these tarts. You should have your own television programme. Vous sur le television, Gaston, make you beaucoup de monnaie. Fantastique!'

The table was crowded with bottles of pink wine, two of them empty, and a variety of custard tarts; a custard tart with bits of ham in it, a custard tart with bits of onion in it, a custard tart with curled-up tomatoes on it and a custard tart with curled-up courgettes on it.

Only Thomas was safe, breast-feeding.

'So you've rounded up the stray,' said Jilly. She whipped her hand in the air and burst into song. 'Round 'em up! Bring 'em in! Raw-w h-ide!'

Robert felt prickles of embarrassment breaking out all over his body. It must be desperate being Jilly.

'He's used to being alone a lot, is he?' said Jo, challenging his mother.

'Yes, when he wants to be,' said his mother, not realizing that Jo thought he might as well be living in an orphanage.

'I was just telling your parents they ought to take you to see the real Father Christmas,' said Jilly, dishing out the food. 'Concorde from Gatwick in the morning, up to Lapland, snowmobiles waiting, and whoosh, you're in Father Christmas's cave twenty minutes later. He gives the children a present, then back on Concorde and home in time for dinner.

It's in the Arctic Circle, you see, which makes it more real than mucking about in Harrods.'

'It sounds very educational,' said his father, 'but I think the school fees will have to take priority.'

'Josh would murder us if we didn't take him,' said Jim.

'I'm not surprised,' said his father.

Josh made the sound of a massive explosion and punched the air.

'Smashing through the sound barrier,' he shouted.

'Which one of these tarts do you fancy?' Jilly asked Robert.

They all looked equally disgusting.

He glanced at his mother with her copper hair spiralling down towards the suckling Thomas, and he could feel the two of them blending together like wet clay.

'I want what Thomas is having,' he said. He hadn't meant to say it out loud, it just slipped out.

Jim, Jilly, Roger, Christine, Jo and Josh brayed like a herd of donkeys. Roger looked even angrier when he was laughing.

'Mine's a breast-milk,' said Jilly, raising her glass drunkenly.

His parents smiled at him sympathetically.

'I'm afraid you're on solids now, old man,' said his father. 'I've got used to wishing I was younger, but I didn't expect you to start quite yet. You're still supposed to be wishing you were older.'

His mother let him sit on the edge of her chair and kissed him on the forehead.

'It's perfectly normal,' Jo reassured his parents, who she knew had hardly ever seen a child. 'They're not usually that direct about it, that's all.' She allowed herself a last hiccup of laughter.

Robert tuned out of the babble around him and gazed at his brother. Thomas's mouth was busy and then quiet and then busy, massaging the milk from their mother's breast.

Robert wanted to be there, curled up in the hub of his senses, before he knew about things he had never seen – the length of the Nile, the size of the moon, what they wore at the Boston Tea Party – before he was bombarded by adult propaganda, and measured his experience against it. He wanted to be there too, but he wanted to take his sense of self with him, the sneaky witness of the very thing that had no witnesses. Thomas was not witnessing himself doing things, he was just doing them. It was an impossible task to join him there as Robert was now, like somersaulting and standing still at the same time. He had often brooded on that idea and although he didn't end up thinking he could do it, he felt the impossibility receding as the muscles of his imagination grew more tense, like a diver standing on the very edge of the board before he springs. That was all he could do: drop into the atmosphere around Thomas, letting his desire for observation peel away as he got closer to the ground where Thomas lived, and where he had once lived as well. It was hard to do it now, though, because Jilly was on to him again.

'Why don't you stay here with us, Robert?' she suggested. 'Jo could drive you back tomorrow. You'd have more fun playing with Josh than going home and being dead jealous of your baby brother.'

He squeezed his mother's leg desperately.

Eventually Gaston returned, distracting Jilly with the dessert, a slimy mound of custard in a puddle of caramel.

'Gaston, you're ruining us,' wailed Jilly, slapping his incorrigible, egg-beating wrist.

Robert leant in close to his mother. '*Please* can we go now,' he whispered in her ear.

'Right after lunch,' she whispered back.

'Is he pleading with you?' said Jilly, wrinkling her nose.

'As a matter of fact he is,' said his mother.

'Go on, let him have a sleep-over,' insisted Jilly.

'He'll be well looked after,' said Jo, as if this was some kind of novelty.

'I'm afraid we can't. We have to go and see his grandmother in her nursing home,' said his mother, not mentioning that they were going there in three days' time.

'It's funny,' said Christine, 'Megan doesn't seem to feel any jealousy yet.'

'Give her a chance,' said his father, 'she's only just discovered rage.'

'Yeah,' laughed Christine. 'Maybe it's because I'm not really owning my pregnancy.'

'That must help,' sighed his father. Robert could tell that his father was now viciously bored. Immediately after lunch, they left the Packers with an urgency rarely seen outside a fire brigade.

'I'm starving,' he said, as their car climbed up the driveway.

They all burst out laughing.

'I wouldn't dream of criticizing your choice of friend,' said his father, 'but couldn't we just get the video instead.'

'I didn't choose him,' Robert protested, 'he just . . . stuck to me.'

He spotted a restaurant by the roadside where they had a late lunch of extremely excellent pizzas and salad and orange juice. Poor Thomas had to have milk again. That was all he ever got, milk, milk, milk.

'My favourite was the London house speech,' said Robert's father. He put on a very silly voice, not particularly like Jilly's but like her attitude. '"It looked huge when we bought it, but by the time we put in the guest suite and the exercise room and the sauna and the home office and the cinema, you know, there really wasn't that much room."

'Room for what?' asked his father, amazed. 'Room for room. This is the room room, for having room in. Next time we climb onto our coat hangers in London to sleep like a family of bats, let's appreciate that we're not just a few bedrooms away from real civilization, but a room room away.

'"I said to Jim," his father continued imitating Jilly, "I hope we can afford this, because I like the lifestyle – the restaurants, the holidays, the shopping – and I'm not going to give them up. Jim assures me that we can afford both."

'And this was the killer,' said his father – '"He knows that if we can't afford it, I'll divorce him." She's un-fucking-believable. She isn't even attractive.'

'She is amazing,' said his mother. 'But I felt in their own quiet way that Christine and Roger had a lot to offer too. When I said that I used to talk to my children when I was pregnant, she said –' his mother put on a shrill Australian accent – '"Hang on! A baby is after the birth. I'm not going to talk to my pregnancy. Roger would have me committed."'

Robert imagined his mother talking to him when he had been sealed up in her womb. Of course he wouldn't have known what her blunted syllables were meant to mean, but he was sure he would have felt a current flowing between them, the contraction of a fear, the stretch of an intention. Thomas was still close to those transfusions of feeling; Robert was getting explanations instead. Thomas still knew how to understand the silent language which Robert had almost lost as the wild margins of his mind fell under the sway of the verbal empire. He was standing on a ridge, about to surge downhill, getting faster, getting taller, getting more words, getting bigger and bigger explanations, cheering all the way. Now Thomas had made him glance backwards and lower his sword for a moment while he noticed everything that he had lost as well. He had become so caught up in building sentences that he had almost forgotten the barbaric days when thinking was like a splash of colour landing on a page. Looking back, he could still see it: living in what would now feel like pauses: when you first open the curtains and see the whole landscape covered in snow and you catch your breath and pause before breathing out again. He couldn't get the whole thing back, but maybe he wouldn't rush down the slope quite yet, maybe he would sit down and look at the view.

'Let's get out of this sorry town,' said his father, chucking back his small cup of coffee.

'I've just got to change him first,' said his mother, gathering up a bulging bag covered in sky-blue rabbits.

Robert looked down at Thomas, slumped in his chair, staring at a picture of a sailing boat, not knowing what a picture was and not knowing what a sailing boat was, and he could feel the drama of being a giant trapped in a small incompetent body.

5

Walking down the long, easily washed corridors of his grandmother's nursing home, the squeak of the nurse's rubber soles made his family's silence seem more hysterical than it was. They passed the open door of a common room where a roaring television masked another kind of silence. The crumpled, paper-white residents sat in rows. What could be making death take so long? Some looked more frightened than bored, some more bored than frightened. Robert could still remember from his first visit the bright geometry decorating the walls. He remembered imagining the apex of a long yellow triangle stabbing him in the chest, and the sharp edge of that red semicircle slicing through his neck.

This year they were taking Thomas to see his grandmother for the first time. She wouldn't be able to say much, but then neither would Thomas. They might get on really well.

When they went into the room, his grandmother was sitting in an armchair by the window. Outside, too close to the window, was the thick trunk of a slightly yellowing poplar tree and beyond it, the bluish cypress hedge that hid part of the car park. Noticing the arrival of her family, his grandmother organized her face into a smile, but her eyes remained detached from the process, frozen in bewilderment and pain. As her lips broke open he saw her blackened and broken teeth. They didn't look as if they could manage anything solid. Perhaps that was why her body seemed so much more wasted than when he had last seen her.

They all kissed his grandmother's soft, rather hairy face. Then his mother held Thomas close to his grandmother and said, 'This is Thomas.'

His grandmother's expression wavered as she tried to negotiate between the strangeness and the intimacy of his presence. Her eyes made Robert feel as if she was scudding through an overcast sky, breaking briefly into clear space and then rushing back through thickening veils into the milky blindness of a cloud. She didn't know Thomas and he didn't know her, but she seemed to have a sense of her connection with him. It kept disappearing, though, and she had to fight to get it back. When she was about to speak, the effort of working out what to say in these particular circumstances wiped her out. She couldn't remember who she was in relation to all the people in the room. Tenacity didn't work any more; the harder she grasped at an idea, the faster it shot away.

Finally, uncertainly, she wrapped her fingers around something, looked up at his father and said, 'Does . . . he . . . like me?'

'Yes,' said Robert's mother instantly, as if this was the most natural question in the world.

'Yes,' said his grandmother, the pool of despair in her eyes flooding back into the rest of her face. It wasn't what she had meant to ask, but a question which had broken through. She sank back into her chair.

After what he had heard that morning Robert was struck by her question, and by the fact that it seemed to be addressed to his father. On the other hand, he was not surprised that his mother had answered it instead of him.

That morning he had been playing in the kitchen while his mother was upstairs packing a bag for Thomas. He hadn't noticed that the monitor was still on, until he heard Thomas waking up with a few short cries, and his mother going into Thomas's bedroom and talking to him soothingly. Before he could gauge whether she was even sweeter to Thomas when he was not around, his father's voice came blasting over the receiver.

'I can't believe this fucking letter.'

'What letter?' asked his mother.

'That scumbag Seamus Dourke is trying to get Eleanor to make the gift of this property absolute during her lifetime. I had arranged for the solicitor to put it on an elastic band of debt. In her will the debt is waived and the house is transferred irrevocably to the charity, but during her lifetime the charity has been lent the value of this property, and if she recalls the debt the place returns to her. She agreed to set things up that way on the grounds that she might get ill and need the money to look after herself, but needless to say, I also hoped she would come to her senses and realize that this joke charity was doing a lot of harm to us and no good to anyone else, except Seamus. Talk about the luck of the Irish. There he was, a National Health nurse changing bedpans in County Meath, until my mother airlifted him from the Emerald Isle and made him the sole beneficiary of an enormous tax-free income from a New Age hotel masquerading as a charity. It makes me sick, completely sick.'

His father was shouting by now.

'Sweetheart, you're ranting,' said his mother. 'Thomas is getting upset.'

'I have to rant,' said his father, 'I've just seen this letter. She was always a lousy mother, but I thought she might take a holiday towards the end of her life, feel that she'd achieved enough by way of betrayal and neglect, and that it was time to have a break, play with her grandchildren, let us stay in the house, that sort of thing. What really terrifies me is realizing how much I loathe her. When I read this letter, I tried to loosen my shirt so that I could breathe, but then I realized it was already loose enough, I just felt as if a noose was tightening around my neck, a noose of loathing.'

'She's a confused old woman,' said Robert's mother.

'I know.'

'And we're seeing her later today.'

'I know,' said his father, much more quietly now, almost inaudibly. 'What I really loathe is the poison dripping from generation to generation. My mother felt disinherited because of her stepfather getting all her mother's money, and now, after thirty years of consciousness-raising workshops and personal-growth programmes, she has found Seamus Dourke to stand in for her stepfather. He's really just the incredibly willing instrument of her unconscious. It's the monotony that drives me mad. I'd rather cut my throat than inflict the same thing on my children.'

'You won't,' his mother answered.

'If you can imagine anything . . .'

Robert had leant closer to the monitor, trying to make out his father's fading voice, only to hear it growing louder behind him as his parents made their way downstairs.

'. . . the result would be my mother,' his father was saying.

'King Lear and Mrs Jellyby,' his mother laughed.

'On the heath,' said his father, 'a quick rut between the feeble tyrant and the fanatical philanthropist.'

He had run from the kitchen, not wanting his parents to know that he had heard their conversation on the monitor. He sat on the knowledge all morning, but when his grandmother had stared at his father, as if she was talking about him, and asked, 'Does he like me?' Robert couldn't help having the mad idea that she had overheard the same conversation as him.

Although he didn't understand everything his father had

said that morning, he understood enough to feel cracks opening in the ground. And now, in the silence that followed his grandmother's shrewd unintentional question, he could feel her misery, and he could feel his mother's desire for harmony, and he could feel the strain in his father's self-restraint. He wanted to do something to make everything all right.

His grandmother was taking about half an hour to ask if Thomas had been christened yet.

'No,' said his mother, 'we're not having a formal christening. The trouble is that we don't really think that children are steeped in sin, and a lot of the ceremony seems to be based on the idea that they're fallen and need to be saved.'

'Yes,' said his grandmother. 'No.'

Thomas started to shake the tiny silver dumbbell he had rediscovered in the creases of his chair. It made a strange high tinkling sound as he waved it jerkily around his head. Soon enough, he banged it against his forehead. After a delay in which he seemed to be trying to work out what had happened, he started to cry.

'He doesn't know whether he hit himself or whether the dumbbell hit him,' said Robert's father.

His mother took sides against the dumbbell and said, 'Naughty dumbbell,' kissing Thomas's forehead.

Robert hit himself on the side of the head and fell off his grandmother's bed theatrically. Thomas wasn't as amused as he had hoped he would be.

His grandmother held her arms out in pleading sympathy, as if Thomas was expressing something that she felt as well, but didn't want to be reminded of. Robert's mother lifted Thomas gently into his grandmother's lap. Seduced by the novelty of his position, Thomas stopped crying and looked searchingly at his grandmother. She seemed to be calmed by his presence. He sat on her lap, giving her what she needed, and they sank together into speechless solidarity. The rest of the family fell silent as well, not wanting to show up the non-speakers. Robert felt his father hovering over his grandmother, resisting saying what was on his mind. In the end it was his grandmother who spoke, not quite fluently but much better than before, as if her speech, abandoning the hopelessly blocked highway of longing, had stolen out under cover of darkness and silence.

'I want you to know,' she said, 'that I'm very . . . unhappy . . . at not being able to communicate.'

His mother reached out and touched her knee.

'It must be horrible for you,' said his father.

'Yes,' said his grandmother, staring at the faraway floor.

Robert didn't know what to do. His father hated his own mother. He couldn't join him and he couldn't condemn him. His grandmother had done her family some wrong, but she was suffering horribly. Robert could only fall back on how things were before they had been darkened by his father's disappointment. Those cloudless days when he was just meant to love his grandmother; he was not sure they had ever existed, but he was sure they didn't exist now. It was still too unfair to gang up against his frightened grandmother, even if she was leaving the house to Seamus.

He hopped down from the bed and sat on the arm of his grandmother's chair, taking her hand in his, like he used to when she first fell ill. That way she could tell him things without having to speak, her thoughts flooding into him in pictures.

The bridges were burnt and broken and everything his grandmother wanted to say got banked up on one side of a ravine, never taking form, never moving on. She felt a perpetual pressure, a scratching behind her eyeballs, like a dog pleading to be let in, a fullness that could only escape in tears and sighs and jagged gestures.

Under the bruise of feeling there was a brutal instinct to

stay alive, like a run-over snake thrashing on a hot road, or blind roots pumping sap into a bleeding stump.

Why was she being tortured? They had sewn her into a sack and thrown her into the bottom of a boat, chains wrapped around her feet. She must have done something very bad to be teased by the oarsmen as they rowed her out into the bay. Something very bad which she couldn't remember.

He tried to break off. It was too much. He didn't let go of her hand, he just tried to close down, but it was impossible to break the connection completely.

He noticed that his grandmother was crying. She gave his hand a squeeze.

'I am . . . no.' She couldn't say it. A carefully threaded thought unstrung itself and scattered across the floor. She couldn't get it back. Something opaque clung to her all the time. Her head had been sealed in a dirty plastic bag; she wanted to tear it off but her hands were tied.

'I . . . am,' she tried again. 'Brave. Yes.'

The evening light was on the other side of the building and the room was growing dimmer. They were all lost for words, except for Thomas who had none to lose. He leant against his grandmother's arms, looking at her with his cool objective gaze. His example balanced the atmosphere. They sat in the fading light of the almost peaceful room, feeling sympathetic and a little bored. Robert's grandmother sank into a quieter anguish, like someone deep in the broken springs of a chair, watching a dust storm coat the world in a blunt grey film.

After knocking on the door and not waiting for a reply, a nurse squeaked in with a trolley of food and slid a clattering tray onto the mobile table next to the bed. Robert's mother lifted Thomas back into her arms, while his father wheeled the table into position and removed the tin hood from the main dish. The sweaty grey fish and leaky ratatouille might have made a greedy man pause, but for his grandmother, who would rather have starved to death anyway, all food was equally unwelcome, and so she gave Robert's hand a last squeeze and broke the circuit which had introduced so many violent pictures into his imagination, and picked up her fork with the strange flat obedience of despair. She manoeuvred a flake of fish onto her fork and began to lift it towards her mouth. Then she stopped and lowered the fork again, staring at his father.

'I can't . . . find my mouth,' she said with emergency precision.

His father looked frustrated, as if his mother had found a trick to stop him from being angry with her, but Robert's mother immediately picked up the fork and smiled and said, 'Can I help you, Eleanor?' in the most natural way.

His grandmother's shoulders crumpled a little further at the thought that it had come to that. She nodded and his mother started to feed her, still holding Thomas on her other arm. His father, temporarily frozen, came to his senses and took Thomas from Robert's mother.

After a few more mouthfuls his grandmother shook her head and said, 'No,' and leant back in her chair exhausted. In the silence that followed, his father handed Thomas back to his mother and sat down next to his grandmother.

'I hesitate to mention this,' said his father, pulling a letter out of his pocket.

'I think you should keep on hesitating,' said his mother quickly.

'I can't,' he said to her, 'hesitate any longer.' He turned back to Robert's grandmother. 'Brown and Stone have written to me saying that you intend to make an outright gift of Saint-Nazaire to the Foundation. I just want to say that I think that leaves you very exposed. You can barely afford to stay here and if you needed any more medical care you would go broke very quickly.'

Robert hadn't thought his grandmother could look any more unhappy, but somehow her features managed to yield a fresh impression of horror.

'I . . . really . . . I . . . really . . . no.'

She covered her face with her hands and screamed.

'I really do object . . .' she wailed.

His mother put her arm around his grandmother without glancing at his father. His father put the letter back in his pocket and looked at his shoes with perfect contempt.

'It's all right,' said his mother. 'Patrick just wants to help you, he's worried that you may give too much away too soon, but nobody's questioning that you can do what you like with the Foundation. The lawyers only told him because you've asked him to help you in the past.'

'I . . . need . . . to rest now,' said his grandmother.

'We'll leave, then,' said his mother.

'Yes.'

'I'm sorry I've upset you,' sighed his father. 'I just don't see what the hurry is: Saint-Nazaire is going to the Foundation in your will anyway.'

'I think we should drop this subject,' said his mother.

'Fine,' he agreed.

Robert's grandmother allowed herself to be kissed by each of them in turn. Robert was the last to say goodbye to her.

'Don't . . . leave me,' she said.

'Now?' he asked, confused.

'No . . . don't . . . no.' She gave up.

'I won't,' he said.

Any discussion of their visit to the nursing home seemed too hazardous, and they started the drive home in silence. Soon enough, though, his father's determination to talk took over. He tried to keep things general, he tried to keep away from the subject of his mother.

'Hospitals are very shocking places,' he said, 'full of poor deluded fools who aren't looking for groundless celebrity or obscene quantities of money, but think the point of life is to help other people. Where do they get these ideas from? We must send them on an empowerment weekend workshop with the Packers.'

Robert's mother smiled.

'I'm sure Seamus could organize it, give it a shamanic angle,' said his father, dragged irresistibly out of his orbit. 'Mind you, although hospitals may be awash with cheerful saints, I would rather shoot myself in the head than experience the erosion of self we witnessed this afternoon.'

'I thought Eleanor did very well,' said his mother. 'I was very moved when she said that she was brave.'

'What can drive a man mad is being forced to have the emotion which he is forbidden to have at the same time,' said his father. 'My mother's treachery forced me to be angry, but then her illness forced me to feel pity instead. Now her recklessness makes me angry again but her bravery is supposed to smother my anger with admiration. Well, I'm a simple sort of a fellow, and the fact is that I remain *fucking angry,* he shouted, banging the steering wheel.

'Who is King Lear?' asked Robert from the back seat.

'Did you overhear our conversation this morning?' asked his mother.

'Yes.'

'Eavesdropping,' said his father.

'No I wasn't,' he objected. 'You left the monitor on.'

'Oh, yes,' said his mother, 'so I did. Anyway, it hardly matters now, does it, darling?' she asked his father sweetly. 'Since you're screaming that you're "fucking angry" at the top of your voice.'

'King Lear,' said his father, 'is a petulant tyrant in Shakespeare who gives everything away and is then surprised when Goneril and Regan – or Seamus Dourke, as I prefer to think of them – refuse him the care he requires and boot him out.'

'And who's Mrs Jellybean?'

'Jellyby. She's a compulsive do-gooder who writes indignant letters about orphans in Africa, while her own children fall into the fireplace at the other end of the drawing room.'

'And what's a rut?'

'Well, the idea is that if you combined these two characters you would get someone like Eleanor.'

'Oh,' said Robert, 'it's quite complicated.'

'Yes,' said his father. 'The thing is that Eleanor is trying to buy herself a front-row seat in heaven by giving all her money to "charity" but, as you can see, she has in fact bought herself a ticket to hell.'

'I don't think it's that clever to turn Robert against his grandmother,' said his mother.

'I don't think it was that clever of her to make it inevitable.'

'You're the one who feels betrayed – she's your mother.'

'She's lied to all of us,' his father insisted. 'At every stage she told me that such and such a thing was destined for Robert, but one by one these little concessions to family feeling were ripped from their pedestals and sucked into the black hole of the Foundation.'

Robert's mother let some time pass in silence and then said, 'Well, at least we didn't have *my* mother to stay this year.'

'Yes, you're right,' said his father, 'we must cultivate gratitude.'

The atmosphere settled down a little after this moment of harmony. They climbed the lane towards the house. The sunset was simple that evening, without clouds to make mountains and chambers and staircases, just a clear pink light around the hill tops, and an edge of moon hanging in the darkening sky. As they rumbled down the rough drive, Robert felt a sense of home which he knew he must learn to set aside. Why was his grandmother causing so much trouble? The scramble for a front-row seat in heaven seemed unbearably expensive. He looked at Thomas in his baby chair and wondered if he was closer to 'the source' than the rest of them, and whether it was a good thing if he was. His grandmother's impatience to be reabsorbed into a luminous anonymity suddenly filled him with the opposite impatience: to live as distinctively as he could before time nailed him to a hospital bed and cut out his tongue.

AUGUST 2001

6

By day, when Patrick heard the echoing bark of the unhappy dog on the other side of the valley, he imagined his neighbour's shaggy Alsatian running back and forth along the split-cane fence of the yard in which he was trapped, but now, in the middle of the night, he thought instead of all the space into which the rings of yelping howling sound were expanding and dissipating. The crowded house compressed his loneliness. There was no one he could go to, except possibly, or rather impossibly (or, perhaps, possibly), Julia, back again after a year.

As usual, he was too tired to read and too restless to sleep. The tower of books on his bedside table seemed to provide for every mood, except the mood of agitated despair he was invariably in. *The Elegant Universe* made him nervous. He didn't want to read about the curvature of space when he was already watching the ceiling shift and warp under his exhausted gaze. He didn't want to think about the neutrinos streaming through his flesh – it seemed vulnerable enough already. He had started but finally had to abandon Rousseau's *Confessions*. He had all the persecution mania he could handle without importing any more. A novel pretending to be the diary of one of Captain Cook's officers on his first voyage to Hawaii was too well researched to bear any resemblance to life. Weighed down by the tiny variations of emblems on the Victualling Board's biscuits, Patrick had started to feel thoroughly depressed, but when a second narrative, written by a descendant of the first narrator, living in twenty-first-century Plymouth and taking a holiday in Honolulu, had set up a ludic counterpoint with the first narrative, he thought he was going to go mad. Two works of history, one a history of salt and the other a history of the entire world since 1500 BC, competed for a place at the bottom of the pile.

Also as usual, Mary had gone to sleep with Thomas, leaving Patrick split between admiration and abandonment. Mary was such a devoted mother because she knew what it felt like not to have one. Patrick also knew what it felt like, and as a former beneficiary of Mary's maternal overdrive, he sometimes had to remind himself that he wasn't an infant any more, to argue that there were real children in the house, not yet horror-trained; he sometimes had to give himself a good talking-to. Nevertheless, he waited in vain for the maturing effects of parenthood. Being surrounded by children only brought him closer to his own childishness. He felt like a man who dreads leaving harbour, knowing that under the deck of his impressive yacht there is only a dirty little twin-stroke engine: fearing and wanting, fearing and wanting.

Kettle, Mary's mother, had arrived that afternoon and, as usual, immediately found a source of friction with her daughter.

'How was your flight?' asked Mary politely.

'Ghastly,' said Kettle. 'There was an awful woman next to me on the plane who was terribly proud of her breasts, and kept sticking them in her child's face.'

'It's called breast-feeding, Mummy,' said Mary.

'Thank you, darling,' said Kettle. 'I know it's all the rage now, but when I was having children the talk was of getting one's figure back. A clever woman was the one who went to a party looking as if she'd never been pregnant, not the one with her breasts hanging out, at least not for breast-feeding.'

As usual, the bottle of Tamazepan squatted on his bedside table. He definitely had a Tamazepan problem, namely, that it wasn't strong enough. The side effects, the memory loss, the dehydration, the hangover, the menace of nightmarish withdrawals, all that worked beautifully. It was just the sleep that was missing. He went on swallowing the pills in order not to confront the withdrawal. He remembered, in the distant past, a leaflet saying not to take Tamazepan for more than thirty consecutive days. He had been taking it every night for three years in larger and larger doses. He would be 'perfectly happy', as people said when they meant the opposite, to suffer horribly, but he never seemed to find the time. Either it was one of the children's birthdays, or he was appearing in court, already hung-over, or some other enormous duty required the absence of hallucination and high anxiety. Tomorrow, for instance, his mother was coming to lunch. Both mothers at once: not an occasion for bringing on any additional psychosis.

And yet he still cherished the days when additional psychosis had been his favourite pastime. His second year at Oxford was spent watching the flowers pulse and spin. It was during that summer of alarming experiments that he had met Julia. She was the younger sister of a dull man on the same staircase in Trinity. Patrick, already in the early stages of a mushroom trip, had been hurriedly refusing his invitation to tea, when he saw through the half-open door a neck-twistingly pretty girl hugging her knees in the window seat. He veered towards a 'quick cup of tea' and spent the next two hours staring idiotically at the unfairly lovely Julia, with her rose-pink cheeks and dark blue eyes. She wore a raspberry T-shirt which showed her nipples, and faded blue jeans frayed open a few inches under the back pocket and above her right knee. He swore to himself that when she was old enough he would seduce her, but she pre-empted his timid resolution by seducing him the same evening. They had made time-lapse, slow-motion and technically illegal (she was only sixteen the following week) love. They had fallen upwards, disappeared down rabbit holes, watched clocks go anticlockwise and run away from policemen who weren't chasing them. When they went to Greece he helped to stash the acid in his favourite hiding place: between her legs. He thought that things would cascade from one adventure to another, but now the stammering ecstasy of their love-making seemed like a miracle of freedom belonging to a lost world. Nothing had ever been as spontaneously intimate again, especially not, he kept reminding himself, conversation with the harder, drier Julia who was staying with him now. And yet, there she was, just down the corridor, bruised but still pretty. Should he go? Should he risk it? Should they mount a joint retrospective? Would the intensity come back once their bodies intertwined? The idea was insane. He would have to walk past Robert, the insomniac observation-freak, past the ferocious Kettle, past Mary, who hovered like a dragonfly over the surface of sleep in case she missed the slightest inflection of her baby's distress, and then into Julia's room (the corner of her door scraped the floor), which had probably already been invaded by her daughter Lucy anyway. He was paralysed, as usual, by equal and opposite forces.

Everything was as usual. That was depression: being stuck, clinging to an out-of-date version of oneself. During the day, when he played with the children, he was very close to being what he appeared to be, a father playing with his children, but at night he was either aching with nostalgia or writhing with self-rejection. His youth had sprinted away in its Airmax Nike trainers (only Kettle's youth still wore winged sandals), leaving a swirl of dust and a collection of fake antiques. He tried to remind himself what his youth had really been like, but all he could remember was the abundance of sex and the sense of potential greatness, replaced, as his view closed in on the present, by the disappearance of sex and the sense of wasted potential. Fearing and wanting, fearing and wanting. Perhaps he should take another twenty milligrams of Tamazepan. Forty milligrams, as long as he drank a lot of red wine for dinner, sometimes purchased a couple of hours of sleep; not the gorgeous oblivion which he craved, but a sweaty, turbulent sleep laced with nightmares. Sleep, in fact, was the last thing he wanted if it was going to usher in those dreams: strapped to a chair in the corner of the room watching his children being tortured while he screamed curses at the torturer, or begged him to stop. There was also a diet version, the Nightmare Lite, in which he threw himself in front of his sons just in time to have his body shredded by gunfire, or dismembered by ravenous traffic. When he wasn't woken by these shocking images, he dozed off dreamlessly, only to wake a few minutes later, gasping for air. The price he paid for the sedation he needed to drop off, was that his breathing seized up, until an emergency unit in his back brain sent a screaming ambulance to his frontal lobes and jolted him back into consciousness.

His dreams, dreadful enough in their own right, were almost always accompanied by a defensive analytic sequel. Johnny, his child-psychologist friend, had said this was 'lucid dreaming', in which the dreamer acknowledged that he was dreaming. What was he protecting his children from? His own sense of being tortured, of course. The in-dream dream seminars always reached such reasonable conclusions.

He was obsessed, it was true, with stopping the flow of poison from one generation to the next, but he already felt that he had failed. Determined not to inflict the causes of his suffering on his children, he couldn't protect them from the consequences. Patrick had buried his own father twenty years ago and hardly ever thought about him. At the peak of his kindness David had been rude, cold, sarcastic, easily bored; compulsively raising the hurdle at the last moment to make sure that Patrick cracked his shins. It would have been too flagrant for Patrick to become a disastrous father, or to get a divorce, or to disinherit his children; instead they had to live with the furious, sleepless consequence of those things. He knew that Robert had inherited his midnight angst and refused to believe that there was a midnight-angst gene which furnished the explanation. He remembered talking endlessly about his insomnia at a time when Robert had wanted to copy everything about him. He also saw, with a mixture of guilt and satisfaction and guilt about the satisfaction, the gradual shift in Robert from empathy and loyalty towards hatred and contempt for Eleanor and her philanthropic cruelty.

One great relief was that they wouldn't be seeing the Packers this year. Josh had been taken out of school for three weeks and lost the habit of pretending that he and Robert were best friends. During that period of heady freedom, Patrick and Robert had run into Jilly in Holland Park and found out that she was getting a divorce from Jim.

'The glitter's off the diamond,' she admitted. 'But at least I get to keep the diamond,' she added with a triumphant little hoot. 'It's awful about Roger being sent to prison. Hadn't you heard? It's an open prison, one of the posh ones. Still, it isn't great, is it? They got him for fraud and tax evasion. Basically, for doing what everyone else does, but not getting away with it. Christine's in bits, with the two kids and everything. She can't even afford a nanny. I said to her, "Get a divorce, it really bucks you up." Mind you, I forgot she wouldn't be getting a huge settlement. I don't know how much it *does* buck you up without a fortune thrown in. I sound awful, don't I? But you've got to be realistic. The doctor's put me on these pills; I can't stop talking. You'd better just walk away, or I'll have you pinned down here all day listening to me wittering on. It's funny, though, thinking of us last year, all sat around the pool in St Trop, having the time of our lives, and now everyone going their separate ways. Still, we've got the children, haven't we? That's the main thing. Don't forget that Josh is still your best friend,' she shouted at Robert as they left.

Thomas had started speaking over the last year. His first word was 'light', followed soon afterwards by 'no'. All those atmospheres evaporated and got so convincingly replaced, it was hard to remember the beginning, when he was speaking not so much to tell a story as to see what it was like to come out of silence into words. Amazement was gradually replaced by desire. He was no longer amazed by seeing, for instance, but by seeing what he wanted. He spotted a broom hundreds of yards down the street, before the rest of them could even see the sweeper's fluorescent jacket. Hoovers hid behind doors in vain; desire had given him X-ray vision. Nobody could wear a belt for long if he was in the room, it was commandeered for an obscure game in which Thomas, looking solemn, waved the buckle around, humming like a machine. If they ever made it out of London, his parents sniffed the flowers and admired the view, Robert looked for good climbing trees, and Thomas, who wasn't yet far enough from nature to have turned it into a cult, hurtled across the lawn towards the limp coils of a hose lying almost invisibly in the uncut grass.

At his first birthday party last week, Thomas had been attacked for the first time, by a boy called Eliot. A commotion suddenly drew Patrick's attention to the other side of the drawing room. Thomas, who was walking along unsteadily with his wooden rabbit on a string, had just been pushed over by a bruiser from his playgroup, and had the string wrenched from his hand. He let out a cry of indignation and then burst into tears. The thug wandered off triumphantly with the undulating rabbit clattering behind him on uneven wheels.

Mary swooped down and lifted Thomas off the ground. Robert went over to check that he was all right, on the way to recapture the rabbit.

Thomas sat on Mary's lap and soon stopped crying. He looked thoughtful, as if he was trying to introduce the novelty of being attacked into his frame of reference. Then he wriggled off Mary's knee and back down to the ground.

'Who was that dreadful child?' said Patrick. 'I don't think I've ever seen such a sinister face. He looks like Chairman Mao on steroids.'

Before Mary could answer, the bruiser's mother came over.

'I'm sorry about that,' she said. 'Eliot is so competitive, just like his dad. I hate to repress all that drive and energy.'

'You're relying on the penal system for that,' said Patrick.

'He should try knocking me over,' said Robert, practising his martial arts moves.

'Let's not go global with this rabbit thing,' said Patrick.

'Eliot,' said the bruiser's mother, in a special false voice, 'give Thomas his rabbit back.'

'No,' growled Eliot.

'Oh, dear,' said his mother, delighted by his tenacity.

Thomas had transferred his focus to the fire tongs which he was dragging noisily out of their bucket. Eliot, convinced that he must have stolen the wrong thing, abandoned the rabbit and headed for the tongs. Mary picked up the string of the rabbit and handed it to Thomas, leaving Eliot revolving next to the bucket, unable to decide what he should be fighting for. Thomas offered the rabbit string to Eliot who refused it and waddled over to his mother with a cry of pain.

'Don't you want the tongs?' she asked coaxingly.

Patrick hoped he would handle things more wisely with Thomas than he had with Robert, not infuse him with his own anxieties and preoccupations. The hurdles were always raised at the last moment. He was so tired now. The hurdles always raised . . . of course . . . he would think that . . . He was chasing his tail now . . . the dog was barking on the other side of the valley . . . the inner and outer worlds ploughing into each other . . . he was almost falling asleep . . . perchance to dream . . . fuck that. He sat up and finished the thought. Yes, even the most enlightened care carried a shadow. Even Johnny (but then, he was a child psychologist) reproached himself for making his children feel that he really understood them, that he knew what they were feeling before they knew themselves, that he could read their unconscious impulses. They lived in the panoptic prison of his sympathy and expertise. He had stolen their inner lives. Perhaps the kindest thing Patrick could do was to break up his family, to offer his children a crude and solid catastrophe. All children had to break free in the end. Why not give them a hard wall to kick against, a high board to jump from. Christ, he really must get some rest.

After midnight, the wonderful Dr Zemblarov was never far from his thoughts. A Bulgarian who practised in the local village, he spoke in extremely rapid, heavily accented English. 'In our culture, we have only this,' he would say, signing an elaborate prescription, '*la pharmacologic*. If we lived in the *Pacifique*, maybe we could dance, but for us there is only the chemical manipulation. When I go back to Bulgaria, for example, I take *de l'amphetamine*. I drive I drive I drive, I see my family, I drive I drive I drive, and I come back to Lacoste.' The last time Patrick had hesitantly asked for more Tamazepan, Dr Zemblarov reproached him for being so shy. '*Mais il faut toujours demander*. I take it myself when I travel.

L'administration want to limit us to thirty days, so I will put "one in the evening and one at night", which naturally is not true, but it will avoid you to come here so often. I will also give you Stillnox, which is from another family – the hypnotics! We also have the barbiturate family,' he added with an appreciative smile, his pen hovering over the page.

No wonder Patrick was always tired, and could only offer short bursts of child care. Today, Thomas had been in pain. Some more teeth were bullying their way through his sore gums, his cheeks were red and swollen and he was rushing about looking for distractions. In the evening, Patrick had finally contributed a quick tour of the house. Their first stop was the socket in the wall under the mirror. Thomas looked at it longingly and then anticipated his father by saying, 'No, no, no, no, no.' He shook his head earnestly, piling up as many 'no's as he could between him and the socket, but desire soon washed away the little dam of his conscience, and he lunged towards the socket, improvising a plug with his small wet fingers. Patrick swept him off his feet and hauled him further down the corridor. Thomas shouted in protest, planting a couple of sharp kicks in his father's testicles.

'Let's go and see the ladder,' gasped Patrick, feeling it would be unfair to offer him anything much less dangerous than electrocution. Thomas recognized the word and calmed down, knowing that the frail, paint-spattered aluminium ladder in the boiler room had its own potential for injury and death. Patrick held him lightly by the waist while he monkeyed up the steps, almost pulling the ladder back on them. As he was lowered to the ground, Thomas burst into a drunken run, reeling his way towards the boiler. Patrick caught him and prevented him from crashing into the water tank. He was completely exhausted by now. He'd had enough. It wasn't as if he hadn't contributed to the baby care. Now he needed a holiday. He staggered back into the drawing room, carrying his wriggling son.

'How are you?' asked Mary.

'Done in,' said Patrick.

'I'm not surprised, you've had him for a minute and a half.'

Thomas hurtled towards his mother, buckling at the last minute. Mary caught him before his head hit the floor and put him back on his feet.

'I don't know how you cope without a nanny,' said Julia.

'I don't know how I would cope with one. I've always wanted to look after the children myself.'

'Motherhood takes some people that way,' said Julia. 'I must say, it didn't in my case, but then I was so *young* when I had Lucy.'

To show that she too went mad in the sun-drenched south, Kettle had come down to dinner wearing a turquoise silk jacket and a pair of lemon-yellow linen trousers. The rest of the household, still wearing their sweat-stained shirts and khaki trousers, left her just where she wanted to be, the lonely martyr to her own high standards.

Thomas slapped his hands over his face as she came in.

'Oh, it's too sweet,' said Kettle. 'What's he doing?'

'Hiding,' said Mary.

Thomas whipped his hands away and stared at the others with his mouth wide open. Patrick reeled back, thunderstruck by his reappearance. It was Thomas's new game. It seemed to Patrick the oldest game in the world.

'It's so relaxing having him hide where we can all see him,' said Patrick. 'I dread the moment when he feels he has to leave the room.'

'He thinks we can't see him because he can't see us,' said Mary.

'I must say, I do sympathize,' said Kettle. 'I rather wish people saw things exactly as I do.'

'But you know that they don't,' said Mary.

'Not always, darling,' said Kettle.

'I'm not sure that it's a story of the self-centred child and the well-adjusted adult,' Patrick had made the mistake of theorizing. 'Thomas knows that we don't see things as he does, otherwise he wouldn't be laughing. The joke is the shift in perspective. He expects us to flow into his point of view when he covers his face, and back into our own when he whips his hands away. We're the ones who are stuck.'

'Honestly, Patrick, you always make everything so intellectual,' Kettle complained. 'He's just a little boy playing a game. Apropos of hiding,' she said, in the manner of someone taking the wheel from a drunken driver, 'I remember going to Venice with Daddy before we were married. We were trying to be discreet because one was expected to make an effort in those days. Well, of course the first thing that happened was that we ran into Cynthia and Ludo at the airport. We decided to behave rather like Thomas and pretend that if we didn't look at them they couldn't see us.'

'Was it a success?' asked Patrick.

'Not at all. They shouted our names across the airport at the top of their voices. I would have thought it was perfectly obvious that we didn't want to be spotted, but tact was never Ludo's forte. Anyway, we made all the right noises.'

'But Thomas does want to be spotted, that's his big moment,' said Mary.

'I'm not saying it's exactly the same situation,' said Kettle, with a little splutter of irritation.

'What are the "right noises"?' Robert had asked Patrick on the way into dinner.

'Anything that comes out of Kettle,' he replied, half hoping she would hear.

It didn't help that Julia was so unfriendly to Mary, not that it would have helped if she had been friendly. His loyalty to Mary was not in question (or was it?); what was in question was whether he could last without sex for one more second. Unlike the riotous appetites of adolescence, his present cravings had a tragic tinge, they were cravings for the appetites, metacravings, wanting to want. The question now was whether he would be able to sustain an erection, rather than whether he could ever get rid of the damn thing. At the same time the cravings had to cultivate simplicity, they had to collapse into an object of desire, in order to hide their tragic nature. They were not cravings for things which he could get, but for capacities which he would never have back. What would he do if he did get Julia? Apologize for being exhausted, of course. Apologize for being tied up. He was having (get it off your chest, dear, it'll do you good) a midlife crisis, and yet he wasn't, because a midlife crisis was a cliché, a verbal Tamazepan made to put an experience to sleep, and the experience he was having was still wide awake – at three thirty in the fucking morning.

He didn't accept any of it: the reduced horizons, the fading faculties. He refused to buy the pebble spectacles his Magoo-standard eyesight pleaded for. He loathed the fungus which seemed to have invaded his bloodstream, blurring everything. The impression of sharpness which he still sometimes gave was a simulation. His speech was like a jigsaw puzzle he had done a hundred times, he was just remembering what he had done before. He didn't make fresh connections any more. All that was over.

From down the corridor, he heard Thomas starting to cry. The sound sandpapered his nerves. He wanted to console Thomas. He wanted to be consoled by Julia. He wanted Mary to be consoled by consoling Thomas. He wanted everyone to be all right. He couldn't bear it any longer. He threw the bedclothes aside and paced the room.

Thomas soon settled down, but his cries had set off a reaction which Patrick could no longer control. He was going to go to Julia's room. He was going to turn the narrow allotment of his life into a field of blazing poppies. He opened the door slowly, lifting it on its hinges so that it didn't whine. He pulled it closed again with the handle held down so that it didn't click. He released the tongue slowly into the groove. The corridor was glowing with child-friendly light. It was as bright as a prison yard. He walked down it, heel-to-toe, all the way to the end, to Lucy's partially open door. He wanted to check first that she was still in her room. Yes. Fine. He doubled back to Julia's door. His heart was thumping. He felt terrifyingly alive. He leant close to the door and listened.

What was he going to do next? What would Julia do if he went into her room? Call the police? Pull him into bed whispering, 'What took you so long?' Perhaps it was a little tactless to wake her at four in the morning. Maybe he should make an appointment for the following evening. His feet were getting cold, standing on the hexagonal tiles.

'Daddy.'

He turned around and saw Robert, pale and frowning in the doorway of his bedroom.

'Hi,' whispered Patrick.

'What are you doing?'

'Good question,' said Patrick. 'Well, I heard Thomas crying . . .' That much was true. 'And I wondered if he was all right.'

'But why are you standing outside Julia's room?'

'I didn't want to disturb Thomas if he had gone back to sleep,' Patrick explained. Robert was too intelligent for this rubbish, but perhaps he was a shade too young to be told the truth. In a couple of years Patrick could offer him a cigar and say, 'I'm having this rather awkward *mezzo del camin* thing, and I need a quick affair to buck me up.' Robert would slap him on the back and say, 'I completely understand, old man. Good luck and happy hunting.' In the meantime, he was six years old and the truth had to be hidden from him.

As if to save Patrick from his predicament, Thomas let out another wail of pain.

'I think I'd better go in,' said Patrick. 'Poor Mummy has been up all night.'

He smiled stoically at Robert. 'You'd better get some sleep,' he said, kissing him on the forehead.

Robert turned back into his room, unconvinced.

The safety plug in Thomas's cluttered room cast a faint orange glow across the floor. Patrick picked his way towards the bed into which Mary carried Thomas every night out of his hated cot, and lowered himself onto the mattress, pushing half a dozen soft toys onto the floor. Thomas writhed and twisted, trying to find a comfortable position. Patrick lay on his side, teetering on the edge of the bed. He certainly wasn't going to get any sleep in this precarious sardine tin, but if he could just let his mind glide along, he might get some rest; if he could go omnogogic, gaining the looseness of dreams without their tyranny, that would be something. He was just going to forget about the Julia incident. What Julia incident?

Perhaps Thomas wouldn't be a wreck when he grew up. What more could one ask?

He was beginning to glide along in half-thoughts . . . quarter-thoughts, counting down . . . down.

Patrick felt a violent kick land on his face. The warm metallic rush of blood flooded his nose and the roof of his mouth.

'Jesus,' he said, 'I think I've got a nosebleed.'

'Poor you,' mumbled Mary.

'I'd better go back to my room,' he whispered, rolling

backwards onto the floor. He replaced Thomas's velveteen bodyguards and clambered to his feet. His knees hurt. He probably had arthritis. He might as well move into his mother's nursing home. Wouldn't that be cosy?

He slouched back down the corridor, pressing his nostril with the knuckle of his index finger. There were spots of blood on his pyjamas: so much for the field of poppies. It was five in the morning now, too late for one half of life and too early for the other. No prospect of sleep. He might as well go downstairs, drink a gallon of healthy, organic coffee and pay some bills.

7

Kettle, wearing dark glasses and an enormous straw hat, was already sitting at the stone table. Using her expired boarding pass as a bookmark, she closed her copy of James Pope-Hennessy's biography of Queen Mary and put it down next to her plate.

'It's like a dream,' said Patrick, easing his mother's wheelchair into position, 'having you both here at the same time.'

'Like . . . a . . . dream,' said Eleanor, generalizing.

'How are you, my dear?' asked Kettle, bristling with indifference.

'Very . . .'

The effort that Eleanor put into producing, after some time, a high-pitched 'well' gave an impression of something quite different, as if she had seen herself heading towards 'mad' or 'miserable' and just managed to swerve at the last moment. Her radiant smile uncovered the dental bomb site Patrick had so often begged her to repair. It was no use: she was not about to waste money on herself while she could still draw a charitable breath. The tiny amount of spare income she had left was being saved up for Seamus's sensory-deprivation tanks. In the meantime she was well on her way to depriving herself of the sensation of eating. Her tongue curled and twisted among shattered crags, searching forlornly for a whole tooth. There were several no-go areas too sensitive for food to enter.

'I'm going to help with the lunch,' said regretful, duty-bound Patrick, bolting across the lawn like a swimmer hurrying to the surface after too long a dive.

He knew that it was not really his mother he needed to escape but the poisonous combination of boredom and rage he felt whenever he thought about her. That, however, was a long-term project. 'It may take more than one lifetime,' he warned himself in a voice of simpering tenderness. Just looking at the next few minutes, he needed to put as many literal-minded yards between himself and his mother as he could manage. That morning, in the nursing home, he had found her sitting by the door with her bag on her knees, looking as if she had been ready for hours. She handed him a faint pencil-written note. It said that she wanted to transfer Saint-Nazaire to the Foundation straight away and not, as things stood, after her death. He had managed to postpone things last year, but could he manage it again? The note said she 'needed closure' and wanted his help and his 'blessing'. Seamus's rhetoric had left its fingerprints all over the prose. No doubt he had a closure ritual lined up, a Native American trance dance which would close its own closure with a macrocosmic and microcosmic, a father sky and mother earth, a symbolic and actual, an immediate and eternal booting out of Patrick and his family from Saint-Nazaire. At the centre of a dogfight of contradictory emotions, Patrick could sometimes glimpse his longing to get rid of the fucking place. At some point he was going to have to drop the whole thing, he was going to have to come back to Saint-Nazaire for a healing-drum weekend, to ask Seamus to help him let go of his childhood home, to put the 'trans' into what seemed so terribly personal.

As he crossed from the terrace into the olive grove, Patrick imagined himself extolling to a group of neo-shamen and neo-shawomen the appropriateness, the challenge, and

'I never would have believed this possible, but I have to use the word "beauty", of coming back to this property in order to achieve closure in the letting-go process (sighs of appreciation). There was a time when I resented and, yes, I must admit, hated Seamus and the Foundation and my own mother, but my loathing has been miraculously transformed into gratitude, and I can honestly say (little catch in his throat) that Seamus has been not only a wonderful teacher and drum guide, but also my truest friend (the pitter-patter of applause and rattles).'

Patrick ditched his little fantasy with a sarcastic yelp and sat down on the ground with his back to the house, leaning against the knotted grey trunk of an old bifurcating olive tree that he had used all his life to hide and to think. He had to keep reminding himself that Seamus was not a straightforward crook who had cheated a little old lady out of her money. Eleanor and Seamus had corrupted each other with the extravagance of their good intentions. Seamus might have continued to do some good, changing bedpans in Navan – the only town in Ireland to be spelt the same way backwards – and Eleanor could have lived on Ryvita and given her income to the blind, or to medical research, or to the victims of torture, but instead they had joined forces to produce a monument of pretension and betrayal. Together they were going to save the world. Together they were going to heighten consciousness by dumbing down an already dangerously dumb constituency. Whatever good there was in Seamus was being destroyed by Eleanor's pathological generosity, and whatever good had been in Eleanor was being destroyed by Seamus's inane vision.

What had turned Eleanor into such a goody-goody? Patrick felt that Eleanor's loathing for her own mother was at the root of her overambitious altruism. Eleanor had told him the story of being taken by her mother to her first big party. It took place in Rome just after the Second World War. Eleanor was a fifteen-year-old girl back for the holidays from her boarding school in Switzerland. Her mother, a rich American and a dedicated snob, had divorced Eleanor's dissolute, charming and untitled father and married a dwarfish and ill-tempered French duke, Jean de Valençay, obsessed with questions of rank and genealogy. On the tattered stage of a near-communist Republic, and entirely subsidized by his wife's recent industrial wealth, he was all the keener to insist on the antiquity of his bloodline. On the night of the party, Eleanor sat in her mother's immense Hispano-Suiza, parked next to a bombed-out building, round the corner from the glowing windows of Princess Colonna's house. Her stepfather had been taken ill but, languishing in an ornate Renaissance bed which had been in his family since his wife bought it for him the month before, he made his wife swear that she wouldn't enter the Princess's house until after the Duchessa di Dino, over whom she had precedence. Precedence, it turned out, meant that her mother had to arrive late. They waited in the car. In the front, next to the driver, was a footman, periodically sent round to check if the inferior Duchessa had arrived. Eleanor was a shy and idealistic girl, happier talking to the cook than to the guests who were being cooked for, but she was still quite impatient and curious about the party.

'Can't we just go? We're not even Italian.'

'Jean would kill me,' said her mother.

'He can't afford to,' said Eleanor.

Her mother froze with fury. Eleanor regretted what she had just said, but also felt a twinge of adolescent pride at giving precedence to honesty over tact. She looked out of the glass cage of her mother's car and saw a tramp stumbling towards them in torn brown clothes. As he grew closer, she saw the skeletal sharpness of his face, the out-sized hunger in his eyes. He shuffled up to the car and tapped on the window, pointing pleadingly to his mouth, raising his hands in prayer, pointing again to his mouth.

Eleanor looked over at her mother. She was staring straight ahead, waiting for an apology.

'We've got to give him some money,' said Eleanor. 'He's starving.'

'So am I,' said her mother, without turning her head. 'If this Italian woman doesn't show up soon, I'm going to go crazy.'

She tapped the glass separating her from the front seat and waved impatiently at the footman.

When they eventually got inside the house, Eleanor spent the party in her first flush of philanthropic fever. Her rejection of her mother's values fused with her idealism to produce an intoxicating vision of herself as a barefoot saint: she was going to dedicate her life to helping others, as long as they weren't related to her. A few years later, her mother speeded Eleanor along the path of self-denial by allowing herself to be bullied, as she lay dying of cancer, into leaving almost all of her vast fortune outright to Eleanor's stepfather. He had protested that the original will, in which he only had the use of her fortune during his lifetime, was an insult to his honour since it implied that he might cheat his stepdaughters by disinheriting them. He, in turn, broke the promise he had made to his dying wife and left the loot to his nephew. Eleanor was by then too implicated in her spiritual quest to admit how bewildered she was about the loss of all that money. The resentment was being passed on to Patrick, carefully preserved like one of the antiques which Jean loved to collect at his wife's expense. Her mother had liked dukes whereas Eleanor liked would-be witch doctors, but regardless of the social decline the essential formula remained the same: rip off the children for the sake of some cherished self-image, the grande dame, or the holy fool. Eleanor had pushed on to the next generation the parts of her experience she wanted to get rid of: divorce, betrayal, mother-hatred, disinheritance; and clung to an idea of herself as part of the world's salvation, the Aquarian Age, the return to primitive Christianity, the revival of shamanism – the terms shifted over the years, but Eleanor's role remained the same: heroic, optimistic, visionary, proud of its humility. The result of her psychological apartheid was to keep both the rejected and aspirant parts of herself frozen. On the night of that Roman party, she had borrowed some money from a family friend and dashed outside to find the starving tramp whose life she was going to save. A few corners later, she found that the streets had not recovered as quickly from six years of war as the merrymakers she had left behind. She couldn't help feeling conspicuous among the rats and the rubble, dressed in her sky-blue ball gown with a large banknote gripped in her eager fist. Shadows shifted in a doorway, and a splash of fear sent her shivering back to her mother's car. Fifty-five years later, Eleanor still hadn't worked out a realistic way to act on her desire to be good. She still missed the feast without relieving the famine. When things went wrong, and they always did, the bad experiences were not allowed to inform the passionate teenager; they were exiled to the bad-experience dump. A secret half of Eleanor grew more bitter and suspicious, so that the visible half could remain credulous and eager. Before Seamus there had been a long procession of allies. Eleanor handed her life over to them with complete trust and then, within a few hours of their last moment of perfection, they were suddenly rejected, and never mentioned again. What exactly they had done to deserve exile was never mentioned either. Illness was producing a terrifying confluence of the two selves which Eleanor had gone to such trouble to keep apart. Patrick was curious to know whether the cycle of trust and rejection would remain intact. After all, if Seamus crossed over into the shadows, Eleanor might want to dismantle the Foundation as vehemently as she had wanted to set it up. Maybe he could delay things for another year. There he was, still hoping to hang on to the place.

Patrick could remember wandering around the rooms and gardens of his grandmother's half-dozen exemplary houses. He had watched a world-class fortune collapse into the moderate wealth that his mother and his aunt Nancy enjoyed from a relatively minor inheritance they received before their mother caved in to the lies and bullying of her second husband. Eleanor and Nancy looked rich to some people, living at good addresses, one in London and one in New York, each with a place in the country, and neither of them needing to work, or indeed shop, wash, garden or cook for themselves, but in the history of their own family they were surviving on loose change. Nancy, who still lived in New York, combed the catalogues of the world's auction houses for images of the objects she should have owned. On the last occasion Patrick visited her on 69th Street, she had scarcely offered him a cup of tea before getting out a sleek black catalogue from Christie's, Geneva. It had just arrived and inside was a photograph of two lead jardinières, decorated with gold bees almost audibly buzzing among blossoming silver branches. They had been made for Napoleon.

'We didn't even used to comment on them,' said Nancy bitterly. 'Do you know what I'm saying? There were so many beautiful things. They used to just sit on the terrace in the rain. A million and a half dollars, that's what the little nephew got for Mummy's garden tubs. I mean, wouldn't you like to have some of these things to give to your children?' she asked, carrying over a new set of photograph albums and catalogues, to syncopate the sale price with the sentimental significance of what had been lost.

She went on decanting the poison of her resentment into him for the next two hours.

'It was thirty years ago,' he would point out from time to time.

'But the little nephew sells something of Mummy's every week,' she growled in defence of her obsession.

The continuing drama of deception and self-deception made Patrick violently depressed. He was only really happy when Thomas first greeted him with a burst of uncomplicated love, throwing open his arms in welcome. Earlier that morning, he had carried Thomas around the terrace, looking for geckos behind the shutters. Thomas grabbed every shutter as they passed, until Patrick unhooked it and creaked it open. Sometimes a gecko shot up the wall towards the shelter of a shutter on the upper floor. Thomas pointed, his mouth rounded with surprise. The gecko was the trigger to the real event, the moment of shared excitement. Patrick tilted his head until his eyes were level with Thomas's, naming the things they came across. 'Valerian . . . Japonica . . . Fig tree,' said Patrick. Thomas stayed silent until he suddenly said, 'Rake!' Patrick tried to imagine the world from Thomas's point of view, but it was a hopeless task. Most of the time, he couldn't even imagine the world from his own point of view. He relied on nightfall to give him a crash course in the real despair that underlay the stale, remote, patchily pleasurable days. Thomas was his antidepressant, but the effect soon wore off as Patrick's lower back started to ache and he caved in to his terror of early death, of dying before the children were old enough to earn a living, or old enough to handle the bereavement. He had no reason to believe that he would die prematurely; it was just the most flagrant and uncontrollable way of letting his children down. Thomas had become the great symbol of hope, leaving none for anyone else.

Thank goodness Johnny was coming later in the month. Patrick felt sure that he was missing something which Johnny could illuminate for him. It was easy to see what was sick, but it was so difficult to know what it meant to be well.

'Patrick!'

They were after him. He could hear Julia calling his name. Perhaps she could come and join him behind the olive tree, give him a very quick blow job, so that he felt a little lighter and calmer during lunch. What a great idea. Standing outside her door last night. The tangle of shame and frustration. He clambered to his feet. Knees going. Old age and death. Cancer. Out of his private space into the confusion of other people, or out of the confusion of his private space into the effortless authority of his engagement with others. He never knew which way it would go.

'Julia. Hi, I'm over here.'

'I've been sent to find you,' said Julia, walking carefully over the rougher ground of the olive grove. 'Are you hiding?'

'Not from you,' said Patrick. 'Come and sit here for a few seconds.'

Julia sat down next to him, their backs against the forking trunk.

'This is cosy,' she said.

'I've been hiding here since I was a child. I'm surprised there isn't a dent in the ground,' said Patrick. He paused and weighed up the risks of telling her.

'I stood outside your door last night at four in the morning.'

'Why didn't you come in?' said Julia.

'Would you have been pleased to see me?'

'Of course,' she said, leaning over and kissing him briefly on the lips.

Patrick felt a surge of excitement. He could imagine pretending to be young, rolling around among the sharp stones and the fallen twigs, laughing manfully as mosquitoes fed on his naked flesh.

'What stopped you?' asked Julia.

'Robert. He found me hesitating in the corridor.'

'You'd better not hesitate next time.'

'Is there going to be a next time?'

'Why not? You're bored and lonely; I'm bored and lonely.'

'God,' said Patrick, 'if we got together, there would be a terrifying amount of boredom and loneliness in the room.'

'Or maybe they have opposite electrical charges and they'd cancel each other out.'

'Are you positively or negatively bored?'

'Positively,' said Julia. 'And I'm absolutely and positively lonely.'

'You may have a point, then,' smiled Patrick. 'There's something very negative about *my* boredom. We're going to have to conduct an experiment under strictly controlled conditions to see whether we achieve a perfect elimination of boredom or an overload of loneliness.'

'I really should drag you back to lunch now,' said Julia, 'or everyone will think we're having an affair.'

They kissed. Tongues. He'd forgotten about tongues. He felt like a teenager hiding behind a tree, experimenting with real kissing. It was bewildering to feel alive, almost painful. He felt his pent-up longing for closeness streaming through his hand as he placed it carefully on her belly.

'Don't get me going now,' she said, 'it's not fair.'

They climbed groaning to their feet.

'Seamus had just arrived when I came to get you,' said Julia, brushing the dust off her skirt. 'He was explaining to Kettle what went on during the rest of the year.'

'What did Kettle make of that?'

'I think she's decided to find Seamus charming so as to annoy you and Mary.'

'Of course she has. It's only because you've got me all flustered that I hadn't worked that out already.'

They made their way towards the stone table, trying not to smile too much or to look too solemn. Patrick felt himself sliding back under the microscope of his family's attention. Mary smiled at him. Thomas threw out his arms in welcome. Robert gazed at him with his intimidating, knowledgeable eyes. He picked up Thomas and smiled at Mary, thinking, 'A man may smile and smile and be a villain.' Then he sat down next to Robert, feeling as he did when he defended an obviously guilty client in front of a famously difficult judge. Robert noticed everything. Patrick admired his intelligence, but far from short-circuiting his depression as Thomas did, Robert made him more aware of the subtle tenacity of the destructive influence that parents had on their children – that he had on his children. Even if he was an affectionate father, even if he wasn't making the gross mistakes his parents had made, the vigilance he invested in the task created another level of tension, a tension which Robert had picked up. With Thomas he would be different – freer, easier, if one could be free and easy while feeling unfree and uneasy. It was all so hopeless. He really must get a decent night's sleep. He poured himself a glass of red wine.

'It's good to see you, Patrick,' said Seamus, rubbing him on the back.

Patrick felt like punching him.

'Seamus has been telling me all about his workshops,' said Kettle. 'I must say they sound absolutely fascinating.'

'Why don't you sign up for one?' said Patrick. 'It's the only way you'll see the place in the cherry season.'

'Ah, the cherries,' said Seamus. 'Now, they're something

really special. We always have a ritual around the cherries – you know, the fruits of life.'

'It sounds very profound,' said Patrick. 'Do the cherries taste any better than they would if you experienced them as the fruits of a cherry tree?'

'The cherries . . .' said Eleanor. 'Yes . . . no . . .' She rubbed out the thought hastily with both hands.

'She loves the cherries. They're grand, aren't they?' said Seamus, clasping Eleanor's hand in his reassuring grip. 'I always take her a bowl in the nursing home, freshly picked, you know.'

'A handsome rent,' said Patrick, draining his glass of wine.

'No,' said Eleanor, panic-stricken, 'no rent.' Patrick realized he was upsetting his mother. He couldn't even go on being sarcastic. Every avenue was blocked. He poured himself another glass of wine. One day he was going to have to drop the whole thing, but just for now he was going to go on fighting; he couldn't stop himself. Fight with what, though? If only he hadn't gone to such trouble to make his mother's folly legally viable. She had handed him, without any sense of irony, the task of disinheriting himself, and he had carried it out carefully. He had sometimes thought of putting a hidden flaw in the foundations. He had sat in the multi-jurisdictional meetings with *notaires* and solicitors, discussing ways of circumventing the forced inheritance of the Napoleonic code, the best way to form a charitable foundation, the tax consequences and the accountancy procedures, and he had never done anything except refine the plan to make it stronger and more efficient. The only way out was that elastic band of debt which Eleanor was now proposing to snip. He had really put it in for her protection. He had tried to set aside the hope that she would take advantage of it, but now that he was about to lose that hope, he realized that he had been cultivating it secretly, using it to keep him at a small but fatal distance from the truth. Saint-Nazaire would soon be gone for ever and there was nothing he could do about it. His mother was an unmaternal idiot and his wife had left him for Thomas. He still had one reliable friend, he sobbed silently, splashing more red wine into his glass. He was definitely going to get drunk and insult Seamus, or maybe he wasn't. In the end, it was even harder to behave badly than to behave well. That was the trouble with not being a psychopath. Every avenue was blocked.

A scene was unfolding around him, no doubt, but his attention was so submerged that he could hardly make out what was going on. If he clawed his way up the slippery well shaft, what would he find anyway, except Kettle extolling Queen Mary's child-rearing methods, or Seamus radiating Celtic charisma? Patrick looked over the valley, a gauntlet of memory and association. In the middle of the view was the Mauduits' ugly farmhouse, its two big acacia trees still growing in the front yard. When he was a child he had often played with the oafish Marcel Mauduit. They used to fashion spears out of the pale green bamboos that flanked the stream at the bottom of the valley. They flung them at little birds which managed to leave several minutes before the bamboo clattered onto the abandoned branch. When Patrick was six years old Marcel invited him to watch his father beheading a chicken. There was nothing more curious and amusing than watching a chicken run around in silly circles looking for its head, Marcel explained. You really had to see it for yourself. The boys waited in the shade of the acacia trees. An old hatchet was stuck at a handy angle among the criss-cross cuts on the surface of a brownish plane tree stump. Marcel danced around like an Indian with a tomahawk, pretending to decapitate his enemies. In the distance, Patrick could hear the panic in the chicken coop. By the time Marcel's father arrived, gripping a hen by the neck, her wings beating uselessly against his vast belly, Patrick was beginning to side with her. He wanted this one to get away. He could see that she knew what was going on. She was held down sideways, her neck stuck over the edge of the stump. Monsieur Mauduit brought the hatchet down so that her head flopped neatly at his feet. Then he put the rest of her quickly on the ground and, with an encouraging pat, set her off on a frantic dash for freedom, while Marcel jeered and laughed and pointed. Elsewhere, the hen's eyes stared at the sky and Patrick stared at her eyes.

With his fourth glass of wine, Patrick found his imagination tilting towards Victorian melodrama. Dark scenes formed of their own accord, but he did nothing to stop them. He saw the bloated figure of a drowned Seamus floating in the Thames. His mother's wheelchair seemed to have lost control and was bouncing down the coastal path towards a Dorset cliff. Patrick noted the magnificent National Trust backdrop as she pitched forwards over the edge. One day he really must drop the whole thing, get real, get contemporary, accept the facts, but just for the moment he would go on imagining himself putting the last touches to a forged will, while Julia, seated on the edge of his desk, bemused him with the complexity of her undergarments. Just for now, he would have another little splash of wine.

Thomas leant forward in Mary's lap, and with her usual perfect intuition, she immediately handed him a biscuit. He sank back on her chest convinced, as he was hundreds of times a day, that he would never need something without being given it. Patrick scanned himself for jealousy, but it wasn't there. There was plenty of dark emotion but no rivalry with his infant son. The trick was to keep up a high level of loathing for his own mother, leaving no room to feel jealous of Thomas getting the solid foundations his father so obviously lacked. Thomas leant forwards a second time and, with an enquiring murmur, held out his biscuit to Julia, offering her a bite. Julia looked at the wet and blunted biscuit, made a face and said, 'Yuk. No thank you very much.'

Patrick suddenly realized that he couldn't make love to someone who missed the point of Thomas's generosity so completely. Or could he? Despite his revulsion, he felt his lust running on, not unlike a beheaded chicken. He had now achieved the pseudo-detachment of drunkenness, the little hillock before the swamps of self-pity and memory loss. He saw that he really must get well, he couldn't go on this way. One day he was going to drop the whole thing, but he couldn't do that until he was ready, and he couldn't control when he would be ready. He could, however, get ready to be ready. He sank back in his chair and agreed at least to that: his business for the rest of the month was to get ready to be ready to be well.

8

'How are you?' asked Johnny, lighting a cheap cigar.

The flaring match brought a patch of colour into the black and white landscape cast by the moonlight. The two men had come outside after dinner to talk and smoke. Patrick looked at the grey grass and then up at a sky bleached of stars by the violence of the moon. He didn't know where to begin. The previous evening he had somehow managed to transcend the 'Yuk' incident, stealing into Julia's bed after midnight and staying there until five in the morning. He had slept with Julia in a speculative haze which his impulsiveness and greed failed to abolish. Too busy asking himself what adultery felt like, he had almost forgotten to notice what Julia felt like. He wondered what it meant to be back inside a woman who, apart from the relatively faint reality of her limbs and skin, was above all a site of nostalgia. What it certainly did not mean was Time Regained. Being a pig in the trough of a disreputable emotion turned out to fall short of the spontaneous timelessness of involuntary memory and associative thinking. Where were the uneven cobblestones and silver spoons and silver doorbells of his own life? If he stumbled across them, would floating bridges spring into being, with their own strange sovereignty, belonging to neither the original nor the repeated, the past nor the fugitive present, but to some kind of enriched present capable of englobing the linearity of time? He had no reason to think so. He felt deprived not only of the ordinary magic of intensified imagination, but of the even more ordinary magic of immersion in his own physical sensations. He wasn't going to scold himself for a lack of particularity in experiencing his sexual pleasure. All sex was prostitution for both participants, not always in the commercial sense, but in the deeper etymological sense that they stood in for something else. The fact that this was sometimes done so effectively that there were weeks or months in which the object of desire and the person one happened to be in bed with seemed identical could not prevent the underlying model of desire from beginning to drift away, sooner or later, from its illusory home. The strangeness of Julia's case was that she stood in for herself, as she had been twenty years ago, a pre-drift lover.

'Sometimes a cigar is just a cigar,' said Johnny, realizing that Patrick didn't want to answer his question.

'When's that?' said Patrick.

'Before you light it – after that, it's a symptom of unreconstructed orality.'

'I wouldn't be having this cigar unless I'd given up smoking,' said Patrick. 'I want to make that absolutely clear.'

'I completely understand,' said Johnny.

'One of the burdens of being a child psychologist,' said Patrick, 'is that if you ask someone how they are, they tell you. Instead of saying that I feel fine, I have to give you the real answer: *not* fine.'

'Not fine?'

'Bad, chaotic, terrified. My emotional life seems to cascade into wordlessness in every direction, not only because Thomas hasn't taken up words yet and Eleanor has already been abandoned by them, but also, internally, I feel the feebleness of everything I can control surrounded by the immensity of everything I can't control. It's very primitive and very strong. There's no wood left for the fire that keeps the wild animals at bay, that sort of thing. But also something even more confusing – the wild animals are a part of me that's winning. I can't stop them from destroying me without destroying them, but I can't destroy them without destroying myself. Even that makes it sound too organized. It's really more like a cartoon of cats fighting: a spinning blackness with exclamation marks flying off it.'

'You sound as if you have a good grasp of what's going on,' said Johnny.

'That should be a strength, but since I'm trying to communicate how little grasp I have of what's going on, it's a hindrance.'

'It's not a hindrance to your telling me about the chaos. It's only a hindrance if you're trying to manifest it.'

'Perhaps I do want to manifest it, so that it takes some concrete form, instead of it being this enormous state of mind.'

'I'm sure it does take some concrete form.'

'Hmm . . .'

Patrick scanned the concrete forms, the insomnia, the heavy drinking, the bouts of overeating, the constant longing for solitude which, if achieved, made him desperate for company, not to mention (or should he mention it? He felt the heavy gravitational field of confession surrounding Johnny) last night's adulterous incident.

He could remember only a few hours ago concluding that it had been a mistake, and beginning to imagine the mature discussion he was going to have with Julia. Now that the tide of alcohol was rising again, he was becoming more and more convinced that he had simply gone to bed with the wrong attitude. He must do better. He would do better.

'I must do better,' said Patrick.

'Do what better?'

'Oh, everything,' said Patrick vaguely.

He certainly wasn't going to tell Johnny, and then have his inflamed appetites placed in some pathological context or, worse, in a therapeutic programme. On the other hand, what was the point of his friendship with Johnny if it wasn't truthful? They had been friends for thirty years. Johnny's parents had known his parents. They knew each other's lives in depth. If Patrick had been wondering whether to commit suicide, he would have asked Johnny's opinion. Maybe he could shift the conversation away from his own mental health and onto one of their favourite topics: the way that time was grinding down their generation. Their shorthand for this process was 'the retreat from Moscow', thanks to the vivid picture they both had of the straggling survivors of Napoleon's army limping, bloodstained and bootless, through a landscape of frozen horses and dying men. Out of professional curiosity, Johnny had recently attended a reunion dinner of their year at school. He reported back to Patrick. The captain of the First XI was now a crack-head. The most brilliant student of their year was buried in the middle ranks of the civil service. Gareth Williams couldn't come because he was in a mental hospital. Their most 'successful' contemporary was the head of a merchant bank who, according to Johnny, 'failed to register on the authenticity graph'. That was the graph that Johnny cared about, the one that would determine whether, in his own eyes, he ended up in a roadside ditch or not.

'I'm sorry to hear that you've been feeling bad,' said Johnny, before Patrick could get him onto the safe ground of collective disappointment, sell-out and loss.

'I slept with Julia last night,' said Patrick.

'Did that make you feel better?'

'It made me wonder if I was feeling better. It was perhaps just a little bit too cerebral.'

'That's what you "must do better".'

'Exactly. I didn't know whether to tell you. I thought I might have to stop if we worked out exactly what was going on.'

'You've worked it out already.'

'Up to a point. I know that Thomas is making me revisit my own infancy in a way that Robert never did. Maybe it's the prominence of that old prop, a mother who needs mothering, which has lent so much authenticity to this revival. In any case, a deep sense of ancestral gloom stalks the night, and I would rather spend it with Julia who, instead of the primal chaos I feel on my own, offers the relatively innocuous death of youth.'

'It all sounds very allegorical – Primal Chaos and the Death of Youth. Sometimes a woman is just a woman.'

'Before you light her up?'

'No, no, that's a cigar,' said Johnny.

'Honestly, there are no easy answers. Just when you think you've worked something out . . .'

Patrick could hear the whining of a mosquito in his right ear. He turned his head and blew smoke in its direction. The sound stopped.

'Obviously, I would love to have real, embodied, fully present experiences – especially of sex,' Patrick went on, 'but, as you've pointed out, I'm taking refuge in an allegorical realm where everything seems to represent a well-known syndrome or conflict. I remember complaining to my doctor about the side effects of the Ribavirin he prescribed for me. "Oh, yes, that's known," he said with a kind of tremendous, uninfectious calm. Mind you, when I told him about a side effect that wasn't known, he dismissed it by saying, "I've never heard of that before." I think I'm trying to be like him, to immunize myself against experience by concentrating on phenomena. I keep thinking, "That's known," when in fact

I feel the opposite, that it's alien and menacing and out of control.'

Patrick felt a sharp sting. 'Fucking mosquitoes,' he said, slapping the back of his neck rather too hard. 'I'm being eaten alive.'

'I've never heard of that before,' said Johnny sceptically.

'Oh, it's *known*,' Patrick assured him. 'It's quite standard among the highlanders of Papua New Guinea. The only question is whether they make you eat yourself alive.'

Johnny let this prospect drown in silence.

'Listen,' said Patrick, leaning forward, and speaking more rapidly than before, 'I'm not in any serious doubt that everything I'm going through at the moment corresponds with the texture of my infancy in some way. I'm sure that my midnight angst resembles some free fall I felt in my cot when, for my own good, and so as to save me from becoming a manipulative little monster, my parents did exactly what suited them and ignored me. As you know, my mother only paves the road to hell with the best intentions, so we can assume that my father was the advocate of the character-building advantages of a will-breaking upbringing. But how can I really know and what good would it do me to find out?'

'Well, for a start, you're not using your powers of persuasion to keep Mary away from Thomas. Without any sense of connection with your own infancy, you almost certainly would be. It's true that the hardest maps to draw up are the very early ones, the first two years. We can only work with inferences. If, for example, someone had an acute intolerance of being kept waiting, felt a perpetual hunger which eating turned into a bloated despair, and was kept awake by hypervigilance . . .'

'Stop! Stop!' sobbed Patrick. 'It's all true.'

'That would imply a certain quality of early care,' Johnny

went on, 'different from the kind of omnipotent fantasy world that Eleanor wants to perpetuate with her "non-ordinary reality" and her "power animals". We are always "the veils that veil us from ourselves", but looking into infancy, with no memories and no established sense of self, it's *all veils*. If the privation is bad enough, there's nobody there to have the insights. It's a question of reinforcing the best false self you can lay your hands on – the authenticity project is not an option. But that's not your case. I think you can afford to lose control, to go into the free fall. If the past was going to destroy you it already would have.'

'Not necessarily. It might have been waiting for just the right moment. The past has all the time in the world. It's only the future which is running out.'

He emptied the wine bottle into his glass.

'And the wine,' he added.

'So,' said Johnny, 'you're going to try to "do better" tonight?'

'Yes. My conscience isn't rebelling in quite the way I expected. I'm not trying to punish Mary by going to bed with Julia – I'm just looking for a little tenderness. I think Mary would almost be relieved if she knew. It's a burden to someone like her not being able to give me what I need.'

'You're really doing her a favour,' said Johnny.

'Yes,' said Patrick, 'I don't like to boast about it, but I'm helping her out. She won't need to feel guilty about abandoning me.'

'If only more people had your sense of generosity,' said Johnny.

'I think quite a lot of people do,' said Patrick. 'Anyway, these philanthropic impulses run in my family.'

'All I feel like saying,' said Johnny, 'is that there's no point to your free fall unless it produces some insight. This is the time for Thomas to develop secure attachment. If you can make it through to his third birthday without destroying your marriage or making Mary feel depressed, that would be a great achievement. I think Robert is already well grounded. Anyway, he has that amazing talent for mimicry which he uses to play with whatever weighs on his mind.'

Before Patrick had time to respond, he heard the screen door swing open and snap back again on its magnetic strip. Both men fell silent and waited to see who was coming out of the house.

'Julia,' said Patrick, as she came into view, swishing across the grey grass, 'come and join us.'

'We've all been wondering what you're up to,' said Julia. 'Are you baying at the moon, or working out the meaning of life?'

'Neither,' said Patrick, 'there's too much baying in this valley already, and we worked out the meaning of life years ago: "Walk tall and spit on the graves of your enemies". Wasn't that it?'

'No, no,' said Johnny. 'It was "love thy neighbour as thyself".'

'Oh, well, given how much I love myself, it amounts to pretty much the same thing.'

'Oh, darling,' said Julia, resting her hands on Patrick's shoulders, 'are you your own worst enemy?'

'I certainly hope so,' said Patrick. 'I dread to think what would happen if somebody else turned out to be better at it than me.'

Johnny ground his crackling, splitting cigar into the ashtray.

'I might head for bed,' he said, 'while you decide whose grave to spit on.'

'Eenee, meenee, minee, mo,' said Patrick.

'Do you know, Lucy's generation don't say, "Catch a

nigger by the toe" any more; they say, "Catch a tiger by the toe". Isn't it sweet?'

'Have they rewritten "Rock a bye, Baby" as well? Or is the cradle still allowed to fall?' asked Patrick. 'God,' he added, looking at Johnny, 'it must be difficult for you hearing a person's unconscious breaking through every sentence.'

'I try not to hear it,' said Johnny, 'when I'm on holiday.'

'But you don't succeed.'

'I don't succeed,' smiled Johnny.

'Has everyone gone to bed?' asked Patrick.

'Everyone except Kettle,' Julia replied. 'She wanted to have a little heart-to-heart; I think she's in love with Seamus. She's been to tea in his cottage for the last two afternoons.'

'She *what*?' said Patrick.

'She's stopped talking about Queen Mary's widowhood and started talking about "opening up to one's full potential".'

'That bastard. He's going to try to get Mary disinherited as well,' said Patrick. 'I'm going to have to kill him.'

'Wouldn't it be more efficient to kill Kettle before she changes her will?' asked Julia.

'Good thinking,' said Patrick. 'My judgement was clouded by emotion.'

'What is this?' said Johnny. 'An evening with the Macbeths? What about just letting her open to her full potential?'

'Jesus,' said Patrick, 'who have you been reading recently? I thought you were a realist, not a human-potential moron who claims to see El Dorados of creativity in every flower arrangement. Even in the hands of a psychotherapeutic genius, Kettle's peak would be joining a tango class in Cheltenham, but with Seamus her "full potential" is to be fully ripped off.'

'The potential which Kettle hasn't realized – and she's not alone,' said Johnny, 'has nothing to do with hobbies, or even achievements, it's to do with being able to enjoy anything at all.'

'Oh, that potential,' said Patrick. 'You're right, of course, we all need to work on that.'

Julia grazed his thigh discreetly with her fingernails. Patrick felt a half-erection creep its way into the most inconvenient possible position among the folds of his underwear. Not particularly wanting to struggle with his trousers in front of Johnny, he waited confidently for the problem to disappear. He didn't have to wait long.

Johnny got to his feet and said good night to Patrick and Julia.

'Sleep well,' he added, starting out towards the house.

'One may be too busy opening up to one's full potential,' said Patrick in a racy version of his Kettle voice.

As soon as they heard Johnny entering the house, Julia climbed astride Patrick's lap, facing him with her hands dangling lightly over his shoulders.

'Does he know?' she asked.

'Yes.'

'Is that a good idea?'

'He won't tell anyone.'

'Maybe, but now it's too late for us not to tell anyone. I can't believe we're already into who knows what, that's all. We've only just been to bed together and it's already a problem of knowledge.'

'It's always a problem of knowledge.'

'Why?'

'Because there was this garden, right? And this apple tree . . .'

'Oh, honestly, that has nothing to do with it. That's a different kind of knowledge.'

'They came together. In the absence of God, we have the

omniscience of gossip to keep us preoccupied with who knows what.'

'I'm not in fact preoccupied with who knows what, I'm preoccupied with how we feel for each other. I think you want it to be about knowledge because you're more at home in your head than in your heart. Anyhow, you didn't have to tell Johnny.'

'Whatever,' said Patrick, suddenly drained of all desire to prove a point or win an argument. 'I often think there should be a superhero called Whateverman. Not an action hero like Superman or Spiderman, but an inaction hero, a hero of resignation.'

'Is there a comma between "Whatever" and "Man"?'

'Only when he can be bothered to speak, which, believe me, isn't often. When someone screams, "There's a meteor headed straight for us! It's the end of all life on Earth!", he says, "Whatever, man," with a comma in between. But when he is invoked, during an episode of ethnic cleansing, or paranoid schizophrenia, as in, "This is a job for Whateverman", it's all in one word.'

'Does he have a cloak?'

'God, no. He wears the same old jeans and T-shirt year in year out.'

'And this fantasy is all in the service of not admitting that you were wrong to tell Johnny.'

'It was wrong if it upset you,' said Patrick. 'But when my oldest friend asked me what was going on, it would have been glib to leave out the most important fact.'

'Poor darling, you're just too—'

'Authentic,' Patrick interrupted. 'That's always been my trouble.'

'Why don't you bring some of that authenticity upstairs?' asked Julia, leaning forwards and giving Patrick a long slow kiss.

He was grateful that she made it impossible for him to answer her question. He wouldn't have known what to say. Was she mocking his shallow disembodied presence the night before? Or hadn't she noticed? The problem of other minds. Christ, he was at it again. They were kissing. Get into it. Picture of himself getting into it. No, not the picture, the thing in itself. Whatever that was. Who was to say that authenticity lay in being oblivious to the reflective aspect of the mind? He was speculative. Why suppress that in favour of what was, in the end, just a picture of authenticity, a cliché of into-it-ness?

Julia broke off the kiss.

'Where have you gone?' she asked.

'I was lost in my head,' he admitted. 'I think I was thrown by your request for me to bring my authenticity upstairs – there's just so much of it, I'm not sure I can manage.'

'I'll help,' said Julia.

They untangled themselves and walked back into the house, holding hands, like a couple of moon-struck teenagers.

When they reached the landing and were about to slip into Julia's bedroom, they heard stifled giggling from Lucy's bedroom, followed by a crescendo of hushing. Transformed from furtive lovers into concerned parents, they walked down the corridor with a new authority. Julia tapped gently on the door and immediately pushed it open. The room was dark, but light from the corridor fell across a crowded bed. All of Lucy's indispensable soft toys, her white rabbit and her blue-eyed dog and, incredibly, the chipmunk she had chewed religiously since her third birthday, were scattered in various buckled postures across the bedspread, and replaced, inside the bed, by a live boy.

'Darling?' said Julia.

The children made no sound.

'It's no use pretending to be asleep. We heard you down the corridor.'

'Well,' said Lucy, sitting up suddenly, 'we're not doing anything wrong.'

'We didn't say you were,' said Julia.

'This is the most outrageous subplot,' said Patrick. 'Still, I don't see why they shouldn't sleep together if they want to.'

'What's a subplot?' asked Robert.

'Another part of the main story,' said Patrick, 'reflecting it in some more or less flagrant way.'

'Why are *we* a subplot?' asked Robert.

'You're not,' said Patrick. 'You're a plot in your own right.'

'We've got so much to talk about,' said Lucy, 'we just couldn't wait until tomorrow.'

'Is that why you two are still up?' asked Robert. 'Because you've got so much to talk about. Is that why you said we were a subplot?'

'Listen, forget I ever said it,' said Patrick. 'We're all each other's subplots,' he added, trying to confuse Robert as much as possible.

'Like the moon going round the earth,' said Robert.

'Exactly. Everyone thinks they're on the earth, even when they're on somebody else's moon.'

'But the earth goes round the sun,' said Robert. 'Who's on the sun?'

'The sun is uninhabitable,' said Patrick, relieved that they had travelled so far from the original motive of his comment. 'Its only plot is to keep us going round and round.'

Robert looked troubled and was about to ask another question when Julia interrupted him.

'Can we return to our own planet for a second?' she asked. 'I suppose I don't mind you sharing a bed, but remember we're going to Aqualand tomorrow, so you must go straight to sleep.'

'What else would we do?' said Lucy, starting to giggle. 'Smudging?'

She and Robert made sounds of extravagant revulsion and collapsed in a heap of limbs and laughter.

9

Patrick ordered another double espresso and watched the waitress weave her way back to the bar, only momentarily transfixed by a vision of her sprawled across one of the tables, gripping its sides while he fucked her from behind. He was too loyal to linger over the waitress when he was already involved in a fantasy about the girl in the black bikini on the other side of the cafe, her eyes closed and her legs slightly parted, absorbing the beams of the morning sun, still as a lizard. He might never recover from the look of intense seriousness with which she had examined her bikini line. An ordinary woman would have reserved that expression for a bathroom mirror, but she was a paragon of self-absorption, running her finger along the inside edge of her bikini, lifting it and realigning it still closer to the centre, so that it interfered as little as possible with the total nudity which was her real object. The mass of holiday-makers on the Promenade Rose, shuffling forward to claim their coffin-sized plot of beach, might as well not have existed; she was too fascinated by the state of her tan, her wax job, her waistline, too in love with herself to notice them. He was in love with her too. He was going to die if he didn't have her. If he was going to be lost, and it looked as if he was, he wanted to be lost inside her, to drown in the little pool of her self-love – if there was room.

Oh, no, not that. Please. A piece of animated sports equipment had just walked up to her table, put his pack of red Marlboros and his mobile phone next to her mobile phone and pack of Marlboro Lights, kissed her on the lips and sat down, if that was the right term for the muscle-bound bouncing with which he eventually settled into the chair next to hers. Heartbreak. Disgust. Fury. Patrick skimmed over the ground of his immediate emotions and then forced himself upwards into the melancholy sky of resignation. Of course she was spoken for a million times over. In the end it was a good thing. There could be no real dialogue between those who still thought that time was on their side and those who realized that they were dangling from its jaws, like Saturn's children, already half-devoured. Devoured. He could feel it: the dull efficiency of a praying mantis tearing arcs of flesh from the still living aphid it has clamped between its forelegs; the circular hobbling of a wildebeest, reluctant to lie down with the lion who hangs confidently from his neck. The fall, the dust, the last twitch.

Yes, in the end it was a good thing that Bikini Girl was spoken for. He lacked the pedagogic patience and the particular kind of vanity which would have enabled him to opt for the cheap solution of being a youth vampire. It was Julia who had got him used to sex during her fortnight's stay, and it was among the time refugees of her blighted generation that he must look for lovers. With the possible exception, of course, of the waitress who was now weaving her way back towards him. There was something about the shop-worn sincerity of her smile which suited his mood. Or was it the stubborn pout of the labial mould formed by her jeans? Should he get a shot of brandy to tip into his espresso? It was only ten thirty in the morning, but there were already several misty-cold glasses of beer blazing among the round tables. He only had two days of holiday left. They might as well be debauched. He ordered the brandy. At least that way she would be back soon. That's how he liked to think of her, weaving back and forth on his behalf, tirelessly attending to his clumsy search for relief.

He turned towards the sea, but the harsh glitter of the water blinded him and, while he shielded his eyes from the sun, he found himself imagining all the people on that body-packed curve of blond sand, shining with protective lotions, playing with bats and balls, lolling in the placid bay, reading on their towels and mattresses, all being blasted by a fierce wind and blown into a fine veil of sparkling sand, and the collective murmur, pierced by louder shouts and sharper cries, falling silent.

He must rush down that beach to shelter Mary and the children from ruin, give them a few more seconds of life with the decomposing shield of his own body. He struggled so hard to get away from his roles as a father and a husband, only to miss them the moment he succeeded. There was no better antidote to his enormous sense of futility than the enormous sense of purpose which his children brought to the most obviously futile tasks, such as pouring buckets of sea water into holes in the sand. Before he managed to break away from his family, he liked to imagine that once he was alone he would become an open field of attention, or a solitary observer training his binoculars on some rare species of insight usually obscured by the mass of obligations that swayed before him like a swarm of twittering starlings. In reality solitude generated its own roles, not based on duty but on hunger. He became a cafe voyeur, drunk with desire, or a calculating machine compulsively assessing the inadequacy of his income.

Was there any activity which didn't freeze into a role? Could he listen without being a listener, think without being a thinker? No doubt there was a flowing world of present participles, of listening and thinking, rushing along beside him, but it was part of the grim allegorical tinge of his mentality that he sat with his back to this glittering torrent, staring at a world of stone. Even his affair with Julia seemed to have *The Sorrows of Adultery* carved on its plinth. Instead of thrilling him with his own audacity, it reminded him of how little he had left. After they had started sleeping together, his days were spent sprawled on a pool-side lounger, feeling that he might as well have been splayed in a roadside ditch, discouraging the excitement of some hungry rats, rather than turning down the demands of his adorable children. His guilt-fuelled bouts of charm towards Mary were as flagrant as his row-picking arguments. The margin of freedom he had gained with Julia was soon filled with the concrete of another role. She was his mistress, he was her married man. She would struggle to get him away, he would struggle to keep her in the mistress slot without tearing his family apart. They were already in a perfectly structured situation, with ultimately opposed interests. Its currency was deception: of Mary, of each other, and of themselves. It was only in the immediate greed of a bed that they could find any common ground. He was amazed by the amount of defeat and inconvenience that already surrounded his affair with Julia. The only sane action would be to end it straight away, to define it as a summer fling and not try to elaborate it into a love affair. The terrible thing was that he had already lost control of the situation. He only felt well when he was in bed with her, when he was inside her, when he was coming inside her. Kneeling on the floor, that had been good, when she had sat in the armchair with her knees up and her legs spread. And the night of the thunder storm, the air awash with free ions, when she stood in the window, gasping at the lightning, and he stood behind her and . . . and here came his brandy, thank God.

He smiled at the waitress. What was the French for 'How

about it, darling?' Something, something, something, *chérie*. He'd better stick to the French for 'Same again' – stay on safe ground. Yes, he was lost because he liked everything about Julia: the smell of tobacco on her breath, the taste of her menstrual blood. He couldn't rely on revulsion of any sort to set him free. She was kind, she was careful, she was accommodating. He was going to have to rely on the machine of their situation to grind them down, as he knew it would.

'*Encore la même chose*,' he called to the waitress, swirling his finger over his empty glass while she unloaded her tray at a nearby table. She nodded. She was the waitress, and he was the waiter waiting for the waitress. Everyone had their role.

He could feel the *fin de saison*, the lassitude of the beaches and restaurants, the sense that it was time to get back to school and to work, back to the big cities; and among the residents, relief at the subsiding numbers, the fading heat. All his guests had left Saint-Nazaire. Kettle had left in triumph, knowing she would be the first to return. She had signed up for Seamus's Basic Shaman workshop and then, in a kind of shopper's euphoria, decided to stay on for the Chi Gong course given by a pony-tailed martial artist whose photograph she pored over whenever there was someone to watch her. Seamus had given her a book called *The Power of Now*, which she kept face down beside her deck chair, not as reading material, obviously, but as a badge of allegiance to the power that now ran Saint-Nazaire. She had taken him up for the simple reason that it was the most annoying thing she could think of doing. It occupied the time when she was not criticizing Mary for the way she brought up the children. Mary had learned to walk away, to make herself unavailable for half-days at a time. Kettle had never known what to do with those fallow periods until she decided to become a fan of Seamus's Transpersonal Foundation.

The Power of Now only disappeared when Anne Whitling, an old friend of Kettle's, wearing her own vast straw hat with an Isadora Duncan-length scarf trailing dangerously behind it, talked her way down the coast from one of the fashionable Caps. Her profound inability to listen to anyone else was unhappily married to a hysterical concern about what other people thought of her. When Thomas started babbling excitedly to Mary about the hose that was coiled next to the pool house, Anne said, 'What's he saying? What's he saying? If he's saying my nose is too big, I'm going to commit.' This charming abbreviation, which Patrick had never heard before, made him imagine bloodstained articles about men's fear of commitment. Should he commit to his marriage? Or commit to Julia? Or just commit?

How could he go on feeling so awful? And how could he stop? Stealing a picture from his senile mother was one obvious way to cheer himself up. The last two valuable paintings she owned were a pair of Boudins, making up complementary views of the beach at Deauville, and worth approximately two hundred thousand pounds. He had to rap himself over the knuckles for assuming that he would inherit the Boudins in 'the normal course of events'. Only three days ago, just after waving an exhilarating farewell to Kettle, he had received another of Eleanor's faint, painstaking, pencil-written notes, saying that she wanted the Boudins sold and the money used to build Seamus's sensory-deprivation annex. Things just weren't moving along fast enough for the Kubla Khan of the mindless realms.

He could imagine himself in some distant past thinking he ought to 'keep the Boudins in the family', feeling sentimental about those banked-up clouds, the atmosphere of a lost yet vividly present world, the cultural threads radiating from those Normandy beaches. Now they might as well have been two cash dispensers in the wall of his mother's nursing home. If he was going to have to walk away from Saint-Nazaire, it would put a spring in his step to know that the sale of the Boudins and the sale of the London flat and a preparedness to move to Queen's Park would allow him to save Thomas from the converted cupboard in which he now slept and offer him an ordinary-sized children's bedroom in a terraced house on a main road, no more than a two-hour traffic jam from his brother's school. Anyway, the last thing he needed was a view of a beach at the other end of France when he could so easily admire the carcinogenic inferno of Les Lecques through the amber lens of his second cognac. 'The sea meets the sky here as well, thank you very much, Monsieur Boudin,' he muttered to himself, already a little light-headed.

Did Seamus know about the note? Had he written it himself? Whereas Patrick was simply going to ignore Eleanor's request to make the gift of Saint-Nazaire absolute in her own lifetime, he was going to make a more drastic refusal in the case of the Boudins: steal them. Unless Seamus had written evidence that Eleanor wanted to give the paintings to the Foundation, any contest would come down to his word against Seamus's. Luckily, Eleanor's post-stroke signature looked like an incompetent forgery. Patrick felt confident that he could run legal circles around the visionary Irishman, even if he was unable to win a popularity contest against him when it was judged by his own mother. It was really, he assured himself, as he briskly ordered a '*dernier cognac*', like a man with better things to do than get blind drunk before lunch, really just a question of how to unhook these two oily ATMs from the wall.

The light on the Promenade Rose rained down on him like a shower of hot needles. Even behind his dark glasses his eyeballs ached. He was really quite . . . the coffee and the brandy . . . a little jet-engine whistle. 'Walkin' on the beaches / Lookin' at the peaches / Na, na-na, na-na-na-na-na'. Where was that from? Press Retrieve. Nothing happens, as usual. Gerard Manley Hopkins? He cackled wildly.

He must have a cigar. Must have, must have, must have, on a must-have basis. When was a cigar just a cigar? Before you must have it.

With any luck, he should arrive back at the Tahiti Beach (Irish accent) just in toyem for a syphilized battle of whine. 'God bless Seamus,' he added piously, making a puking sound at the foot of a squat bronze lamppost. Puns: the symptom of a schizoid personality.

Here was the *tabac*. The red cylinder. Whoops. '*Pardon, Madame.*' What was it with these big, tanned, wrinkly French women with chunky gold jewellery, orange hair and caramel-coloured poodles? They were *everywhere*. Unlock the glass cabinet. '*Celui-là*,' pointing to a Hoyo de Monterey. The little guillotine. Snip. Do you have something more serious at the back of the shop? *Un vrai guillotine. Non, non, Madame, pas pour les cigars, pour les clients!* Snap.

More hot needles. Hurry to the next patch of pine shade. Maybe he should have one more teeny-weeny brandy before going back to his family. Mary and the boys, he loved them so much, it made him want to cry.

He stopped at Le Dauphin. Coffee, cognac, cigar. Just as well to get these chores out of the way, then he'd be free to enjoy the rest of the day. He lit his cigar and as the thick smoke trickled back out of his mouth he felt he was being shown a pattern, like a rug unrolling in a rug shop. He had taken Mary, a good woman, and made her into an instrument of torture, a weird echo of Eleanor forty years ago: never available, always exhausted by her dedication to an altruistic project which didn't include him. He had achieved this by the ironic device of rejecting the sort of woman who would have made a bad mother, like Eleanor, and choosing one who was such a good mother that she was incapable of letting one drop of her love escape from her children. He could see that his obsession with not having enough money was only the material form of his emotional privation. He had known these facts for years, but just at that moment he felt that his grasp of them was especially subtle and clear and that his understanding gave him complete mastery of the situation. A second mouthful of heavy blue Cuban smoke drifted into the air. He was entranced by the sense of his own detachment, as if he had been set free by an instinctual expertise, like a seabird that breaks into flight just before a wave crashes onto the rock where it was perched.

The feeling passed. With only orange juice for breakfast, the six espressos and four glasses of brandy were having a bar brawl in his stomach. What was he doing? He had given up smoking. He flung the cigar towards the gutter. Whoops. '*Pardon*, *Madame*.' My God, it was the same woman, or almost the same woman. He might have set fire to her poodle. The newspaper headlines didn't bear thinking about . . . *Anglais intoxiqué . . . incendie de caniche . . .*

He must call Julia. He could live without her as long as he knew that she couldn't live without him. That was the deal the furiously weak made between their permanent disappointment and their temporary consolations. He looked at it with some disgust but knew that he would sign the contract anyway. He must make sure she was waiting for him, missing him, longing for him and expecting him in her flat on Monday night.

The nearest phone booth, a doorless and piss-scented wastepaper basket, was smouldering in full sunlight on the next corner. The blue plastic burnt his hand as he dialled the number.

'I can't come to the phone at the moment, but please leave a message . . .'

'Hello? Hello? It's Patrick. Are you hiding behind your machine? . . . OK, I'll call you tomorrow. I love you.' He'd almost forgotten to say that.

So, she wasn't in. Unless she was in bed with another man, sniggering at his tentative phone message. If he had one thing to say to the world, it was this: never, never have a child without first getting a reliable mistress. And don't be deceived by the false horizons – 'when the breastfeeding is over; when he spends the whole night in his own bed; when he goes to university'. Like a team of run-away horses, the empty promises hauled a man over shattered stone and giant cactuses while he prayed for the tangled reins to snap. It was all over, there was no comfort in marriage, just duty and obligation. He sank down on the nearest bench, needing to pause before he saw his family again. The cerulean huts and parasols of the Tahiti Beach were already in view, tunnelling deep into his memory. He had been Thomas's age when he first went there and Robert's when his memories became most intense: those pedalo rides which he expected to grind up on African beaches; jumping up and down on the sand-castles carefully assembled for him by foreign au pairs; being allowed to order his own drinks and ice creams as his chin cleared the wooden counter for the first time. As a teenager, he had taken books to the beach. They helped to hide his bulging trunks while he stared from behind his wraparound shades at the first blush of topless sunbathing to pass over the pale sands of Les Lecques. Since then the Tahiti had grown thinner and thinner, until the whole beach was nearly abolished by the sea. In his twenties, he had watched the municipality rebuild it with thousands of tons of imported pebbles. Every Easter, sand was dredged from the bay and spread over the artificial beach by teams of bulldozers, and every winter storms clawed it back into the bay.

He leant forward and rested his chin on his hands. The

initial impact of the coffee and brandy was dying out, leaving him only with a doomed nervous energy, like a flung stone bouncing over the water a few times before sinking beneath its surface. He looked wearily at the simulacrum of the original beach, if 'original' was the word for the beach he had known when he was the same age as his children were now. He let this pitifully local definition melt away, and tumbled back through geological time to the perfect boredom of the first beach, with its empty rock pools and its simple molecules not knowing what to do with themselves for billions of years on end. Can anyone think of anything to do other than jostle around? Rows of blank faces, like asking a group of old friends to suggest a new restaurant on a Sunday night. Seen from this primal shore, the emergence of human life looked like Géricault's *Raft of the Medusa*, greenish ghosts drowning in a frigid ocean of time.

He really needed another drink to recover from the chaos of his imagination. And some food. And some sex. He needed to get grounded, as Seamus would say. He needed to rejoin his own species, the rows and rows of belching animals on the beach with only a razor blade or a wax job between them and a great thick pelt; paying with agonizing back pains for their pretentious upright posture, but secretly longing to hobble along with their knuckles dragging in the sand, squealing and grunting, fighting and fucking. Yes, he needed to get real. Only consideration for the white-haired old lady with swollen ankles further down the bench prevented him from raining punches on his clenched pectorals and letting out a territorial bellow. Consideration and, of course, his growing sense of liverish gloom and midday hangover.

He hauled himself up and scraped his way along the last few hundred yards to the Tahiti. Swaying towards him over the smooth pink concrete, an almost naked girl with overpoweringly perfect breasts and a diamond nestling in her navel, locked her eyes onto his and smiled, raising both her arms, ostensibly to wrap her long blonde hair into a loose coil above her head, but really to simulate the way her limbs would be arranged if she were lying on a bed with her arms thrown back. Oh, God, why was life so badly organized? Why couldn't he just hoist her onto a hot car bonnet and tear off that turquoise excuse for a bikini bottom? She wanted it, he wanted it. Well, anyway, he wanted it. She probably wanted exactly what she had, the power to disturb every heterosexual man – and let's not forget our lesbian colleagues, he added with mayoral unction – who she scythed through as she strolled back and forth between her depressing boyfriend and her nippy little car. She walked by, he staggered on. She might as well have chopped off his genitals and chucked them in the sand. He could feel the blood running down his legs, hear the dogs squabbling over the unexpected meat. He wanted to sit down again, to lie down, to bury himself deep underground. He was finished as a man. He envied the male spider who was eaten straight after fertilizing the female, rather than consumed bit by bit like his human counterpart.

He paused at the head of the broad white ladder that led down to the Tahiti Beach. He could see Robert running back and forth with a bucket, trying to fill a leaking moat. Thomas was lying in his mother's arms, sucking his thumb, holding his raggie and watching Robert with his strange objective gaze. They were happy because they had the undivided attention of their mother, and he was unhappy because he had her undivided inattention. That, at least, was the local reason, but hardly the original beach of his unhappiness. Never mind the original beach. He had to step down onto this one and be a father.

'Hello, darling,' said Mary, with that permanently exhausted smile in which her eyes didn't participate. They inhabited a harder world in which she was trying to survive the ceaseless demands of her sons, and the destructive effect on a solitary nature of spending years without a moment of solitude.

'Hi,' said Patrick. 'Shall we have lunch?'

'I think Thomas is about to fall asleep.'

'Right,' said Patrick, sinking down onto his lounger. There was always a good reason to frustrate his desires.

'Look,' said Robert, showing Patrick a swelling on his eyelid, 'I got a mosquito bite.'

'Don't be too hard on mosquitoes,' sighed Patrick, 'only the pregnant females whine, whereas women never stop whining, even after they've had several children.'

Why had he said that? He seemed to be full of zoological misogyny today. If anyone was whining it was him. It certainly wasn't true of Mary. He was the one who suffered from a seething distrust of women. His sons had no reason to share it. He must try to pull himself together. The least he could do was contain his depression.

'I'm sorry,' he said, 'I don't know why I said that. I'm feeling awfully tired.'

He smiled apologetically all round.

'It looks as if you need some help with that moat,' he suggested to Robert, picking up a second bucket.

They walked back and forth, pouring sea water into the sand until Thomas fell asleep in his mother's arms.

AUGUST 2002

10

From the blue paddling pool where he had been playing contentedly a moment before, Thomas suddenly dashed across the sand, glancing over his shoulder to see if his mother was following him. Mary pushed her chair back and bolted after him. He was so fast now, faster every day. He was already on the top step and only had to cross the Promenade Rose to reach the traffic. She leapt up three steps at a time and just caught him as he reached the corner of the parked car that hid him from the drivers cruising along the seaside road. He kicked and wriggled as she lifted him in the air.

'Never do that,' she said, almost in tears. 'Never do that. It's *so* dangerous.'

Thomas gurgled with laughter and excitement. He had discovered this new game yesterday when they arrived back at the Tahiti Beach. Last year he used to double back if he got more than three yards away from her.

As Mary carried him from the road to the parasol he shifted into another mode, sucking his thumb and patting her face affectionately with his palm.

'Are you all right, Mama?'

'I'm upset that you ran into the road.'

'I'm going to do something so dangerous,' said Thomas proudly. 'Yes, I am.'

Mary couldn't help smiling. Thomas was so charming.

How could she say she was sad when she was happy the

next minute? How could she say she was happy when a minute later she wanted to scream? She had no time to draw up a family tree of every emotion that rushed through her. She had spent too long in a state of shattering empathy, tuned in to her children's vagrant moods. She sometimes felt she was about to forget her own existence completely. She had to cry to reclaim herself. People who didn't understand thought that her tears were the product of a long-suppressed and mundane catastrophe, her terminal exhaustion, her huge overdraft or her unfaithful husband, but they were in fact a crash course in the necessary egotism of someone who needed to get a self back in order to sacrifice it again. She had always been like that. Even as a child she only had to see a bird land on a branch in order for its wild heartbeat to replace her own. She sometimes wondered if her selflessness was a distinction or a pathology. She had no final answer to that either. Patrick was the one who worked in a world where judgements and opinions had to be given with an air of authority.

She sat Thomas down in the stacked plastic chairs of his place at the table.

'No, Mama, I don't want to sit in the double chairs,' said Thomas, climbing down and smiling mischievously as he set off towards the steps again. Mary recaptured him immediately and lifted him back into the chairs.

'No, Mama, don't pick me up, it's really unbearable.'

'Where do you pick up these phrases?' Mary laughed.

Michelle, the owner, came over with their grilled *dorade* and looked at Thomas reproachfully.

'*C'est dangereux, ça*,' she scolded him.

Yesterday Michelle had said she would have spanked her children for running towards the road like that. Mary was always getting useless advice. She couldn't spank Thomas under any circumstances. Apart from the nausea she felt at the idea, she thought that punishment was the perfect way of masking the lesson it was supposed to enforce; all the child remembered was the violence, replacing the parent's justified distress with his own.

Kettle was a supreme source of useless advice, fed by the deep wells of her own uselessness as a mother. She had always tried to smother Mary's independent identity. It was not that she had treated Mary as a doll – she was too busy being one herself to do that – but as a kind of venture-capital fund: someone who was initially worthless, but who might one day pay off, if she married a big house or a big name. She had made it clear that marrying a barrister who was about to lose a medium-sized house abroad fell short of the bonanza she had in mind. Kettle's disappointment in the adult Mary was only the sequel to the disappointment she felt at her birth. Mary was not a boy. Girls who weren't boys were such a let-down. Kettle pretended that Mary's father was desperate for a boy, whereas the desperation had really belonged to her own father, a soldier who preferred trench warfare to female company and only agreed to the minimum necessary contact with the weaker sex in the hope of producing a male heir. Three daughters later he retired to his study.

Mary's father, on the contrary, had been delighted with her just as she was. His shyness intermeshed with hers in a way that set them both free. Mary, who hardly spoke for the first twenty years of her life, loved him for never making her feel that her silence was a failure. He understood that it came from a kind of over-intensity, a superabundance of impressions. The gap between her emotional life and social convention was too wide for her to cross. He had been the same way when he was young, but gradually learnt to present something that was not quite himself to the world. Mary's violent authenticity brought him back to his own core.

Mary remembered him vividly but her memories were

embalmed by his early death. She was fourteen when he died of cancer. She was 'protected' from his illness by an ineffectual secrecy which made the situation more worrying than it was anyway. The secrecy had been Kettle's contribution, her substitute for sympathy. After Henry died, Kettle told Mary to 'be brave'. Being brave meant not asking for sympathy now either. There would have been no point in asking for it, even if the opportunity had not been blocked. Their experiences were essentially so different. Mary was utterly lost in loss, lost in imagining her father's suffering, lost in the madness of knowing that only he could have understood her feelings about his death. At the same time, confusingly, so much of their relationship had been spent in silent communion that there seemed to be no reason for it to stop. Kettle only appeared to be sharing the same bereavement. She was in fact suffering from the latest instalment of her inevitable disappointment. It was so unfair. She was too young to be a widow, and too old to start again on acceptable terms. It was in the wake of her father's death that Mary had got the full measure of her mother's emotional sterility and learnt to despise her. The crust of pity which she had formed since then had grown thinner when she had children of her own. It was now in constant danger of being torn apart by fresh eruptions of fury.

Kettle's most recent contribution had been to apologize for not getting Thomas a present for his second birthday. She had searched 'high and low' (translation: rung Harrods) 'for some of those marvellous reins you used to have as a child'. After Harrods let her down, she was too tired to look for anything else. 'They're bound to come back into fashion,' she said, as if she might give Thomas a pair when he was twenty or thirty, or whenever the world came to its senses and started stocking child reins again.

'I suppose Granny's a great disappointment to you, not getting you any reins,' she said to Thomas.

'No, I don't want any reins,' said Thomas, who had taken to ritually contradicting the latest statement he heard. Kettle, not knowing this, was astonished.

'Nanny used to swear by them,' she resumed.

'And I used to swear at them,' said Mary.

'You didn't, as a matter of fact,' said Kettle. 'Unlike Thomas, you weren't encouraged to swear like a drunken sailor.'

It was true that the last time they had visited Kettle in London, Thomas had said, 'Oh, no! Bloody fucking hell, my washing machine is on again,' and then pretended to turn it off by pressing the disconnected bell next to Kettle's fireplace.

He had heard Patrick say 'bloody fucking hell' that morning, after reading a letter from Sotheby's. The Boudins, it turned out, were fakes.

'What a waste of moral effort,' said Patrick.

'It wasn't a waste. You didn't know they were fakes before you decided not to steal them.'

'I know, that's just it: it would have been such an easy decision if I had known. "Steal from my own mother? Never!" I could have thundered right at the beginning, instead of spending a year wondering whether to be some kind of intergenerational Robin Hood, correcting an imbalance with my virtuous crime. My mother managed to make me hate myself for being honourable,' said Patrick, clasping his head between his hands. 'How conflicted was that? And how unnecessary.'

'What's Dada talking about?' asked Thomas.

'I'm talking about your fucking grandmother's fake paintings.'

'No, she's not my fucking grandmother,' said Thomas, shaking his head solemnly.

'Seamus is not the first person to have bamboozled her

into parting with the little money that *my* fucking grandmother left her. Some art dealer in Paris pulled off that facile trick thirty years ago.'

'No, she's not your fucking grandmother,' said Thomas, 'she's my fucking grandmother.'

Property was another thing Thomas had taken up recently. For a long time he had no sense of owning things, now everything belonged to him.

Mary was alone with Thomas for the first week of August. Patrick was detained in London by a difficult case which she suspected should be called Julia versus Mary, but was pretending to be called something else. How could she say she was jealous of Julia when the next moment she was not? Sometimes, in fact, she was grateful to her. She didn't want Patrick to be taken away, nor did she think he would be. Mary was both naturally jealous and naturally permissive, and the only way these two sides of her could collaborate was by cultivating the permissiveness. That way Patrick never really wanted to leave her, and so her jealousy was satisfied as well. The flow chart looked simple enough, except for two immediate complications. First, there were the times when she was overwhelmed with nostalgia for the erotic life they had shared before she became a mother. Her passion had peaked, naturally, when it was organizing its own extinction, during the time when she was trying to get pregnant. Secondly, she was angered when she felt that Patrick was deliberately worsening their relations in order to invigorate his adultery. There it was: he needed sex, she couldn't provide it, he was going to look elsewhere. Infidelity was a technicality, but disloyalty introduced a fundamental doubt, a terminal atmosphere.

It was the first time Robert had been away from home for more than a night. He was devastatingly relaxed on his first evening at his friend Jeremy's when they spoke on the telephone. Of course she was pleased, of course it was a sign of his confidence in his parents' love that he felt the love was there even when they were not. Still, it was strange to be without him. She could remember him at Thomas's age, when he still ran away in order to be chased and still hid in order to be found. Even then he had been more introspective than Thomas, more burdened. He had been, on the one hand, the inhabitant of a pristine paradise that Thomas would never know, and on the other hand, a prototype. Thomas had benefited from learned mistakes and the more precise hopes that followed them.

'I've had enough now,' said Thomas, starting to climb down from his chairs.

Mary waved at Michelle but she was serving another customer. She held back a plate of chips for this moment. If Thomas saw them earlier he ate no fish, if he saw them now he stayed for a second five-minute sitting. Mary couldn't catch Michelle's attention and Thomas continued his descent.

'Do you want some chips, darling?'

'No, Mama, I don't. Yes, I do want some chips,' Thomas corrected himself.

He slipped and bumped his chin against the table top.

'Mama take you,' he said, spreading his arms out.

She lifted him up and sat him on her lap, rocking him gently. Whenever he was hurt he reverted to calling himself 'you', although he had discovered the proper use of the first person singular six months ago. Until then, he had referred to himself as 'you' on the perfectly logical grounds that everyone else did. He also referred to others as 'I', on the perfectly logical grounds that that was how they referred to themselves. Then one week 'you want it' turned into 'I want it'. Everything he did at the moment – the fascination with danger, the assertion of ownership, the ritual contradiction, the desire to do things for himself – was about this explosive transition from being 'you' to being 'I', from seeing himself through his parents' eyes to looking through his own. Just for now, though, he was having a grammatical regression, he wanted to be 'you' again, his mother's creature.

'It's so difficult because your will is what gets you through life,' Sally had said last night. 'Why would you want to break your child's will? That's what our mothers wanted to do. That's what it meant to be "good" – being broken.'

Sally, Mary's American friend, was her greatest ally; also a mother showered in useless advice, also determined to give her children uncompromised support, to roll the boulder of her own upbringing out of the way so that they could run free. This task was surrounded by hostile commentary: stop being a doormat; don't be a slave to your children; get your figure back; keep your husband happy; get back 'out there'; go to a party, spending your whole time with your children drives you literally mad; increase your self-esteem by handing your children over to someone else and writing an article saying that women should not feel guilty about handing their children over to someone else; don't spoil your children by giving them what they want; let the little tyrants cry themselves to sleep, when they realize that crying is useless they'll stop; anyway, children love boundaries. Below this layer came the confusing rumours: never use paracetamol, always use paracetamol, paracetamol stops homeopathy from working, homeopathy doesn't work, homeopathy works for some things but not for others; an amber necklace stops their teeth hurting; that rash could be an allergy to cow's milk, it could be an allergy to wheat, it could be an allergy to the air quality, London has become five times more polluted in the last ten years; nobody really knows, it'll probably just go away. Then there were the invidious comparisons and the plain lies: my daughter sleeps all through the night; she hasn't needed nappies since she was three weeks old; his mother breast-fed him till he was five; we're so lucky, they've both got guaranteed places at the Acorn; her best friend at school is Cilla Black's granddaughter.

When all these distractions could be ignored, Mary tried to hack through the dead wood of her own conditioning, through the overcompensation, through the exhaustion and the irritation and the terror, through the tension between dependency and independence which was alive in her as well as her children, which she had to recognize but could give no time to, and get back, perhaps, to the root of an instinct for love, and try to stay there and to act from there.

She felt that Sally was roped to the same cliff face as her, and that they could rely on each other. Sally had sent through a fax last night but Mary hadn't had time to read it yet. She had torn it from the fax machine and squeezed it into her rucksack. Perhaps when Thomas had a sleep – when he had a sleep, that moment into which the rest of life was supposed to be artfully crammed. By the time it came around, she was usually too desperate for sleep herself to break away from his rhythm and do anything different.

The chips had already lost their power to hold Thomas and he was climbing back down the chairs. Mary took his hand and let him lead her back to the steps he had dashed up earlier. They wandered down the Promenade Rose together hand in hand.

'It's lovely and smooth on my feet,' said Thomas. 'Oh,' he suddenly stopped in front of a row of wilted cactuses, 'what's that called?'

'It's some kind of cactus, darling. I don't know the specific name.'

'But I want to know the specific name,' said Thomas.

'We'll have to look it up in my book when we get home.'

'Yes, Mama, we'll . . . Oh! What's that boy doing?'

'He's got a water pistol.'

'For watering the flowers.'

'Well, yes, that would be a good use for it.'

'It's for watering the flowers,' he informed her.

He loosened his hand and walked ahead of her. Although they were constantly together, she often didn't get to look at him for hours on end. He was either too close for her to see the whole of him, or she was focused on the dangerous elements in the situation and had no time to appreciate the rest. Now she could see him whole, without anxiety, looking adorable with his hooped blue T-shirt and khaki trousers and his determined walk. His face was astonishingly beautiful. She sometimes worried about the kind of attention it would attract, and the kind of impact he would get used to having. She could remember when he had first opened his eyes in the hospital. They were blazing with an inexplicably strong sense of intention; a drive to make sense of the world, in order to house another kind of knowledge which he already had. Robert had arrived with a completely different atmosphere, a sense of emotional intensity, of trouble that needed working out.

'Oh,' said Thomas pointing, 'what's that funny man doing?'

'He's putting on his mask and snorkel.'

'It's my mask and snorkel.'

'Well, it's very nice of you to let him use it.'

'I let him use it,' said Thomas. 'He can use it, Mama.'

'Thank you, darling.'

He marched on. He was being munificent now, but in about ten minutes his energy would collapse and everything would start to go wrong.

'Shall we go back to the beach and have a little rest?'

'I don't want a little rest. I want to go to the playground. I love the playground so much,' he said, breaking into a run.

The playground was uninhabitable at this time of day, its

dangerous climbing frame led to a metal slide hot enough to fry an egg on. Next to it, a plastic pony squeaked unbearably on a coiled spring. When they arrived at the wooden gate, Mary reached out and swung it open for Thomas.

'No, Mama, I do it,' he said with a sudden wail of misery.

'OK, OK,' said Mary.

'No, I do it,' said Thomas, pulling open with some difficulty the gate, made heavier by a metal plaque displaying eight playground rules, four times as many rules as rides. They made the transition to a pink rubber surface masquerading as tarmac. Thomas climbed the curved bars up to the platform above the slide, and then dashed over to the other opening, opposite a fireman's pole which he couldn't possibly get down on his own. Mary hurried around the climbing frame to meet him. Would he really jump? Was he really going to misjudge his capacities to that extent? Was she pumping fear into a situation where only play was needed? Was it an instinct to anticipate disaster, or was every other mother in the world more relaxed than her? Was it worth pretending to be relaxed, or was pretence always a bad thing? Once Mary was standing beside the pole, Thomas moved back to the slide and quickly pulled himself down. He tipped over at the end of his run and banged his head on the edge. The shock fused with his exhaustion to produce a long moment of silence; his face flushed and he let out a long scream, his pink tongue quivering in his mouth, and his eyes thickly glazed with tears. Mary felt, as usual, that a javelin had been flung into her chest. She picked him up in her arms and held him close, reassuring them both.

'Raggie with a label,' he sobbed. She handed him a Harrington square with the label still on it. A raggie without a label was not just unconsoling but doubly upsetting because of its tantalizing resemblance to the ones which still had labels.

She walked back swiftly to the beach, carrying him in her arms. He shuddered and grew quiet, clasping Raggie and sucking his thumb with the same hand. The adventure was over, the exploration had gone to its limit and ended the only way it could, involuntarily. She laid him down on a mattress under a parasol and curled up next to him, closing her eyes and lying completely still. She heard him suck his thumb more intensely as he settled, and then she could tell from the change in his breathing that he had fallen asleep. She opened her eyes.

Now she had an hour, perhaps two, in which to answer letters, pay her taxes, keep in touch with her friends, revive her intellect, take some exercise, read a good book, think of a brilliant money-making scheme, take up yoga, see an osteopath, go to the dentist and get some sleep. Sleep, remember sleep? The word had once referred to great haunches of unconsciousness, six, eight, nine-hour slabs; now she fought for twenty-minute scraps of disturbing rest, rest which reminded her that she was fundamentally done in. Last night she was kept awake by an overwhelming terror that some harm would come to Thomas if she fell asleep. She was rigid with resistance all night, like a sentry who knows that death is the penalty for nodding off on his watch. Now she really had to get some muddling, hangover-like afternoon sleep, soaked in unpleasant dreams, but first she was going to read Sally's fax, as a sign of her independence, which she often felt was even less well established than Thomas's, since she couldn't test its limits as wildly as he could. It was a practical fax, as Sally had warned her, with the dates and times of her arrival at Saint-Nazaire, but then at the end Sally added, 'I came across this quotation yesterday, from Alexander Herzen. "We think the purpose of a child is to grow up because it does grow up. But its purpose is to play, to enjoy itself, to be a child. If we merely look to the end of the process, the purpose of life is death."'

Yes, that was what she had wanted to say to Patrick when they had been alone with Robert. Patrick had been so concerned with shaping Robert's mind, with giving him a transfusion of scepticism, that he had sometimes forgotten to let him play, enjoy himself and be a child. He let Thomas follow his own course, partly because he was preoccupied with his own psychological survival, but also because Thomas's desire for knowledge outstripped any parental ambition. With him she thought, as she closed her eyes after a last glance at Thomas's sleeping face, it was so clear that playing and enjoying himself were identical with learning to master the world around him.

11

'Where has my willie gone?' said Thomas, lying on his blue towel after his bath.

'It's disappeared,' said Mary.

'Oh! There it is, Mama,' he said, uncrossing his legs.

'That's a relief,' said Mary.

'It certainly is a relief,' said Thomas.

After playing in his bath he was reluctant to get back into the padded cell of a nappy. Pyjamas, the dreadful sign that he was expected to go to sleep, sometimes had to wait until he was asleep to be put on. Any sense that Mary was in a hurry made him take twice as long to go to bed.

'Oh, no! My willie's disappeared again,' said Thomas. 'I really am upset about it.'

'Are you, darling?' said Mary, noticing him experiment with the phrase she had used yesterday when he threw a glass on the kitchen floor.

'Yes, Mama, it's driving me crazy.'

'Where can it have gone?' asked Mary.

'I don't believe it,' he said, pausing for her to appreciate the gravity of the loss. 'Oh, there it is!' He gave a perfect imitation of the reassured cheerfulness with which she rediscovered a milk bottle or a lost shoe.

He started to jump up and down and then dropped onto the bed, rolling among the pillows.

'Be careful,' said Mary, watching him bounce too near the metal guards that surrounded the edge of the bed.

It was hard to stay ready for a sudden catch, to keep scanning for sharp corners and hard edges, to let him go to the limit of his adventure. She really wanted to lie down now, but the last thing she should do was to show any sign of exasperation or impatience.

'I am an acrobat at the circus,' said Thomas, trying to do a forward roll but keeling over. 'Mama say, "Be careful, little monkey."'

'Be careful, little monkey,' Mary repeated her line obediently. She must get him a director's chair and a megaphone. He was always being told what to do, now it was his turn.

She felt drained by the long day, most of all by visiting Eleanor in her nursing home. Mary had tried to mask her sense of shock when she arrived with Thomas in Eleanor's room. All of Eleanor's upper teeth were missing from one side of her mouth and only three dangled like black stalactites from the other. Her hair, which she used to have washed every other day, was reduced to a greasy chaos stuck to her now visibly bumpy skull. As Mary leant over to kiss Eleanor, she was assailed by a stench that made her want to reach for the portable changing mat she carried in her rucksack. She must restrain her maternal drive, especially in the presence of a proven champion of maternal self-restraint.

Eleanor's decay was underlined by her loss of equality with Thomas. Last year, neither of them could talk properly or walk steadily; Eleanor had lost enough teeth to leave her with roughly the same number as Thomas had gained; her new need for incontinence pads matched his established need for nappies. This year, everything had changed. Thomas wouldn't need nappies for much longer, Eleanor needed more than she was currently using; only his back molars still had to work their way through, her back molars would soon be the only teeth she had left; he was getting so fast that his mother could hardly keep up, Eleanor could hardly keep herself up in her chair and would soon be bedridden. Mary paused on top of the icy slopes of potential conversation. The already strained assumption that they shared an enthusiasm for Thomas's progress now looked like a covert insult. It was no use reminding her of Robert either, her former ally, now the disciple of his father's hostility.

'Oh, no!' said Thomas to Eleanor. 'Alabala stole my halumbalum.'

Thomas, who was so often stuck with adults in a traffic jam of incomprehensible syllables, sometimes answered back with a little private language of his own. Mary was used to this sweet revenge and also intrigued by the emergence of Alabala, a recent creation who seemed to be falling into the classic role of doing naughty things to and for Thomas, and was accompanied by his conscience, a character called Felan. He looked up at Eleanor with a smile. It was not returned. Eleanor stared at Thomas with horror and suspicion. What she saw was not the ingenuity of a child but the harbinger of her worst fear: that soon, on top of being unable to make herself understood, she would not be able to understand anybody else. Mary moved in quickly.

'He doesn't only talk nonsense,' she said. 'One of his favourite phrases at the moment – I think you'll detect Patrick's influence – ' she tried another complicit smile, 'is "absolutely unbearable".'

Eleanor's body lurched forward a couple of inches. She gripped the wooden arms of her chair and looked at Mary with furious concentration.

'Absolute-ly un-bearable,' she spat out, and then fell back, adding a high, faint, 'Yes.'

Eleanor turned again towards Thomas, but this time she looked at him with a kind of greed. A moment ago, he seemed to be announcing the storm of gibberish that would soon enshroud her, but now he had given her a phrase which she understood perfectly, a phrase she couldn't have managed on her own, describing exactly how she felt.

Something similar happened when Mary read out a list of audio books that Eleanor might want sent from England. Eleanor's method for choosing the books bore no obvious relation to their authors or categories. Mary droned through the titles of works by Jane Austen and Proust, Jeffrey Archer and Jilly Cooper, without any signs of interest from Eleanor. Then she read out the title *Ordeal of Innocence* and Eleanor started nodding her head and flapping her hands acquisitively, as if she were splashing water onto her chest. *Harvest of Dust* elicited the same surges of excitement. Stimulated by these unexpected communications, Eleanor remembered the note she had written earlier, and handed it to Mary with her shaking, liver-spotted hand.

Mary made out the faint words, in pencil-written block capitals, '*WHY SEAMUS DOES NOT COME*?'

Mary suspected the reason, but could hardly believe it. She hadn't expected Seamus to be so flagrant. His opportunism always seemed to be blended with the genuine delusion that he was a good man, or at least a strong desire to be mistaken for one. And yet here he was, only a fortnight after the final transfer of Saint-Nazaire to the Foundation, dropping his benefactor like a sack on a skip.

She remembered what Patrick had said when he finally used the power of attorney his mother had given him to sign over the house: 'These people who want to crawl unburdened to their graves just don't make it. There is no second childhood, no licence for irresponsibility.' He then got blind drunk.

Mary looked at Eleanor's face. It was impacted with misery. Her eyes were veiled like the eyes of a recently dead fish, but in her case the dullness seemed to stem from the effort of staying disconnected from reality. Mary could see now that her missing teeth were really a suicidal gesture, with the violent passivity of a hunger strike. They could so easily have been replaced, it must have taken great stubbornness to stay in the vortex of self-neglect, week after week, as they fell out, one by one, ignoring the medical profession, the antidepressants, the nursing home and the remains of her own will to live.

Mary felt pierced by a sense of tragedy. Here was a woman who had abandoned her family for a vision and for a man, and now the man and the vision had abandoned her. She could remember Eleanor telling her, when she could still speak adequately, that she and Seamus had known each other in 'previous lifetimes'. One of these previous lifetimes had taken place on something called a 'skelig', some kind of Irish seaside mound, which Seamus had taken Eleanor to see early in his financial courtship, on that unforgettable, blustery day when he took her hand and said, 'Ireland needs you.' Once Eleanor realized, in a 'past-life recall', that she had lived as Seamus's wife on the very skelig they visited, during the Dark Ages, when Ireland was a beacon of Christianity in that muddle of pillage and migration, her immediate family, with whom she had a relatively shallow past, began to slip from view. And once Seamus visited Saint-Nazaire, he realized that France needed him even more than Ireland needed Eleanor. The house had been a convent in the seventeenth century, and a second 'past-life recall' established that Eleanor was (it seemed obvious once you were told) the mother superior. The noun, Mary remembered thinking, had stayed stuck in front of the adjective ever since. Seamus, amazingly, was the abbot of a local monastery at exactly the same time. And so they had been thrown together again, this time in a 'spiritual friendship' which had been misinterpreted and caused a great scandal in the area.

When Eleanor told her all this, in an oppressive parody of girls' talk, Mary decided not to argue. Eleanor believed more or less anything, as long as it was untrue. It was part of her charitable nature to rush belief to the unbelievable, like emergency aid. She clearly needed to inhabit these historical novels to make up for the disappointment of a passion which was not being acted out in the bedroom (it had evolved too much for that) but was having a thrilling enough time at the Land Registry. It had all seemed so ridiculous to Mary at the time; now she wished she could stick back the peeling wallpaper of Eleanor's credulity. Under the dreadful sincerity of the original confession was that need to be needed which Mary recognized so well.

'I'll ask him,' she said, covering Eleanor's hand gently with her own. Although she hadn't seen him yet, she knew that Seamus was in his cottage. 'Perhaps he's been ill, or in Ireland.'

'Ireland,' Eleanor whispered.

When they were walking back to the car, Thomas stopped and shook his head. 'Oh, dear,' he said. 'Eleanor is not very well.'

Mary loved his straightforward sympathy for suffering. He hadn't yet learned to pretend that it wasn't going on, or to blame the person who was having it. He fell asleep in the car and she decided she might as well go straight to Seamus's cottage.

'Well, now, that's a terrible thing,' said Seamus. 'I thought with the family being here and everything, that Eleanor wouldn't want to see me so much. And, to be honest with you Mary, the Pegasus Press have been breathing down my neck. They want to put my book in their spring catalogue. I've got so many ideas, it's just getting them down. Do you think *Drumbeat of my Heart* or *Heartbeat of my Drum* is better?'

'I don't know,' said Mary. 'It depends which one you mean, I suppose.'

'That's good advice,' said Seamus. 'Talking of drums, we're very pleased with your mother's progress. She's taken to the soul-retrieval work like a duck to water. I just got an email from her saying she wants to come to the autumn intensive.'

'Amazing,' said Mary. She was nervous that the monitor wouldn't work. The green light seemed to be winking in the usual way, but she had never used it in the car before.

'Soul retrieval is something I think Eleanor could benefit from immensely. I'm just thinking aloud now,' said Seamus, swivelling excitedly in his chair and blocking Mary's view of a leathery old Inuit woman, with a pipe dangling from her mouth, that radiated from his computer screen. 'If your mother were to lead a ceremony with Eleanor at the centre of the circle, that could be hugely powerful with all the, you know, connections.' He spread the fingers of both his hands and intermeshed them tenderly.

Poor Seamus, thought Mary, he wasn't really a bad man, he was just a complete idiot. She sometimes became a little competitive with Patrick about who had the most annoying mother. Kettle gave nothing away, Eleanor gave everything away; the results were indistinguishable for the family, except that Mary had 'expectations', made fantastically remote by the robustness of her meticulously selfish mother, who thought of nothing but her own comfort, rushed to the doctor every time she sneezed and 'treated' herself to a holiday once a month to get over the disappointment of the last one. Patrick's disinheritance had nudged him ahead in the bad-mother stakes, but perhaps Seamus was planning to eliminate that advantage by taking Kettle's money as well. Was he, after all, really a bad man doing a brilliant impersonation of an idiot? It was hard to tell. The connections between stupidity and malice were so tangled and so dense.

'I'm seeing more and more connections,' said Seamus, twisting his fingers around each other. 'To be honest with you, Mary, I don't think I'll write another book. It can do your head in.'

'I bet,' said Mary. 'I couldn't even begin to write a book.'

'Oh, I've done the beginning,' said Seamus. 'In fact, I've done several beginnings. Perhaps it's all beginnings, do you know what I mean?'

'With each new heartbeat,' said Mary. 'Or drumbeat.'

'That's right, that's right,' said Seamus.

Thomas's waking cry burst through the monitor. Mary was relieved to know that she was in range.

'Oh, dear, I'm going to have to leave.'

'I'll definitely try to see Eleanor in the next few days,' said Seamus, accompanying her to the door of his cottage. 'I really appreciate what you said about the heartbeat and being in the moment – it's given me a lot of ideas.'

He opened the door, setting off a tinkling of chimes. Mary looked up and saw three Chinese pictographs clustered around a dangling brass rod.

'Happiness, Peace and Prosperity,' said Seamus. 'They're inseparable.'

'I'm sorry to hear that,' said Mary. 'I was rather hoping to get the first two on their own.'

'Ah, but what is prosperity?' said Seamus, walking with her towards the car. 'Ultimately, it's having something to eat when you're hungry. That's the prosperity that was denied to Ireland, for instance, during the 1840s, and that's still denied to millions of people around the world.'

'Gosh,' said Mary. 'There's not a lot I can do about the Irish in the 1840s. But I could give Thomas his "ultimate prosperity" – or can I go on calling it "lunch"?'

Seamus threw back his head and let out a guffaw of wholesome laughter.

'I think that would be simpler,' he said, giving Mary's back an unwelcome rub.

She opened the door and took Thomas out of his car seat.

'How is the little man?' said Seamus.

'He's very well,' said Mary. 'He has a lovely time here.'

'Well, I'm sure that's down to your excellent mothering,' said Seamus, his hand by now burning a hole in the back of her T-shirt. 'But I'd also say that with the soul work, it's very important to create a safe environment. That's what we do here. Now, maybe Thomas is picking that up, you know, at some level.'

'I expect he is,' said Mary, reluctant to deny Thomas a compliment, even when it was really intended by Seamus for himself. 'He's very good at picking things up.'

She managed to stand out of Seamus's range, holding Thomas in her arms.

'Ah,' said Seamus, framing the two of them with a large parenthetical gesture, 'the mother-and-child archetype. It makes me think of my own mother. She had the eight of us to look after. At the time I think I was preoccupied with little ways of getting more than my fair share of the attention.' He chuckled indulgently at the memory of this younger, less enlightened self. 'That was definitely a big dynamic in my family; but looking back from where I'm standing now, what amazes me is how she went on giving and giving. And you know, Mary, I've come to the conclusion that she was tapping into a universal source, into that archetypal mother-and-child energy. Do you know what I mean? I want to put something about that in my book. It all ties in with the shamanic work – at some level. It's just getting it down. I'd welcome any thoughts about that: moments when you've felt supported by something beyond the level of, you know, personal sacrifice.'

'Let me think about it,' said Mary, suddenly realizing where

Seamus had learned his little ways of getting mothers to hand over their resources to him. 'In the meantime, I really must make Thomas some lunch.'

'Of course, of course,' said Seamus. 'Well, it's been grand talking to you, Mary. I really feel that we've connected.'

'I feel I've learned a lot as well,' said Mary.

She now knew, for instance, that his feeble promise to 'try to visit Eleanor in the next few days' meant that he would not visit her today, or tomorrow, or the next day. Why would he waste his 'little ways' on a woman who only had a couple of fake Boudins to her name?

She carried Thomas into the kitchen and put him down on the counter. He took his thumb out of his mouth and looked at her with a subtle expression which hovered between seriousness and laughter.

'Seamus is a very funny man, Mama,' he said.

Mary burst out laughing.

'He certainly is,' she said, kissing him on the forehead.

'He certainly is a very funny man!' said Thomas, catching her laughter. He scrunched up his eyes in order to laugh more seriously.

No wonder she was tired after seeing Eleanor and Seamus on the same day, no wonder it was difficult to extort any more vigilance from her aching body and her blanched mind. Something had happened today; she hadn't quite got the measure of it, but it was one of those sudden dam bursts which were the only way she ever ended a long period of conflict. She had no time to work it out while Thomas was still bouncing naked in the middle of the bed.

'That was a very big jump,' said Thomas, climbing to his feet again. 'You certainly are impressed, Mama.'

'Yes, darling. What would you like to read tonight?'

Thomas stopped in order to concentrate on a difficult task.

'Let's talk reasonably about lollipops,' he said, retrieving a phrase from an old book of Patrick's which had got stuck down in Saint-Nazaire.

'Dr Upping and Dr Downing?'

'No, Mama, I don't want to read that.'

Mary took *Babar and Professor Grifiton* from the shelf and climbed over the guard onto the bed. They had a ritual of reviewing the day, and Mary threw out the usual question, 'What did we do today?' Thomas stopped bouncing as she had hoped.

Thomas lowered his voice and shook his head solemnly.

'Peter Rabbit has been eating my grapes,' he said.

'No!' said Mary, shocked.

'Mr McGregor will be very angry with Seamus.'

'Why Seamus? I thought it was Peter Rabbit who took the grapes.'

'No, Mama, it was Seamus.'

Whatever it was that Thomas was 'picking up', it wasn't the sense of a 'safe environment' that Seamus had boasted about creating for 'the soul work'. It was the atmosphere of theft. If Seamus was prepared to treat Eleanor with so little ceremony, when she had set off the prosperity chime in his life with such a resounding tinkle, why would he bother to honour her promises to his defeated rivals? His imagination was teeming with competing siblings, and he had adopted Patrick and Mary for the purposes of triumphing over them in an archaic contest for which neither of them had received his commando training. What was the point of an old woman who couldn't even buy him a sensory-deprivation tank? And what was the point of her descendants cluttering up his Foundation during August?

12

'But I don't understand, said Robert, watching Mary pack. 'Why do we have to leave?'

'You know why,' said Mary.

He sat on the edge of the bed, his shoulders rounded and his hands wedged under his thighs. If there had been time, she would have sat beside him and hugged him and let him cry again, but she had to get on with the packing while Thomas was sleeping.

Mary hadn't slept for the last two days, equally tormented by the atmosphere of loss and the longing to leave. Houses, paintings, trees, Eleanor's teeth, Patrick's childhood and her children's holidays: to her tired mind they all seemed to be piled up like the wreckage from a flood. She had spent the last seven years watching Patrick's childhood like a rope inching through his clenched hands. Now she wanted to get the hell out. It was already too late to stop Robert from identifying with Patrick's sense of injustice, but she could still save Thomas from getting tangled in the drama of disinheritance. The family was being split in half and it could only come back together if they left.

Patrick had gone to say goodbye to Eleanor. He had promised not to make any irrevocably bitter speeches in case he never saw her again. If he had enough warning of her death, he would doubtless fly down to hold her hand, but it was unrealistic to think that the rest of them would be checking into the Grand Hôtel des Bains to mount a deathbed vigil in the nursing home. Mary had to admit that she looked forward to Eleanor dropping out of their lives altogether.

'Would we get the house if we killed Seamus?' asked Robert.

'No,' said Mary, 'it would go to the next director of the Foundation.'

'That's so unfair,' said Robert. 'Unless I became the director. Yes! I'm a genius!'

'Except that you would have to direct the Foundation.'

'Oh, yeah, that's true,' said Robert. 'Well, maybe Seamus will repent.' He adopted a thick Irish accent. 'I can only apologize, Mary. I don't know what came over me, trying to steal the house from you and the little ones, but I've come to moi senses now and I want you to know that even if you can find it in your heart to forgive me for the agony I've caused you, I shall never be able to forgive myself.' He broke down sobbing.

She knew his fake sobbing was close to being real. For the first time since Thomas was born she felt that Robert was the one who needed her most. His great strength was that he was even more interested in playing with what was going on than he was in wasting his time trying to control it – although he did quite a lot of that as well. His playfulness had collapsed for a few days and been replaced entirely by wishing and longing and regretting. Now she saw it coming back. She could never quite get used to the way he pieced together impersonations out of the things he overheard. Seamus had become his latest obsession, and no wonder. She was too exhausted to do anything but give him a laborious smile and fold the swimming trunks she had unpacked for him less than a week before. Everything had happened so fast. On the day he arrived with Robert, Patrick had found a note asking if Kevin and Anette could have 'some space' in the house. Seamus had dropped in the next morning at breakfast to get his answer.

'I hope I'm not interrupting,' he called out.

'Not at all,' said Patrick. 'It's good of you to come so quickly. Would you like some coffee?'

'I won't, thank you, Patrick. I've really been abusing the caffeine lately in an attempt to get myself going with the writing, you know.'

'Well, I hope you don't mind if I go ahead and abuse some caffeine without you.'

'Be my guest,' said Seamus.

'Is that what I am?' asked Patrick, like a greyhound out of the slips. 'Or are you in fact my guest during this one month of the year? That's the crux of the matter. You know that the terms of my mother's gift included letting us have the house for August, and we're not going to put up with having your friends billeted on us.'

'Well, now, "terms" is a very legalistic way of putting it,' said Seamus. 'There's nothing in writing about the Foundation providing you with a free holiday. I have a genuine sympathy for the trouble you've had in accepting your mother's wishes. That's why I've been prepared to put up with a lot of negativity from your side.'

'We're not discussing the trouble I've had with my mother's wishes, but the trouble you're having with them. Let's not stray from the subject.'

'They're inseparable.'

'Everything looks inseparable to a moron.'

'There's no need to get personal. They're inseparable because they both depend on knowing what Eleanor wanted.'

'It's obvious what she wanted. What isn't clear is whether you can accept the part that doesn't suit you.'

'Well, I have a more global vision than that, Patrick. I see the problem in holistic terms. I think we all need to find a solution together, you and your family, and Kevin and Anette, and me. Perhaps we could do a ritual expressing what we bring to this community and what we expect to take from it.'

'Oh, no, not another ritual. What is it with you people and rituals? What's wrong with having a conversation? When I spent my teenage years in what has become your cottage, there were two bedrooms. Why don't you put your friends up in your own spare room?'

'That's now my study and office space.'

'God forbid they should invade your private space.'

Thomas wriggled down from Mary's arms and started to explore. His desire to move made her even more aware of how paralysed the rest of them had become. She took no pleasure in seeing Patrick frozen in a kind of autumnal adolescence: dogmatic and sarcastic, resentful of his mother's actions, still secretly thinking of Seamus's cottage as the teenage den in which he spent half a dozen summers of semi-independence. Only Thomas, because he hadn't been given any coordinates on this particular grid, could slip to the floor and let his mind flow wherever it wanted. Seeing him get away gave Mary a certain remoteness from the scene being played out by Patrick and Seamus, even though she could feel a sullen violence taking over from Seamus's usual inane affability.

'Did you know,' said Patrick, addressing Seamus again, 'that among the caribou herdsmen of Lapland, the top shaman gets to drink the urine of the reindeer that has eaten the magic mushrooms, and his assistant drinks the urine of the top shaman, and so on, all the way down to the lowest of the low who scramble in the snow, pleading for a splash of twelfth-generation caribou piss?'

'I didn't know that,' said Seamus flatly.

'I thought it was your special field,' said Patrick, surrised. 'Anyhow, the irony is that the premier cru, the first hit, is much the most toxic. Poor old top shaman is reeling and sweating, trying to get all the poison out, whereas a few damaged livers later, the urine is harmless without having lost its hallucinogenic power. Such is the human attachment to status that people will sacrifice their peace of mind and their precious time in order to pickaxe their way towards what turns out to be a thoroughly poisonous experience.'

'That's all very interesting,' said Seamus, 'but I don't see what it has to do with our immediate problem.'

'Only this: that out of what I admit is pride, I am not prepared to be at the bottom of the pissing hierarchy in this "community".'

'If you don't want to be part of this community, you don't have to stay,' said Seamus quietly.

There was a pause.

'Good,' said Patrick. 'Now at least we know what you really want.'

'Why don't *you* go away,' shouted Robert. 'Just leave us alone. This is my grandmother's house, and we have more right to be here than you do.'

'Let's calm down,' said Mary, resting a hand on Robert's shoulder. 'We aren't going to leave in the middle of the children's holidays, whether we come here next year or not. We could compromise over your friends, perhaps. If you sacrifice your office for a week, we could put them up for the last week of our stay. That seems fair enough.'

Seamus faltered between the momentum of his anger and his desire to look reasonable.

'I'll have to get back to you on that,' he said. 'To be honest with you, I'm going to have to process some of the negative feelings I'm having at the moment, before I can come to a decision.'

'You process away,' said Patrick, getting up to bring the conversation to an end. 'Be my guest. Do a ritual.'

He moved round the table, and spread his arms as if to herd Seamus out of the house, but then he came to a halt.

'By the way,' he said, leaning close, 'Mary tells me that you've dropped Eleanor now that she's given you the house. Is that true? After all she's done for you, you might pop in on her.'

'I don't need any lectures from you on the importance of my friendship with Eleanor,' said Seamus.

'Listen, I know she's not great company,' said Patrick, 'but that's just part of the treasure trove of things you have in common.'

'I've had just about enough of your hostile attitude,' said Seamus, his face flushing crimson. 'I've tried to be patient—'

'Patient?' Patrick interrupted. 'You've tried to billet your sidekicks on us and you've tossed Eleanor on the scrap heap because there's nothing more you can screw out of her. Anyone who thinks that "patient" is the word to describe that sort of thing should be doing English as a foreign language rather than signing a book contract.'

'I don't have to stand for these insults,' said Seamus. 'Eleanor and I created this Foundation, and I know that she wouldn't want anything to undermine its success. What's so tragic, in my opinion, is that you don't see how central the Foundation is to your mother's life's purpose, and you don't realize what an extraordinary woman she is.'

'You're so wrong,' said Patrick. 'I couldn't wish for a more extraordinary mother.'

'It's fairly obvious where all this is heading,' said Mary. 'Let's take some time to cool off. I don't see any point in more acrimony.'

'But, darling,' said Patrick, 'acrimony is all we've got left.'

It was certainly all he had left. She knew that it would fall on her to rescue a holiday from the wreckage left by Patrick's disdain. The expectation that she would be tirelessly resourceful and at the same time completely sympathetic to Patrick was not one she could either put up with or disappoint.

As she hoisted Thomas into her arms, she felt again the extent to which motherhood had destroyed her solitude. Mary had lived alone through most of her twenties and stubbornly kept her own flat until she was pregnant with Robert. She had such a strong need to distance herself from the flood of others. Now she was very rarely alone, and if she was, her thoughts were commandeered by her family obligations. Neglected meanings piled up like unopened letters. She knew they contained ever more threatening reminders that her life was unexamined.

Solitude was something she had to share with Thomas for the moment. She remembered a phrase Johnny once quoted about the infant being 'alone in the presence of its mother'. That had stayed with her, and sitting with Thomas after the row between Patrick and Seamus, while he played with his favourite hose, holding it sideways and watching the silvery arc of water splash to the ground, Mary could feel the pressure to encourage him to be useful, to water the plants and to keep the mud from splattering his trousers, but she didn't give in to it, seeing a kind of freedom in the uselessness of his play. He had no outcome in mind, no project or profit, he just liked watching the water flow.

It would have made perfect sense for her to make room for nostalgia now that the departure she had longed for seemed inevitable, but she found herself looking at the garden and the view and the cloudless sky with a cold eye. It was time to go.

Back in the house, she went to her own room for a

moment's rest, and found Patrick already sprawled on the bed with a glass of red wine beside him.

'You weren't very friendly this morning,' he said.

'What do you mean?' said Mary. 'I wasn't unfriendly. You were wrapped up in arguing with Seamus.'

'Well, the Thermopylae buzz is wearing off,' said Patrick.

She sat down on the edge of the bed and stroked his hand absently.

'Do you remember, back in the Olden Days, when we used to go to bed together in the afternoon?' asked Patrick.

'Thomas has only just gone to sleep.'

'You know that's not the real reason. We're not grinding our teeth with frustration, promising we'll jump into bed the moment we get the chance: it isn't even a possibility.' Patrick closed his eyes. 'I feel as if we're shooting down a gleaming white tunnel . . .' he said.

'That was yesterday, on the way from the airport,' said Mary.

'A bone with the marrow sucked out,' Patrick persevered. 'Nothing is ever the same again, however often you repeat that magical phrase to the waitress in the cocktail bar.'

'Never, in my case,' said Mary.

'Congratulations,' said Patrick, falling abruptly silent, his eyes still closed.

Was she being unsympathetic? Should she be giving him a charity blow job? She felt that these pleas for attention were timed to be impossible, so as to keep him self-righteously unfaithful. Patrick would have been horrified if she had started to make love to him. Or would he? How could she find out while she was incapable of taking any sexual initiative? The whole thing had died for her, and she couldn't blame his affair for the collapse. It had happened the moment Thomas was born. She couldn't help marvelling at the strength of the severance. It had the authority of an instinct, redirecting her resources from the spent, enfeebled, damaged Patrick to the thrilling potential of her new child. The same thing had happened with Robert, but only for a few months. This time her erotic life was subsumed in intimacy with Thomas. Her relationship with Patrick was dead, not without guilt and duty turning up at the funeral. She sank down on the bed next to him, stared at the ceiling for a few seconds of empty intensity and then closed her eyes as well. They lay on the bed together, floating in shallow sleep.

'Oh, God,' said Mary to Robert, getting up from the floor where she had been kneeling next to the open suitcase, 'I still haven't cancelled Granny and Sally.'

'I must say it's frightfully disappointing,' said Robert in his Kettle voice.

'Let's see if you're right,' said Mary, sitting down next to him to dial her mother's number.

'Well, I must say it *is* disappointing,' said Kettle, making Mary cover the mouthpiece while she tried to suppress her laughter. 'Perfect,' she whispered to Robert. He raised his arms in triumph.

'Why don't you come anyway?' said Mary to her mother. 'Seamus seems to enjoy your company even more than we do. Which is saying a lot,' she added after too long a pause.

Sally said she would come to see them all in London instead, and then took the view that it was 'great news'.

'To an outsider that place looks like a beautiful bell jar with the air being sucked out. You have to get out before you blow up.'

'She's happy for us,' said Mary.

'Well, gee,' said Robert, 'I hope she loses her house so we can be happy for her.'

When Patrick returned, he put a piece of paper on top of the suitcase Mary was struggling to close and sank down onto the chair by the door. She picked the paper up and saw that it was one of Eleanor's faint pencil-written notes.

MY WORK HERE IS OVER. I WANT TO COME HOME. PLEASE FIND A NURSING HOME IN KENSINGTON?

She gave the note to Robert.

'It's difficult to know which sentence gave me most pleasure,' said Patrick. 'Eleanor's tiny store of unshamanic capital will be dismembered in rather less than a year if she moves to Kensington. After that, if she has the bad taste to stay alive, guess who will be expected to keep her vegetating in the Royal Borough?'

'I like the question mark,' said Mary.

'Eleanor's real genius is for putting our emotional and moral impulses into total conflict. Again and again she makes me hate myself for doing the right thing, she makes virtue into its own punishment.'

'I suppose we have to protect her from the horror of knowing that Seamus was really only interested in her money.'

'Why?' said Robert. 'It serves her right.'

'Listen,' said Patrick, 'what I saw today was someone who is terrified. Terrified of dying alone. Terrified that her family will abandon her, as Seamus has done. Terrified that she's fucked up, that she's been sleepwalking through a replica of her mother's behaviour. Terrified by the impotence of her convictions in the face of real suffering, terrified of everything. If we agree to her request, she can switch from philanthropy to family. Essentially, neither of them works any more, but the switch might give her a little relief before she settles back into hell.'

Nobody spoke.

'Let's hope that it's purgatory rather than hell,' said Mary.

'I'm not very up on these things,' said Patrick, 'but if purgatory is a place where suffering refines you rather than degrades you, I see no sign of it.'

'Well, maybe it can be purgatory for us at least.'

'I don't understand,' said Robert. 'Is Granny going to come and live with us?'

'Not in the flat,' said Mary. 'In a nursing home.'

'And we're going to have to pay?'

'Not yet,' she replied.

'But that way Seamus wins completely,' said Robert. 'He gets the house and we get the cripple.'

'She's not a cripple,' said Mary, 'she's an invalid.'

'Oh, sorry,' said Robert, 'that makes all the difference. Lucky us.' He put on his compère voice. 'Today's lucky winners, the Melrose family from London, will be taking home our fabulous first prize. This amazing *invalid* can't speak, can't walk *and* she can't control her bowels.' Robert made the sound of delirious applause, and then changed to a solemn but consoling tone. 'Bad luck, Seamus,' he said, putting his arm around an imaginary contestant, 'you played well, but in the end, they beat you in the Slow Death round. You won't be going home empty-handed, though, because we're giving you this private hamlet in the South of France, with thirty acres of gorgeous woodland, a giant swimming pool and several garden areas for the kiddies to play in . . .'

'That was amazing,' said Mary. 'Where did that pop up from?'

'I don't think Seamus knows yet,' said Patrick. 'She made me read a postcard saying that he was going to come and see her after the family had left. So he still hasn't seen her yet.'

'And did she look as if that might change her mind?'

'No,' said Patrick. 'She smiled when she gave me the note.'

'The mechanical smile, or the radiant one?'

'Radiant,' said Patrick.

'It's worse than we thought,' said Mary. 'She's not just running away from the truth about Seamus's motives, she's making another sacrifice. The only thing she had left to give him was her absence. It's unconditional love, the thing people usually keep for their children, if they can do it at all. In this case the children are the sacrifice.'

'There's an awful Christian stench to it as well,' said Patrick. 'Being useful and affirming her worthlessness at the same time – all in the service of wounded pride. If she stays here she has to pay attention to Seamus's betrayal, but this way we're the ones who are betrayed. I can't get over her stubbornness. There's nothing like doing God's will to make people pig-headed.'

'She can't speak or move,' said Mary, 'but look at the power she has.'

'Yeah,' said Patrick. 'All this chattering that takes place in between is nothing compared to the crying and groaning that takes place at either end of life. It drives me crazy: we're controlled by one wordless tyrant after another.'

'But where are we going for our holidays next year?' asked Robert.

'We can go anywhere,' said Patrick. 'We're no longer prisoners of this Provençal perfection. We're jumping out of the postcard, we're hitting the road.' He sat down next to Robert on the bed. 'Bogotá! Blackpool! Rwanda! Let your imagination roam. Picture the fugitive Alaskan summer breaking out among the potholes of the tundra. Tierra del Fuego is nice at this time of year. No competition for the beaches there, except from those hilarious, blubbery sea lions. We've had enough of the predictable pleasures of the Mediterranean, with its pedalos and its *pizzas au feu de bois*. The world is our oyster.'

'I hate oysters,' said Robert.

'Yeah, I slipped up there,' said Patrick.

'Well, where do you want to go?' asked Mary. 'You can choose anywhere you like.'

'America,' said Robert. 'I want to go to America.'

'Why not?' said Patrick. 'That's where Europeans traditionally go when they've been evicted.'

'We're not being evicted,' said Mary, 'we're finally getting free.'

AUGUST 2003

13

Would America be just like he'd imagined it? Along with the rest of the world, Robert had lived under a rain of American images most of his life. Perhaps the place had already been imagined for him and he wouldn't be able to see anything at all.

The first impression that came his way, while the plane was still on the ground at Heathrow, was a sense of hysterical softness. The flow of passengers up the aisle was blocked by a red-haired woman sagging at the knees under her own weight.

'I cannot go there. I cannot get in there,' she panted. 'Linda wants me to sit by the window, but I cannot fit in there.'

'Get in there, Linda,' said the enormous father of the family.

'Dad!' said Linda, whose size spoke for itself.

That certainly seemed typical of something he had seen before in London's tourist spots: a special kind of tender American obesity; not the hard-won fat of a gourmet, or the juggernaut body of a truck driver, but the apprehensive fat of people who had decided to become their own airbag systems in a dangerous world. What if their bus was hijacked by a psychopath who hadn't brought any peanuts? Better have some now. If there was going to be a terrorist incident, why go hungry on top of everything else?

Eventually, the Airbags dented themselves into their seats.

Robert had never seen such vague faces, mere sketches on the immensity of their bodies. Even the father's relatively protuberant features looked like the remnants of a melted candle. As she squeezed into her aisle seat, Mrs Airbag turned to the long queue of obstructed passengers, a brown smudge of tiredness radiating from her faded hazel eyes.

'Thank you for your patience,' she groaned.

'It's sweet of her to thank us for something we haven't given her,' said Robert's father. 'Perhaps I should thank her for her agility.'

Robert's mother gave him a warning look. It turned out they were in the row behind the Airbags.

'You're going to have to put the armrests down for takeoff,' Linda's father warned her.

'Mom and me are sharing these seats,' giggled Linda. 'Our tushes are expanding!'

Robert peeped through the gap in the seats. He didn't see how they were going to get the armrests down.

After meeting the Airbags, Robert's sense of softness spread everywhere. Even the hardness of some of the faces he saw on that warm and waxy arrival afternoon, in the flag-strewn mineral crevasses of mid-town Manhattan, looked to him like the embittered softness of betrayed children who had been told to expect everything. For those who were prepared to be consoled there was always something to eat; a pretzel stall, an ice-cream cart, a food-delivery service, a bowl of nuts on the counter, a snack machine down the corridor. He felt the pressure to drift into the mentality of grazing cattle, not just ordinary cattle but industrialized cattle, neither made to wait nor allowed to.

In the Oak Bar, Robert saw a row of men as pale and spongy as mushrooms, all standing on the broad stalks of their khaki trousers in front of the cigar cabinet. They seemed to be playing at being men. They sniggered and whispered, like schoolboys who were expecting to be caught out, to be made to remove the cushions they had stuffed under their pastel button-down shirts, and unpeel the plastic caps which made them look as if they were already bald. Watching them made Robert feel so grown up. He saw the old lady on the next table drape her powdered lips over the edge of her cocktail glass and suck the pink liquid expertly into her mouth. She looked like a camel trying to hide its braces. In the convex reflection of the black ceramic bowl in the window he saw people come and go, yellow cabs surge and slip, the spinning wheels of the park carriages approaching until they grew as small as the wheels of a wristwatch, and disappeared.

The park was bright and warm, crowded with sleeveless dresses and jackets hooked over shoulders. Robert felt the heightened alertness of arrival being eroded by exhaustion, and the novelty of New York overlaid by the sense that he had seen this new place a thousand times before. Whereas the London parks he knew seemed to insist on nature, Central Park insisted on recreation. Every inch was organized for pleasure. Cinder paths looped among the little hills and plains, past a zoo and a skating rink, quiet zones, sports fields and a plethora of playgrounds. Headphoned rollerbladers pursued a private music. Teenagers scaled small mounds of bronze-grey rocks. A flute player's serpentine music echoed damply under the arch of a bridge. As it faded behind them, it was replaced by the shrill mechanical tooting of a carousel.

'Look, Mama, a carousel!' said Thomas. 'I want to go on it. I can't resist doing that, actually.'

'OK,' said Robert's father with a tantrum-avoiding sigh.

Robert was delegated to take Thomas for a ride, sitting on the same horse as him and fastening a leather belt around his waist.

'Is this a real horse?' said Thomas.

'Yes,' said Robert. 'It's a huge wild American horse.'

'You be Alabala and say it's a wild American horse,' said Thomas.

Robert obeyed his brother.

'No, Alabala!' said Thomas sharply, waving his index finger. 'It's a carousel horse.'

'Whoops, sorry,' said Robert as the carousel set in motion.

Soon it was going fast, almost too fast. Nothing about the carousel in Lacoste had prepared him for these rearing snorting horses, their nostrils painted red and their thick necks twisted out ambitiously towards the park. He was on a different continent now. The frighteningly loud music seemed to have driven all the clowns on the central barrel mad, and he could see that instead of being disguised by a painted sky studded with lights, heavily greased rods were revolving overhead. Along with the violence of the ride, this exposed machinery struck him as typically American. He didn't really know why. Perhaps everything in America would show this genius for being instantly typical. Just as his body was being tricked by a second afternoon, every surprise was haunted by this sense of being exemplary.

Soon after they left the carousel, they came across a vibrant middle-aged woman bent over her lapdog.

'Do you want a cappuccino?' she asked, as if it must be a tremendous temptation. 'Are you ready for a cappuccino? Come on! Come on!' She clapped her hands together ecstatically.

But the dog strained backwards on his leash, as if to say, 'I'm a Dandie Dinmont, I don't drink cappuccino.'

'I think that's a clear "no",' said Robert's father.

'Shh . . .' said Robert.

'I mean,' said Thomas, removing his thumb from his mouth as he reclined in his stroller, 'I think that's a clear no.' He chuckled. 'I mean, it's incredible. The little doggie doesn't want a cappuccino!' He put his thumb back in his mouth and played with the smooth label of his raggie.

After another five minutes his parents were ready to head back to the hotel, but Robert caught a glimpse of some water and ran forward a little further.

'Look,' he said, 'a lake.'

The landscaping created the impression that the far shore of the lake lapped against the base of a double-towered West Side skyscraper. Under the gaze of this perforated cliff, T-shirted men hauled metal boats past reedy islands, girlfriends photographed each other laughing among the oars, immobile children bulged in blue life jackets.

'Look,' said Robert, not quite able to express how astonishingly typical it all seemed.

'I want to go on the lake,' said Thomas.

'Not today,' said Robert's father.

'But I want to,' he screamed, tears instantly beading his eyelids.

'Let's go for a run,' said Robert's father, grabbing the stroller and sprinting down an avenue of bronze statues, Thomas's protests gradually replaced by cries of 'Faster!'

By the time they caught up with him, Robert's father was bent double over the handles of the stroller, getting his breath back.

'The selection committee must have been based in Edinburgh,' he gasped, nodding at the giant statues of Robert Burns and Walter Scott, stooped beneath the weight of their genius. A little further on a much smaller sprightly Shakespeare sported a period costume.

The Churchill Hotel where they were staying had no room service, and so Robert's father went out to buy a kettle and some 'basic provisions'. When he got back, Robert could smell the fresh whiskey on his breath.

'Jesus,' said his father, fishing a box out of his shopping

bag, 'you go out to buy a kettle and you come back with nothing less than a Travel Smart Hot Beverage Maker.'

Like Linda's and Mom's unconstrained tushes, phrases seemed to feel entitled to take up as much room as they could. Robert watched his father unloading tea and coffee and a bottle of whiskey from a brown-paper bag. The bottle had already been drunk from.

'Look at these filthy curtains,' said his father, seeing Robert calculating the proportion of the bottle that was already empty. 'The reason why the rest of New York is breathing lovely clean air is that we've got these special pollution filters in our room sucking all the dirt out of the atmosphere. Sally said that the decoration in this place "grows on you" – that's exactly what I'm worried about. Try not to touch any of the surfaces.'

Robert, who had been excited to be staying in any hotel at all, started to look sceptically at his surroundings. A Chinese carpet in mouse's-underbelly pink, with a medallioned pictogram at the centre, gave way to the greasy French provincial upholstery of the sofa and armchair. Above the sofa, against the buttercup walls, an Indian tapestry of women dancing rigidly by a well, with some cows in the foreground, stood opposite a big painting of two ballerinas, one in a lemon-yellow and the other in a rose-pink tutu. The bath was as cratered as the moon. The chrome had greyed on the taps and the enamel was stained. If you didn't really need a bath before getting in it, you certainly would afterwards. The view from his parents' room, where Thomas was bouncing up and down on the bed shouting, 'Look at me! I'm an astronaut!', gave onto a rusty air-conditioning system that throbbed a few feet beneath the ill-fitting window. From the drawing room, where he was going to sleep on the sofa bed with Thomas (or, knowing Thomas, where his father was going to sleep after Thomas had taken over his mother's bed), there was a perfect view of the Sheetrock that covered the neighbouring skyscraper.

'It's like living in a quarry,' said his father, splashing a couple of inches of whiskey into a glass. He strode over to the window and pulled down the grey plastic blind. The pole holding the blind crashed down onto the drawing room's air-conditioning unit with a hollow clang.

'Bloody hell,' he said.

Robert's mother burst out laughing. 'It's only for a few nights,' she said. 'Let's go out to dinner. Thomas isn't going to get back to sleep for ages. He had three hours on the plane. What about you, darling?' she asked Robert.

'I want to motor on. Can I have a Coca-Cola?'

'No,' said his mother, 'you're quite excited enough already.'

'Apple and cinnamon flavour,' muttered Robert's father, as he continued to unpack the shopping. 'I couldn't find any oats that taste of oats or apples that taste of apples, only oats that taste of apples. And cinnamon, of course, to blend with the toothpaste. A less sober man might end up brushing his teeth with oats, or having a bowl of toothpaste for breakfast – without noticing. It's enough to drive you mad. If there aren't any additives they boast about that too. I saw a packet of camomile tea that said "Caffeine Free". Why would camomile have any caffeine in it?' He took out the last package.

'Morning Thunder,' said Robert's mother. 'Isn't Thomas enough morning thunder already?'

'That's your trouble, darling, you think Thomas can substitute for everything: tea, coffee, work, social life . . .' He let the list hurtle on in silence, and then quickly buried the remark in more general commentary. 'Morning Thunder is very literary, it just has added quotations.' He cleared his throat and read out loud, '"*Born often under another sky, placed in the middle of an always moving scene, himself driven by an irresistible torrent which draws all about him, the American has no time to tie himself to anything, he grows accustomed only to change, and ends by regarding it as the natural state of man. He feels the need of it, more he loves it; for the instability, instead of meaning disaster to him, seems to give birth only to miracles all about him.*" – Alexis de Tocqueville.

'So you see,' he said, ruffling Robert's hair, 'wanting to "motor on" is in perfect keeping with the mood of this country, at least in 1840, or whatever.'

Thomas clambered onto a table whose protective circle of glass was about a foot less wide than the table itself, leaving the mulberry polyester tablecloth exposed at the edges.

'Let's go out to a restaurant,' said Robert's mother, lifting him gently into her arms.

Robert felt the sense of almost violent silence in the lift, made up of the things that his parents were not saying to each other, but also caused by the aroma of mental illness surrounding the knobbly headed lift operator who informed them with pride, rather than the apologies Robert felt they deserved, that the lift had been installed in 1926. Robert liked some things to be old – dinosaurs, for instance, or planets – but he liked his lifts brand new. The family's longing to escape the red velveteen cage was explosive. While the madman jerked a brass lever back and forth, the lift lurched around in the vicinity of the ground floor and finally came to rest only an inch or two below the lobby.

In the fading light, they walked over glittering pavements, steam surging from corner drains and giant grilles replacing the paving stones for feverishly long stretches. Robert refused to give in to the cowardice of avoiding them altogether, but he walked on them reluctantly, trying to make himself lighter. Gravity had never seemed so grave.

'Why do the pavements glitter?' he asked.

'God knows,' said his father. 'It's probably the added iron, or the crushed quotations. Or maybe they've just had the caffeine sucked right out of them.'

Apart from a few yellowing newspaper articles displayed in the window, and a handwritten sign saying *GOD BLESS OUR TROOPS*, Venus Pizza gave no hint of the disgusting food that was being prepared indoors. The ingredients of the salads and pizzas seemed to fit in with the unreflecting expansion which Robert had been noticing since Heathrow. A list would start out reasonably enough with feta and tomato and then roll over the border into pineapple and Swiss cheese. Smoked chicken burst in on what had seemed to be a seafood party, and 'all the above' were served with French fries and onion rings.

'Everything is "mouthwatering",' said Robert. 'What does that mean? That you need a huge glass of water to wash away the taste?'

His mother burst out laughing.

'It's more like a police report on what they found in someone's dustbin than a dish,' his father complained. 'The suspect was obviously a tropical-fruit freak with a hearty love of Brie and shellfish,' he muttered in an American accent.

'I thought French fries were called Freedom fries now,' said Robert.

'It's cheaper to write *GOD BLESS OUR TROOPS* than reprint a hundred menus,' said his father. 'Thank goodness Spain joined the coalition of the willing, otherwise we'd be saying things like, "Mine's a Supreme Court omelette with some Freedom fries on the side." English muffins will probably survive the purge, but I wouldn't go round asking for Turkish coffee after the way they behaved. I'm sorry.' Robert's father sank back into the booth. 'I had such a love affair with America, I suppose I feel jilted by its current incarnation. Of course it's a vast and complex society, and I have great faith in its powers of self-correction. But where are they? What happened to rioting? Satire? Scepticism?'

'Hi!' The waitress wore a badge saying KAREN. 'Have you guys made a menu selection? Oh,' she sighed, looking at Thomas, 'you are gorgeous.'

Robert was mesmerized by the strange hollow friendliness of her manner. He wanted to set her free from the obligation to be cheerful. He could tell she really wanted to go home.

His mother smiled at her and said, 'Could we have a Vesuvio without the pineapple chunks or the smoked turkey or . . .' She started laughing helplessly. 'I'm sorry . . .'

'Mummy!' said Robert, starting to laugh as well.

Thomas scrunched up his eyes and rocked back and forth, not wanting to be left out. 'I mean,' he said, 'it's incredible.'

'Maybe we should approach this from the other direction,' said Robert's father. 'Could we have a pizza with tomato, anchovy and black olives.'

'Like the pizzas in Les Lecques,' said Robert.

'We'll see,' said his father.

Karen tried to master her bewilderment at the poverty of the ingredients.

'You want mozzarella, right?'

'No thanks.'

'How about a drizzle of basil oil?'

'No drizzle, thank you.'

'OK,' she said, hardened by their stubbornness.

Robert slid across the Formica table and rested his head sideways on the pillow of his folded arms. He felt he had been trapped all day in an argument with his body: confined on the plane when he was ready to run around, and running around now when he should have been in bed. In the corner a television with the sound turned down enough to be inaudible, but too little to be silent, radiated diagonally into the room. Robert had never seen a baseball game before, but he had seen films in which the human spirit triumphed over adversity on a baseball field. He thought he could remember one in which some gangsters tried to make a sincere baseball star deliberately lose a game, but at the last moment, just when he was about to throw the whole thing away and the groans of disappointment from the crowd seemed to express the whole unsatisfactoriness of a world in which there was nothing left to believe in, he went into a trance and remembered when he had first hit a ball a long way, into the middle of a wheat field in the middle of America. He couldn't betray that amazing slow-motion sky-bound feeling from his childhood, and he couldn't betray his mother who always wore an apron and told him not to lie, and so he hit the ball right out of the stadium, and the gangsters looked a bit like Karen when she took the pizza order, only much angrier, but his girlfriend looked proud of him, even though the gangsters were standing either side of her, because she was basically like his mother with much more expensive peach-coloured clothes, and the crowd went crazy because there was something to believe in again. And then there was a car chase and the gangsters, whose reflexes were not honed by a lifetime in sports and whose bad character turned into bad driving on a crucial bend, crashed their car and exploded.

In the game on television the gangsters seemed to be having much more success and the ball hardly got hit at all. Every few minutes advertisements interrupted the play and then the words WORLD SERIES in huge gold letters spun out of nowhere and glinted on the screen.

'Where's our wine?' said his father.

'Your wine,' Robert's mother corrected him.

He saw his father clench his jaw and swallow a remark. When Karen arrived with the bottle of red wine, his father started drinking decisively, as if the remark he had not made was stuck in his throat. Karen gave Robert and Thomas huge glasses of ice stained with cranberry juice. Robert sipped his drink listlessly. The day had been unbearably long. Not just the pressurized biscuit-coloured staleness of the flight, but the Immigration formalities as well. His father, who had joked that he was going to describe himself as an 'international tourist' on the grounds that that was how President Bush pronounced 'international terrorist', managed to resist the temptation. He was nevertheless taken into a side room by a black female Immigration officer after having his passport stamped.

'She couldn't understand why an English lawyer was born in France,' he explained in the taxi. 'She clasped her head and said, "I'm just trying to get a concept of your life, Mr Melrose." I told her I was trying to do the same thing and that if I ever wrote an autobiography I'd send her a copy.'

'Oh,' said Robert's mother, 'so that's why we waited an extra half-hour.'

'Well, you know, when people hate officialdom, they either become craven or facetious.'

'Try craven next time, it's quicker.'

When the pizzas finally arrived Robert saw that they were hopeless. As thick as nappies, they hadn't been adjusted to the ninety per cent reduction in ingredients. Robert scraped all the tomato and anchovy and olives into one corner and made two mouthfuls of miniature pizza. It was not at all like the delicious, thin, slightly burnt pizza in Les Lecques but somehow, because he had thought it might be, he had opened a trap door into the summers he used to have and would never have again.

'What's wrong?' asked his mother.

'I just want a pizza like the ones in Les Lecques.' He was assailed by injustice and despair. He really didn't want to cry.

'Oh, darling, I so understand,' she said, touching his hand.

'I know it seems far-fetched in this mad restaurant, but we're going to have a lovely time in America.'

'Why is Bobby crying?' said Thomas.

'He's upset.'

'But I don't want him to cry,' said Thomas. 'I don't want him to!' he screamed, and started crying himself.

'Fucking hell,' said Robert's father. 'I knew we should have gone to Ramsgate.'

On the way back to the hotel, Thomas fell asleep in his stroller.

'Let's cut to the chase,' said Robert's father, 'and not pretend we're going to sleep with each other. You take both of the boys into the bedroom and I'll take the sofa bed.'

'Fine,' said Robert's mother, 'if that's what you want.'

'There's no need to introduce exciting words like "want". It's what I'm realistically anticipating.'

Robert fell asleep immediately, but woke up again when the red digits on the bedside clock said 2:11. His mother and Thomas were still asleep but he could hear a muffled sound from the drawing room. He found his father on the floor in front of the television.

'I put my back out unfolding that fucking sofa bed,' he said, doing push-ups with his hips still pressed to the carpet.

The bottle of whiskey was on the glass table, three-quarters empty next to a ravaged sheet of Codis painkillers.

'I'm sorry about the Venus Pizza,' said his father. 'After going there, and shopping at Carnegie Foods and watching a few hours of this delinquent network television, I've come to the conclusion that we should probably fast during our holiday here. Factory farming doesn't stop in the slaughter-house, it stops in our bloodstreams, after the Henry Ford food missiles have hurtled out of their cages into our open mouths and dissolved their growth hormones and their genetically modified feed into our increasingly wobbly bodies. Even when the food isn't "fast", the bill is instantaneous, dumping an idle eater back on the snack-crowded streets. In the end, we're on the same conveyor belt as the featherless, electrocuted chickens.'

Robert found his father vaguely frightening, with his bloodshot eyes and the sweat stains on his shirt, twisting the corkscrew of his own talk. Robert knew that he wasn't being communicated with, but allowed to listen to his father practising speeches. All this time while he had been asleep, his father had been pacing up and down a mental courtroom, prosecuting.

'I liked the Park,' said Robert.

'The Park's nice,' his father conceded, 'but the rest of the country is just people in huge cars wondering what to eat next. When we hire a car you'll see that it's really a mobile dining room, with little tables all over the place and cup holders. It's a nation of hungry children with real guns. If you're not blown up by a bomb, you're blown up by a Vesuvio pizza. It's absolutely terrifying.'

'Please stop,' said Robert.

'I'm sorry. I just feel . . .' His father suddenly seemed lost. 'I just can't sleep. The Park is great. The city is breathtakingly beautiful. It's just me.'

'Is whiskey going to be part of the fast?'

'Unfortunately,' said his father, imitating the mischievous way that Thomas liked to say that word, 'the whiskey is something *very* pure and can't reasonably be included in the war against corruption.'

'Oh,' said Robert.

'Or war *on* corruption, as they would say here. War on terror; war on crime; war on drugs. I suppose if you're a pacifist here you have to have a war on war, or nobody would notice.'

'Daddy,' Robert warned him.

'I'm sorry, I'm sorry.' He grabbed the remote control. 'Let's turn off this mind-shattering rubbish and read a story.'

'Excellent,' said Robert, jumping onto the sofa bed. He felt he was pretending to be more cheerful than he was, a little bit like Karen. Perhaps it was infectious, or something in the food supply.

14

'Oh, Patrick, why weren't we told that the lovely life we had was going to end?' said Aunt Nancy, turning the pages of the photograph album.

'Weren't you told that?' said Patrick. 'How maddening. But then again, it didn't end for the people who might have told you. Your mother just ruined it by trusting your stepfather.'

'Do you know the worst thing about that – I'm going to use the word "evil" – '

'Popular word these days,' murmured Patrick.

' – man?' Nancy continued, only briefly closing her eyelids to refuse admittance to Patrick's distracting remark. 'He used to grope me in the back of Mummy's car while she was at home dying of cancer. He had Parkinson's by then, so he had a shaky grip, if you know what I'm saying. After Mummy died, he actually asked me to marry him. Can you believe that? I just laughed, but sometimes I think I should have accepted. He only lasted two more years, and I might have been spared the sight of the little nephew's removal men carrying my dressing table out of my bedroom, while I lay in bed, on the morning of Jean's death. I said to the brutes in blue overalls, "What are you doing? Those are my hairbrushes." "We were told to take everything," they grunted, and then they threw me out of bed, so they could load that on the van as well.'

'It might have been even more traumatic to marry someone you loathed and found physically disgusting,' said Patrick.

'Oh, look,' said Nancy, turning a page of the album, 'here's Fairley, where we spent the beginning of the war, while Mummy was still stuck in France. It was the most divine house on Long Island. Do you know that uncle Bill had a one-hundred-and-fifty-acre garden; I'm not talking about woods and fields, there were plenty of those as well. Nowadays people think they're God almighty if they have a ten-acre garden on Long Island. There was *the* most beautiful pink marble throne in the middle of the topiary garden where we used to play grandmother's footsteps. It used to belong to the Emperor of Byzantium . . .' She sighed. 'All lost, all the beautiful things.'

'The thing about things is that they just keep getting lost,' said Patrick. 'The Emperor lost his throne before Uncle Bill lost his garden furniture.'

'Well, at least Uncle Bill's children got to sell Fairley,' Nancy flared up. 'They didn't have it stolen.'

'Listen, I'm the first to sympathize. After what Eleanor did, we're the most financially withered branch of the family,' said Patrick. 'How long were you separated from your mother?' he asked, as if to introduce a lighter note.

'Four years.'

'Four years!'

'Well, we went to America two years before the war started. Mummy stayed in Europe trying to get the really good things out of France and England and Italy, and she only made it to America two years after the Germans invaded. She and Jean escaped via Portugal and when they arrived I remember that her shoe trunk had fallen overboard from the fishing boat they hired to get them across to New York. I thought that if you could get away from the Germans and only lose a trunk with nothing in it but shoes, you weren't having such a bad war.'

'But how did you feel about not seeing her all that time?'

'Well, you know, I had the oddest conversation with Eleanor a couple of years before she had her stroke. She told me that when Mummy and Jean arrived at Fairley, she rowed out to the middle of the lake and refused to talk to them because she was so angry that Mummy had abandoned us for four years. I was shocked because I couldn't remember anything about it. I mean, that would have been a big deal in our young lives. But all I remember is Mummy's shoes getting lost.'

'I guess everybody remembers what's important to them,' said Patrick.

'She told me that she hated Mummy,' said Nancy. 'I mean, I didn't know that was *genetically* possible.'

'Her genes probably just stood by horrified,' said Patrick. 'The story Eleanor always told me was that she hated your mother for sacking the two people she loved and depended on: her father and her nanny.'

'I tied myself to the car when Nanny was being driven away,' said Nancy competitively.

'Well, there you have it – didn't you feel a little gene-defying twinge . . .'

'No! I blamed Jean. He was the one who persuaded Mummy that we were too old to have a nanny.'

'And your father?'

'Well, Mummy said that she just couldn't afford to keep him any more. Every week he would drive her crazy with some new extravagance. In the run-up to Ascot, for instance, he didn't just buy a racehorse, he bought a stable of racehorses. Do you know what I'm saying?'

'Those were the days,' said Patrick. 'I'd love to be in a position to be irritated by Mary buying a couple of dozen racehorses, rather than getting in a blind panic when Thomas needs a new pair of shoes.'

'You're exaggerating.'

'It's the only extravagance I can still afford.'

The telephone rang, drawing Nancy into a study next to her library, and leaving Patrick on the soft sofa dented by the weight of the red leather album, with 1940 stamped in gold on its spine.

The image of Eleanor rowing out to the middle of the lake and refusing to talk to anyone fused in Patrick's imagination with her present condition, bedridden and cut off from the rest of the world.

The day after she had settled into her thickly carpeted, overheated, nursing tomb in Kensington, Patrick was rung by the director.

'Your mother would like to see you straight away. She thinks she's going to die today.'

'Is there any reason to believe she's right?'

'There's no medical reason as such, but she is very insistent.'

Patrick hauled himself out of his chambers and went over to see Eleanor. He found her crying from the unspeakable frustration of having something so important to say. After half an hour, she finally gave birth to, 'Die today,' delivered with all the stunned wonder of recent motherhood. After that, hardly a day passed without a death promise emerging from half an hour's gibbering, weeping struggle.

When Patrick complained to Kathleen, the perky Irish nurse in charge of Eleanor's floor, she clasped his forearm and hooted, 'She'll probably outlive us all. Take Dr MacDougal on the next floor. When he was seventy, he married a lady half his age – she was a lovely lady, so friendly. Well, the next year, it was quite tragic really, he got the Alzheimer's and moved in here. She was ever so devoted, came to see him every day. Anyway, if she didn't get breast cancer the following year. She was dead three years after marrying him, and he's still upstairs, *going strong*.'

After a final hoot of laughter, she left him standing alone in the airless corridor next to the locked dispensary.

What depressed him even more than the inaccuracy of Eleanor's predictions was the doggedness of her self-deception and her spiritual vanity. The idea that she had any special insight into the exact time of her death was typical of the daydreams that ruled her life. It was only in June, after she had fallen over and broken her hip, that she began to take a more realistic attitude about the degree of control she could have over her death.

Patrick went to visit her in the Chelsea and Westminster Hospital after her fall.

Eleanor had been given morphine for breakfast, but her restlessness was unsubdued. The desperate need to get out of bed, which had produced several falls, bruising her right temple purple-black, leaving her nose swollen and red, staining her right eyelid yellow and eventually fracturing her hip, made her, even now, reach for the bar on the side of her Evans Nesbit Jubilee bed and try to pull herself up with those flabby white arms bruised by fresh puncture marks Patrick could not help envying. A few clear phrases reared up like Pacific islands from a mumbling moaning ocean of meaningless syllables.

'I have a rendezvous,' she said, making a renewed surge towards the end of the bed.

'I'm sure whoever you have to meet will come here,' said Patrick, 'knowing that you can't move.'

'Yes,' she said, collapsing back on the bloodstained pillows for a moment, but lurching forwards again and wailing, 'I have a rendezvous.'

She was not strong enough to stay up for long, and soon resumed a slow writhing motion on the bed, and the long haul through another stretch of murmurous, urgent nonsense. And then 'No longer' appeared, not attached to anything else. She ran her hands down her face in exasperation, looking as if she wanted to cry but was being let down by her body in that respect as well.

At last she managed it.

'I want you to kill me,' she said, gripping his hand surprisingly hard.

'I'd love to help,' said Patrick, 'but unfortunately it's against the law.'

'No longer,' shouted Eleanor.

'We're doing all we can,' he said vaguely.

Looking for solace in practicality, Patrick tried to give his mother a sip of pineapple juice from the plastic glass on her bedside table. He eased his hand under the top pillow and lifted her head, tipping the juice gently towards her peeling lips. He felt himself being transformed by the tenderness of the act. He had never treated anyone so carefully except his own children. The flow of generations was reversed and he found himself holding his useless, treacherous, confused mother with exquisite anxiety. How to lift her head, how to make sure she didn't choke. He watched her roll the sip of juice around her mouth, an alarmed and disconnected look on her face, and he willed her to succeed while she tried to remind her throat how to swallow.

Poor Eleanor, poor little Eleanor, she wasn't well at all, she needed help, she needed protection. There was no obstacle, no interruption to his desire to help her. He was amazed to see his argumentative, disappointed mind overwhelmed by a physical act. He leant over further and kissed her on the forehead.

A nurse came in and saw the glass in Patrick's hand.

'Did you give her some of the Thicken Up?' she asked.

'Some what?'

'Thicken Up,' she said, tapping a tin of that name.

'I don't think my mother wants to thicken up,' said Patrick. 'You haven't got a tin called "Waste Away", have you?'

The nurse looked shocked, but Eleanor smiled.

'Aste way,' she echoed.

'She had a very good breakfast this morning,' the nurse persevered.

'Orce,' said Eleanor.

'Forced?' Patrick suggested.

She turned her wild-eyed face towards him and said, 'Yes.'

'When you get back to the nursing home, you can stop eating if you want to,' said Patrick. 'You'll have more control over your fate.'

'Yes,' she whispered, smiling.

She seemed to relax for the first time. And so did Patrick. He was going to guard his mother from having more horrible life imposed on her. Here at last was a filial role he could throw himself into.

Patrick looked at Nancy's other photograph albums, over a hundred identical red-leather volumes dated from 1919 to 2001, ranged in the shelves directly in front of him. The rest of the room was lined with decorative blocks of leather books and, lower down, glossy books on the art of decoration. Even the two doors, one into the hall and the other into the study where Nancy was talking on the phone, did not interrupt the library theme. Their backs were crowded with the spines of false books resting on trompe l'œil shelves perfectly aligned with the real shelves, so that when the doors were closed the room generated an impressive claustrophobia. The blast of resentment and nostalgia coming from Nancy, undiminished since he last saw her eight years before, made Patrick all the more determined not to live in the has-been world enshrined in the wall of albums – let alone in the might-have-been realm where Nancy's imagination burnt even more ferociously. There seemed little point in trying to give her a bracing lecture on the value of staying contemporary when she wouldn't even stick to the past as it was, but preferred a version cleansed of the injustice which had been done to her nearly forty years earlier. The afterglow of plutocracy was no more alluring to him than a pile of dirty dishes after a dinner party. Something had died, and its death was tied in with the tenderness he had felt for Eleanor when he helped her drink that glass of pineapple juice in hospital.

Seeing his aunt made him marvel again at how different she was from her sister. And yet their attitudes of extreme worldliness and extreme unworldliness had a common origin in a sense of maternal betrayal and financial disappointment. The blame had been reattributed to her stepfather by Nancy, while Eleanor had tried to unload the sense of betrayal onto Patrick. Unsuccessfully, he now liked to think, although after only a few hours with his aunt he felt like a recovering alcoholic who has been given a cocktail shaker for his birthday.

The tall clear windows looked onto a broad lawn sloping down to an ornamental pond and spanned by a wooden Japanese bridge. From where he sat he could see Thomas trying to hang over the side of the bridge, gently restrained by Mary while he pointed at the exotic waterfowl rippling across the bright coin of water. Or perhaps there were koi carp giving depth to the Japanese theme. Or some samurai armour gleaming in the mud. It was dangerous to underestimate Nancy's decorative thoroughness. Robert was writing his diary in the little pond-side pagoda.

Several shelves of unreadable classics creaked open and Nancy strode back into the room.

'That was our rich cousin,' she said, as if invigorated by contact with money.

'Which one?'

'Henry. He says you're going to his island next week.'

'That's right,' said Patrick. 'We're just paw whi-te trash throwin' oursef on the cha-ri-tee of our American kin.'

'He wanted to know if your children were well behaved. I told him they hadn't broken anything yet. "How long have they been there?" he asked. When I said you arrived about two hours ago, he said, "Oh, for God sakes, Nancy, what kind of a sample is that? I'm ringing back tomorrow for a full report." I guess not everybody has the world's most important collection of Meissen figurines.'

'I don't suppose he will either, after Thomas has been to stay.'

'Don't say that!' said Nancy. 'Now you're making me nervous.'

'I didn't know Henry had become so pompous. I haven't seen him in at least twenty years; it was really very hospitable of him to let us come. As a teenager he belonged to that familiar type, the complacent rebel. I suppose the rebel was defeated by the army of Meissen figurines. Who can blame him for surrendering? Imagine the gleaming hordes of porcelain milkmaids clearing the brow of the hill and flooding the bowl of the valley, and poor Henry with only a rolled-up portfolio statement to beat them off.'

'You get awfully carried away by your imagination,' said Nancy.

'Sorry' said Patrick. 'I haven't been in court for three weeks. The speeches pile up . . .'

'Well, your ancient aunt is going to have a rest now. We're going to Walter's and Beth's for tea, and I'd better be on top form for that. Don't let the children walk on the grass barefoot, or go into the woods at all. I'm afraid this part of Connecticut is a Lyme disease hot spot, and the ticks are just dreadful this year. The gardener tries to keep the poison ivy out of the garden, but he can't control the woods. Lyme disease is just horrible. It's recurring and if it goes untreated it can destroy your life. There's a little boy who lives in the village here and he's really not at all well. He has psychotic fits and things. Beth just takes the antibiotics round the clock. She "self-medicates". She says it's safer to assume you're always in danger.'

'Grounds for perpetual war,' said Patrick. '*Tout ce qu'il y a de plus chic.*'

'Well, if you want to put it that way.'

'I think I do. Not necessarily to her face.'

'Necessarily *not* to her face,' Nancy flared up. 'She's one of my oldest friends and besides, she's the most powerful of the Park Avenue women and it's not a good idea to cross her.'

'I wouldn't dream of it,' said Patrick.

After Nancy had left, Patrick walked over to the drinks tray and, so as not to leave a dirty glass, drank several gulps of bourbon from a bottle of Maker's Mark. He sank back into an armchair and stared out of the window. The impenetrable New England countryside looked pretty enough, but was in fact packed with more dangers than a Cambodian swamp. Mary already had several pamphlets on Lyme disease – named after a Connecticut town only a few miles away – and so there was no need to rush out and tell the family.

'It's safer to assume you're always in danger.' Some verbal tic made him want to say, 'It's safer to assume you're safe unless you're in danger', but he was quickly won over by the plausibility of paranoia. In any case, he now felt in danger all the time. Danger of liver collapse, marital breakdown, terminal fear. Nobody ever died of a feeling, he would say to himself, not believing a word of it, as he sweated his way through the feeling that he was dying of fear. People died of feelings all the time, once they had gone through the formality of materializing them into bullets and bottles and tumours. Someone who was organized like him, with utterly chaotic foundations, a quite strongly developed intellect and almost nothing in between desperately needed to develop the middle ground. Without it, he split into a vigilant day mind, a bird of prey hovering over a landscape, and a helpless night mind, a jellyfish splattered on the deck of a ship. 'The Eagle and the Jellyfish', a fable Aesop just couldn't be bothered to write. He guffawed with abrupt, slightly deranged laughter and got up to take another gulp of bourbon from the bottle. Yes, the middle ground was now occupied by a lake of alcohol. The first drink centred him for about twenty minutes and then the rest brought his night mind rushing over the landscape like the dark blade of an eclipse.

The whole thing, he knew, was a humiliating Oedipal drama. Despite the superficial revolution in his relations with Eleanor, a local victory of compassion over loathing, the underlying impact she had made on his life remained undisturbed. His fundamental sense of being was a kind of free fall, a limitless dread, a claustrophobic agoraphobia. Doubtless there was something universal about fear. His sons, despite their lavish treatment from Mary, had moments of fear, but these were temporary afflictions, whereas Patrick felt that fear was the ground he stood on, or the groundlessness he fell into, and he couldn't help connecting this conviction with his mother's absolute inability to concentrate on another human being. He had to remind himself that the defining characteristic of Eleanor's life was her incompetence. She wanted to have a child and became a lousy mother; she wanted to write children's stories and became a lousy writer; she wanted to be a philanthropist and gave all her money to a self-serving charlatan. Now she wanted to die and she couldn't do that either. She could only communicate with people who presented themselves as the portals to some bombastic generalization, like 'humanity' or 'salvation', something the mewling, puking Patrick must have been unable to do. One of the troubles with being an infant was the difficulty of distinguishing incompetence from malice, and this difficulty sometimes returned to him in the drunken middle of the night. It was now beginning to invade his view of Mary as well.

Mary had been a devoted mother to Robert, but after the absorption of the first year she had resurfaced as a wife, if only because she wanted another child. With Thomas, perhaps because she knew that he was her last child, she seemed to be trapped in a Madonna and Child force field, preserving a precinct of purity, including her own rediscovered virginity. Patrick was in the unenviable role of Joseph in this enduring, unendurable Bethlehem. Mary had completely withdrawn her attention from him and the more he requested it the more he appeared in the light of an imposturous rival to his younger son. He had turned elsewhere, to Julia, and once that had collapsed, to the oblivious embrace of alcohol. He must stop. At his age he either had to join the resistance or become a collaborator with death. There was no room to play with self-destruction once the juvenile illusion of indestructibility had evaporated.

Oh dear, he'd made rather too much progress with the Maker's Mark. The logical thing to do was to take this bottle upstairs and pour the rest of it into the depleted bottle of bourbon hidden in his rucksack, and then nip into town to buy another one for Nancy's drinks table. He would, of course, have to make convincing inroads into the new bottle so that it resembled the old bottle before he had almost finished it. Practically anything was less complicated than being a successful alcoholic. Bombing Third World countries – now there was an occupation for a man of leisure. 'It's all right for some,' he muttered, weaving his way across the room. He was arguably just a teeny-weeny bit too drunk for this time of day. His thoughts were cracking up, going staccato, getting overtrumped just as he was about to pick up the trick.

Check: family in the garden. Check: silence in the hall. Run up the stairs, close the door, get the rucksack, decant the bourbon – all over his hand. Hide the empty on top of cupboard. Car keys. Down and out. Tell family? Yes. No. Yes. No! Get in car. Ding ding ding. Fucking American car safety ding ding. Safer to assume sudden violent death. Police no please no police, p-l-e-a-s-e. Slip away over crunchy nutritious gravel. Cruise control, out of control. Suggestible suggestions. Jump the tracks, get out of the syllable cruncher and into, into the sunlit death-trap countryside. Better pave the whole thing over. Angry posses of ordinary citizens with chain saws and concrete mixers. 'We've lived in fear for long enough! We've got a right to protect our families! It says in the Bible, "The wild places shall be made tame. And the people shall have dominion over the ticks."'

He was drifting along in his silvery blue Buick LeSabre, screaming in a hillbilly accent. He couldn't stop. He couldn't stop anything. He couldn't stop the car, he couldn't stop drinking, he couldn't stop the Koncrete Klux Klan. A bright red Stop sign slipped by as he merged quietly with the main road into town. He parked next to the Vino Veritas liquor store. The car had somehow locked itself, just to be on the safe side. Ding ding ding. Keys still in the ignition. He arched backwards trying to ease the dull pain in his lower back. Eroded vertebrae? Swollen kidneys? 'We have to think our way out of the box of our habitual dichotomies,' he purred, in the smug tones of a self-help tape. 'It's not an *either* vertebrae *or* kidneys situation, it's a *both* kidneys *and* vertebrae situation. Think outside the box! Be creative!'

And here, straight ahead of him, across the railway tracks, down among the playing fields, was another *both and* situation. Both the exuberant sentimentality of American family life unfolding among the brightly coloured tubes and slides and swings of a playground, with its soft wood-chip landing sites and, on a large area of grass beyond the chain-link fence, two pot-bellied policemen training an Alsatian to tear apart any sick fucks who thought to disturb the peace and prosperity of New Milton. One policeman held the dog by the collar, the other stood at the far end of the green with a huge padded arm guard. The Alsatian streaked across the grass, leapt onto the padded arm and shook his head savagely from side to side, his growling just audible through the humid air pierced by the cries of children and the sonic solicitude of safety-conscious cars. Did the children feel safer, or just feel that it was safer to assume they were always in danger? A Botero-shaped family munching soft buns at a round-cornered picnic table looked on as the first policeman hurried across the green and tried to detach the keen young Alsatian from his colleague's arm. The second policeman was by now floundering on the grass trying to persuade the dog that he was not a sick fuck but one of the good guys.

Vino Veritas had three sizes of Maker's Mark. Not sure which one he was supposed to replace, Patrick bought all three.

'Better be safe than sorry,' he explained to the salesman.

'You'd better believe it,' said the salesman with a fervour that catapulted Patrick back into the parking lot.

He was already in another phase of drunkenness. Sweatier, sadder, slower. He needed *both* another drink *and* a huge amount of coffee, so that he could stand up at Walter and Beth's, or indeed anywhere. He was in fact certain, he might as well admit it, that the smallest bottle of Maker's Mark was not the one he had to replace. He hadn't been able to resist buying the baby bottle to complete the family. Ding ding ding. He unpeeled the red faux-wax cap and uncorked the bottle. As the bourbon slipped down his throat, he pictured a flaming beam crashing through the floors and ceilings of a building, spreading fire and wreckage. What a relief.

The Better Latte Than Never coffee shop lived up to the maddening promise of its name. Patrick sailed past the invitation to a skinny caramel grande vanilla frapuccino in a transparent plastic cup jam-packed with mouthwatering ice and strawberry-flavoured whipped cream, and ordered some black coffee. He moved along the assembly line.

'Have a great one!' said Pete, a heavy-jawed blond beast in an apron, sliding the coffee across the counter.

Old enough to remember the arrival of 'Have a nice day', Patrick could only look with alarm on the hyperinflation of 'Have a great one'. Where would this Weimar of bullying cheerfulness end? 'You have a profound and meaningful day now,' he simpered under his breath as he tottered across the room with his giant mug. 'Have a blissful one,' he snapped as he sat at a table. 'You all make sure you have an all-body orgasm,' he whispered in a Southern accent, 'and make it last.' Because you deserve it. Because you owe it to yourself. Because you're a unique and special person. In the end, there was only so much you could expect from a cup of coffee and an uneatable muffin. If only Pete had confined himself to realistic achievements. 'Have a cold shower,' or 'Try not to crash your car.'

He was back in the inflammatory, deranged drunkenness he had lost in the hot parking lot. Yes yes yes. After a few gallons of coffee there'd be no stopping him. Across the room, a voluptuous medical student in a pink cardigan and faded jeans was working on her computer. Her mobile phone was on the slate ledge of the Heat and Glow fireplace, next to the Walkman and the complicated drink. She sat on her chair with her knees raised and her legs wide open as if she had just given birth to her Hewlett Packard, *The Pathology of*

Disease squashing some loose notes on the edge of the table. He must have her, on a must-have basis. She was so relaxed in her body. He stared at her and she looked back at him with a calm even gaze. She smiled. It was absolutely terrifying how perfect she was. He looked away and smiled bashfully at his kneecap. He couldn't bear her being friendly. It made him want to cry. She was practically a doctor, she could probably completely save him. His sons would miss him at first, but they'd get over it. Anyway, they could come and stay. She was obviously an incredibly warm and loving person.

The Oedipal vortex had him caught like a dead leaf in its compulsory spin, wanting one consolation after another. Some languages kept the ideas of desire and privation apart, but English forced them into the naked intimacy of a single syllable: want. Wanting love to ease the want of love. The war on want which made one want more. Whiskey was no better at looking after him than his mother had been, or his wife had become, or the pink cardigan would be if he lurched across the room, fell to his knees and begged her for mercy. Why did he want to do that? Where was the Eagle now? Why wasn't he coolly registering the feeling of attraction and reabsorbing it into a sense of his present state of mind, or beyond that, into the simple fact of being alive? Why rush naively towards the objects of his thoughts, when he could stay at their source? He closed his eyes and slumped in his chair.

So, here he was in the magnificence of the inner realm, no longer chasing after pink cardigans and amber bottles, but watching thoughts flick open like so many fans in a hot crowded room. He was no longer jumping into the painted scenes, but noticing the flicking, noticing the heat, noticing that drunkenness gave a certain predominance to images in his otherwise predominantly verbal mind, noticing that the conclusion he was looking for was not blackout and orgasm, but knowledge and insight. The trouble was that even when the object of pursuit changed, the anguish of pursuit remained. He found himself hurtling towards a vacuum rather than hurtling away from it. Big deal. In the end he was better off galloping after the syrupy mirage of a hot fuck. He opened his eyes. She was gone. Want in both directions. Directions delusions anyway. A universe of want. Infinite melancholy.

The scraping chair. Late. Family. Tea. Try not to think. Think: don't think. Madness. Ding ding ding. Cruise control, out of control. Please stop thinking. Who's asking? Who's being asked?

When he drew up to the house, the Others were arranged around Nancy's car in a tableau of reproach and irritation.

'You wouldn't believe what happened to me in New Milton,' he said, wondering what he would say if anybody asked.

'We were about to leave without you,' said Nancy. 'Beth can't stand people being late; they just drop right off her guest list.'

'A slobbering thought,' said Patrick. 'I mean sobering thought,' he corrected himself. Neither version was heard above the sound of crunching gravel and slamming doors. He climbed into the back of Nancy's car and slumped next to Thomas, wishing he had the baby bottle of Maker's Mark to nurse him through tea. During the journey he dozed superficially until he felt the car slow down and come to a halt. When he clambered out he found himself surrounded by unpunctuated woodland. The Berkshire Hills rolled off in every direction, like a heavy swell in a green and yellow ocean, with Walter and Beth's white clapboard ark cresting the nearest wave. He felt seasick and land-bound at the same time.

'Unbelievable,' he muttered.

'I know,' said Nancy. 'They pretty much own the view.'

The tea party unfolded for Patrick in an unreliable middle distance. One moment he felt as glazed over as an aquarium on television, the next he was drowning. There were maids in uniform with eyeball aching white shoes. A small Hispanic butler. Sweet brown cinnamony iced tea. Park Avenue gossip. People laughing about something Henry Kissinger had said at dinner on Thursday.

Then the garden tour began. Walter went ahead, sometimes unlocking his arm from Nancy's in order to clip an impertinent shoot with the secateurs he held in his suede-gloved hand. He certainly wouldn't be doing any gardening if it hadn't been done already. He bore the same relation to the gardening as a mayor to the housing development on which he cuts the inaugural ribbon. Beth followed with Mary and the children. She was persistently modest about the garden and sometimes downright dissatisfied. When she came to a topiary deer that stood on the edge of a flower bed, she said, 'I hate it! It looks like a kangaroo. I pour vinegar on it to try to kill it off. The climate here is impossible: we're up to our waists in snow until the middle of May, and two weeks later we're living in Vietnam.'

Patrick dragged behind the rest of the party, trying to pretend he was in a horticultural trance, leaning over to stare blindly at a nameless flower, hoping he looked like the shade of Andrew Marvell rather than a stale drunk who dreaded being drawn into conversation. The vast lawn turned into a box maze, a topiary zoo (from which the doomed kangaroo was excluded) and finally a lime grove.

'Look, Dada! A *sanglier*!' said Thomas, pointing to a curly haired, heavy snouted bronze boar, with legs that looked too delicate to bear the weight of its pendulous belly and massive tusked head.

'Yes, darling,' said Patrick.

Wild boar had always been French for Patrick and he was heartbroken that they were French for Thomas as well. How could he have retained that word over the whole year? Was he thinking of the wild boar at Saint-Nazaire trotting across the garden to eat the fallen figs, or snuffling among the vines at night, looking for ripe grapes? No, he wasn't. *Sanglier* was just a word for the animal in the statue. He had already turned his back on it and was running down the lime grove pretending to be an aeroplane. Patrick's heartbreak was all his own, and even that was hollow. He no longer felt a corrosive nostalgia for Saint-Nazaire; its loss just clarified the real failure: that he couldn't be the sort of father he wanted to be, a man who had transcended his ancestral muddle and offered his children unhaunted love. He had made it out of what he thought of as Zone One, where a parent was doomed to make his child experience what he had hated most about his life, but he was still stuck in Zone Two, where the painstaking avoidance of Zone One blinded him to fresh mistakes. In Zone Two giving was based on what the giver lacked. Nothing was more exhausting than this deficiency-driven, overcompensating zeal. He dreamt of Zone Three. He sensed that it was there, just over the hill, like the rumour of a fertile valley. Perhaps his present chaos was the final rejection of an unsustainable way of being. He must stop drinking, not tomorrow but later this afternoon when the next opportunity arose.

Strangely excited by this glint of hope, Patrick continued to hang back. The tour drifted on. A stone Diana stood at the far end of the grove, eternally hunting the bronze boar at the other end. Behind the house, a springy wood-chip path meandered through an improved wood. Patches of light shivered on the denuded ground between the broad trunks of oaks and beeches. Beyond the wood they passed a hangar where huge fans, consuming enough electricity to run a small village, kept agapanthus warm in the winter. Next to the hangar was a hen house somewhat larger than Patrick's London flat, and so strangely undefiled that he couldn't help wondering if these were genetically modified hens which had been crossed with cucumbers to stop them from defecating. Beth walked over the fresh sawdust, under the red heat lamps, and discovered three speckled brown eggs in the laying boxes. Every plate of scrambled eggs must cost her several thousand dollars. The truth was that he hated the very rich, especially since he was never going to be one of them. They were all too often only the shrill pea in the whistle of their possessions. Without the editorial influence of the word 'afford', their desires rambled on like unstoppable bores, relentless and whimsical at the same time. They could give the appearance of generosity to all sorts of emotional meanness – 'Do borrow the fourth house we never get round to using. We won't be there ourselves, but Carmen and Alfonso will look after you. No, really, it's no trouble at all, and besides it's about time we got our money's worth out of those two. We pay them a fortune and they never do a stroke of work.'

'What are you muttering about?' said Nancy, who was clearly annoyed that Patrick had underperformed as an admiring guest.

'Oh, nothing,' said Patrick.

'Isn't this hen house divine?' she prompted him.

'It would be a privilege to live here,' said Patrick, catching up abruptly with his social duties.

When the garden tour ended, with a gift of eggs, the visit ended as well. On the way back to Nancy's, Patrick was confronted by his decision not to go on drinking. It was all very well to decide not to drink when he had no choice, but in a few minutes he would be able to climb into the Buick's private liquor store. What did it matter if he started stopping tomorrow? He knew that it somehow mattered completely.

If he went on now he would be hung over tomorrow morning and the whole day would begin with a poisonous legacy. But more than that, he wanted to cultivate the faint hope he had felt in the garden. If he stopped tomorrow it would be from an excess of shame, a nastier and less reliable motivation. What, on the other hand, was Zone Three? His mind was occluded by tension; he couldn't reconstruct the hope.

Back in Nancy's library, he stared out of the window, feeling that he was being stared at in turn by the bottle of bourbon he had replaced on the drinks tray. It would be so much neater to bring it down to the level the empty one had started at. Just as he was about to give in, Nancy came into the room and sank with a theatrical sigh into the armchair opposite him.

'I feel we haven't really talked about Eleanor,' she said. 'I think I'm frightened of asking because I was so shocked when I last saw her.'

'You heard about the fall?'

'No!'

'She broke her hip and went into hospital. When I went to see her she started asking me to kill her. She hasn't stopped asking me since. Every time I go . . .'

'Oh, come on,' said Nancy, 'I really don't think that's fair! I mean, it's all too Greek. There must be some special Furies for children who kill their parents.'

'Yeah,' said Patrick. 'Wormwood Scrubs.'

'Oh, God,' said Nancy, twisting in her chair. 'It's so complicated. I mean, I know I wouldn't want to go on living if I couldn't speak, or move, or read, or watch a movie.'

'I have no doubt that helping her to die would be the most loving thing to do.'

'Well, I don't want you to misinterpret me, but maybe we should rent an ambulance and drive her to Holland.'

'Arriving in Holland isn't in itself fatal,' said Patrick.

'Oh, please, let's not talk about it any more. I find it too upsetting. I really couldn't bear it if I ended up like that.'

'Do you want a drink?' asked Patrick.

'Oh, no. I don't drink,' said Nancy. 'Didn't you know? I watched it destroy Daddy's life. But do help yourself if you want one.'

Patrick imagined one of his children saying, 'I watched it destroy Daddy's life.' He noticed that he was leaning forward in his chair.

'I might help myself by not having one,' he said, sinking back and closing his eyes.

15

Mary could hardly believe that Patrick and Robert were in one thinly carpeted motel room and she and Thomas were in another, with plastic wraps on the plastic glasses, and Sanitized For Your Protection sashes on the plastic loo seats, and a machine down the corridor whose shuddering ejaculations of ice reminded her unwillingly of the state of her marriage. She could hear the steady hum of the freeway thickening in the early morning. It was the perfect soundtrack to the quick, slick flow of her anxiety. At about four in the morning a phrase had started clicking like a metronome she was too tired to reach out and stop: 'Interstate-inner state, interstate-inner state.' Sleeplessness was the breeding ground of these sardonic harmonies; ice machine-marriage; interstate-inner state. It was enough to drive you mad. Or was it enough to stop you from going mad? Making connections. She could hardly believe that her family was haemorrhaging more money in order to have a horrible time in one of America's migratory nowheres. So much road and so few places, so much friendliness and so little intimacy, so much flavour and so little taste. She longed to get the children back home to London, away from the thin rush of America and back to the density of their ordinary lives.

Patrick had kept up the tradition of getting them thrown out of somewhere rather lovely quite a long time before the end of the holidays. Saint-Nazaire last year, Henry's island this year. Of course she was delighted that he had stopped drinking, but the effect in the first week was to make him behave like other people when they were blind drunk: explosive, irascible, despairing. All the boils were being lanced at once, the kidney dishes overflowing. Henry was certainly a nightmare, but he was also some sort of relation and, above all, a host who was providing a playground for the children, with its own harbour and beaches and sailing boats and motor boats and, to Thomas's undying amazement, its own petrol pump.

'I mean, it's unbelievable, Henry has his own petrol pump!' Thomas said several times a day, opening his palms and shaking his head. Robert was in a statistical frenzy of acres and bedrooms, totting up the immensity of Henry's domain, but both boys were mainly having a wonderful time dashing briefly into the freezing water and going out in Henry's speedboats, riding the wake behind the big ferries which served the public islands.

The only thing which went wrong was everything else. During the first lunch Henry asked Mary to remove Thomas from the dining room when his monologue on the moral necessity of increasing Israel's nuclear-strike capacity was interrupted by Thomas's impersonation of a petrol pump.

'The Syrians are filling their pants right now and they're right to be . . .' Henry was saying gleefully.

'Bvvvv,' said Thomas. 'Bvvvv . . .'

'I'm sure you're familiar with the phrase, "Children should be seen and not heard",' said Henry.

'Who isn't?' said Mary.

'I've always thought it was too liberal,' said Henry, craning his neck out of his shirt to emphasize his bon mot.

'You'd rather not see him either?' said Mary, suddenly furious. She picked Thomas up and carried him out of the room rapidly, Henry's unmolested monologue resuming its flow behind her.

'When Admiral Yamamoto had finished his attack on Pearl Harbor, he had the wisdom to be more apprehensive than triumphant. "Gentlemen," he said, "we have roused a sleeping dragon." It is that thought that should be uppermost in the minds of the world's international terrorists and their state sponsors. With an arsenal of tactical nuclear weapons, not just a deterrent nuclear shield, Israel will send a clear message to the region that it stands shoulder to shoulder . . .'

She burst onto the lawn picturing Henry as one of those unknotted balloons Thomas liked to watch swirling flatulently around the room until it suddenly flopped to the ground in wrinkled exhaustion.

'I'm letting go of a balloon, Mama,' said Thomas, spinning his hand in tight circles.

'How did you know I was thinking about a balloon?' said Mary.

'I did know that,' said Thomas, tilting his head to one side and smiling.

These borderless moments happened often enough for Mary to get used to them, but she couldn't quite shake off her surprise at how precise they were.

By silent agreement the two of them walked away from the house to the little rocky beach at the foot of the lawn. Mary sat down on a small patch of silvery white sand among rocks festooned with beaded black seaweed.

'Will you look after me for a long time?' asked Thomas.

'Yes, darling.'

'Until I'm fourteen?'

'As long as you want me to,' she said. 'As long as I can . . .' she added. He had asked her the other day if she was going to die and she had said, 'Yes, but not for a long time, I hope.' His discovery of her mortality blew away the dust which had dimmed the menace of it in her own mind and made it glare at her again with all its root horror restored. She loathed death for making her let him down. Why couldn't he play a little longer? Why couldn't he feel safe a little longer? She had recovered her balance to some extent, attributing his interest in death to the transition from infancy to childhood, but also wondering if Patrick's impatience with that transition was making it happen sooner than necessary. Robert had been through the same sort of crisis when he was five; Thomas was only three.

Thomas sat down on her lap and sucked his thumb, fingering the smooth label of his raggie with the other hand. He was minutes away from sleep. Mary sat back on her heels and made herself calm. She could do things for Thomas that she couldn't do for herself or anyone else, not even Robert. Thomas needed her for his protection, that was obvious enough, but she needed him for her sense of virtue. When she felt gloomy he made her want to be cheerful, when she was drained he made her find new wells of energy, when she was exasperated she searched for a deeper patience. She sat there as still as the rocks around her and waited while he dropped off.

However hot the day became, the sea here was a refrigerator throwing off a sceptical little breeze. She liked the feeling that Maine was basically inhospitable, that it would soon shake out its summer visitors, like a dog on a beach. In the chink between two winters the northern light sparkled hungrily on the sea. She imagined it stretched out like a gaunt El Greco saint. The thought made her want to paint again. She wanted to make love again. She wanted to think again, if she was going to start making lists, but somehow she had lost her independence. Her being was fused with Thomas's. She was like someone whose clothes had been stolen while she was having a swim, and now she didn't know how to get out of this tiring beautiful pool.

After Thomas had been asleep for five minutes she was able to move to a more comfortable position. She sat against the bank at the bottom of the lawn and placed him lengthwise between her legs, as if he was still being born, still the wrong way round. She formed a canopy with his raggie to protect him from the sun, and leant back and closed her eyes and tried to rest, but her thoughts looped back tightly enough onto Kettle's remote style of mothering and the part it played in producing her own fanatical availability. She thought of her nanny, her kind, dedicated nanny, solving one little problem after the next, inhabiting a nursery world without sex or art or intoxicants or conversation, just practical kindness and food. Of course looking after a child made her feel like the nanny who had looked after her when she was a child. And of course it made her determined to be unlike Kettle who had failed to look after her. Personality seemed to her at once absurd and compulsive: she remained trapped inside it even when she could see through it. Her thoughts on mothers and mothering twisted around, following the thread of a knot they couldn't untie.

For some reason, sitting by this black sea with its slightly chill breeze made her feel she could see everything very clearly. Thomas was asleep and nobody else knew exactly where she was. For the first time in months nobody knew how to make any demands on her and in that sudden absence of pressure she could appreciate the family's tropical atmosphere of unresolved dependency. Eleanor like a sick child pleading with Patrick to 'make it stop'; Thomas like a referee pushing his parents apart if Patrick ever tried to get close to her indifferent body; Robert keeping his diary, keeping his distance. She was at the eye of the storm, with her need to be needed making her appear more self-sufficient than she really was.

In reality she couldn't survive on the glory of satisfying other people's unreasonable demands. Her passion for self-sacrifice sometimes made her feel like a prisoner who meekly digs the trench for her own execution. Patrick needed a revolution against the tyranny of dependency, but she needed one against the tyranny of self-sacrifice. Although she was overstretched and monopolized, an appeal to her best instincts only drove her further into the trap. The protests which might be expected to come from Robert's sibling rivalry came instead from the relatively unstable Patrick. It was bad luck that she had become disgusted by the slightest sign of need in Patrick at a time when he had Thomas as well as Eleanor to stimulate his own sense of helplessness. Patrick accused her of overindulging Thomas, but if Thomas was ready to do without certain maternal comforts, Patrick must be even readier. Perhaps he was no longer ripe but rotten. Perhaps a psychic gangrene had set in and it was the smell of corruption that revolted her.

That evening she excused herself from dinner and stayed with Thomas, leaving Patrick and Robert to face the roused dragon of Henry's table talk on their own. Even before dinner, as she sat on the faded pink cushions of the window seat, the panes of the bay window around her bleeding and glittering in the sea-reflected evening light, with the children behaving beautifully and Patrick smiling over a glass of mineral water, she knew she couldn't stand more than a few minutes of Henry's address to the nation. He was on a whirlwind tour of foreign policy, heading east from Israel, through the Stans and the Formers, and on his way to the People's Republics. She had a dreadful feeling that he intended to get to North Korea before bedtime. No doubt he had a cunning plan to nuke North Korea before it nuked South Korea and Japan. She didn't want to hear it.

After his bath, Thomas wanted to climb into her bed and

she didn't have the heart to refuse him. They snuggled up together reading *The Wind in the Willows*. Thomas fell asleep as Rat and Mole started to drift down the river after their picnic. When Patrick came into the room she realized that she had also dropped off with the book on her lap and her reading glasses still on.

'I so nearly had a fight with Henry,' said Patrick, striding into the room with his clenched fists still looking for a destination.

'Oh dear, what was it this evening?' she asked.

Patrick was always saying that their erotic, conversational and social lives were over, that they were just parental bureaucrats. Well, here she was, shattered and abruptly woken, but ready for a lively conversation.

'North Korea.'

'I knew it.'

'You always know everything. No wonder you felt you could miss dinner.'

Everything she said was wrong. No matter what she did, Patrick felt abandoned. She tried again.

'I mean, I just had a feeling before dinner that North Korea would be next.'

'That's what Henry thinks: North Korea is next. You should form a coalition.'

'Did you argue with him, or are you going to have to argue with me instead?'

'We relied heavily on the democratic miracle of agreeing to disagree. Henry hates free speech but, partly as a result of that, he isn't free to say so. He banged on about how lucky we were not to live in a country where you could be shot for holding the wrong opinions.'

'He wants to shoot you.'

'Exactly.'

'Great. That'll make our holiday more fun.'

'More fun? Don't you have to be having fun in the first place to have more fun?'

'I think the children are having fun.'

'Oh, well, that's all that matters,' said Patrick with rigid piety. 'I did hint to Henry,' he continued, pacing up and down at the end of the bed, 'that I felt the present administration's foreign policy was made up of projection. That America is the rogue state with a fundamentalist president, and several thousand times the weapons of mass destruction of all other nations combined, et cetera, et cetera.'

'How did that go down?' Mary wanted to keep him going, keep the aggression political.

'Incredulous laughter. A lot of neck-craning. False smiles. Reminded me of "a certain event which played no small part in our lives over here". I said that 9/11 was one of the most shocking things in history, but that its exploitation, what I'd like to call 9/12, was just as shocking in its own way. The tracer bullet was the use of the word "war" on the following day. War is an activity between nation states. A word the British government spent thirty years carefully avoiding in its struggle with the IRA. Why give the standing of a nation state to a few hundred homicidal maniacs, unless you're going to use them as the pretext to make war with some real nation states? Henry said, "I think that's a distinction that would be lost on Joe Six-Pack. We had a war to sell to the American public." That was the trouble with our conversation – my accusations are his assumptions, selling war to the American public, testing new weapons, stimulating the military-industrial complex, using public money to demolish a country which the cabinet's pet corporations benefit from rebuilding and so forth. He loves it all, so he can't be caught making hollow apologies.'

'How was Robert?'

'An excellent junior counsel,' said Patrick. 'He made the

no-proven-links point and played pretty skilfully with the idea of "innocent lives". He asked Henry whether innocence was exclusively American. Again, the trouble is that for Henry the answer is really "Yes", so it's hard to get him on the run. He didn't bother to pretend much, except about free speech.'

'How did he answer Robert?'

'Oh, he just said that he could see that I'd "trained" him. He obviously thought we were the tag team from hell. The thing that ruffled him was my last bombing mission, in which I said that a really "developed" nation, as opposed to a merely powerful one, might bother to imagine the impact of two per cent of the world's population consuming fifty per cent of its resources, of the rapid extinction of every species of non-American culture and so forth. I got a little bit carried away and also said that the death of nature was a high price to pay for adding the few last curlicues of convenience to the lives of the very rich.'

'It's amazing he didn't throw us out,' said Mary.

'Don't worry, I'll try again tomorrow. I'll get him in the end. I can see now what upsets him. Politics is an exciting game, but money is sacred.'

She could tell that Patrick was serious. His sense of tension was so extreme that he had to destroy something, and this time it wasn't going to be himself.

'Do you mind not getting us thrown out for a couple of days? I've only just finished unpacking.' She tried to sound breezy.

'And you're comfortably installed with your lover as usual,' said Patrick.

'God, for a man who claims not to suffer from jealousy . . .'

'I don't suffer from jealousy, I suffer from rage. It's more fundamental. Loss produces anger first, possessiveness afterwards.'

'Before the rage, there's anxiety,' said Mary, feeling she

knew what she was talking about. 'Anyway, I think you move through all three, even if one is usually dominant. It's not like shopping, you can't just opt for rage.'

'You'd be surprised.'

'I know you prefer anger because you think it's less humiliating.'

'I don't prefer anger,' shouted Patrick, 'but I get it anyway.'

'I mean prefer it to the neighbouring emotions.'

Thomas, disturbed by Patrick's shouting, shifted in the bed and muttered to himself inaudibly.

'You're straying from the point,' said Patrick, more quietly. 'As usual we can't sleep together because you're in bed with our three-year-old son.'

'We can sleep together,' sighed Mary, 'I'll move him over to the side.'

'I want to make love to a woman, not a sighing heap of guilt and resignation,' hissed Patrick, in an ineffective whisper.

Thomas sat up blearily.

'No, Dada, you stop talking nonsense!' he shouted. 'And Mama, stop upsetting Dada!'

He collapsed back on the pillow and fell asleep again, his work done. A silence fell over the room, which Patrick was the first to interrupt.

'I wasn't talking nonsense . . .' he began.

'Oh, for God's sake,' said Mary. 'You don't have to win an argument with him as well. Can't you hear what he's saying? He wants us to stop arguing, not for you to start arguing with him.'

'Sure,' said Patrick in his suddenly bored way. 'I'll go to his bed, although I don't know why I call it "his" bed. I might as well stop pretending and call it mine.'

'You don't have to . . .'

'No – I do have to,' said Patrick and ducked out of the room.

He had abandoned her abruptly, but failed to transfer his sense of abandonment to her. She felt relieved, angry, guilty, mournful. The cloudscape of her emotional life was so rolling and rapid that she couldn't help marvelling at, sometimes envying, people who were 'out of touch with their feelings'. How did they do it? Right now she wouldn't mind knowing.

Her bedroom had a terrace built above the bay window of the drawing room where she had been sitting before dinner. She walked up to the French windows and imagined herself throwing them open, contemplating the stars, having an epiphany.

It wasn't going to happen. Her body had started its landslide towards sleep. She took one last glance out of the window and wished she hadn't. A thin streak of cloud was crossing the moon in a way that reminded her of the elision in *Un Chien Andalou* between the same image and a razor blade slicing open an eyeball. Her vision was the end of vision. Was she blinded by something she couldn't see, or blinded by seeing something she couldn't bear to look at? She was too tired to work anything out. Her thoughts were just threats, sleep just the rubble of wakefulness.

She got into bed and was covered by a thin layer of broken rest. Soon afterwards, she was disturbed by hearing Patrick slink back into the room. She could feel him staring at her to see if she was awake. She gave nothing away. He eventually settled on the other side of Thomas, who lay in the middle like the sword placed between the unmarried in a medieval bed. Why couldn't she reach out to Patrick? Why couldn't she make a nest of pillows for Thomas on one side of the bed and stay with Patrick on the other? She had no charity left for Patrick. In fact, for the first time in her marriage she could picture herself and the children living alone in the flat while Patrick was off somewhere, anywhere, being miserable.

The next day she was shocked by her coldness, but she soon got used to it.

She had always known it was there, the alternative to the warmth which struck everyone as so typical. Now she took it up like a hermit moving into a cave. She resisted Patrick's rashes of nervous charm without effort. It was too tiring to move back and forth to the jumpy rhythm of his moods. She might as well stay where she was. He was going to ruin their holiday, but first he wanted to make her agree that fighting with Henry was a sign of his splendid integrity rather than his uncontrollable irritation. She refused. By that evening it was clear that Patrick's agreement to disagree with Henry was in peril.

'It's going to be tough to make conversation if you don't stop attacking everything I say,' said plain-speaking Henry. 'Let's stick to talking family.'

'That proven formula for goodwill and unity,' said Patrick with one of his short barking laughs.

'You're as bad as Yasser Arafat,' said Henry. 'You think peace and defeat are the same thing. I'm just trying to extend some hospitality here. You don't have to accept it, if you've got an ideological problem with that.' Henry chuckled at the word 'ideological', which for him was as inherently comic as the word 'bottom' to an exuberant four-year-old.

'That's right,' said Patrick, 'we don't.'

'But we'd like to,' said Mary quickly.

'Speak for yourself,' said Patrick.

'I am,' she said, 'and unlike you I'm also trying to speak for the children.'

'Are you? Only this morning Thomas was saying that Henry is "a very funny man" and, as you know, Robert's nickname for him is "Hitler". I doubt you're even speaking for yourself after you were thrown out of lunch yesterday.'

That had been that. They left the next morning. She

expected Patrick to be stubborn and proud and destructive, but she hadn't yet forgiven him for including the children in his final explosive charge.

The ice machine in the motel corridor produced another juddering emission of cubes just the other side of the thin bedroom wall. The interstate's mosquito whine had given way to a hornet drone. Thomas stirred beside her and then, with his usual prompt transition to full desire, he sat up and said, 'I want you to read me a story.' She obediently picked up the copy of *The Wind in the Willows* which they had started reading in Maine.

'Do you remember where we were?' asked Mary.

'Ratty was saying to Moley that he was a plain pig,' said Thomas, rounding his eyes in amazement. 'But, actually, he's a rat.'

'That's right,' laughed Mary. Rat and Mole were on their way back to River Bank in the gathering darkness of a December afternoon. Mole had just smelt the traces of his old home and was overwhelmed by longing and nostalgia. Rat had pressed on to River Bank, his own home, assuming Mole would want to go there as well. Then Mole broke down and told Rat about his homesickness. Mary reread the sentence they had finished with the night before.

'The Rat stared straight in front of him, saying nothing, only patting Mole gently on the shoulder. After a time he muttered gloomily, "I see it all now! What a pig I've been! A pig – that's me! Just a pig – a plain pig!"'

'I mean . . .' Thomas began.

There was a knock on the door. Mary put the book down and asked who it was.

'Bobby!' said Thomas. 'I knew it was you because – well, because it is you!'

Robert sat down on the bed with his shoulders slumped, ignoring his brother's reasoning.

'I hate this place,' he said.

'I know,' said Mary, 'but we'll move on this morning.'

'Again,' groaned Robert. 'We've been to three motels since the Prosecuting Attorney got us thrown off that brilliant island. We might as well get a mobile home.'

'I'm going to ring Sally after breakfast and ask her if we could go to Long Island a few days earlier than planned.'

'I don't want to go to Long Island, I want to go home,' said Robert.

'Moley smells his home and he wants it,' said Thomas, leaning forward to support his brother's case.

They agreed that if they couldn't go straight to Long Island, they would tell Patrick they wanted to go back to England.

'No more magic of the open road,' said Robert. 'Please.'

When she rang Sally there was no answer in Long Island. Eventually she found her in New York.

'We had to come back to the city because our water tank burst and flooded the apartment downstairs. Our neighbours are suing us, so we're suing the plumbers who only put the tank in last year. The plumbers are suing the tank company for defective design. And the residents are suing the building, even though they're all on vacation, because the water was cut off for two days instead of two hours, which caused them a lot of mental stress in Tuscany and Nantucket.'

'Gosh,' said Mary. 'What's wrong with mopping up and getting a new water tank?'

'That is *so* English,' said Sally, delighted by Mary's quaint stoicism.

Mary explained at breakfast that there wasn't really room in the New York apartment, but Sally said they were welcome to all squeeze in somehow.

'I don't want to squeeze in,' said Robert, 'I want to fly out.'

'We're on an aeroplane now,' said Thomas, thrusting his arms out like wings, 'and Alabala is in the cockpit!'

'Oh-oh,' said Robert, 'we'd better catch the next flight.'

'He's on the next flight as well,' said Thomas, as surprised as anyone by Alabala's resourcefulness.

'How did he manage that?' said Robert.

Thomas glanced sideways for a moment to look for the explanation.

'He used his ejector seat,' he said, making an ejector-seat noise, 'and then Felan stopped the next plane and Alabala got on!'

'There's the little matter of our unrefundable tickets,' said Patrick.

'We could have bought new ones with the money we've spent in these disgusting motels,' said Robert.

'You've taught him to argue too well,' said Mary.

'There's no one to argue with, is there?' said Patrick. 'I think we're all sick of America by now.'

16

After her fall, Eleanor's ceaseless pleas for death had forced Patrick to look into the legalities of euthanasia and assisted suicide. Once again, as with his own disinheritance, he became the legal servant of his mother's repulsive demands. Superficially, there was something more attractive about getting rid of Eleanor than there had been about losing Saint-Nazaire, but then the obscenity of what he was being asked to do would break through the stockade of practicalities with Jacobean vigour. Even if a nursing home was not the usual setting for a *Revenger's Tragedy*, he felt the perils of usurping God's monopoly on vengeance just as keenly as he would have in the catacombs of an Italian castle. He tried to pull himself together, to examine his motives scrupulously. The dead were not dogged enough to make ghosts without the guilt of the living. His mother was like a rock fall blocking a mountain pass. Perhaps he could clear her out of the way, but if his intentions were murderous, her ghost would haunt the pass for ever.

He decided to have nothing to do with organizing her death. Asking him to help her die was the last and nastiest trick of a woman who had always insisted, from the moment he was born, that she was the one who needed cheering up. And then he would visit Eleanor again and see that the cruellest thing he could do was to leave her exactly where she was. He tried to remain angry so he could forbid himself to help, but compassion tortured him as well. The compassion was far harder to bear and he came to think of his vengefulness as a relatively frivolous state of mind.

'Go on, do yourself a favour, get homicidal,' he muttered to himself as he dialled the number of the Voluntary Euthanasia Society.

Before going to America, he kept his research secret. He didn't tell Mary because they never discussed anything important without having a row. He didn't tell Julia because his affair with her was in the final stages of its decay. In any case, secrecy was essential in a country where helping someone to die could be punished with fourteen years' imprisonment. He read articles in the papers about nurses sent to jail for generous injections. The Voluntary Euthanasia Society, despite its promising name, was unable to help. It was a campaigning organization trying to change the legislation. Patrick could remember reading about Arthur Koestler and his wife using the plastic bags provided by Exit to asphyxiate themselves in their house in Montpelier Square. The lady who answered the phone at the Voluntary Euthanasia Society had no knowledge of an organization called Exit. She couldn't even comment on most of his questions, because her advice might be construed as suicide 'counselling', an offence under the same statute that punished assisting and aiding. She hadn't heard of an organization called Dignitas either and couldn't tell him how to get in touch with it. The Everlasting was not the only one to have 'fixed his canon 'gainst self-slaughter', Patrick couldn't help thinking as the fruitless conversation dragged to a close. Directory Inquiries, careless of the legal consequences, gave him the number of Dignitas a few minutes later.

He rang Switzerland, his pulse racing. The calm voice which answered the phone in German turned out to speak English as well, and promised to send some information.

When Patrick pressed him on the legal points, he said that it was not a matter of euthanasia, administered by the doctor, but of assisted suicide administered by the patient. The barbiturate would be prescribed if a Swiss doctor was convinced that it was warranted and that the suicide was entirely voluntary. If Patrick wanted to make progress while he waited for the membership forms to arrive, he should get a letter of consent from Eleanor and a doctor's report on her condition. Patrick pointed out that his mother could no longer write and he doubted that she could give herself an injection either.

'Can she sign?'

'Just.'

'Can she swallow?'

'Just.'

'So, maybe we can help.'

Patrick felt a surge of excitement after his telephone call to Switzerland. Signing and swallowing, those were the keys to the kingdom, the code for the missile launch. There wasn't much time before Eleanor lost them. He dreaded the precious barbiturate dribbling uselessly down her shining chin. As to her signature, it now formed an Alpine silhouette reminiscent of Thomas's earliest stabs at writing. Patrick paced up and down the drawing room of his flat. He was 'working at home', and had waited for Robert to go to school and for Mary to take Thomas to Holland Park before carrying on with his secret research. Now the whole flat was his to bounce around; there was nobody to be efficient for, nobody to be friendly to. Just as well, since he couldn't stop pacing, couldn't stop repeating, 'Sign and swallow, sign and swallow,' like a chained parrot in the corner of an overstuffed room. He felt increasingly tense, having to pause and breathe out slowly to expel the feeling that he was about to faint. There was a sinister, knife-grinding quality to his excitement. He was going to give Eleanor exactly what she wanted. But should he be wanting it quite so much as well?

He recognized the signature of his murderous longings and felt duly troubled. What seemed new, but then admitted that it had been there all along, was his own desire for a glass of barbiturate. 'To cease upon the midnight with no pain' – rearranged a little, it might almost be the chemical name for that final drink: Sismidnopin.

'Oh, my God! You've got a bottle of Sismidnopin! Can I have some?' he suddenly squealed as he reached the end of the corridor and spun round to pace back again. His thoughts were all over the place, or rather they were in one place dragging everything towards them. He imagined a modest little protest march, starting out in Hampstead with a few ethical types trying to ban unnecessary suffering, and then swelling rapidly as it flowed down to Swiss Cottage, until soon every shop was closed and every restaurant empty and all the trains stood still and the petrol pumps were unattended, and the whole population of London was flowing towards Whitehall and Trafalgar Square and Parliament Square, cursing unnecessary suffering and screaming for Sismidnopin.

'Why should a dog, a cat have death,' he wailed front stage, 'and she . . .'. He forced himself to stop. 'Oh, shut up,' he said, collapsing on a sofa.

'I'm just trying to help my old mum,' he cajoled himself in a new voice. 'She's a bit past her sell-by date, to be honest. Not enjoying life as much as she used to. Can't even watch the old goggle box. Eyes gone. No use reading to her, just gets her agitated. Every little thing frightens her, even her own happy memories. Terrible situation, really.'

Who was talking? Who was he talking to? He felt taken over.

He breathed out slowly. He was feeling way too tense. He was going to give himself a heart attack, finishing off the wrong person by mistake. He could see that he was breaking into fragments because the simplicity of his situation – son asked to kill mother – was unbearable; and the simplicity of her situation – person dreads every second of her existence – was more unbearable still. He tried to stay with it, to think about what didn't bear thinking about: Eleanor's experience. He felt her writhing on the bed, begging for death. He suddenly burst into tears, all his evasions exhausted.

The rivalry between revenge and compassion ended during that morning in his flat, and he was left with a more straightforward longing for everyone in his family to be free, including his mother. He decided to press ahead with getting a medical report before his trip to America. There was little point in applying to the nursing home's doctor, whose entire mission was to keep patients alive despite their craving for a lethal injection. Dr Fenelon was Patrick's family doctor, but he had not taken care of Eleanor before. He was a sympathetic and intelligent man whose Catholicism had not yet stood in the way of useful prescriptions and rapid specialist appointments. Patrick was used to thinking of him as grown up and was bewildered to hear him speak of his ethics classes at Ampleforth, as if he had allowed a priest to spray his teenage sketch of the world with an Infallible fixative.

'I still believe that suicide is a sin,' said Dr Fenelon, 'but I no longer believe that people who want to commit suicide are being tempted by the Devil, because we now know that they're suffering from a disease called depression.'

'Listen,' said Patrick, trying to recover as unobtrusively as possible from finding the Devil on the guest list, 'when you can't move, can't speak, can't read, and know that you're losing control of your mind, depression is not a disease, it's the only reasonable response. It's cheerfulness that would require a glandular dysfunction, or a supernatural force to explain it.'

'When people are depressed, we give them antidepressants,' Dr Fenelon persevered.

'She's already on them. It's true that they gave a certain enthusiasm to her loathing of life. It was only after she started taking them that she asked me to kill her.'

'It can be a great privilege to work with the dying,' Dr Fenelon began.

'I don't think she's going to start working with the dying,' Patrick interrupted. 'She can't even stand up. If you mean that it's a great privilege for you, I have to say that I'm more concerned about her quality of life than yours.'

'I mean,' said the doctor, with more equanimity than Patrick's sarcasm might have deserved, 'that suffering can have a transfiguring effect. One sees people, after an enormous struggle, breaking through to a kind of peacefulness they've never known before.'

'There has to be some sense of self to experience the peacefulness – that's precisely what my mother is losing.'

Dr Fenelon sat back in his buttoned leather chair with a sympathetic nod, exposing the crucifix he kept on the shelf behind him. Patrick had often noticed it before, but it now seemed to be mocking him with its brilliant inversion of glory and suffering, making the thing it was natural to be disgusted by into the central meaning of life, not just the mundane meaning of forcing a person to reflect more deeply, but the entirely mysterious meaning of the world being redeemed from sin because Jesus got on the wrong side of the law two thousand years ago. What did it mean that the world had been redeemed from sin? It obviously didn't mean that there was any less sin. And how was Christ's nasty, kinky execution supposed to be responsible for this redemption which, as far as Patrick could tell, hadn't taken place? Until then he had only been dazzled by the irrelevance of Christianity in his own life, but now he found himself loathing it for threatening to cheat Eleanor of a punctual death. After some more schoolboy reminiscences, Dr Fenelon agreed to compile a report on Eleanor's condition. What use was made of it was none of his affair, he assured himself, and made an appointment to meet Patrick at the nursing home two days later.

Patrick went to tell his mother the good news and prepare her for the doctor's visit.

'I want . . .' she howled, and then half an hour later, 'Swiss . . . land.'

Patrick braced himself for his impatience with his mother's impatience.

'Everything is going as fast as possible,' he answered smoothly.

'You . . . ook . . . like . . . my . . . son,' Eleanor managed eventually.

'There's a simple explanation for that,' said Patrick. 'I am your son.'

'No!' said Eleanor, sure of her ground at last.

Patrick left with the even more pressing sense that Eleanor would soon be too senile to consent.

When he took Dr Fenelon into Eleanor's fetid room the next day, she was in a state of hysterical cheerfulness which Patrick had never seen before but immediately understood. She thought that she had to be on best behaviour, to win the doctor over, to show him that she was a good girl who deserved a favour. She stared at him adoringly. He was her liberator, her angel of death. Dr Fenelon asked Patrick to stay, to help him understand Eleanor's incoherent speech. He was impressed by the good quality of her reflexes, the absence of bed sores and the general condition of her skin. Patrick looked away from the white wrinkled expanse of her belly, feeling that he really shouldn't be allowed to see so much of his mother, and certainly didn't want to. He was driven mad by her eagerness. Why couldn't she manifest the misery he had spent the last week labouring to put into words? She never tired of letting him down. He imagined the unbearably upbeat report that Dr Fenelon would be dictating on his return to the surgery. That evening he composed a letter of consent but he couldn't face seeing his mother again straight away. In any case, Fenelon's report wouldn't arrive before the family left on their American holiday and so Patrick resolved to let the whole thing drop until his return.

In America he tried not to think about a situation he could make no progress with, but he knew that the secret of his macabre project was alienating him from the rest of his family. After sobering up, he clung to his somewhat drunken vision of Zone Three in Walter and Beth's garden. Whenever he tried to define Zone Three, he could only think of it as a generosity that was not based on compensation or duty. Even though he could not quite describe it, he clung to this fragile intuition of what it might mean to be well.

It was only on the plane back to England that he finally told Mary what was going on. Thomas was asleep and Robert was watching a movie. At first Mary said nothing beyond sympathizing with the trouble Patrick had been through. She didn't know whether to voice her suspicion that Patrick had been so busy examining his own motives that he might not have looked carefully enough at Eleanor's. Wanting to die was one of the most commonplace things about life, but dying was something else. Eleanor's demands for help were not an offer to clear herself out of the way, but the only way she had left to keep herself at the centre of her family's attention. And did she really understand that she would have to do the killing herself? Mary felt sure that Eleanor was imagining an infinitely wise doctor with a gaze as deep as a mountain lake, leaning over to give her a fatal good-night kiss, not a tumbler of bitter barbiturates she had to hoist to her own lips. Eleanor was the most childish person Mary knew, including Thomas.

'She won't do it,' she finally said to Patrick. 'She won't swallow. You'll have to get some special air ambulance, and take her to see the Swiss doctors, and get the prescription, and then she won't do it.'

'If she makes me take her to Switzerland for nothing, I'll kill her,' said Patrick.

'I'm sure that would suit her perfectly,' said Mary. 'She wants death taken out of her hands, not put into them.'

'Whatever,' said Patrick with an impatient sigh. 'But I have to treat her as if she really meant the only thing she ever manages to say.'

'I'm sure she's sincere about wanting to die,' said Mary. 'I'm just not sure she's up to it.'

From within the hub of his headphones, Robert sensed that his parents were having a heated conversation. He took off his headset and asked them what they were talking about.

'Just about Granny – how we can help her,' said Mary.

Robert put his headphones back on. As far as he was concerned Eleanor was just someone who was not yet dead. His parents no longer took him or Thomas to see her because they said it was too disturbing. It was an effort for him to remember, ages ago, being close to her, and it wasn't an effort that seemed worth making. Sometimes, in the presence of his other grandmother, his indifference to Eleanor was taken by surprise and, in contrast to the tight little knot of Kettle's selfishness, he would remember Eleanor's softness and the great aching bruise of her good intentions. Then he would forget how unfair it was that Eleanor had cheated them of Saint-Nazaire and feel how unfair it was for Eleanor being Eleanor – not just her dire circumstances, but being who she was. In the end it was unfair on everyone being who they were because they couldn't be anyone else. It wasn't even that he wanted to be anybody else, it was just a horrible thought that he couldn't be, in an emergency. He took off his headphones again, as if they were the thing that was limiting him. The comedy about the talking dog who became President of the United States wasn't that good anyway. Robert switched channels to the map. It showed their plane hovering near the Irish coast, south of Cork. Then it expanded to show London and Paris and the Bay of Biscay. The next scale included Casablanca and Djibouti and Warsaw. How long was this informational feast going to go on? Where were they in relation to the moon? The only thing anybody wanted to know finally came up: 52 minutes to arrival. They were flying through seven fat hours, pumped full of darkening time zones. Speed; height; temperature; local time in New York; local time in London. They told you everything, except the local time on the plane. Watches just couldn't keep up with those warped, enriched minutes. They ought to flip their dials round and say NOW until they could get back on the ground and start counting distinctly again.

He longed to get back on the ground as well, back home to London. Losing Saint-Nazaire had made London into his total home. He had heard about children who pretended they had been adopted and that their real parents were much more glamorous than the dreary people they lived with. He had done something similar with Saint-Nazaire, pretending it was his real home. After the shock of losing it, he had gradually relaxed into the knowledge that he really belonged among the sodden billboards and giant plane trees of his native city. Compared to the density of New York, London's backward glance at the countryside and the rambling privacy of its streets seemed to be the opposite of what a city was for, and yet he longed to get back to the greasy black mud of the parks, the rained-out playgrounds and paddocks of dead leaves, the glance at his scratchy school uniform in the hall mirror, the clunk of the car door on the way to school. Nothing seemed more exotic than the depth of those feelings.

A stewardess told Mary she must wake Thomas for the landing. Thomas woke up and Mary gave him a bottle of milk. Halfway through, he unplugged the bottle and said, 'Alabala is in the cockpit!' His eyes rounded as he looked up at his brother. 'He's going to land the plane!'

'Oh-oh,' said Robert, 'we're in trouble.'

'The captain says, "No, Alabala, you are *not* allowed to land the plane," said Thomas, thumping his thigh, "but Felan is allowed to land the plane."

'Is Felan in there too?'

'Yes, he is. He's the co-pilot.'

'Really? And who's the pilot?'

'Scott Tracy.'

'So this is an International Rescue plane?'

'Yes. We have to rescue a pentatenton.'

'What's a pentatenton?'

'Well, it's a hedgehog, actually, and it's fallen in the river!'

'In the Thames?'

'Yes! And it doesn't know how to swim, so Gordon Tracy has to rescue it with Thunderbird 4.'

Thomas thrust out his hand and moved the submarine through the muddy waters of the Thames.

Robert hummed the theme tune from *Thunderbirds*, drumming on the armrest between them.

'Perhaps you could get her to sign the letter of consent,' said Patrick.

'OK,' said Mary.

'At least we can assemble all the elements . . .'

'What elements?' asked Robert.

'Never mind,' said Mary. 'Look, we're about to land,' she said, trying to infuse the glinting fields, congested roads and small crowds of reddish houses with an excitement they were unlikely to generate on their own.

On the day of their arrival, the Dignitas membership form and Dr Fenelon's report emerged from the heap of letters in the hall. Sprawled exhausted on the black sofa, Patrick read through the Dignitas brochures.

'All the people in the cases they quote have agonizing terminal diseases or can only move one eyelid,' he commented. 'I'm worried she may just not be ill enough.'

'Let's get everything together and see what they think about her case,' said Mary.

Patrick gave her the letter of consent he had written before leaving for America and she set off with it to the nursing home. In the upper corridor the cleaners had wedged open the doors to air the rooms. Through the doorway Eleanor looked quite calm, until she detected another presence entering the room and stared with a kind of furious blankness in the direction of the newcomer. When Mary announced who she was, Eleanor grabbed the side rail of her barred bed and tried to heave herself up, making desperate mumbling sounds. Mary felt that she had interrupted Eleanor's communion with some other realm in which things were not quite as bad as they were on planet Earth. She suddenly felt that both ends of life were absolutely terrifying, with a quite frightening stretch in between. No wonder people did what they could to escape.

There was no point in asking Eleanor how she was, no point in trying to make conversation, and so Mary plunged in with a summary of what had been going on with the rest of them. Eleanor seemed horrified to be placed within the coordinates of her family. Mary quickly moved on to the purpose of her visit, suggesting that she read the letter out loud.

'If you feel it's what you want to say, you can sign it,' she said.

Eleanor nodded.

Mary got up and closed the door, glancing down the corridor to check that there were no nurses on their way. She pulled her chair close to Eleanor's bed and placed her chin over the hand rail, holding the letter on Eleanor's side of the bars. She began to read with surprising nervousness.

*I have had several strokes over the last few years,
each one leaving me more shattered than the last.
I can hardly move and I can hardly speak. I am
bedridden and incontinent. I feel uninterrupted
anguish and terror and frustration at my own
immobility and uselessness. There is no prospect
of improvement, only of drifting into dementia,
the thing I dread most. I can already feel my
faculties betraying me. I do not look on death
with fear but with longing. There is no other
liberation from the daily torture of my existence.
Please help me if you can.
yours sincerely,*

'Do you think that's fair?' asked Mary, trying not to cry.

'No . . . es,' said Eleanor with great difficulty.

'I mean a fair description.'

'Es.'

They gripped each other's hands for a while, saying nothing. Eleanor looked at her with a kind of dry-eyed hunger.

'Do you want to sign it?'

'Sign,' said Eleanor, swallowing hard.

When Mary broke out into the streets, along with her sense of physical relief at getting away from the smell of urine and boiled cabbage, and the waiting-room atmosphere in which death was the delayed train, she felt grateful that there had been a moment of communication with Eleanor. In that gripped hand she had felt not just an appeal but a determination that made her wonder if she was right to doubt Eleanor's preparedness to commit suicide. And yet there was something fundamentally lost about Eleanor, a sense that she had neither engaged in the mundane realm of family and friendship and politics and property, nor had she engaged with the realm of contemplation and spiritual fulfilment; she had simply sacrificed one to the other. If she belonged to the tribe who always heard the siren call of the choice they were about to lose, she was bound to feel an absolute need to stay alive once suicide had been perfectly organized for her. Salvation would always be elsewhere. Suddenly it would be more spiritual to stay alive – to learn patience, remain in the refining fires of suffering, whatever. More dreadful life would be imposed on her and it would inevitably seem more spiritual to die – to be reunited with the source, stop being a burden, meet Jesus at the end of a tunnel, whatever. The spiritual, because she had never committed herself to it any more effectively than to the rest of life, was subject to endless metamorphosis without losing its theoretical centrality.

When Mary got home, Thomas ran out into the hall to greet her. He wrapped his arms around her thigh with some difficulty, due to the Hoberman sphere, a multicoloured collapsible dodecahedron frame, which he had allowed to close around his neck and wore as a spiky helmet. His hands were clad in a pair of socks and he was holding a battery-operated propeller fan of fairy lights acquired on a visit to the Chinese State Circus on Blackheath.

'We're on Earth, aren't we, Mama?'

'Most of us,' said Mary, thinking of the look she had glimpsed on Eleanor's face through the open door of her room.

'Yes, I did know that,' said Thomas wisely. 'Except astronauts who are in outer space. And they just float about because there's no gravity!'

'Did she sign?' said Patrick, appearing in the doorway.

'Yes,' said Mary, handing him the letter.

Patrick sent the letter and membership form and doctor's report to Switzerland and waited for a couple of days before ringing to find out if his mother's application was likely to be successful.

'In this case I think we will be able to help,' was the answer he received. He stubbornly refused to get involved with his emotions, letting panic and elation and solemnity lean on the doorbell while he only glanced at them from behind closed curtains, pretending not to be at home. He was helped by the storm of practical demands which enveloped the family during the next week. Mary told Eleanor the news and was answered with a radiant smile. Patrick arranged a flight for the following Thursday. The nursing home was told that Eleanor was moving, without being told where. A consultation was booked with a doctor in Zurich.

'We could all go on Wednesday to say goodbye,' said Patrick.

'Not Thomas,' said Mary. 'It's been too long since he's seen her and the last time he made it very clear that he was upset. Robert can still remember her when she was well.'

None of Mary's close friends could look after Thomas on Wednesday afternoon and she was finally forced to ask her mother.

'Of course I'll do anything I can to help,' said Kettle, feeling that if ever there was a time to make all the right noises, it was now. 'Why don't you drop him off at lunchtime? Amparo can make him some lovely fish fingers and you can all come to tea after you've said goodbye to poor old Eleanor.'

When Wednesday came round Mary brought Thomas to the door of her mother's flat.

'Your mother is not here,' said Amparo.

'Oh,' said Mary, surprised and at the same time wondering why she was surprised.

'She go out to buy the cakes for tea.'

'But she'll be back soon . . .'

'She has lunch with a friend and then she come back, but don't you worry, I look after the little boy.'

Amparo reached out her child-greedy, ingratiating hands. Thomas had met her only once before and Mary handed him over with some reluctance but above all with a sense of terminal boredom. Never again, she would never ask her mother to help again. The decision seemed as irrevocable and overdue as a slab of cliff falling into the sea. She smiled at Amparo and handed over Thomas, not reassuring him too much in case it made him think there was something troubling about his situation.

The thing to do is the thing to do, thought Thomas, heading towards the disconnected bell beside the fireplace in the drawing room. He liked to stand on the small chair and press the bell and then let in whoever came to the fireplace-door. By the time Amparo had said goodbye to Mary and caught up with him, he was welcoming a visitor.

'It's Badger!' he said.

'Who is this Badger?' said Amparo with precautionary alarm.

'Mr Badger is not in the habit of smoking cigarettes,' said Thomas, 'because they make him grow bigger and smaller. So he smokes cigars!'

'Oh, no, my darling, you must not smoke,' said Amparo. 'It's very bad for you.'

Thomas climbed onto the small chair and pressed the bell again.

'Listen,' he said, 'there's somebody at the door.'

He leapt down and ran around the table. 'I'm running to open the door,' he explained, coming back to the fireplace.

'Be careful,' said Amparo.

'It's Lady Penelope,' said Thomas. 'You be Lady Penelope!'

'Would you like to help me with the hoovering?' said Amparo.

'Yes, m'lady,' said Thomas in his Parker voice. 'You'll find a thermos of hot chocolate in your hat box.' He howled with pleasure and flung himself on the cushions of the sofa.

'Oh, my God, I just tidy this,' wailed Amparo.

'Build me a house,' said Thomas, pulling the cushions onto the floor. 'Build me a house!' he shouted when she started to put them back. He lowered his head and frowned severely. 'Look, Amparo, this is my grumpy face.'

Amparo caved in to his desire for a house and Thomas crawled into the space between two cushions and underneath the roof of a third.

'Unfortunately,' he remarked once he had settled into position, 'Beatrix Potter died a long time ago.'

'Oh, I'm sorry, darling,' said Amparo.

Thomas hoped that his parents would live for a very long time. He wanted them to be immortalized. That was a word he had learnt in his *Children's Book of Greek Myths*. Ariadne was immortalized when she was turned into a star by Dionysus. Immortalized meant that she lived for ever – except that she was a star. He didn't want his parents to turn into stars. What would be the point of that? Just twinkling away.

'Just twinkling away,' he said sceptically.

'Oh, my God, you come with Amparo to the bathroom.'

He couldn't understand why Amparo stood him by the loo and tried to pull his trousers down.

'I don't want to do peepee,' he said flatly and started to walk away. The truth was that Amparo was quite difficult to have a conversation with. She didn't seem to understand anything. He decided to go on an expedition. She trailed behind him, wittering on.

'No, Amparo,' he said, turning on her, 'leave me alone!'

'I can't leave you, darling. You have to have an adult with you.'

'No! I!' said Thomas. 'You are frustrating me!'

Amparo bent double with laughter. 'Oh, my God,' she said. 'You know so many words.'

'I have to talk, otherwise my mouth gets clogged up with bits and pieces of words,' said Thomas.

'How old are you now, darling?'

'I'm three,' said Thomas. 'How old did you think I was?'

'I thought you were at least five, you're such a grown-up boy.'

'Hum,' said Thomas.

He saw that there was no prospect of shaking her off and so he decided to treat her the way his parents treated him when they wanted to bring him under control.

'Shall I tell you an Alabala story?' he said.

They were back in the drawing room. He sat Amparo down on an armchair and climbed into his cushion cave.

'Once upon a time,' he began, 'Alabala was in California and he was driving along with his mummy and there was an earthquake!'

'I hope this story has a happy ending,' said Amparo.

'No!' said Thomas. 'You don't interrupt me!' He sighed and began again. 'And the ground opened up and California fell into the sea, which was not very convenient, as you can imagine. And there was a huge tidal wave, and Alabala said to his mummy, "We can surf to Australia!" And so they did, and Alabala was allowed to drive the car.' He searched the ceiling for inspiration and then added with all the naturalness of suddenly remembering. 'When they arrived on the beach in Australia, Alan Razor was there giving a concert!'

'Who is Alan Razor?' asked Amparo, completely lost.

'He's a composer,' said Thomas. 'He has helicopters and violins and trumpets and drills, and Alabala played in the concert.'

'What did he play?'

'Well, he played a hoover, actually.'

When Kettle returned from her lunch, she found Amparo clutching her sides, thinking she was helpless with laughter at the thought of a hoover being played at a concert, but in fact hysterical at having her idea of what children should be like disrupted by being with Thomas.

'Oh, dear,' she panted, 'he's really an amazing little boy.'

While the two women struggled not to look after him, Thomas was at last able to have some time to himself. He decided that he never wanted to be an adult. He didn't like the look of adults. Anyway, if he became an adult what would happen to his parents? They would become old, like Eleanor and Kettle.

The intercom buzzed and Thomas leapt to his feet.

'I'll answer it!' he said.

'It's too high up,' said Kettle.

'But I want to!'

Kettle ignored him and pressed the intercom to let the others into the building. Thomas screamed in the background.

'What was that screaming about?' asked Mary when she arrived in the flat.

'Granny wouldn't let me press the button,' said Thomas.

'It's not a child's toy,' said Kettle.

'No, but he's a child playing,' said Mary. 'Why not let him play with the intercom?'

Kettle thought of rising above her daughter's argumentative style, but decided against it.

'I can't do anything right,' she said, 'so we might as well assume I'm wrong – then there won't be any need to point it out. I've only just come in, so I'm afraid tea isn't ready. I rushed home from a lunch that I couldn't get out of.'

'Yes,' laughed Mary. 'We saw you gazing through the shop windows when we were trying to park the car. Don't worry, I won't ask you to help with the children again.'

'I'll make the tea, if you like,' said Amparo, offering Kettle the opportunity to stay with her family.

'It's all right,' snapped Kettle. 'I'm still capable of making a pot of tea.'

'Am I being childish?' said Thomas, approaching his father.

'No,' said Patrick. 'You're being a child. Only grown-ups can be childish, and my God, we take advantage of the fact.'

'I see,' said Thomas, nodding wisely.

Robert was slumped in an armchair feeling despondent. He'd had enough of both his grandmothers to last him a lifetime.

Kettle tottered back in, laying the tray down with a groan of relief.

'So, how was your mother?' she asked Patrick.

'She only spoke two words,' he answered.

'Did they make any sense?'

'Perfect sense: "Do nothing."'

'You mean she doesn't want to . . . to go to Switzerland?' asked Kettle, emphasizing a code she knew the children were excluded from.

'That's right,' said Patrick.

'That's a bit of a muddle,' said Kettle.

Mary felt the effort she was putting into avoiding her favourite word: 'disappointment'.

'It's something we're all entitled to feel ambivalent about,' said Patrick. 'Mary saw it all along. I suppose she was less invested in the results, or just clearer. Anyhow, I intend to take this last instruction very seriously indeed. I will do nothing.'

'Do nothing!?' said Thomas. 'I mean, how do you do nothing? Because if you *do* nothing, you do something!'

Patrick burst out laughing. He picked up Thomas and put him on his knee and kissed the top of his head.

'I shan't be visiting her again,' said Patrick. 'Not out of spite, but out of gratitude. She's made us a gift and it would be ungracious not to accept it.'

'A gift?' said Kettle. 'Aren't you reading rather too much into those two words.'

'What else is there to do but read too much into things?' said Patrick breezily. 'What a poor, thin, dull world we'd live in if we didn't. Besides, is it possible? There's always more meaning than we can lay our hands on.'

Kettle was transfixed by several kinds of indignation at once, but Thomas filled the silence by jumping off his father's knee and shouting, 'Do nothing! Do nothing!' as he circled the table laden with cakes and tea.

AT LAST

For Bo

1

'Surprised to see me?' said Nicholas Pratt, planting his walking stick on the crematorium carpet and fixing Patrick with a look of slightly aimless defiance, a habit no longer useful but too late to change. 'I've become rather a memorial-creeper. One's bound to at my age. It's no use sitting at home guffawing over the ignorant mistakes of juvenile obituarists, or giving in to the rather monotonous pleasure of counting the daily quota of extinct contemporaries. No! One has to "celebrate the life": there goes the school tart. They say he had a good war, but I know better! – that sort of thing, put the whole achievement in perspective. Mind you, I'm not saying it isn't all very moving. There's a sort of swelling orchestra effect to these last days. And plenty of horror, of course. Padding about on my daily rounds from hospital bed to memorial pew and back again, I'm reminded of those oil tankers that used to dash themselves onto the rocks every other week and the flocks of birds dying on the beaches with their wings stuck together and their bewildered yellow eyes blinking.'

Nicholas glanced into the room. 'Thinly attended,' he murmured, as if preparing a description for someone else. 'Are those people your mother's religious friends? Too extraordinary. What colour would you call that suit? Aubergine? *Aubergine à la crème d'oursin?* I must go to Huntsman and get one knocked up. What do you mean, you have no

Aubergine? Everyone was wearing it at Eleanor Melrose's. Order a mile of it straight away!

'I suppose your aunt will be here soon. She'll be an all too familiar face amidst the Aubergines. I saw her last week in New York and I'm pleased to say I was the first to tell her the tragic news about your mother. She burst into tears and ordered a *croque monsieur* to swallow with her second helping of diet pills. I felt sorry for her and got her asked to dinner with the Blands. Do you know Freddie Bland? He's the smallest billionaire alive. His parents were practically dwarfs, like General and Mrs Tom Thumb. They used to come into the room with a tremendous fanfare and then disappear under a console table. Baby Bland has taken to being serious, the way some people do in their senile twilight. She's decided to write a book about Cubism, of all ridiculous subjects. I think it's really part of her being a perfect wife. She knows what a state Freddie used to get into over her birthday, but thanks to her new hobby, all he has to do now is get Sotheby's to wrap up a revolting painting of a woman with a face like a slice of watermelon by that arch fake Picasso, and he knows she'll be over the moon. Do you know what Baby said to me? At breakfast, if you please, when I was almost defenceless.' Nicholas put on a simpering voice:

'"Those divine birds in late Braque are really just an excuse for the sky."

'"Such a good excuse," I said, choking on my first sip of coffee, "so much better than a lawn mower or a pair of clogs. It shows he was in complete control of his material."

'Serious, you see. It's a fate I shall resist with every last scrap of my intelligence, unless Herr Doktor Alzheimer takes over, in which case I'll have to write a book about Islamic art to show that the towel-heads have always been much more civilized than us, or a fat volume on how little we know about Shakespeare's mother and her top-secret Catholicism. Something serious.

'Anyhow, I'm afraid Aunt Nancy rather bombed with the Blands. It must be hard to be exclusively social and entirely friendless at the same time. Poor thing. But do you know what struck me, apart from Nancy's vibrant self-pity, which she had the nerve to pretend was grief, what struck me about those two girls, your mother and your aunt, was that they are, were – my life is spent wobbling between tenses – completely American. Their father's connection with the Highlands was, let's face it, entirely liquid and after your grandmother sacked him he was hardly ever around. He spent the war with those dimwits the Windsors in Nassau; Monte Carlo after the war, and finally foundered in the bar of White's. Of the tribe who are blind drunk every day of their lives from lunch until bedtime, he was by far the most charming, but frustrating I think as a father. At that level of drunkenness one's essentially trying to embrace a drowning man. The odd eruption of sentimentality for the twenty minutes the drink took him that way was no substitute for the steady flow of self-sacrificing kindness that has always inspired my own efforts as a father. With what I admit have been mixed results. As I'm sure you know, Amanda hasn't spoken to me for the last fifteen years. I blame her psychoanalyst, filling her never very brilliant little head with Freudian ideas about her doting Papa.'

Nicholas's rotund style of delivery was fading into an increasingly urgent whisper, and the knuckles of his blue-veined hands were white from the effort of holding himself upright. 'Well, my dear, we'll have another little chat after the ceremony. It's been marvellous finding you on such good form. My condolences and all that, although if ever there was a "merciful release", it was in the case of your poor mother. I've become something of a Florence Nightingale in my old age, but even the Lady with the Lamp had to beat a retreat in the face of that terrifying ruin. It's bound to act as a brake on the rush to get me canonized but I prefer to pay visits to people who can still enjoy a bitchy remark and a glass of champagne.'

He seemed about to leave but then turned back. 'Try not to be bitter about the money. One or two friends of mine who've made a mess of that side of things have ended up dying in National Health wards and I must say I've been very impressed by the humanity of the mostly foreign staff. Mind you, what is there to do with money except spend it when you've got it or be bitter about it when you haven't? It's a very limited commodity in which people invest the most extraordinary emotions. What I suppose I really mean is *do* be bitter about the money; it's one of the few things it can do: siphon off some bitterness. Do-gooders have sometimes complained that I have too many *bêtes noires*, but I need my *bêtes noires* to get the *noire* out of me and into the *bêtes*. Besides, that side of your family has had a good run. What is it now? Six generations with every single descendant, not just the eldest son, essentially idle. They may have taken on the camouflage of work, especially in America where everyone has to have an office, if only to swivel about with their shoes on the desk for half an hour before lunch, but there's been no necessity. It must be rather thrilling, although I can't speak from experience, for you and your children, after this long exemption from competition, to get stuck in. God knows what I would have made of my life if I hadn't divided my time between town and country, between home and abroad, between wives and mistresses. I have divided time and now doth time divide me, what? I must take a closer look at these religious fanatics your mother surrounded herself with.'

Nicholas hobbled off with no pretence that he expected any response other than silent fascination.

When Patrick looked back on the way that illness and dying had torn apart Eleanor's flimsy shamanic fantasies, Nicholas's 'religious fanatics' seemed to him more like credulous draft-dodgers. At the end of her life Eleanor had been thrown into a merciless crash-course in self-knowledge, with only a 'power animal' in one hand and a rattle in the other. She had been left with the steepest practice of all: no speech, no movement, no sex, no drugs, no travel, no spending, hardly any food; just alone in silent contemplation of her thoughts. If contemplation was the word. Perhaps she felt that her thoughts were contemplating her, like hungry predators.

'Were you thinking about her?' said a soft Irish voice. Annette rested a healing hand on Patrick's forearm and tilted her understanding head to one side.

'I was thinking that a life is just the history of what we give our attention to,' said Patrick. 'The rest is packaging.'

'Oh, I think that's too stark,' said Annette. 'Maya Angelou says that the meaning of our lives is the impact we have on other people, whether we make them feel good or not. Eleanor always made people feel good, it was one of her gifts to the world. Oh,' she added with sudden excitement, gripping Patrick's forearm, 'I only made this connection on the way in: we're in Mortlake crematorium to say farewell to Eleanor, and guess what I took to read to her on the last occasion I saw her. You'll never guess. *The Lady of the Lake*. It's an Arthurian whodunit, not very good actually. But that says it all, doesn't it? Lady of the lake – Mortlake. Given Eleanor's connection with water and her love of the Arthurian legends.'

Patrick was stunned by Annette's confidence in the consoling power of her words. He felt irritation being usurped by despair. To think that his mother had chosen to live among these resolute fools. What knowledge was she so determined to avoid?

'Who can say why a crematorium and a bad novel should

have vaguely similar names?' said Patrick. 'It's tantalizing to be taken so far beyond the rational mind. I tell you who would be very receptive to that sort of connection: you see the old man over there with the walking stick. Do tell him. He loves that kind of thing. His name is Nick.' Patrick dimly remembered that Nicholas loathed this abbreviation.

'Seamus sends his best,' said Annette, accepting her dismissal cheerfully.

'Thank you.' Patrick bowed his head, trying not to lose control of his exaggerated deference.

What was he doing? It was all so out of date. The war with Seamus and his mother's Foundation was over. Now that he was an orphan everything was perfect. He seemed to have been waiting all his life for this sense of completeness. It was all very well for the Oliver Twists of this world, who started out in the enviable state it had taken him forty-five years to achieve, but the relative luxury of being brought up by Bumble and Fagin, rather than David and Eleanor Melrose, was bound to have a weakening effect on the personality. Patient endurance of potentially lethal influences had made Patrick the man he was today, living alone in a bedsit, only a year away from his latest visit to the Suicide Observation Room in the Depression Wing of the Priory Hospital. It had felt so ancestral to have delirium tremens, to bow down, after his disobedient youth as a junkie, to the shattering banality of alcohol. As a barrister he was reluctant nowadays to kill himself illegally. The alcohol felt deep, humming down the bloodline. He could still remember, when he was five, taking a donkey ride among the palm trees and the packed red and white flowerbeds of Monte Carlo's Casino Gardens, while his grandfather sat on a green bench shaking uncontrollably, clamped by sunlight, a stain spreading slowly through the pearl-grey trousers of his perfectly cut suit.

Lack of insurance forced Patrick to pay for his own stay

in the Priory, exhausting all his funds in a thirty-day gamble on recovery. Unhelpfully short from a psychiatric point of view, a month was still long enough for him to become immediately infatuated with a twenty-year-old patient called Becky. She looked like Botticelli's Venus, improved by a bloody trellis of razor cuts crisscrossing its way up her slender white arms. When he first saw her in the lounge of the Depression Wing, her radiant unhappiness sent a flaming arrow into the powder keg of his frustration and emptiness.

'I'm a self-harming resistant depressive,' she told him. 'They've got me on eight different kinds of pills.'

'Eight,' said Patrick admiringly. He was down to three himself: the daytime antidepressant, the nighttime antidepressant, and the thirty-two oxazepam tranquillizers a day he was taking to deal with the delirium tremens.

In so far as he could think at all on such a high dose of oxazepam, he could think only of Becky. The next day, he heaved himself off his crackling mattress and slouched to the Depression Support Group in the hope of seeing her again. She was not there, but Patrick could not escape from joining the circle of tracksuited depressives. 'As to sports, let our wear do it for us,' he sighed, slumping down in the nearest chair.

An American called Gary kicked off the sharing with the words, 'Let me give you a scenario: suppose you were sent to Germany for work, and suppose a friend you hadn't heard from in a long time called you up and came to visit with you from the States . . .' After a tale of shocking exploitation and ingratitude, he asked the group what he should say to this friend. 'Cut them out of your life,' said the bitter and abrasive Terry, 'with friends like that, who needs enemies?'

'Okay,' said Gary, relishing his moment, 'and suppose I told you that this "friend" was my mother, what would you say then? Why would that be so different?'

Consternation raced through the Group. A man, who had been feeling 'completely euphoric' since his mother had come over on Sunday and taken him out to buy a new pair of trousers, said that Gary should never abandon his mother. On the other hand, there was a woman called Jill who had been 'for a long walk by the river I wasn't supposed to come back from – well, put it this way, I did come back *very wet*, and I said to Dr Pagazzi, who I love to bits, that I thought it had something to do with my mother and he said, "We're not even going to go there."' Jill said that, like her, Gary should have nothing to do with his mother. At the end of the session, the wise Scottish moderator tried to shield the group from this downpour of self-centred advice.

'Someone once asked me why mothers are so good at pushing our buttons,' he said, 'and the answer I gave was, "Because they put them there in the first place." '

Everyone nodded gloomily, and Patrick asked himself, not for the first time, but with renewed desperation, what it would mean to be free, to live beyond the tyranny of dependency and conditioning and resentment.

After the Support Group, he saw a caved-in, illicitly smoking, barefooted Becky go down the staircase beyond the laundry. He followed her and found her crumpled on the stairs, her giant pupils swimming in a pool of tears. 'I hate this place,' she said. 'They're going to throw me out because they say I've got a bad attitude. But I only stayed in bed because I'm so *depressed*. I don't know where I'm going to go, I can't face going back to my parents.'

She was screaming to be saved. Why not run away with her to the bedsit? She was one of the few people alive who was more suicidal than him. They could lie on the bed together, Priory refugees, one convulsing while the other slashed. Why not take her back and let her finish the job for him? Her bluest veins to bandage, her whitening lips to kiss. No no no no no. He was too well, or at least too old.

These days he could only remember Becky with deliberate effort. He often watched his obsessions pass over him like so many blushes, and by doing nothing about them, watched them fade. Becoming an orphan was a thermal on which this new sense of freedom might continue to rise, if only he had the courage not to feel guilty about the opportunity it presented.

Patrick drifted towards Nicholas and Annette, curious to see the outcome of his matchmaking.

'Stand by the graveside or the furnace,' he heard Nicholas instructing Annette, 'and repeat these words, "Goodbye, old thing. One of us was bound to die first and I'm delighted it was you!" That's my spiritual practice, and you're welcome to adopt it and put it into your hilarious "spiritual tool box".'

'Your friend is absolutely priceless,' said Annette, seeing Patrick approaching. 'What he doesn't realize is that we live in a loving universe. And it loves you too, Nick,' she assured Nicholas, resting her hand on his recoiling shoulder.

'I've quoted Bibesco before,' snapped Nicholas, 'and I'll quote him again: "To a man of the world, the universe is a suburb".'

'Oh, he's got an answer to everything, hasn't he?' said Annette. 'I expect he'll joke his way into heaven. St Peter loves a witty man.'

'Does he?' said Nicholas, surprisingly appeased. 'That's the best thing I've heard yet about that bungling social secretary. As if the Supreme Being would consent to spend eternity surrounded by a lot of nuns and paupers and parboiled missionaries, having his lovely concerts ruined by the rattle of spiritual tool boxes and the screams of the faithful, boasting about their crucifixions! What a relief that an enlightened command has finally reached the concierge at the Pearly Gates: "For Heaven's sake, send Me a conversationalist!"'

Annette looked at Nicholas with humorous reproach.

'Ah,' he said, nodding at Patrick, 'I never thought I'd be so grateful to see your impossible aunt.' He lifted his stick and waved it at Nancy. She stood in the doorway looking exhausted by her own haughtiness, as if her raised eyebrows might not be able to stand the strain much longer.

'Help!' she said to Nicholas. 'Who are these peculiar people?'

'Zealots, Moonies, witch-doctors, would-be terrorists, every variety of religious lunatic,' explained Nicholas, offering Nancy his arm. 'Avoid eye contact, stick close to me and you may live to tell the tale.'

Nancy flared up when she saw Patrick. 'Of all the days *not* to have the funeral,' she said.

'Why?' he asked, confused.

'It's Prince Charles's wedding. The only other people who might have come will be at Windsor.'

'I'm sure you'd be there as well, if you'd been invited,' said Patrick. 'Don't hesitate to nip down with a Union Jack and a cardboard periscope if you think you'd find it more entertaining.'

'When I think how we were brought up,' wailed Nancy, 'it's too ridiculous to think what my sister did with . . .' She was lost for words.

'The golden address book,' purred Nicholas, gripping his walking stick more tightly as she sagged against him.

'Yes,' said Nancy, 'the golden address book.'

2

Nancy watched her infuriating nephew drift towards his mother's coffin. Patrick would never understand the fabulous way that she and Eleanor had been brought up. Eleanor had stupidly rebelled against it, whereas it had been ripped from Nancy's prayerfully clasped hands.

'The golden address book,' she sighed again, locking arms with Nicholas. 'I mean, for example, Mummy only ever had one car accident in her entire life, but even then, when she was hanging upside down in the buckled metal, she had the Infanta of Spain dangling next to her.'

'That's very in-depth, I must say,' said Nicholas. 'A car accident can get one tangled up with all sorts of obscure people. Picture the commotion at the College of Heralds if a drop of one's blood landed on the dashboard of a lorry and mingled with the bodily fluids of the brute whose head had been dashed against the steering wheel.'

'Do you always have to be so facetious?' snapped Nancy.

'I do my best,' said Nicholas. 'But you can't pretend that your mother was a fan of the common man. Didn't she buy the entire village street that ran along the boundary wall of the Pavillon Colombe, in order to demolish it and expand the garden? How many houses was that?'

'Twenty-seven,' said Nancy, cheering up. 'They weren't all demolished. Some of them were turned into exactly the right kind of ruin to go with the house. There were follies and grottos, and Mummy had a replica made of the main house, only fifty times smaller. We used to have tea there, it was like something out of *Alice in Wonderland*.' Nancy's face clouded over. 'There was a horrible old man who refused to sell, although Mummy offered him far too much for his poky little house, and so there was an inward bulge following the line of the old wall, if you see what I'm saying.'

'Every paradise demands a serpent,' said Nicholas.

'He did it just to annoy us,' said Nancy. 'He put a French flag on the roof and used to play Edith Piaf all day long. We had to smother him in vegetation.'

'Maybe he liked Edith Piaf,' said Nicholas.

'Oh, don't be funny! Nobody could like Edith Piaf at that volume.'

Nicholas sounded sour to Nancy's sensitive ear. So what if Mummy hadn't wanted ordinary people pressing up against her property? It was hardly surprising when everything else was so divine. Fragonard had painted *Les Demoiselles Colombe* in that garden, hence the necessity for having Fragonards in the house. The original owners had hung a pair of big Guardis in the drawing room, hence the authenticity of getting them back.

Nancy couldn't help being haunted by the splendour and the wreckage of her mother's family. One day she was going to write a book about her mother and her aunts, the legendary Jonson Sisters. She had been collecting material for years, fascinating bits and pieces that just needed to be organized. Only last week, she had sacked a hopeless young researcher – the tenth in a succession of greedy egomaniacs who wanted to be paid in advance – but not before her latest slave had discovered a copy of her grandmother's birth certificate. According to this wonderfully quaint document, Nancy's grandmother had been 'Born in Indian Country'. How could the daughter of a young army officer, born at this unlikely address, have guessed, as she tottered about among the creaky pallet beds and restless horses of an adobe fort in the Western Territories, that her own daughters would be tottering along the corridors of European castles and filling their houses with the debris of failed dynasties – splashing about in Marie-Antoinette's black marble bath, while their yellow Labradors dozed on carpets from the throne room of the imperial palace in Peking? Even the lead garden tubs on the terrace of the Pavillon Colombe had been made for Napoleon. Gold bees searching through silver blossoms, dripping in the rain. She always thought that Jean had made Mummy buy those tubs to take an obscure revenge on Napoleon for saying that his ancestor, the great Duc de Valençay, was 'a piece of shit in a silk stocking'. What she liked to say was that Jean kept up the family tradition, minus the silk stocking. Nancy gripped Nicholas's arm even more tightly, as if her horrid stepfather might try to steal him as well.

If only Mummy hadn't divorced Daddy. They had such a glamorous life in Sunninghill Park, where she and Eleanor were brought up. The Prince of Wales used to drop in all the time, and there were never less than twenty people staying in the house, having the best fun ever. It was true that Daddy had the bad habit of buying Mummy extremely expensive presents, which she had to pay for. When she said, 'Oh, darling, you shouldn't have,' she really meant it. She grew nervous of commenting on the garden. If she said that a border needed a little more blue, a couple of days later she would find that Daddy had flown in some impossible flower from Tibet which bloomed for about three minutes and cost as much as a house. But before the drink took over, Daddy was handsome and warm and so infectiously funny that the food often arrived shaking at the table, because the footmen were laughing too much to hold the platters steadily.

When the Crash came, lawyers flew in from America to

ask the Craigs to rack their brains for something they could do without. They thought and thought. They obviously couldn't sell Sunninghill Park. They had to go on entertaining their friends. It would be too cruel and too inconvenient to sack any of the servants. They couldn't do without the house in Bruton Street for overnight stays in London. They needed two Rolls-Royces and two chauffeurs because Daddy was incorrigibly punctual and Mummy was incorrigibly late. In the end they sacrificed one of the six newspapers that each guest received with their breakfast. The lawyers relented. The pools of Jonson money were too deep to pretend there was a crisis; they were not stock-market speculators, they were industrialists and owners of great blocks of urban America. People would always need hardened fats and dry-cleaning fluids and somewhere to live.

Even if Daddy had been too extravagant, Mummy's marriage to Jean was a folly that could only be explained by the resulting title – she was definitely jealous of Aunt Gerty being married to a grand duke. Jean's role in the Jonson story was to disgrace himself, as a liar and a thief, a lecherous stepfather and a tyrannical husband. While Mummy lay dying of cancer, Jean threw one of his tantrums, screaming that doubt was being cast on his honour by her will. She was leaving him her houses and paintings and furniture only for his lifetime and then on to her children, as if he couldn't be trusted to leave them to the children himself. He knew perfectly well that they were Jonson possessions . . . and on and on; the morphine, the pain, the screaming, the indignant promises. She changed her will and Jean went back on his word and left everything to his nephew.

God, how Nancy loathed Jean! He had died almost forty years ago, but she wanted to kill him every day. He had stolen everything and ruined her life. Sunninghill, the Pavillon, the Palazzo Arichele, all lost. She even regretted the loss of some of the Jonson houses she would never have inherited, not unless lots of people had died, that is, which would have been a tragedy, except that at least she would have known how to live in them properly, which was more than could be said of some people she could name.

'All the lovely things, all the lovely houses,' said Nancy, 'where have they all gone?'

'Presumably the houses are where they've always been,' said Nicholas, 'but they're being lived in by people who can afford them.'

'But that's just it, I should be able to afford them!'

'Never use a conditional tense when it comes to money.'

Really, Nicholas was being impossible. She certainly wasn't going to tell him about her book. Ernest Hemingway had told Daddy that he really ought to write a book, because he told such funny stories. When Daddy protested that he couldn't write, Hemingway sent a tape-recorder. Daddy forgot to plug the thing in, and when the spools didn't go round, he lost his temper and threw it out of the window. Luckily, the woman it landed on didn't take any legal action and Daddy had another marvellous story, but the whole incident had made Nancy superstitious about tape-recorders. Maybe she should hire a ghost writer. Exorcized by a ghost! That would be original. Still, she had to give the poor ghost an idea of how she wanted it done. It could be theme by theme, or decade by decade, but that seemed to her a stuffy egghead bookworm kind of approach. She wanted it done sister by sister; after all, the rivalry between them was quite the dynamic force.

Gerty, the youngest and most beautiful of the three Jonson Sisters, was definitely the one Mummy was most competitive with. She married the Grand Duke Vladimir, nephew of the last Tsar of Russia. 'Uncle Vlad', as Nancy called him, had helped to assassinate Rasputin, lending his Imperial revolver to Prince Yussopov for what was supposed to be the final kill, but turned out to be only the middle stage between poisoning the energetic priest with arsenic and drowning him in the Neva. Despite many pleas, the Tsar exiled Vladimir for his part in the assassination, making him miss the Russian Revolution and the chance to get bayoneted, strangled or shot by Russia's new Bolshevik masters. Once in exile, Uncle Vlad went on to assassinate himself by drinking twenty-three dry martinis before lunch every day. Thanks to the Russian whimsy of smashing a glass after drinking from it, there was hardly a moment's silence in the house. Nancy had Daddy's copy of a forgotten memoir by Uncle Vlad's sister, the Grand Duchess Anna. It was inscribed in purple ink to 'my dear brother-in-law', although he was in fact her brother's sister-in-law's husband. The inscription seemed to Nancy somehow typical of the generous inclusiveness that had enabled that amazing family to straddle two continents, from Kiev to Vladivostok. Before Uncle Vlad's marriage to Gerty in Biarritz, his sister had to perform the blessing that would traditionally have been performed by their parents. It was a moment they dreaded because it reminded them of the horrifying reason for the absence of their family. The grand duchess described her feelings in *The Palace of Memory*:

> Through the window I could see the great waves pounding the rocks; the sun had gone down. The grey ocean at that moment looked to me as ruthless and indifferent as fate, and infinitely lonely.

Gerty decided to convert to the Russian Orthodox religion, in order to be closer to Vladimir's people. Anna went on:

> Our cousin, the Duke of Leuchtenberg, and I were her sponsors. The ceremony was a long and wearisome one, and I felt sorry for Gerty, who did not understand a word of it.

If her pet ghost could write as well as that, Nancy felt sure she would have a bestseller on her hands. The eldest Jonson Sister was the richest of all: bossy, practical Aunt Edith. While her flighty younger sisters jumped into the pages of an illustrated history book, holding hands with the remnants of some of the world's greatest families, sensible Aunt Edith, who preferred her antiques to arrive in a crate, made a consolidating marriage to a man whose father, like her own, had been on the list of the hundred richest men in America in 1900. Nancy spent the first two years of the war living with Edith, while Mummy tried to get some of her really valuable things into storage in Switzerland before joining her daughters in America. Edith's husband, Uncle Bill, struck an original note by paying with his own money for the presents he gave his wife. One birthday present was a white clapboard house with dark green shutters and two gently curved wings, on a slope of lawn above a lake, at the centre of a ten-thousand-acre plantation. She loved it. That was the sort of useful tip that they never gave you in books called *The Art of Giving*.

Patrick glanced at his unhappy aunt, still complaining to Nicholas by the entrance. He couldn't help thinking of the favourite dictum of the moderator from his Depression Group, 'Resentment is drinking the poison, and hoping that someone else will die'. All the patients had impersonated this sentence in more or less convincing Scottish accents at least once a day.

If he was now standing beside his mother's coffin with uneasy detachment, it was not because he had cherished his aunt's 'golden address book'. As far as Patrick was concerned, the past was a corpse waiting to be cremated, and although his wish was about to be granted in the most literal fashion, in a furnace only a few yards from where he was standing, another kind of fire was needed to incinerate the attitudes which haunted Nancy; the psychological impact of inherited wealth, the raging desire to get rid of it and the raging desire to hang on to it; the demoralizing effect of already having what almost everyone else was sacrificing their precious lives to acquire; the more or less secret superiority and the more or less secret shame of being rich, generating their characteristic disguises: the philanthropy solution, the alcoholic solution, the mask of eccentricity, the search for salvation in perfect taste; the defeated, the idle, and the frivolous, and their opponents, the standard-bearers, all living in a world that the dense glitter of alternatives made it hard for love and work to penetrate. If these values were in themselves sterile, they looked all the more ridiculous after two generations of disinheritance. Patrick wanted to distance himself from what he thought of as his aunt's virulent irrelevance, and yet there was a fascination with status running down the maternal line of his family that he had to understand.

He remembered going to see Eleanor just after she had launched her last philanthropic project, the Transpersonal Foundation. She had decided to renounce the frustration of being a person in favour of the exciting prospect of becoming a Transperson; denying part of what she was, the daughter of one bewildered family and the mother of another, and claiming to be what she was not, a healer and a saint. The impact of this adolescent project on her ageing body was to produce the first of the dozen strokes which eventually demolished her. When Patrick went down to see her in Lacoste after that first stroke, she was still able to speak fluently enough, but her mind had become entirely suspicious. The moment they were alone together in her bedroom, with the tattered curtains under full sail in the evening breeze, she clasped his arm and hissed to him urgently. 'Don't tell anybody my mother was a duchess.'

He nodded conspiratorially. She relaxed her grasp and searched the ceiling for the next worry.

Nancy's instructions, without even a stroke to justify them, would have been the exact opposite. Tell nobody? Tell everybody! Behind the cartoon contrasts of Nancy's worldliness and Eleanor's other-worldliness, Nancy's bulk and Eleanor's emaciation, there was a common cause, a past that had to be falsified, whether by suppression or selective glorification. What was that? Were Eleanor and Nancy individuals at all, or were they just part of the characteristic debris of their class and family?

Eleanor had taken Patrick to stay with her Aunt Edith in the early 1970s when he was twelve. While the rest of the world was worrying about the OPEC crisis, stagflation, carpet bombing, and whether the effects of LSD were permanent, eternal or temporary, they found Edith living in a style which made no concession whatsoever to the fifty years since Live Oak had been given to her. The forty black servants made the slaves in *Gone With The Wind* look like extras on a film set. On the evening that Patrick and Eleanor arrived, Moses, one of the footmen, asked if he could be excused in order to go to his brother's funeral. Edith said no. There were four people at dinner and Moses was needed to serve the hominy grits. Patrick didn't mind if the servant who brought the quail, or the one who took the vegetables around, served the hominy grits as well, but there was a system in place and Edith was not going to allow it to be disrupted. Moses, in white gloves and a white coat, stepped forward silently, tears pouring down his cheeks, and offered Patrick his first taste of grits. He never knew if he would have liked them.

Later, beside a crackling fire in her bedroom, Eleanor raged against her aunt's cruelty. The scene over dinner had been too resonant for her; she could never disentangle the taste of the grits from Moses' tears, or indeed her mother's perfect taste from her own childhood tears. Eleanor's sense that her sanity was rooted in the kindness of servants meant that she would always be on Moses' side. If she had been articulate, this loyalty might have made her political; as it was it made her charitable. Most of all she raged against the way her aunt made her feel as if she were still twelve years old, as she had been when she was a passionate but mute guest at the beginning of the war, staying at Fairley, Bill and Edith's place on Long Island. His mother was hypnotized by the memory of being Patrick's age. Her arrested development always rigorously shadowed his efforts to grow up. In his early childhood she had been preoccupied by how much her nanny meant to her, while failing to provide him with a similar paragon of warmth and trustworthiness.

Looking up from his mother's coffin, Patrick saw that Nancy and Nicholas were planning to approach him again, their instinct for social hierarchy turning a bereaved son into the temporary top dog at his mother's funeral. He rested a hand on Eleanor's coffin, forming a secret alliance against misunderstanding.

'My dear,' said Nicholas, apparently refreshed by some important news, 'I hadn't realized, until Nancy enlightened me, what a serious partygoer your Mama used to be, before she took up her "good works".' He seemed to poke the phrase aside with his walking stick, clearing it from his path. 'To think of shy, religious little Eleanor at the Beistegui Ball! I didn't know her then, or I would have felt compelled to shield her from that stampede of ravenous harlequins.' Nicholas moved his free hand artistically through the air. 'It was a magical occasion, as if the gilded layabouts in one of Watteau's paintings had been released from their enchanted prison and given an enormous dose of steroids and a fleet of speedboats.'

'Oh, she wasn't all that shy, if you know what I'm saying,' Nancy corrected him. 'She had any number of beaux. You know your mother could have made a dazzling marriage.'

'And saved me the trouble of being born.'

'Oh, don't be so silly. You would have been born anyway.'

'Not quite.'

'When I think,' said Nicholas, 'of all the impostors who claim to have been at that legendary party, it's hard to believe that I knew someone who was there and chose never to mention it. And now it's too late to congratulate her on her modesty.' He patted the coffin, as an owner might pat a winning racehorse. 'Which shows the pointlessness of that particular affectation.'

Nancy spotted a white-haired man in a black pinstriped suit and a black silk tie walking down the aisle.

'Henry!' she said, staggering back theatrically. 'We needed some Jonson reinforcements.' Nancy loved Henry. He was so rich. It would have been better if the money had been hers, but a close relation having it was the next best thing.

'How are you, Cabbage?' she greeted him.

Henry kissed Nancy hello, without looking especially pleased to be addressed as 'Cabbage'.

'My God, I didn't expect to see you,' said Patrick. He felt a wave of remorse.

'I didn't expect to see you either,' said Henry. 'Nobody communicates in this family. I'm over here for a few days staying at the Connaught, and when they wheeled in *The Times* with my breakfast this morning, I saw that your mother had died and that there was a ceremony here today. Fortunately, the hotel got me a car straight away and I was able to make it.'

'I haven't seen you since you kindly had us to stay on your island,' said Patrick, deciding to plunge in. 'I think I was rather a nightmare. I'm sorry about that.'

'I guess nobody enjoys being unhappy,' said Henry.

'It always spills over. But we mustn't let a few foreign-policy differences get in the way of the really important things.'

'Absolutely,' said Patrick, struck by how kind Henry was being. 'I'm so glad you've made it here today. Eleanor was very fond of you.'

'Well, I loved your mother. As you know, she stayed with us at Fairley for a couple of years at the beginning of the war and so naturally we became very close. She had an innocent quality that was really attractive; it drew you in and at the same time it kept you at a certain distance. It's hard to explain, but whatever you feel about your mother and this charity she got involved with, I hope you know that she was a good person with the best intentions.'

'Yes,' said Patrick, accepting the simplicity of Henry's affection for a moment, 'I think "innocent" is exactly the right word.' He marvelled again at the effect of projection: how hostile Henry had seemed to him when Patrick was hostile towards everyone; how considerate he seemed now that Patrick had no argument with him. What would it be like to stop projecting? Was it possible at all?

As he turned to leave, Henry reached out and touched Patrick's shoulder.

'I'm sorry for your loss,' he said, with a formality that was by then infused with emotion. He nodded to Nancy and Nicholas.

'Excuse me,' said Patrick, looking back at the entrance of the crematorium, 'I have to say hello to Johnny Hall.'

'Who's he?' asked Nancy, sensing obscurity.

'You may well ask,' scowled Nicholas. 'He wouldn't be anybody at all, if he wasn't my daughter's psychoanalyst. As it is, he's a fiend.'

3

Patrick walked away from his mother's coffin, aware that unless he rushed back hysterically, he had stood beside her for the last time. He had seen the cold damp contents of the coffin the night before, when he paid a visit to Bunyon's funeral parlour. A friendly, blue-suited woman with short white hair had greeted him at the door.

'Hello, love, I heard a taxi and I thought it was you.'

She guided him downstairs. Pink and brown diamond carpet like the bar of a country house hotel. Discreet advertisements for special services. A framed photograph of a woman kneeling by a black box from which a dove was only too pleased to be set free. Bolting upwards in a blur of white wings. Did it return to the Bunyon's dovecote and get recycled? Oh, no, not the black box again. 'We can release a dove for you on the day of your funeral'. Gothic script seemed to warp every letter that passed through the door of the funeral parlour, as if death were a German village. There were stained-glass windows, electrically lit, on the stairs down to the basement.

'I'll leave you with her. If there's anything you need, don't hesitate. I'll be upstairs.'

'Thank you,' said Patrick, waiting for her to turn the corner before stepping into the Willow Chapel.

He closed the door behind him and glanced hurriedly into the coffin, as though his mother had told him it was rude to stare. Whatever he was looking at, it was not the 'her' he had been promised with solemn cosiness a few minutes before. The absence of life in that familiar body, the rigid and rectified features of the face he had known before he even knew his own, made all the difference. Here was a transitional object for the far end of life. Instead of the soft toy or raggie that a child uses to cope with its mother's absence, he was being offered a corpse, its scrawny fingers clutching an artificial white rose whose stiff silk petals were twisted into position over an unbeating heart. It had the sarcasm of a relic, as well as the prestige of a metonym. It stood for his mother and for her absence with equal authority. In either case, it was her final appearance before she retired into other people's memory.

He had better take another look, a longer look, a less theoretical look, but how could he concentrate in this disconcerting basement? The Willow Chapel turned out to be under a busy pavement, pierced by the declamatory brightness of mobile-phone talk and tattooed by clicking heels. A rumbling taxi emerged from the general traffic and splashed a puddle onto the paving stones above the far corner of the ceiling. He was reminded of the Tennyson poem he hadn't thought of for decades, 'Dead, long dead, / Long dead! / And my heart is a handful of dust, / And the wheels go over my head, / And my bones are shaken with pain, / For in a shallow grave they are thrust, / Only a yard beneath the street, / And the hoofs of the horses beat, beat, / The hoofs of the horses beat, / Beat into my scalp and my brain, / With never an end to the stream of passing feet.' He could see why Bunyon's had chosen to call this room the Willow Chapel rather than the Coal Cellar or the Shallow Grave. 'Hello, love, your Mum's in the Coal Cellar,' muttered Patrick. 'We could release a dove in the Shallow Grave, but it would have no chance whatever of escape.' He sat down and rocked his torso over his folded arms. His entrails were in torment, as they had been since hearing about his mother's death three days ago. No need for ten years of psychoanalysis to work out that he felt 'gutted'. He was doing what he always did under pressure, observing everything, chattering to himself in different voices, circling the unacceptable feelings, in this case conveniently embedded in his mother's coffin.

She had left the world with screeching slowness, sliding inch by inch into oblivion. At first he could not help enjoying the comparative quiet of her presence, but then he noticed that he was clinging to the urban noises outside in order not to be drawn into the deep pit of silence at the centre of the room. He must take a closer look, but first he really had to turn down the lights that were glaring through chrome grids in the low polystyrene ceiling. They bleached the glow of the four stout candles impaled on brass stands at the corners of the coffin. He dimmed the spotlights and restored some of the ecclesiastical pomposity to the candles. There was one more thing he had to check. A pink velvet curtain partitioned the room; he had to know what was behind it before he could pay attention to his mother. It turned out to hide a storage area packed with equipment: a grey metal trolley with sensible wheels, some no-nonsense rubber tubes and a huge gold crucifix. Everything needed to embalm a Christian. Eleanor had expected to meet Jesus at the end of a tunnel after she died. The poor man was a slave to his fans, waiting to show crowds of eager dead the neon countryside that lay beyond the rebirth canal of earthly annihilation. It must be hard to be chosen as optimism's master cliché, the Light at the End of the Tunnel, ruling over a glittering army of half-full glasses and silver-lined clouds.

Patrick let the curtain drop reluctantly, acknowledging that he had run out of distractions. He edged towards the coffin, like a man approaching a cliff. At least he knew that this coffin contained his mother's corpse. Twenty years ago, when he had been to see his father's remains in New York, he was shown into the wrong room. 'In loving memory of Hermann Newton'. He had done everything he could to opt out of that bereavement process, but he was not going to evade this one. A cool dry part of his mind was trying to bring his emotions under its aphoristic sway, but the stabbing pain in his guts undermined its ambitions, and confused his defences.

As he stared into the coffin, he felt the encroachment of an agitated animal sadness. He wanted to linger incredulously by the body, still giving it some of the attention it had commanded in life: a shake, a touch, a word, an enquiring gaze. He reached out and put his hand on her chest and felt the shock of its thinness. He leant over and kissed her on the forehead and felt the shock of its coldness. These sharp sensations lowered his defences further, and he was overwhelmed by an expanding rush of sympathy for the ruined human being in front of him. During its fleeting life, this vast sense of tenderness reduced his mother's personality to a detail, and his relationship with her to a detail within a detail.

He sat down again and leant forward over his crossed legs and folded arms to give himself some faint relief from the pain in his stomach. And then he suddenly made a connection. Of course, how strange – how determined. Aged seven, going on his first trip alone abroad with his mother, a few months after his parents' divorce. His first flash of Italy: the white number plates, the blue bay, the ochre churches. They were staying at the Excelsior in Naples, on a waterfront buzzing with waspish motorcycles and humming with crowded trams. From the balcony of their magnificent room, his mother pointed to the street urchins crouched on the roofs, or clinging to the backs of the trams. Patrick, who thought they were in Naples on holiday, was alarmed to hear that Eleanor had come there to save these poor children. There was a marvellous man, a priest called Father Tortelli, who never tired of picking up lost Neapolitan boys and giving them shelter in the refuge that Eleanor had been bankrolling from London. She was now going to see it for the first time. Wasn't it exciting? Wasn't it a good thing to be doing? She showed Patrick a photograph of Father Tortelli: a small, tough, fifty-year-old man in a black skirt who looked as if he was no stranger to the boxing ring. His bearish arms were locked around the fragile, sharp-boned shoulders of two sun-tanned boys in white vests. Father Tortelli was protecting them from the streets, but who was protecting them from Father Tortelli? Not Eleanor. She was providing him with the means to fill his refuge with ever-growing numbers of orphans and runaways. After lunch that day, Patrick had an attack of violent gastroenteritis, and instead of leaving him in luxurious neglect while she went to look after the other children, his mother was made to stay with him and hold his hand while he screamed with pain in the green marble bathroom. No amount of stomach ache could make her stay now. Not that he wanted her to stay, but his body had a memory of its own which it continued to narrate without any reference to his current wishes. What was it that had driven Eleanor to furnish children for her husband and for Father Tortelli, and why was the drive so strong that, after the collapse of her marriage, she immediately replaced a father with a Father, a doctor with a priest? Patrick had no doubt that her motives were unconscious, as unconscious as the somatic memory that had taken him over in the last three days. What could he do but drag these fragments out of the dark and acknowledge them?

After a quiet knock, the door opened and the attendant leant into the room.

'Just to make sure everything is all right,' she whispered.

'Maybe it is,' said Patrick.

The journey back to his flat had a mildly hallucinatory quality, surging through the rainy night in a fluorescent bus, freshly flooded by so many fierce impressions and remote memories. There were two Jehovah's Witnesses on board, a black man handing out leaflets and a black woman preaching at the top of her voice. 'Repent of your sins and take Jesus into your heart, because when you die it will be too late to repent in the grave and you'll burn in the fires of Hell . . .'

A red-eyed Irishman in a threadbare tweed jacket started shouting in counterpoint from a back seat. 'Shut up, you fuckin' bitch. Go suck Satan's cock. You're not allowed to do this, whether you're Muslim, or Christian, or Satanic.' When the man with the leaflets headed for the upper deck, he persisted, investing his accent with a sadistic Southern twang, 'I can see you, Boy. How do you think you'd look with your head under your arm, Boy. If you don't shut that bitch up, I'll adjust your face for you, Boy.'

'Oh, do shut up yourself,' said an exasperated commuter.

Patrick noticed that his stomach pains had gone. He watched the Irishman sway in his seat, his lips continuing to argue silently with the Jehovah's Witness, or with some Jesuit from his youth. Give us a boy till the age of seven and we'll have him for life. Not me, thought Patrick, you won't have me.

As the bus pushed haltingly towards his destination, he thought about those brief but pivotal nights in the Suicide Observation Room, unpeeling one sweat-soaked T-shirt after another, throwing off the sauna of the bedclothes only to shudder in the freezer of their absence; turning the light on and off, pained by the brightness, alarmed by the dark; a poisonous headache lurching around his skull like the lead in a jumping bean. He had brought nothing to read except *The Tibetan Book of the Dead*, hoping to find its exotic iconography ridiculous enough to purge any fantasies he might still cling to about consciousness continuing after death. As it turned out, he found his imagination seduced by a passage from the introduction to the *Chonyid Bardo*, 'O nobly born, when thy body and thy mind were separating, thou must have experienced a glimpse of the Pure Truth, subtle, sparkling, bright, dazzling, glorious, and radiantly awesome, in appearance like a mirage moving across a landscape in springtime in one continuous stream of vibrations. Be not daunted thereby, nor terrified, nor awed. That is the radiance of thine own true nature. Recognize it.' The words had a psychedelic authority that overpowered the materialist annihilation he longed to believe in. He struggled to restore his faith in the finality of death, but couldn't help seeing it as a superstition among superstitions, no more bracingly rational than the rest. The idea that an afterlife had been invented to reassure people who couldn't face the finality of death was no more plausible than the idea that the finality of death had been invented to reassure people who couldn't face the nightmare of endless experience. His delirium tremens collaborated with the poets of the *Bardo* to produce a sensation of seething electrocution as he was goaded towards the abattoir of sleep, terrified that the slaughter of his rational mind would present him with a 'glimpse of the Pure Truth'.

Memories and phrases loomed and flitted like fog banks on a night road. Thoughts threatened him from a distance, but disappeared as he approached them. 'Drowned in dreams and burning to be gone'. Who had said that? Other people's words. Had he already thought 'other people's words'? Things seemed far away and then, a moment later, repetitious. Was it like fog, or was it more like hot sand, something he was labouring through and trying not to touch at the same time? Cold and wet, hot and dry. How could it be both? How could it be other than both? Similes of dissimilarities

– another phrase that seemed to chase itself like a miniature train around a tight circuit. Please make it stop.

A scene that kept tumbling back into his delirious thoughts was his visit to the philosopher Victor Eisen after Victor's near-death experience. He had found his old Saint-Nazaire neighbour in the London clinic, still strapped to the machines that had flat-lined a few days earlier. Victor's withered yellow arms emerged limply from an institutional dressing gown, but as he described what had happened his speech was as rapid and emphatic as ever, saturated by a lifetime of confident opinions.

'I came to a riverbank and on the other side was a red light which controlled the universe. There were two figures either side of it, who I knew to be the Lord of Time and the Lord of Space. They communicated to me directly through their thoughts, without using any speech. They told me that the fabric of Time-Space was torn and that I had to repair it, that the fate of the universe depended on me. I had a tremendous sense of urgency and purpose and I was on my way to fulfil my task when I felt myself being dragged back into my body and I very reluctantly returned.'

For three weeks Victor was won over by the feeling of authenticity that accompanied his vision, but then the habits of his public atheism and the fear that the logical reductions enshrined in his philosophical work might be invalidated made him squeeze his new sense of openness back into the biological crisis he was suffering at the time. He decided that the pressing mission he had been sent on by the controller of the universe was an allegory of a brain running out of oxygen. His mind had been failing, not expanding.

As he lay sweating in that narrow room, thinking about Victor's need to decide what everything meant, Patrick wondered if he could ever make his ego light enough to relax in not having to settle the meaning of things. What would that feel like?

In the meantime, the Suicide Observation Room lived up to its majestic name. In it, he saw that suicide had always formed the unquestioned backdrop to his existence. Even before he had taken to carrying around a copy of *The Myth of Sisyphus* in his overcoat pocket, making its first sentence the mantra of his early twenties, Patrick had greeted the day with the basic question, 'Can anyone think of a good reason not to kill himself?' Since he lived at the time in a theatrical solitude, crowded with mad and mocking voices, he was not likely to get an affirmative answer. Elaborate postponement was the best he could hope for, and in the end the obligation to talk proved stronger than the desire to die. During the next twenty years the suicidal chatter died down to an occasional whisper on a coastal path, or in a quiet chemist. When it returned in full force, it took the form of a grim monologue rather than a surreal chorus. The comparative simplicity of the most recent assault made him realize that he had only ever been superficially in love with easeful death and was much more deeply enthralled by his own personality. Suicide wore the mask of self-rejection; but in reality nobody took their personality more seriously than the person who was planning to kill himself on its instructions. Nobody was more determined to stay in charge at any cost, to force the most mysterious aspect of life into their own imperious schedule.

His month in the Priory had been a crucial period of his life, transforming the crisis that had led to the breakdown of his marriage and the escalation of his drinking. It was disquieting to think how close he had come to running away after only three days, lured by Becky's departure. Before leaving, she had found him in the lounge of the Depression Wing.

'I was looking for you. I'm not meant to speak to anyone,' she said in a mock whisper, 'because I'm a bad influence.'

She gave him a little folded note and a light kiss on the lips before hurrying out of the room.

This is my sister's address. She's away in the States, so I'll be there alone, if you feel like running away from this fucking place and doing something CRAZY. Love Becks.

The note reminded him of the jagged CRAZYs he used to doodle in the margins of his O-level chemistry notes after smoking a joint during the morning break at school. It was out of the question to visit her, he told himself, as he called a minicab service listed in the payphone booth under the back stairs. Was this what they meant by powerless?

'Just don't!' he muttered, closing the door of his minicab firmly to show how determined he was not to pursue a blood-stained festival of dysfunction. He gave the driver the address on Becky's note.

'Well, you must be all right if they let you out,' said the jaunty driver.

'I let myself out. I couldn't afford it.'

'Bit pricey, is it?'

Patrick didn't answer, glazed over with desire and conflict.

'Have you heard the one about the man who goes into the psychiatrist's office?' asked the driver, setting off down the drive and smiling in the rear-view mirror. 'He says, "It's been terrible, Doctor, for three years I thought I was a butterfly, and that's not all, it gets worse: for the last three months I thought I was a moth." "Good God," says the psychiatrist, "what a difficult time you've been having. So, what made you come here today and ask for help?" "Well," says the man, "I saw the light in the window and I felt drawn to it, so I just flew in."'

'That's a good one,' said Patrick, sinking deeper into Becky's imagined nakedness, while wondering how long his latest dose of oxazepam would last. 'Do you specialize in Priory patients because of your sunny temperament?'

'You say that,' said the driver, 'but last year for about four months I literally couldn't get out of bed, literally couldn't see the point in anything.'

'Oh, I'm sorry,' said Patrick.

From Hammersmith Broadway to the Shepherd's Bush roundabout, they talked about the causeless weeping, the suicidal daydreams, the excruciating slowness, the sleepless nights and the listless days. By the time they reached Bayswater, they were best friends and the driver turned round to Patrick and said with the full blast of his restored cheerfulness, 'In a few months you'll be looking back on what you've just been through and saying, "*What* was all that about? What was all that fuss and aggravation about?" That's what happened to me.'

Patrick looked back down at Becky's note. She had signed herself with the name of a beer. Becks. He started to whisper hoarsely under his breath, in a Marlon Brando as Vito Corleone voice, 'The one who comes to you and asks for a meeting, and has the same name as a well-known brand of beer – *she's* the one that wants you to have a relapse . . .'

Not the voices, he mustn't let them kick off. 'It starts off with a little Marlon Brando impersonation,' sighed Mrs Mop, 'and the next thing you know . . .'

'Shut up!' Patrick interrupted.

'What?'

'Oh, not you. I'm sorry.'

They turned into a big square with a central garden. The driver drew up to a white stucco building. Patrick leant sideways and looked out of the window. Becky was on the third floor, beautiful, available and mentally ill.

To think of the things he'd done for a little intimacy; earth flying over his shoulder as he dug his own grave. There were the good women who gave him the care he had never had. They had to be tortured into letting him down, to show that they couldn't really be trusted. And then there were the bad women who saved time by being untrustworthy straight away. He generally alternated between these two broad categories, enchanted by some variant which briefly masked the futility of defending the decaying fortress of his personality, while hoping that it would obligingly rearrange itself into a temple of peace and fulfilment. Hoping and moping, moping and hoping. With only a little detachment, his love life looked like a child's wind-up toy made to march again and again over the precipice of a kitchen table. Romance was where love was most under threat, not where it was likely to achieve its highest expression. If a candidate was sufficiently hopeless, like Becky, she took on the magnetism of the obviously doomed. It was embarrassing to be so deluded, and even more embarrassing to react to the delusion, like a man running away from his own looming shadow.

'I know this sounds a little bit *crazy*, for want of a better word,' said Patrick with a snort of laughter, 'but do you think you could drive me back? I'm not ready yet.'

'Back to the Priory?' said the driver, no longer quite as sympathetic to his passenger.

He doesn't want to know about those of us who have to go back, thought Patrick. He closed his eyes and stretched out in the back seat. 'Talk would talk and go so far askance . . . something, something . . . You don't want madhouse and the whole thing there.' The whole thing there. The wonderful inarticulacy of it, expanding with threat and contracting with ostensive urgency.

On the drive back, Patrick started to feel chest pains which even the violence of his longing for pathological romance could no longer explain. His hands were shaking and he could feel the sweat breaking out on his forehead. By the time he reached Dr Pagazzi's office, he was hallucinating mildly and apparently trapped in a two-dimensional space with no depth, like an insect crawling around a window pane, looking for a way out. Dr Pagazzi scolded him for missing his four o'clock dose of oxazepam, saying that he might have a heart attack if he withdrew too fast. Patrick lifted the dull plastic tub in his shaking hand and knocked back three oxazepam.

The next day he 'shared' his near escape with the Depression Group. It turned out that all of them had nearly run away, or had run away and come back, or thought about running away much of the time. Some, on the other hand, dreaded leaving, but they only seemed superficially opposite to the ones who wanted to run away: everyone was obsessed with how much therapy they needed before they could begin a 'normal life'. Patrick was surprised by how grateful he felt for the sense of solidarity with the other patients. A lifelong habit of being set apart was briefly overturned by a wave of goodwill towards everyone in the group.

Johnny Hall had taken an unassuming seat near the back of the room. Patrick worked his way round the far end of the pew to join his old friend.

'How are you bearing up?' said Johnny.

'Pretty well,' said Patrick, sitting down next to him. 'I have a strange feeling of excitement which I wouldn't admit to anyone except you and Mary. I felt rather knocked out for the first few days, but then I had what I think your profession would call an "insight". I went to the funeral parlour yesterday evening and sat with Eleanor's body. I connected . . . I'll tell you later.'

Johnny smiled encouragingly. 'Christ,' he said, after a pause, 'Nicholas Pratt. I didn't expect to see him.'

'Neither did I. You're so lucky to have an ethical reason not to talk to him.'

'Doesn't everybody?'

'Quite.'

'I'll see you afterwards at the Onslow,' said Johnny, leaving Patrick to the usher who had come up to him and was standing by expectantly.

'We can start whenever you're ready, sir,' said the usher, somehow hinting at the queue of corpses that would pile up unless the ceremony got going right away.

Patrick scanned the room. There were a few dozen people sitting in the pews facing Eleanor's coffin.

'Fine,' he said, 'let's begin in ten minutes.'

'Ten minutes?' said the usher, like a young child who has been told he can do something really exciting when he's twenty-one.

'Yes, there are still people arriving,' said Patrick, noticing Julia standing in the doorway, a spiky effusion of black against the dull morning: black veil, black hat, stiff black silk dress and, he imagined, softer black silk beneath. He immediately felt the impact of her mentality, that intense but exclusive sensitivity. She was like a spider's web, trembling at the slightest touch, but indifferent to the light that made its threads shine in the wet grass.

'You're just in time,' said Patrick, kissing Julia through her scratchy black veil.

'You mean late as usual.'

'No; just in time. We're about to kick off, if that's the phrase I'm looking for.'

'It's not,' she said, with that short husky laugh that always got to him.

The last time they had seen each other was in the French hotel where their affair had ended. Despite their communicating rooms, they could think of nothing to say to each other. Sitting through long meals, under the vault of an artificial sky, painted with faint clouds and garlands of tumbling roses, they stared at a flight of steps that led down to the slapping keels of a private harbour, ropes creaking against bollards, bollards rusting into stone quays; everything longing to leave.

'Now that you're not with Mary, you don't need me. I was . . . structural.'

'Exactly.'

The single word was perhaps too bare and could only be outstripped by silence. She had stood up and walked away without further comment. A gull launched itself from the soiled balustrade and clapped its way out to sea with a piercing cry. He had wanted to call her back, but the impulse died in the thick carpet lengthening between them.

Looking at him now, the freshly bereaved son, Julia decided she felt utterly detached from Patrick, apart from wanting him to find her irresistible.

'I haven't seen you for such a long time,' said Patrick, looking down at Julia's lips, red under the black net of her veil. He remained inconveniently attracted to almost all the women he had ever been to bed with, even when he had a strong aversion to a revival on all other grounds.

'A year and a half,' said Julia. 'Is it true that you've given up drinking? It must be hard just now.'

'Not at all: a crisis demands a hero. The ambush comes when things are going well, or so I'm told.'

'If you can't speak personally about things going well, they haven't changed that much.'

'They have changed, but my speech patterns may take a while to catch up.'

'I can't wait.'

'If there's an opportunity for irony . . .'

'You'll take it.'

'It's the hardest addiction of all,' said Patrick. 'Forget heroin. Just try giving up irony, that deep-down need to mean two things at once, to be in two places at once, not to be there for the catastrophe of a fixed meaning.'

'Don't!' said Julia, 'I'm having enough trouble wearing nicotine patches and still smoking at the same time. Don't take away my irony,' she pleaded, clasping him histrionically, 'leave me with a little sarcasm.'

'Sarcasm doesn't count. It only means one thing: contempt.'

'You always were a quality freak,' said Julia. 'Some of us like sarcasm.'

Julia noticed that she was playing with Patrick. She felt a small tug of nostalgia, but reminded herself sternly that she was well rid of him. Besides, she had Gunther now, a charming German banker who spent the middle of the week in London. It was true that he was married, as Patrick had been, but in every other way he was the opposite: slick, fit, rich and disciplined. He had opera tickets, and bookings in caviar bars and membership of nightclubs, organized by his personal assistant. Sometimes he threw caution to the winds and put on his ironed jeans and his zip-up suede jacket and took her to jazz clubs in unusual parts of town, always, of course, with a big, reassuring, silent car waiting outside to take them back to Hays Mews, just behind Berkeley Square, where Gunther, like all his friends, was having a swimming pool put into the sub-basement of his triple mews house lateral conversion. He collected hideous contemporary art with the haphazard credulity of a man who has friends in the art world. There were artistic black-and-white photographs of women's nipples in his dressing room. He made Julia feel sophisticated, but he didn't make her want to play. The thought simply didn't enter her head when she was with Gunther. He had never struggled to give up irony. He knew, of course, that it existed and he pursued it doggedly with all the silliness at his command.

'We'd better find a seat,' said Patrick. 'I'm not quite sure what's going on; I haven't even had time to look at the order of service.'

'But didn't you organize it?'

'No. Mary did.'

'Sweet!' said Julia. 'She's always so helpful, more like a mother than your own mother really.'

Julia felt her heart rate accelerate; perhaps she had gone too far. She was amazed that her old competition with that paragon of self-sacrifice had suddenly burst out, now that it was so out of date.

'She was, until she had children of her own,' said Patrick amiably. 'That rather blew my cover.'

From fearing that he would take offence, Julia found herself wishing he would stop being so maddeningly calm.

Organ music purred into life.

'Well, real or not, I have to burn the remains of the only mother I'll ever have,' said Patrick, smiling briskly at Julia and setting off down the aisle to the front row where Mary was keeping a seat for him.

4

Mary sat in the front pew of the crematorium staring at Eleanor's coffin, mastering a moment of rebellion. Wondering where Patrick was, she had looked back and seen him bantering flirtatiously with Julia. Now that nothing serious depended on her cultivated indifference, she felt a thud of exasperation. Here she was again, being helpful, while Patrick, in one of the more legitimate throes of his perpetual crisis, bestowed his attention on another woman. Not that she wanted more of his attention; all she wanted from Patrick was for him to be a little freer, a little less predictable. To be fair, and she sometimes wished she could stop being so fair, that's what he wanted as well. She had to remind herself that separation had made them grow closer. No longer hurled together or driven apart by their habitual reactions, they had settled into a relatively stable orbit around the children and around each other.

Her irritation was further blunted when a second backward glance yielded a grave smile from Erasmus Price, her own tiny concession to the consolations of adultery. She had started her affair with him in the South of France, where Patrick had insisted on renting a house during the final disintegration of their marriage, compulsively circling back to the area around his childhood home in Saint-Nazaire. Mary protested against this extravagance in vain; Patrick was in the last phase of his drinking, stumbling around the labyrinth of his unconscious, unavailable for discussion.

The Prices, whose own marriage was falling apart, had sons roughly the same age as Robert and Thomas. Despite these promising symmetries, harmony eluded the two families.

'Anybody who is amazed that "a week is a long time in politics",' said Patrick on the second day, 'should try having the Prices to stay. It turns out to be a fucking eternity. Do you know how he got his wacky name? His father was in the middle of editing the sixty-five-volume Oxford University Press *Complete Works of Erasmus* when his mother interrupted him with the news that she had given birth to a son. "Let's call him Erasmus," he cried, like a man inspired, "or Luther, whose crucial letter to Erasmus I was re-reading only this morning." Given the choice . . .' Patrick subsided.

Mary ignored him, knowing that he was just setting up that day's pretext for more senseless drinking. After Patrick had passed out and Emily Price had gone to bed, Mary sat up late, listening to Erasmus' troubles.

'Some people think that the future belongs to them and that they can lose it,' he said on the first evening, staring into his wine-dark glass, 'but I don't have that sense at all. Even when the work is going well, I wouldn't mind if I could painlessly and instantly expire.'

Why was she drawn to these gloomy men? As a philosopher, at least Erasmus, like Schopenhauer, could make his pessimism into a world view. He cheered up at the mention of the German philosopher.

'My favourite remark of his was the advice he gave to a dying friend: "You are ceasing to be something you would have done better never to become."'

'That must have helped,' said Mary.

'A real nostalgia-buster,' he whispered admiringly.

According to Erasmus his marriage was irreparable; the puzzle for Mary was that it existed at all. As a guest, Emily Price had three main drawbacks: she was incapable of saying please, incapable of saying thank you, and incapable of saying sorry, all the while creating a surge in the demand for these expressions. When she saw Mary applying sunblock to Thomas's sharp pale shoulders, she hurried over and scooped the white cream out of Mary's cupped hand, saying, 'I can't see it without wanting to take some.' By her own account, the same hunger had haunted the birth of her eldest son, 'The moment I saw him, I thought: *I want another one*.'

Emily complained about Cambridge, she complained about her husband and about her sons, she complained about her house, she complained about France and the sun and the clouds and the leaves and the wind and the bottle tops. She couldn't stop; she had to bail out the flooding dinghy of her discontent. Sometimes she set false targets with her complaining: Cambridge was hell, London was great, but when Erasmus applied for a job at London University, she made him withdraw. At the time, she had said that he was too cowardly to apply, but on holiday with the Melroses she admitted the truth, 'I only wanted to move to London so I could complain about the air quality and the schools.'

Patrick was momentarily jolted out of his stupor by the challenge of Emily's personality.

'She could be the centrepiece of a Kleinian Conference – "Talk About Bad Breasts".' He giggled sweatily on the bed while Mary cultivated patience. 'She had a difficult start in life,' he sighed. 'Her mother wouldn't let her use the biros in their house, in case they ran out of ink.' He fell off the bed laughing, knocked his head on the bedside table and had to take a handful of codeine to deal with the bump.

When Mary abandoned tolerance, she did it vehemently. She could feel Emily's underlying sense of privation like the blast from a furnace, but she somehow made the decision to put aside her characteristic empathy, to stay with the annoying consequences and not to feel the distressing causes of Emily's behaviour, especially after Erasmus' clumsy pass, which she hadn't entirely rejected, on the second evening of their endless conversation about marital failure. For a week, they kept each other afloat with the wreckage from their respective marriages. On their return to England it took them two months to admit the futility of trying to build an affair out of these sodden fragments – just long enough for Mary to struggle loyally through Erasmus's latest work, *None the Wiser: developments in the philosophy of consciousness.*

It was the presence of *None the Wiser* on Mary's bedside table that alerted Patrick to his wife's laborious romance.

'You couldn't be reading that book unless you were having an affair with the author,' he guessed through half-closed eyes.

'Believe me, it's virtually impossible even then.'

He gave in to the relief of closing his eyes completely, a strange smile on his lips. She realized with vague disgust that he was pleased to have the huge weight of his infidelity alleviated by her trivial contribution to the other side of the scales.

After that, there was what her mother would have called an 'absolutely maddening' period, when Patrick only emerged from his new blackout bedsit in order to lecture or interrogate her about consciousness studies, sometimes with the slow sententious precision of drunkenness, sometimes with its visionary fever, all delivered with the specious fluency of a man used to pleading a case in public.

'The subject of consciousness, in order to enter the realm of science, must become the object of consciousness, and that is precisely what it cannot do, for the eye cannot perceive itself, cannot vault from its socket fast enough to glimpse the lens. The language of experience and the language of experiment hang like oil and water in the same test tube, never mingling except from the violence of philosophy. The violence of philosophy. Would you agree? Whoops. Don't worry about that lamp, I'll get you a new one.

'Seriously, though, where do you stand on microtubules? Micro-tubular bells. Are you For or Against? Do you think that a theory of extended mind can base itself confidently in quantum non-locality? Do you believe that two linked particles conceived in the warm spiralling quantum womb of a microtubule could continue to inform each other as they rush through vast fields of interstellar darkness; still communicating despite the appearance of *icy separation*? Are you For, or Against? And what difference would it make to experience if these particles did continue to resonate with each other, since it is not particles that we experience?'

'Oh, for God's sake shut up.'

'Who will rid us of the Explanatory Gap?' he shouted, like Henry II requesting an assassin for his troublesome priest. 'And is that gap just a product of our misconstrued discourse?' He ploughed on, 'Is reality a consensual hallucination? And is a nervous breakdown in fact a *refusal to consent*? Go on, don't be shy, tell me what you think?'

'Why don't you go back to your flat and pass out there? I don't want the children seeing you in this state.'

'What state? A state of philosophical enquiry? I thought you would approve.'

'I've got to collect the boys. Please go home.'

'How sweet that you think of it as my home. I'm not in that happy position.'

He would leave, abandoning the consciousness debate for a slamming door. Even 'fucking bitch' had a welcome directness after the twisted use he made of abstract phrases like 'property dualism' to express his shattered sense of home.

She felt less and less guilty about his stormy departures. She dreaded Robert and Thomas asking her about their father's moods, his glaring silences, his declamatory introversion, the spectacle of his clumsiness and misery. The children in fact saw very little of him. He was 'away on business' for the last two months of his drinking and for his month in the Priory. With his unusual talent for mimicry, Robert still managed to impersonate the concerns that Erasmus wrote books about and Patrick used to make veiled attacks on his wife.

'Where do thoughts come from?' he muttered, pacing up and down pensively. 'Before you decide to move your hand where does the decision live?'

'Honestly, Bobby,' said Thomas, letting out a short giggle. 'I expect Brains would know.'

'Well, Mr Tracy,' stammered Robert, bobbing up and down on imaginary strings, 'when you move your hand, your . . . your brain tells you to move your hand, but what tells your brain to tell your hand?'

'That's a real puzzle, Brains,' said Robert, switching to Mr Tracy's basso profundo.

'Weh-well, Mr Tracy,' he returned to the stammering scientist, 'I've invented a machine that may be able to s-solve that puzzle. It's called the Thinkatron.'

'Switch it on, switch it on!' shouted Thomas, swishing his raggie in the air.

Robert made a loud humming sound that gradually grew more threatening.

'Oh, no, it's going to blow up!' warned Thomas. 'The Thinkatron is going to blow up!'

Robert flung himself on the floor with the sound of a huge explosion.

'Gee, Mr Tracy, I guess I must have o-overloaded the primary circuits.'

'Don't worry, Brains,' said Thomas magnanimously, 'I'm

sure you'll work it out. But seriously,' he added to Mary, 'what is the "consciousness debate" that Dada gets so angry about?'

'Oh, God,' said Mary, desperate for someone close to her who didn't want to talk about consciousness. She thought she could put Thomas off by making the subject sound impenetrably learned. 'It's really the philosophical and scientific debate about whether the brain and the mind are identical.'

'Well, of course not,' said Thomas taking his thumb out of his mouth and rounding his eyes, 'I mean, the brain is part of the body and the mind is the outer soul.'

'Quite,' said Mary, amazed.

'What I don't understand,' said Thomas, 'is why things exist.'

'What do you mean? Why there's something rather than nothing?'

'Yes.'

'I have no idea, but it's probably worth staying surprised by that.'

'I am surprised by it, Mama. I'm really surprised.'

When she told Erasmus what Thomas had said about the mind being the 'outer soul', he didn't seem as impressed as she had been.

'It's rather an old-fashioned view,' he commented, 'although the more modern point of view, that the soul is the inner mind, can't be said to have got us anywhere by simply inverting the relationship between two opaque signifiers.'

'Right,' said Mary. 'Still, don't you think it's rather extraordinary for a six-year-old to be so clear about that famously tricky subject?'

'Children often say things that seem extraordinary to us precisely because the big questions are not yet "famously tricky" for them. Oliver is obsessed with death at the moment and he's also only six. He can't bear it, it hasn't become part of How it Is; it's still a scandal, a catastrophic design flaw; it ruins everything. We've got used to the fact of death – although the experience is irreducibly strange. He hasn't found the trick of putting a hood on the executioner, of hiding the experience with the fact. He still sees it as pure experience. I found him crying over a dead fly lying on the windowsill. He asked me why things have to die and all I could offer him was tautology: because nothing lasts for ever.'

Erasmus' need to take a general and theoretical view of every situation sometimes infuriated Mary. All she had wanted was a little compliment for Thomas. Even when she finally told him that she felt there was no point in carrying on with their affair, he accepted her position with insulting equanimity, and then went on to admit that he had 'recently been toying with the Panpsychist approach', as if this unveiling of the wild side of his intellect might tempt her to change her mind.

Mary had decided not to take the children to Eleanor's funeral, but to leave them with her mother. Thomas had no memory of Eleanor and Robert was so steeped in his father's sense of betrayal that the occasion would be more likely to revive faded hostility than to relieve a natural sense of sadness and loss. They had all been together for the last time about two years before in Kew Gardens, during the bluebell season, soon after Eleanor had come back from Saint-Nazaire to live in England. On their way to the Woodland Walk, Mary pushed Eleanor's wheelchair through the twisting Rhododendron Dell, hemmed in by walls of outrageous colour. Patrick hung back, gulping down the odd miniature of Johnny Walker Black Label in moments of feigned fascination with a sprawling pink or orange blossom, while Robert and Thomas explored the gigantic bushes ranged against the slopes on either side. When a golden pheasant emerged onto the path, its saffron-yellow and blood-red feathers shining like enamel, Mary stopped the wheelchair, astonished. The pheasant crossed the hot cinder with the bobbing majesty of an avian gait, the price of a strained talent, like the high head of a swimming dog. Eleanor, crumpled in her seat, wearing old baby-blue flannel trousers and a maroon cardigan with big flat buttons and holes at the elbow, stared at the bird with the alarmed distaste that had taken up residence in her frozen features. Patrick, determined not to talk to his mother, hurried past muttering that he'd 'better keep an eye on the boys'.

Eleanor gestured frantically to Mary to come closer and then produced one of her rare whole sentences.

'I can never forget that he's David's son.'

'I don't think it's his father who haunts him these days,' said Mary, surprised by her own sharpness.

'Haunts . . .' said Eleanor.

Mary was thrusting the wheelchair through the dappled potholes of the Woodland Walk by the time Eleanor was able to speak again.

'Are . . . you . . . all . . . right?'

She asked the same question again and again, with mounting agitation, ignoring the haze of bluebells, mingled with the yellow stalks of wild garlic, under the shifting and swelling shade of the oaks. She was trying to save Mary from Patrick, not out of any insight into her circumstances, but in order to save herself, by some retroactive magic, from David. Mary's attempts to give an affirmative answer tormented Eleanor, since the only answer she could accept was: 'No, I'm not all right! I'm living in hell with a tyrannical madman, just as you did, my poor darling. On the other hand, I sincerely believe that the universe will save us, thanks to the awesome shamanic powers of the wounded healer that you truly are.'

For some reason Mary couldn't quite bring herself to say this, and yet there was still a troubling sisterhood between the two women. Mary recognized certain features of Eleanor's upbringing all too easily: the intense shyness, the all-important nanny, the diffident sense of self, the masochistic attraction to difficult men. Eleanor was the cautionary tale of these forces, a warning against the worthlessness of self-sacrifice when there was almost no self to sacrifice, of dealing with being lost by getting more lost. Above all, she was a baby, not a 'big baby' like so many adults, but a small baby perfectly preserved in the pickling jar of money, alcohol and fantasy.

Since that colourful day in Kew, neither of the boys had been taken to see their grandmother in her nursing home. Patrick stopped visiting her as well, after her excruciating flirtation with assisted suicide two years before. Only Mary persevered, sometimes with the scant dutiful reminder that Eleanor was, after all, her mother-in-law; sometimes with the more obscure conviction that Eleanor was out of balance with her family and that the work of redressing that balance must start straight away, whether Eleanor was able to participate or not. It was certainly strange, as the months wore on, to be talking into space, hoping that she was doing some good, while Eleanor stared ever more rigidly and blankly at the ceiling. And in the absence of any dialogue, she often ran aground on her contempt for Eleanor's failure to protect her child.

She could remember Eleanor describing the first few weeks after she returned from hospital with the infant Patrick. David was so tormented by his son's crying that he ordered her to take the noisy brat to the remotest room in the attic. Eleanor already felt exiled enough in David's beloved Cornwall, at the end of a headland overlooking an impenetrably wooded estuary, and she could hardly believe, as she was thrown out of her bedroom too suddenly to put on her slippers, or to collect a blanket for the baby, that there was a further exile available, a small cold room in the big cold house. For her the building was already sodden with melancholy horror. She had married David in the Truro registry office when she was heavily pregnant with their first child. Overestimating his medical skills, he had encouraged her to have the child at home. Without the incubator that she needed, Georgina died two days later. David sailed his boat out into the estuary, buried her at sea, and then disappeared for three days to get drunk. Eleanor stayed in bed, bleeding and abandoned, staring at the grey water through the bay window of her bedroom. After Georgina's death, she had refused to go to bed with David. One evening he punched her in the back of the knees as she was going upstairs. When she fell, he twisted her arm behind her back and raped her on the staircase. Just as she thought she was finally disgusted enough to leave him, she found that she was pregnant. Up in the attic with the new rape-born baby in her arms, she felt hysterically unconfident. Looking at the narrow bed she was gripped by the fear that if they lay down on it together, she would roll over and asphyxiate him, and so she chose the wooden chair in the corner, next to the empty fireplace, and sat up all night, clutching him in her arms. During those nights in the wooden chair, she was sucked down into sleep again and again, and then woken abruptly by sensing the baby's body sliding down her nightdress towards the precipice of her knees. She would catch him at the last moment, terrified that his soft head was about to crash onto the hard floor; and yet unable to go to the bed they both longed for, in case she crushed him to death.

The days were a little better. The maternity nurse came

in to help, the housekeeper bustled about in the kitchen, and with David out sailing and drinking, the house took on a superficially cheerful atmosphere. The three women fussed over Patrick and when Eleanor was resting back in her own bedroom she almost forgot about the dreadful nights; she almost forgot about the death of Georgina when she closed her eyes and could no longer see the stretch of grey water outside her window, and when she fed the baby from her breasts and they fell asleep together, she almost forgot about the violence that had brought him into the world.

But then one day, three weeks after they came back from hospital, David stayed behind. He was in a dangerous mood from the start; she could smell the brandy in his coffee and see the furious jealousy in his looks. By lunchtime, he had wounded everyone in the house with his cutting remarks, and all the women were anxious, feeling him pacing around, waiting for the chance to hurt and humiliate them. Nevertheless, they were surprised when he strode into the kitchen, carrying a battered leather bag and wearing a surgeon's ill-fitting green pyjamas. He ordered them to clear a space on the scrubbed oak table, unfolded a towel, took out a wooden case of surgical instruments from the bag and opened it next to the towel. He asked for a saucepan of boiling water, as if everything had already been agreed and everyone knew what was going on.

'What for?' said the housekeeper, the first to wake from the trance.

'To sterilize the instruments,' David answered in the tone of a man explaining something very obvious to someone very stupid. 'The time has come to perform a circumcision. Not, I assure you,' he added, as if to allay their innermost fears, 'for religious reasons,' he allowed himself a fleeting smile, 'but for medical ones.'

'You've been drinking,' Eleanor blurted out.

'Only a beaker of surgical spirit,' he quipped, a little giddy from the prospect of the operation; and then, no longer in the mood for fun, 'Bring me the boy.'

'Are you sure it's for the best?' asked the maternity nurse.

'Do not question my authority,' said David, throwing everything into it: the older man, the doctor, the employer, the centuries of command, but also the paralysing dart of his psychological presence, which made it seem life-threatening to oppose him.

His credentials as a murderer were well established in Eleanor's imagination. Late at night, when he was down to one listener, amongst the empty bottles and crushed cigars, David was fond of telling the story of an Indian pig-sticking hunt he had been on in the late nineteen-twenties. He was thrilled by the danger of galloping through the high grass with a lance, chasing a wild boar whose tusks could ruin a horse's legs, throw a rider to the ground and gore him to death. Impaling one of these fast, tough pigs was also a terrific pleasure, more involving than a long-distance kill. The only blemish on the expedition was that one of the party was bitten by a wild dog and developed the symptoms of rabies. Three days from the nearest hospital, it was already too late to help, and so the hunters decided to truss up their foaming and thrashing friend in one of the thick nets originally intended for transporting the bodies of the dead pigs, and to hoist him off the ground, tying the corners of the net to the branches of a big jacaranda tree. It was challenging, even for these hard men, to enjoy the sense of deep relaxation that follows a day of invigorating sport with this parcel of hydrophobic anguish dangling from a nearby tree. The row of lanterns down the dinner table, the quiet gleam of silver, the well-trained servants, the triumph of imposing civilization on the wild vastness of the Indian night, seemed to have been thrown into question. David could only just make out, against a background of screams, the splendid tale of Archie Montcrieff driving a pony and trap into the Viceroy's ballroom. Archie had worn an improvised toga and shouted obscenities in 'an outlandish kind of Cockney Latin', while the pony manured the dance floor. If his father hadn't been such a friend of the Viceroy's he might have had to resign his commission, but as it was, the viceroy admitted, privately of course, that Archie had raised his spirits during 'another damned dull dance'.

When the story was finished, David rose from the table muttering, 'This noise is intolerable,' and went into his tent to fetch his pistol. He walked over to the rabies victim and shot him in the head. Returning to the dumbfounded table, he sat down with a 'feeling of absolute calm' and said, 'Much the kindest thing to do.' Gradually, the word spread around the table: much the kindest thing to do. Rich and powerful men, some of them quite high up in government, and one of them a judge, couldn't help agreeing with him. With the silencing of the screams and a few pints of whisky and soda, it became the general view by the end of the evening that David had done something exceptionally courageous. David would almost smile as he described how he had brought everyone at the table round, and then in a fit of piety, he would sometimes finish by saying that although at the time he had not yet set eyes on a copy of *Gray's Anatomy*, he really thought of that pistol shot as the beginning of his 'love affair with medicine'.

Eleanor felt obliged to hand over the baby to him in the kitchen in Cornwall. The baby screamed and screamed. Eleanor thought there must be dogs whimpering in their kennels a hundred miles away, the screams were so loud and high. All the women huddled together crying and begging David to stop and to be careful and to give the baby some local anaesthetic. They knew this was no operation, it was an attack by a furious old man on his son's genitals; but like the chorus in a play, they could only comment and wail, without being able to alter the action.

'I wanted to say, "You've already killed Georgina and now you want to kill Patrick," ' Eleanor told Mary, to show how bold she would have been if she had said anything at all. 'I wanted to call the police!'

Well, why didn't you? was all that Mary could think, but she said nothing about Eleanor saying nothing; she just nodded and went on being a good listener.

'It was like . . .' said Eleanor, 'it was like that Goya painting of Saturn devouring his son.' Brought up surrounded by great paintings, Eleanor had experienced a late-adolescent crush on the History of Art, rudely guillotined by her disinheritance, and replaced by a proclivity for bright dollops of optimistic symbolism. Nevertheless, she could still remember, when she was twenty, driving through Spain in her first car, and being shocked, on a visit to the Prado, by the black vision of those late Goyas.

Mary was struck by the comparison, because it was unusual for Eleanor to make that sort of connection, and also because she knew the painting well, and could easily visualize the gaping mouth, the staring eyes and the ragged white hair of the old god of melancholy, mad with jealousy and the fear of usurpation, as he fed on the bleeding corpse of his decapitated child. Watching Eleanor plead for exoneration made Mary realize that her mother-in-law could never have protected anyone else when she was so entranced by her own vulnerability, so desperate to be saved. Later in her marriage, Eleanor did manage to get police protection for herself. It was in Saint-Nazaire, just after she learned about her mother's death and, not yet knowing the content of the will, was expecting to get control of a world-class fortune. She had to fly to Rome later that morning for the funeral, and David sat opposite her at the breakfast table, brooding about the possible consequences of his wife's increased independence.

'You're looking forward to getting your hands on all that lovely money,' he said, walking round to her side of the table. She got up, sensing danger. 'But you're not going to,' he added, grabbing her and pressing his thumbs expertly into her throat, 'because I'm going to kill you.'

Almost unconscious, she had managed to knee him in the balls with all her remaining strength. In the reflex of pain, he let go long enough for her to slide across the table and bolt out of the house. He pursued her for a while, but the twenty-three-year age difference took its toll on his tired body and she escaped into the woods. Convinced that he would follow by car, she struggled through the undergrowth to the local police station, and arrived scratched, bleeding and in tears. The two gendarmes who drove her back to the house stood guard over a proud and sulky David while she packed her bags for Rome. She left with relief, but without Patrick, who stayed behind with only the flimsy protection of yet another terrified nanny – they lasted, on average, about six weeks. Eleanor might have been out of reach, but once he had given the nanny a munificent day out, and sent Yvette home, David had the consolation of torturing his son without any interference from the gendarmerie.

In the end, Eleanor's betrayal of the maternal instinct that ruled Mary's own life formed an absolute barrier to the liking she could feel for her. She could remember her own sons at three weeks old: their hot silky heads burrowing their way back into the shelter of her body to soften the shock of being born. The thought of handing them over, before their skin could bear the roughness of wool, to be hacked at with knives by a cruel and sinister man, required a level of treachery that blinded her imagination.

No doubt David had searched hard among the foolish and the meek to find a woman who could put up with his special tastes, but once his depravity was on full display, how could Eleanor escape the charge of colluding with a sadist and a paedophile? She had invited children from other families to spend their holidays in the South of France and, like Patrick, they had been raped and inducted into an underworld of shame and secrecy, backed by convincing threats of punishment and death. Just before her first stroke, Eleanor received a letter from one of those children, saying that after a lifetime of insomnia, self-harm, frigidity, promiscuity, perpetual anxiety and suicide attempts, she had started to lead a more normal life, thanks to seven years of therapy, and had finally been able to forgive Eleanor for not protecting her during the summer she stayed with the Melroses. When she showed the letter to Mary, Eleanor dwelt on the injustice of being made to feel guilty about a category of behaviour she had not even known existed, although it was going on in the bedroom next to hers.

And yet how ignorant could she really have been? The year before the arrival of the letter that so dismayed Eleanor, Patrick had received a letter from Sophie, an old au pair, who had heroically stayed with the Melroses for more than two years, more than twenty times the average endurance shown by the parade of incredulous young foreign women who passed through the house. In her letter, Sophie confessed to decades of guilt about the time she had spent looking after Patrick. She used to hear screams down the corridor of the house in Lacoste, and she knew that Patrick was being tormented, not merely punished or frustrated, but she was only nineteen at the time and she hesitated to intervene. She also confessed that she was terrified of David and, despite being genuinely fond of Patrick and feeling some pity for Eleanor, longed to get away from his grotesque family.

If Sophie knew that something was terribly wrong, how could Eleanor not have known? It was common enough to ignore what was seemingly impossible to ignore, but Eleanor stuck to her blindness with uncommon tenacity. Through all her programmes of self-discovery and shamanic healing, she avoided acknowledging her passion for avoidance. If she had ever discovered her real 'power animals', Mary suspected they would have been the Three Monkeys: See no Evil, Hear no Evil, Speak no Evil. Mary also suspected that these grim vigilantes had been killed off by one of her strokes, flooding her all at once with the fragments of knowledge that she had kept sealed off from each other, like the cells of a secret organization. In a parody of wholeness, the fragments converged when it was too late to make them cohere.

Eleanor was entirely confined to the nursing home for the last two years of her life, rarely leaving her bed. For the first year, Mary went on assuming that at least one of the threads holding Eleanor to her tormented existence was concern for her family, and she continued to reassure her that they were well. Later, she began to see that what really trapped Eleanor was not the strength of her attachments, but rather their weakness: without anything substantial to 'let go' of, she was left with only the volatility of her guilt and confusion. Part of her was aching to die, but she could never find the time; there was no gap between the proliferating anxieties; the desire to die collided instantly with the dread of dying, which in turn gave birth to a renewed desire.

For the second year, Mary was largely silent. She went into the room and wished Eleanor well. What else was there to do?

The last time she had seen her mother-in-law was two weeks ago. By then Eleanor had achieved a tranquillity indistinguishable from pure absence. Gaunt and drawn, her face seemed incapable of any deliberate change. Mary could remember Eleanor telling her, in one of those alienating confidential chats, that she knew exactly when she was going to die. The mysterious source of this information (Astrology? Channelling? A morbid guru? A drumming session? A prophetic dream?) was never unveiled, but the news was delivered with the slightly boastful serenity of pure fantasy. Mary felt that the certainty of death and the uncertainty of both its timing and its meaning were fundamental facts of life. Eleanor, on the other hand, knew exactly when she was going to die and that her death was not final. By the end, as far as Mary could tell, this conviction had deserted Eleanor, along with all the other features of her personality, as if a sandstorm had raged through her, ripping away every sign of comfort, and leaving a smooth and sterile landscape under a dry blank sky.

Still, Eleanor had died on Easter Sunday, and Mary knew that nothing could have pleased her more. Or would have pleased her more, had she known. Perhaps she did know, even though her mind appeared to be fixed in a realm removed from anything as mundane as a calendar. Even then there was still no way of knowing whether that was the day she had been expecting to die.

Mary adjusted her position on the uncomfortable crematorium bench. Where was a convincing and practical theory of consciousness when you really needed it? She glanced back a few rows at Erasmus, but he appeared to have fallen asleep. As she turned back to the coffin a few feet in front of her, Mary's speculations collapsed abruptly. She found herself imagining, with a vividness she couldn't sustain while it was still going on, how it had felt for Eleanor during those two last brutal years, having her individuality annihilated, faculty by faculty, memory by memory.

Her eyes blurred with tears.

'Are you all right?' whispered Patrick, as he sat down next to her.

'I was thinking about your mother,' she said.

'A highly suitable choice,' Patrick murmured, in the voice of a sycophantic shopkeeper.

For some reason Mary started to laugh uncontrollably, and Patrick started laughing too, and they both had to bite their lower lips and keep their shoulders from shaking too wildly.

5

Hoping to master his fit of grief-stricken laughter, Patrick breathed out slowly and concentrated on the dull tension of waiting to begin. The organ sighed, as if bored of searching for a decent tune, and then meandered on resignedly. He must pull himself together: he was here to mourn his mother's death, a serious business.

There were various obstructions in his way. For a long time the feeling of madness brought on by the loss of his French home had made it impossible to get over his resentment of Eleanor. Without Saint-Nazaire, a primitive part of him was deprived of the imaginary care that had kept him sane as a child. He was certainly attached to the beauty of the place, but much more deeply to a secret protection that he dare not renounce in case it left him utterly destroyed. The shifting faces formed by the cracks, stains and hollows of the limestone mountain opposite the house used to keep him company. The line of pine trees along its ridge was like a column of soldiers coming to his rescue. There were hiding places where nobody had ever found him; and vine terraces to jump down, giving him the feeling he could fly when he had to flee. There was a dangerous well where he could drown rocks and clods of earth, without drowning himself. The most heroic connection of all was with the gecko that had taken custody of his soul in a moment of crisis and dashed out onto the roof, to safety and to exile. How could it ever find him again, if Patrick wasn't there any more?

On his last night in Saint-Nazaire there was a spectacular storm. Sheet lightning flickered behind ribbed banks of cloud, making the dark bowl of the valley tremble with light. At first, fat tropical raindrops dented the dusty ground, but soon enough, rivulets guttered down the steep paths, and little waterfalls flowed from step to step on the terraces. Patrick wandered outside into the warm heavy rain, feeling mad. He knew that he had to end his magical contract with this landscape, but the electric air and the violent protest of the storm renewed the archaic mentality of a child, as if the same thick piano wires, hammered by thunder and pelting rain, ran through his body and the land. With water streaming down his face there was no need for tears, no need to scream with the sky cracking overhead. He stood in the drive, among the milky puddles and the murmur of new streams and the smell of the wet rosemary, until he sank to the ground, weighed down by what he was unable to give up, and sat motionless in the gravel and the mud. Forked lightning landed like antlers on the limestone mountain. In that sudden flash, he made out a shape on the ground between him and the wall that ran along the edge of the drive. Concentrating in the murky light, he saw that a toad had ventured out into the watery world beyond the laurel bushes, where Patrick imagined it had been waiting all summer for the rain, and was now resting gratefully on a bar of muddy ground between two puddles. They sat in front of each other, perfectly still.

Patrick pictured the white corpses of the toads he used to see each spring, at the bottom of the stone pools. Around their spent bodies, hundreds of soft black tadpoles clung to the grey-green algae on the walls, or wriggled across the open pond, or overflowed into the runnels that carried the water from pool to pool, between the source and the stream in the crease of the valley. Some of the tadpoles slipped limply down the slope, others swam frantically against the current. Robert and Thomas spent hours each Easter holiday, removing the little dams that formed overnight, and when the covered part of the channel was blocked and the grass around the lower pond flooded, airlifting the stranded tadpoles in their cupped hands. Patrick could remember doing the same thing as a child, and the sense of giant compassion that he used to feel as he released them back into the safety of the pond through his flooding fingers.

In those days there had been a chorus of frogs during the spring nights, and during the day, sitting on the lily pads in the crescent pond, bullfrogs blowing their insides out like bubble gum; but in the system of imaginary protection that the land used to allow him, it was the lucky tree frogs that really counted. If only he could touch one of them, everything would be all right. They were hard to find. The round suckers on the tips of their feet meant that they could hang anywhere in the tree, camouflaged by the bright green of a new leaf or an unripe fig. When he did see one of these tiny frogs, fixed to the smooth grey bark, its brilliant skin stretched over a sharp skeleton, it looked to him like pulsing jewellery. He would reach out his index finger and touch it lightly for good luck. It might have only happened once, but he had thought about it a thousand times.

Remembering that charged and tentative gesture, he now looked with some scepticism at the warty head of the sodden toad in front of him. At the same time, he remembered his A-level Arden edition of *King Lear* with its footnote about the jewel in the head of the toad, the emblem of the treasure hidden in the midst of ugly, muddy, repulsive experience. One day he would live without superstition, but not yet. He reached out and touched the head of the toad. He felt some of the same awe he had felt as a child, but the resurgence of what he was about to lose gave the feeling a self-cancelling intensity. The mad fusion of mythologies created an excess of meaning that might at any moment flip into a world with no meaning at all. He drew away and, like someone returning to the familiar compromises of his city flat after a long exotic journey, recognized that he was a middle-aged man, sitting eccentrically in his muddy driveway in the middle of a thunderstorm, trying to communicate with a toad. He got up stiffly and slouched back to the house, feeling realistically miserable, but still kicking the puddles in defiance of his useless maturity.

Eleanor had given Saint-Nazaire away, but at least she had provided it in the first place, if only as a massive substitute for herself, a motherland that was there to cover for her incapacities. In a sense its loveliness was a decoy, the branches of almond blossom reaching into a cloudless sky, the unopened irises, like paintbrushes dipped in bluc, thc clear amber resin bleeding from the gunmetal bark of the cherry trees – all of that was a decoy, he must stop thinking about it. A child's need for protection would have assembled a system out of whatever materials came to hand, however ritual or bizarre. It might have been a spider in a broom cupboard, or the appearance of a neighbour across the well of a block of flats, or the number of red cars between the front door and the school gates, that took on the burden of love and reassurance. In his case, it had been a hillside in France. His home had stretched from the dark pinewood at the top of the slope, all the way to the pale bamboo that grew beside the stream at its foot. In between were terraces where vine shoots burst from twisted stumps that spent the winter looking like rusted iron, and olive trees rushed from green to grey and grey to green in the combing wind. Halfway down the slope were the cluster of houses and cypresses and the network of pools where he had experienced the most horror and negotiated the most far-fetched reprieves. Even the steep mountainside opposite the house was colonized by his imagination, and not only with the army of trees marching along its crest. Later on, its rejection of human encroachment became an image of his own less reliable aloofness.

Nobody could spend their whole life in a place without missing it when they left. Pathetic fallacies, projections, substitutions and displacements were part of the inevitable traffic between any mind and its habitual surroundings, but the pathological intensity he had brought to these operations made it vital for him to see through them. What would it be like to live without consolation, or the desire for consolation? He would never find out, unless he uprooted the consolatory system that had started on the hillside at Saint-Nazaire and then spread to every medicine cabinet, bed and bottle he had come across since; substitutes substituting for substitutes: the system was always more fundamental than its contents, and the mental act more fundamental still. What if memories were just memories, without any consolatory or persecutory power? Would they exist at all, or was it always emotional pressure that summoned images from what was potentially all of experience so far? Even if that was the case, there must be better librarians than panic, resentment and dismembering nostalgia to search among the dim and crowded stacks.

Whereas ordinary generosity came from a desire to give something to someone, Eleanor's philanthropy had come from a desire to give everything to anyone. The sources of the compulsion were complex. There was the repetition syndrome of a disinherited daughter; there was a rejection of the materialism and snobbery of her mother's world; and there was the basic shame at having any money at all, an unconscious drive to make her net worth and her self-worth converge in a perfect zero; but apart from all these negative forces, there was also the inspiring precedent of her great-aunt Virginia Jonson. With a rare enthusiasm for an ancestor, Eleanor used to tell Patrick all about the heroic scale of Virginia's charitable works; how she made so much difference to so many lives, showing that ardent selflessness which is often more stubborn than open egotism.

Virginia had already lost two sons when her husband died in 1901. Over the next twenty-five years she demolished half the Jonson fortune with her mournful philanthropy. In 1903 she endowed the Thomas J. Jonson Memorial Fund with twenty million dollars and in her will with another twenty-five million, at a time when these were sums of a rare vastness, rather than the typical Christmas bonus of a mediocre hedge-fund manager. She also collected paintings by Titian, Rubens, Van Dyck, Rembrandt, Tintoretto, Bronzino, Lorenzo di Credi, Murillo, Velasquez, Hals, Le Brun, Gainsborough, Romney and Botticelli, and donated them to the Jonson Wing of the Cleveland Art Museum. This cultural legacy was what interested Eleanor least, perhaps because it resembled too closely the private acquisitive frenzy taking place in her own branch of the Jonson family. What she really admired were Virginia's Good Works, the hospitals and YMCAs she built, and above all, the new town she created on a four-hundred-acre site, in the hope of clearing Cleveland's slums by giving ideal housing to the poor. It was named Friendship, after her summer place in Newport. When it was completed in 1926, Virginia addressed a 'Greeting' to its first residents in the *Friendship Messenger*.

> Good morning. Is the sun a little brighter, there in Friendship? Is the air a little fresher? Is your home a little sweeter? Is your housework somewhat easier? And the children – do you feel safer about them? Are their faces a little ruddier; are their legs a little sturdier? Do they laugh and play a lot louder in Friendship? Then I am content.

To Eleanor, there had been something deeply moving about this Queen Victoria of Ohio, a little woman with a puffy white face, always dressed in black, always reclusive, seeking no personal glory for her charitable acts, driven by deep religious convictions, still naming streets and buildings after her dead sons right up to the end – her Albert had his Avenue and her Sheldon had his Close in the safer, child-friendly precincts of Friendship.

At the same time, the coolness of relations between the Jonson sisters and their Aunt Virginia showed that in the opinion of her nieces she had not struck the right balance between the civic-minded and the family-minded. If anyone was going to give away Jonson money, the sisters felt that it should be them, rather than the daughter of a penniless clergyman who had married their Uncle Thomas. They were each left a hundred thousand dollars in Virginia's will. Even her friends did better. She endowed a Trust with two and a half million dollars to provide annuities for sixty-nine friends for the rest of their lives. Patrick suspected that Virginia's talent for annoying Eleanor's mother and her aunts was the unacknowledged source of Eleanor's admiration for her great-aunt. She and Virginia stood apart from the dynastic ambitions of wealth. For them, money was a trust from God that must be used to do good in the world. Patrick hoped that during her frantic silence in the nursing home, Eleanor had been dreaming, at least some of the time, of the place she might occupy next to the great Jonson philanthropist who had Gone Before.

Virginia's meanness to the Jonson Sisters was no doubt underpinned by the knowledge that her brother-in-law would leave each of them with a huge fortune.

Nevertheless, by their generation, the thrill of being rich was already shadowed by the shocks of disinheritance and the ironies of philanthropy. The 1929 Crash came two years after Virginia's death. The poor became destitute, and the white middle classes, who were much poorer than they used to be, fled the inner city for the half-timbered cosiness of Friendship, even though Virginia had built it in memory of a husband who was 'a friend to the Negro race'.

Eleanor's friendship was with something altogether vaguer than the Negro race. 'Friend to the neo-shamanic revival of the Celtic Twilight' seemed less likely to yield concrete social progress. During Patrick's childhood, her charitable focus had resembled Virginia's Good Works much more closely, except that it was devoted overwhelmingly to children. He had often been left alone with his father while Eleanor went to a committee meeting of the Save the Children Fund. The absolute banishment of irony from Eleanor's earnest persona created a black market for the blind sarcasm of her actions. Later, it was Father Tortelli and his Neapolitan street urchins who were the targets of her evasive charity. Patrick could not help thinking that this passion for saving all the children of the world was an unconscious admission that she could not save her own child. Poor Eleanor, how frightened she must have been. Patrick suddenly wanted to protect her.

When Patrick's childhood had ended and the inarticulate echoes of her own childhood faded, Eleanor stopped supporting children's charities, and embarked on the second adolescence of her New Age quest. She showed the same genius for generalization that had characterized her rescue of children, except that her identity crisis was not merely global, but interplanetary and cosmic as well, without sinking one millimetre into the resistant bedrock of self-knowledge. No stranger to 'the energy of the universe', she remained a stranger to herself. Patrick could not pretend that he would have applauded any charitable gift involving all of his mother's property, but once that became inevitable, it was a further pity that it had all gone to the Transpersonal Foundation.

Aunt Virginia would not have approved either. She wanted to bring real benefits to fellow human beings. Her influence on Eleanor had been indirect but strong and, like all the other strong influences, matriarchal. The Jonson men sometimes seemed to Patrick like those diminutive male spiders that quickly discharge their only important responsibility before being eaten by the much larger females. The founder's two sons left two widows: Virginia, the widow of good works, and Eleanor's grandmother, the widow of good marriages, whose second marriage to the son of an English earl launched her three daughters on their dazzling social and matrimonial careers. Patrick knew that Nancy had been intending to write a book about the Jonsons for the last twenty years. Without any tiresome show of false modesty, she had said to him, 'I mean, it would be much better than Henry James and Edith Wharton and those sort of people, because it *really* happened.'

Men who married Jonson women didn't fare much better than the founder's sons. Eleanor's father and her Uncle Vladimir were both alcoholics, emasculated by getting the heiress they thought they wanted. They ended up sitting together in White's, nursing their wounds over a luxurious drink; divorced, discarded, cut off from their children. Eleanor was brought up wondering how an heiress could avoid destroying the man she married, unless he was already too corrupt to be destroyed, or rich enough to be immune. She had chosen from the first category in marrying David, and yet his malice and pride, which were impressive enough to begin with, were still magnified by the humiliation of depending on his wife's money.

Patrick was not one of the Jonson castrati by marriage, but he knew what it was to be born into a matriarchal world, given money by a grandmother he scarcely knew, and cut off by a mother who still expected him to look after her. The psychological impact of these powerful women, generous from an impersonal distance, treacherous up close, had furnished him with one basic model of what a woman should look like and how she would in fact turn out to be. The object of desire generated by this combination was the Hiso Bitch – Hiso was an acronym for high society invented by a Japanese friend of his. The Hiso Bitch had to be a reincarnation of a Jonson Sister: glamorous, intensely social, infinitely rich in the pursuit of pleasure, embedded among beautiful possessions. As if this was not enough (as if this was not too much) she also had to be sexually voracious and morally disoriented. His first girlfriend had been an embryonic version of the type. He still thought sometimes about kneeling in front of her, in the pool of light from the reading lamp, the shining folds of her black silk pyjamas gathered between her splayed legs, a trickle of blood running down her proffered arm, the gasp of pleasure, whispering, 'Too much too much,' the film of sweat on her angular face, the syringe in his hand, her first fix of cocaine. He did his best to addict her, but she was a vampire of a different sort, feeding off the despairing obsession of the men who surrounded her, draining ever more socially assured admirers in the hope of acquiring their sense of belonging, even as she trivialized it in their eyes by making herself seem the only thing worth having and then walking away.

In his early thirties his compulsive search for disappointment brought him Inez, the Sistine Chapel of the Hiso Bitch. She insisted that every one of her cartload of lovers was exclusive to her, a condition she failed to secure from her husband, but successfully extorted from Patrick, who left the relatively sane and generous woman he was living with in order to plunge into the hungry vacuum of Inez's love. Her absolute indifference to the feelings of her lovers made her sexual receptiveness into a kind of free-fall. In the end the cliff he fell off was as flat as the one Gloucester was made to leap off by his devoted son: a cliff of blindness and guilt and imagination, with no beetling rocks at its base. But she did not know that and neither did he.

With her curling blonde hair and her slender limbs and her beautiful clothes, Inez was alluring in an obvious way, and yet it was easy enough to see that her slightly protruding blue eyes were blank screens of self-love on which a small selection of fake emotions was allowed to flicker. She made rather haphazard impersonations of someone who has relationships with others. Based on the gossip of her courtiers, a diet of Hollywood movies and the projection of her own cunning calculations, these guesses might be sentimental or nasty, but were always vulgar and melodramatic. Since she hadn't the least interest in the answer, she was inclined to ask, 'How *are* you?' with great gravity, at least half a dozen times. She was often exhausted by the thought of how generous she was, whereas the exhaustion really stemmed from the strain of not giving away anything at all. 'I'm going to buy six thoroughbred Arab stallions for the Queen of Spain's birthday,' she announced one day. 'Don't you think it's a good idea?'

'Is six enough?' asked Patrick.

'You don't think six is enough? Do you have any idea how much they cost?'

He was amazed when she did buy the horses, less surprised when she kept them for herself and bored when she sold them back to the man she had bought them from. However maddening she was as a friend, it was in the cut and thrust of romance that her talents excelled.

'I've never felt this way before,' she would say with troubled profundity. 'I don't think anybody has really understood me until now. Do you know that? Do you know how important you are to me?' Tears would well up in her eyes as she hardly dared to whisper, 'I don't think I've ever felt at home until now,' nestling in his strong manly arms.

Soon afterwards he would be left waiting for days in some foreign hotel where Inez never bothered to show up. Her social secretary would call twice a day to say that she had been delayed but was really on her way now. Inez knew that this tantalizing absence was the most efficient way to ensure that he would think of nothing but her, while leaving her free to do the same thing at a safe distance. His mind might wander almost anywhere if she was lying in his arms talking nonsense, whereas if he was nailed to the telephone, haemorrhaging money and abandoning all his other responsibilities, he was bound to think of her constantly. When they did eventually meet up, she would hurry to point out how unbearable it had all been for her, ruthlessly monopolizing the suffering generated by her endlessly collapsing plans.

Why would anyone allow himself to be annihilated by such shallowness, unless a buried image of a careless woman was longing for outward form? Lateness, let-down, longing for the unobtainable: these were the mechanisms that turned a powerful matriarchal stimulant into a powerful maternal depressant. Bewildering lateness, especially, took him directly into an early despair, waiting in vain on the stairs for his mother to come, terrified that she was dead.

Patrick suddenly experienced these old emotions as a physical oppression. He ran his fingers along the inside of his collar to make sure that it was not concealing a tightening noose. He couldn't bear the lure of disappointment any longer, or for that matter the lure of consolation, its Siamese twin. He must somehow get beyond both of them, but first he had to mourn his mother. In a sense he had been missing her all his life. It was not the end of closeness but the end of the longing for closeness that he had to mourn. How futile his longing must have been for him to disperse himself into the land at Saint-Nazaire. If he tried to imagine anything deeper than his old home, he just pictured himself standing there, straining to see something elusive, shielding his eyes to watch a dragonfly dip into the burning water at noon, or starlings twisting against the setting sun.

He could now see that the loss of Saint-Nazaire was not an obstacle to mourning his mother but the only possible means to do so. Letting go of the imaginary world he had put in her place released him from that futile longing and took him into a deeper grief. He was free to imagine how terrified Eleanor must have been, for a woman of such good intentions, to have abandoned her desire to love him, which he did not doubt, and be compelled to pass on so much fear and panic instead. At last he could begin to mourn her for herself, for the tragic person she had been.

6

Patrick had little idea what to expect from the ceremony. He had been on a business trip to America at the time of his mother's death and pleaded the impossibility of preparing anything to say or read, leaving Mary to take over the arrangements. He had only arrived back from New York yesterday, just in time to go to Bunyon's funeral parlour, and now that he was sitting in a pew next to Mary, picking up the order of service for thc first time, he realized how unready he was for this exploration of his mother's confusing life. On the front of the little booklet was a photograph of Eleanor in the sixties, throwing her arms out as if to embrace the world, her dark glasses firmly on and no breathalyser test results available. He hesitated to look inside; this was the muddle, the pile-up of fact and feeling he had been trying to outmanoeuvre since the end of Eleanor's flirtation with assisted suicide two years ago. She had died as a person before her body died, and he had tried to pretend that her life was over before it really was, but no amount of anticipation could cheat the demands of an actual death and now, with a combination of embarrassment and fear and evasiveness, he leant forward and slipped the order of service back onto the shelf in front of him. He would find out what was in it soon enough.

He had gone to America after receiving a letter from Brown and Stone LLP, the lawyers for the John J. Jonson

Corporation, known affectionately as 'Triple J'. They had been informed by 'the family' – Patrick now suspected that it was Henry who had told them – that Eleanor Melrose was incompetent to administer her own affairs, and since she was the beneficiary of a trust created by her grandfather, of which Patrick was the ultimate beneficiary, measures should be taken to procure him a US power of attorney in order to administer the money on his mother's behalf. All this was news to Patrick and he was freshly astonished by his mother's capacity for secrecy. In his amazement he failed to ask how much the trust contained and he got onto the plane to New York not knowing whether he would be put in charge of twenty thousand dollars or two hundred thousand.

Joe Rich and Peter Zirkovsky met him in one of the smaller oval-tabled, glass-sided conference rooms of Brown and Stone's offices on Lexington Avenue. Instead of the sulphurous yellow legal pads he was expecting, he found lined cream paper with the name of the firm printed elegantly on the top of each page. An assistant photocopied Patrick's passport, while Joe examined the doctor's letter testifying to Eleanor's incapacity.

'I had no idea about this trust,' said Patrick.

'Your mother must have been keeping it as a nice surprise,' said Peter with a big lazy smile.

'It might be that,' said Patrick tolerantly. 'Where does the income go?'

'Currently we're sending it to . . .' Peter flicked over a sheet of paper, 'the Association Transpersonel at the Banque Populaire de la Côte d'Azur in Lacoste, France.'

'Well, you can stop that straight away,' said Patrick.

'Whoa, slow down,' said Joe. 'We're going to have to get you a power of attorney first.'

'That's why she didn't tell me about it,' said Patrick,

'because she's continuing to subsidize her pet charity in France while I pay for her nursing-home fees in London.'

'She may have lost her competence before she had a chance to change the instructions,' said Peter, who seemed determined to furnish Patrick with a loving mother.

'This letter is fine,' said Joe. 'We're going to have to get you to sign some documents and get them notarized.'

'How much money are we talking about?' asked Patrick.

'It's not a large Jonson trust and it's suffered in the recent stock-market corrections,' said Joe.

'Let's hope it behaves incorrigibly from now on,' said Patrick.

'The latest valuation we have,' said Peter, glancing down at his notes, 'is two point three million dollars, with an estimated income of eighty thousand.'

'Oh, well, still a useful sum,' said Patrick, trying to sound slightly disappointed.

'Enough to buy a country cottage!' said Peter in an absurd impersonation of an English accent. 'I gather house prices are pretty crazy over there.'

'Enough to buy a second room,' said Patrick, eliciting a polite guffaw from Peter, although Patrick could in fact think of nothing he wanted more than to separate the bed from the sit.

Walking down Lexington Avenue towards his hotel in Gramercy Park, Patrick began adjusting to his strange good fortune. The long arm of his great-grandfather, who had died more than half a century before Patrick was born, was going to pluck him out of his cramped living quarters and get him into a place where there might be room for his children to stay and his friends to visit. In the meantime it would pay for his mother's nursing home. It was puzzling to think that this complete stranger was going to have such a powerful influence on his life. Even his benefactor had inherited his money. It had been his father who had founded the Jonson Candle Company in Cleveland, in 1832. By 1845 it was one of the most profitable candle companies in the country. Patrick could remember reading the founder's uninspiring explanation for his success: 'We had a new process of distilling cheap greases. Our competitors were using costly tallow and lard. Candles were high and our profits were large for a number of years.' Later, the candle factory diversified into paraffin, oil treatment and hardening processes, and developed a patented compound that became an indispensable ingredient in dry cleaning around the world. The Jonsons also bought buildings and building sites in San Francisco, Denver, Kansas City, Toledo, Indianapolis, Chicago, New York, Trinidad and Puerto Rico, but the original fortune rested on the hard-headedness of the founder who had 'died on the job', falling through a hatchway in one of his own factories, and also on those 'cheap greases' which were still lubricating the life of one of his descendants a hundred and seventy years after their discovery.

John J. Jonson, Jr., Eleanor's grandfather, was already sixty by the time he finally married. He had been travelling the world in the service of his family's burgeoning business, and was only recalled from China by the death of his nephew Sheldon in a sledging accident at St Paul's School. His eldest nephew, Albert, had already died from pneumonia at Harvard the year before. There were no heirs to the Jonson fortune and Sheldon's grieving father, Thomas, told his brother it was his duty to marry. John accepted his fate and, after a brief courtship of a general's daughter, got married and moved to New York. He fathered three daughters in rapid succession, and then dropped dead, but not before creating a multitude of trusts, one of which was meandering its way down to Patrick, as he had discovered that afternoon.

What did this long-range goodwill mean, and what did it say about the social contract that allowed a rich man to free all of his descendants from the need to work over the course of almost two centuries? There was something disreputable about being saved by increasingly remote ancestors. When he had exhausted the money given to him by a grandmother he scarcely knew, money arrived from a great-grandfather he could never have known. He could only feel an abstract gratitude towards a man whose face he would not have been able to pick out from a heap of sepia daguerreotypes. The ironies of the dynastic drive were just as great as the philanthropic ironies generated by Eleanor, or her Great-Aunt Virginia. No doubt his grandmother and his great-grandfather had hoped to empower a senator, enrich a great art collection or encourage a dazzling marriage, but in the end they had mainly subsidized idleness, drunkenness, treachery and divorce. Were the ironies of taxation any better: raising money for schools and hospitals and roads and bridges, and spending it on blowing up schools and hospitals and roads and bridges in self-defeating wars? It was hard to choose between these variously absurd methods of transferring wealth, but just for now he was going to cave in to the pleasure of having benefited from this particular form of American capitalism. Only in a country free from the funnelling of primogeniture and the levelling of *égalité* could the fifth generation of a family still be receiving parcels of wealth from a fortune that had essentially been made in the 1830s. His pleasure coexisted peacefully with his disapproval, as he walked into his dim and scented hotel, which resembled the film set of an expensive Spanish brothel, with the room numbers sewn into the carpet, on the assumption that the guests were on all fours after some kind of near overdose and could no longer find their rooms as they crawled down the obscure corridors.

The phone was ringing when he arrived in the velvet jewel box of his room, bathed in the murky urine light of parchment lampshades and presumptive hangover. He groped his way to the bedside table, clipping his shin on the bowed legs of a chair designed to resemble the virile effeminacy of a matador's jacket, with immense epaulettes jutting out proudly from the top of its stiff back.

'Fuck,' he said as he answered the phone.

'Are you all right?' said Mary.

'Oh, hi, sorry, it's you. I just got impaled on this fucking matador chair. I can't see anything in this hotel. They ought to hand out miner's helmets at the reception.'

'Listen, I've got some bad news.' She paused.

Patrick lay back on the pillows with a clear intuition of what she was going to say.

'Eleanor died last night. I'm sorry.'

'What a relief,' said Patrick defiantly. 'Amongst other things . . .'

'Yes, other things as well,' said Mary and she gave the impression of accepting them all in advance.

They agreed to talk in the morning. Patrick had a fervent desire to be left alone matched only by his fervent desire not to be left alone. He opened the minibar and sat on the floor cross-legged, staring at the wall of miniatures on the inside of the door, shining in the dazzling light of the little white fridge. On shelves next to the tumblers and wine glasses were chocolates, jellybeans, salted nuts, treats and bribes for tired bodies and discontented children. He closed the fridge and closed the cupboard door and climbed carefully onto the red velvet sofa, avoiding the matador chair as best he could.

He must try not to forget that only a year ago hallucinations had been crashing into his helpless mind like missiles into a besieged city. He lay down on the sofa, clutching a heavily embroidered cushion to his already aching stomach, and slipped effortlessly into the delirious mentality of his little room in the Priory. He remembered how he used to hear the scratch of a metal nib, or the flutter of moth wings on a screen door, or the swish of a carving knife being sharpened, or the pebble clatter of a retreating wave, as if they were in the same room with him, or rather as if he was in the same place as them. There was a broken rock streaked with the hectic glitter of quartz that quite often lay at the foot of his bed. Blue lobsters explored the edges of the skirting board with their sensitive antennae. Sometimes it was whole scenes that took him over. He would picture, for instance, brake lights streaming across a wet road, the smoky interior of a car, the throb of familiar music, a swollen drop of water rushing down the windscreen, consuming the other drops in its path, and feel that this atmosphere was the deepest thing he had ever known. The absence of narrative in these compulsory waking dreams ushered in a more secretive sense of connection. Instead of trudging across the desert floor of ordinary succession, he was plunged into an oceanic night lit by isolated flares of bioluminescence. He surfaced from these states, unable to imagine how he could describe their haunting power to his Depression Group and longing for his breakfast oxazepam.

He could have all that back with a few months of hard drinking, not just the quicksilver swamps of early withdrawal with their poisonous, fugitive, shattering reflections, and the discreet delirium of the next two weeks, but all the group therapy as well. He could still remember, on his third day in the Alcohol and Addiction Group, wanting to dive out of the window when an old-timer had dropped in to share his experience, strength and hope with the trembling foals of early recovery. A well-groomed ex-meths drinker, with white hair and a smoker's orange fingers, he had quoted the wisdom of an even older-timer who was 'in the rooms' when he first 'came round': 'Fear knocked at the door!' (Pause) 'Courage answered the door!' (Pause) 'And there was nobody there!' (Long pause). He could also have more of the Scottish moderator from the Depression Group, with his cute mnemonic for the power of projection: 'you've got what you spot and you spot what you've got'. And then there were the 'rock bottoms' of the other patients to reconsider, the man who woke next to a girlfriend he couldn't remember slashing with a kitchen knife the night before; the weekend guest surrounded by the hand-painted wallpaper he couldn't remember smearing with excrement; the woman whose arm was amputated when the syringe she picked up from the concrete floor of a friend's flat turned out to be infected with a flesh-eating superbug; the mother who abandoned her terrified children in a remote holiday cottage in order to return to her dealer in London, and countless other stories of less demonstrative despair – moments of shame that precipitated 'moments of clarity' in the pilgrim's progress of recovery.

All in all, the minibar was out. His month in the Priory had worked. He knew as deeply as he knew anything that sedation was the prelude to anxiety, stimulation the prelude to exhaustion and consolation the prelude to disappointment, and so he lay on the red velvet sofa and did nothing to distract himself from the news of his mother's death. He stayed awake through the night feeling unconvincingly numb. At five in the morning, when he calculated that Mary would be back from the school run in London, he called her flat and they agreed that she would take over the arrangements for the funeral.

The organ fell silent, interrupting Patrick's daydream. He picked up the booklet again from the narrow shelf in front of him, but before he had time to look inside, music burst out from the speakers in the corners of the room. He recognized the song just before the deep black cheerful voice rang out over the crematorium.

Oh, I got plenty o' nuthin',
An' nuthin's plenty for me.
I got no car, got no mule, I got no misery.
De folks wid plenty o' plenty
Got a lock on dey door,
'Fraid somebody's a-goin' to rob 'em
While dey's out a-makin' more.
What for?

Patrick looked round and smiled mischievously at Mary. She smiled back. He suddenly felt irrationally guilty that he hadn't yet told her about the trust, as if he were no longer entitled to enjoy the song, now that he didn't have quite as much *nuthin'* as before. *More / What for?* was a rhyme that deserved to be made more often.

I got plenty o' nuthin',
An' nuthin's plenty fo' me.
I got de sun, got de moon, got de deep blue sea.
De folks wid plenty o' plenty,
Got to pray all de day.
Seems wid plenty you sure got to worry
How to keep the Debble away,
A-way.

Patrick was entertained by Porgy's insistence on the sinfulness of riches. He felt that Eleanor and Aunt Virginia would have approved. After all, before they became masters of the universe, usurers were consigned to the seventh circle of Hell. Under a rain of fire, their perpetually restless hands were a punishment for hands that had made nothing useful or good in their lifetime, just exploited the labour of others.

Even from the less breezy position of being one of the *folks wid plenty o' plenty*, and at the cost of buying into the fantasy that folks with *plenty o' nuthin'* didn't also have to worry about keeping the *Debble* away, Eleanor would have endorsed Porgy's views. Patrick renewed his concentration for the final part of the song.

Never one to strive
To be good, to be bad –
What the hell! I is glad
I's alive.
Oh, I got plenty o' nuthin'
An' nuthin's plenty fo' me.
I got my gal, got my song,
Got Hebben de whole day long.
(No use complainin'!)
Got my gal, got my Lawd, got my song!

'Great choice,' Patrick whispered to Mary with a grateful nod. He picked up the order of service again, finally ready to look inside.

7

How nauseating, thought Nicholas, a Jew being sentimental on behalf of a Negro: you lucky fellows, you've got plenty o' nuthin', whereas we're weighed down with all this international capital and these wretched Broadway musical hits. When an idea is floundering, Nicholas said to himself, practising for later, songwriters always wheel out the celestial bodies. 'De things dat I prize / Like de stars in de skies / All are free.' No surprises there – one couldn't expect to get much rent from a hydrogen bomb several million light-years away. It was hard enough persuading a merchant banker to cough up a decent rent for one's lovely Grade II listed Queen Anne dower house in Shropshire, without asking him to drive to the moon for the weekend. Talk about too far from London, and nothing to do when one got there, except bounce around while the oxygen runs out. There was such a thing as the way of the world. Sixty per cent of the *Titanic*'s first-class passengers survived; twenty-five per cent of the second-class passengers, and no one from steerage. That was the way of the world. 'Sure is grateful, boss,' simpered Nicholas under his breath, 'I got de deep blue sea.'

Oh, God, what was going on now? The ghastly 'Spiritual Tool Box' was going up to the lectern. He could hardly bear it. What was he doing here? In the end, he was just as sentimental as silly old Ira Gershwin. He had come for David Melrose. In many ways David had been an obscure failure, but his presence had possessed a rare and precious quality: pure contempt. He bestrode middle-class morality like a colossus. Other people laboured through the odd bigoted remark, but David had embodied an absolute disdain for the opinion of the world. One could only do one's best to keep up the tradition.

For Erasmus the most interesting lines were undoubtedly, *Never one to strive / To be good, to be bad / What the hell! I is glad / I's alive.* Nietzsche was there, of course, and Rousseau (inevitably), but also the Diamond Sutra. Porgy was unlikely to have read any of them. Nevertheless, it was legitimate to think in terms of the pervasive influence of a certain family of ideas, of non-striving and of a natural state that preceded rule-based morality and in some sense made it redundant. Maybe he could see Mary after the funeral. She had always been so receptive. He sometimes thought about that.

Thank goodness there were people who were happy with nothing, thought Julia, so that people like her (and everyone else she had ever met), could have *more*. It was virtually impossible to think of a sentence that made a positive use of that dreadful word 'enough', let alone one that started raving about 'nothing'. Still, the song was rather perfect for Patrick's dotty mother, as well as being an upbeat disinheritance anthem. Hats off to Mary, as usual. Julia sighed with admiration. She assumed that Patrick had been feeling too 'mad' to do anything practical, and that Mother Mary had been asked to step in.

Really, thought Nancy, it was too ridiculous to turn to the Gershwin brothers when one's own godfather was the divine Cole Porter. Why had Mummy wasted him on indifferent

Eleanor when Nancy, who really appreciated his glamour and wit, might have had him all to herself? Not that *Porgy and Bess* didn't have its glamorous side. She had gone to a big New York opening with Hansie and Dinkie Guttenburg and had the best time ever, going backstage to congratulate everybody. The real stars weren't at all overawed by meeting a ferociously handsome German prince with a severe stutter, but you could tell that some of the little chorus girls didn't know whether to curtsy, start a revolution, or poison his wife. She would definitely include that scene in her book, it was such a coming together of everything fun, unlike this drab funeral. Really, Eleanor was letting the family down and letting herself down as well.

Annette was stunned, as she walked down the aisle towards the lectern, by the appropriateness, the serendipity and the synchronicity of that wonderful, spiritual song. Only yesterday she had been sitting with Seamus at their favourite power point on the terrace at Saint-Nazaire (actually they had decided that it was the heart chakra of the entire property, which made perfect sense when you thought about it), celebrating Eleanor's unique gifts with a glass of red wine, and Seamus had mentioned her incredibly strong connection with the African-American people. He had been privileged to be present at several of Eleanor's past-life regressions and it turned out that she had been a runaway slave during the American Civil War, trying to make her way to the abolitionist North with a young baby in her arms. She'd had the most terrible time of it, apparently, only travelling at night, in the dead of winter, hiding in ditches and living in fear of her life. And now, the very next day, at Eleanor's funeral, a man who was obviously the descendant of a slave was singing those marvellous lyrics. Perhaps – Annette almost came to a halt, overwhelmed by further horizons of magical coincidence

– perhaps he was the very baby Eleanor had carried to freedom through the ditches and the night, grown into a splendid man with a deep and resonant voice. It was almost unbearably beautiful, but she had a task to perform and with a regretful tug she extracted herself from the amazing dimension to which her train of thought had transported her, and stood squarely at the lectern, unfolding the pages she had been carrying in the pocket of her dress. She fingered the amber necklace she had bought at the Mother Meera gift shop when she had gone for *darshan* with the avatar of Talheim. Feeling mysteriously empowered by the silent Indian woman whose gaze of unconditional love had X-rayed her soul and set her off on the healing path she was still following today, Annette addressed the group of mourners in a voice torn between an expression of pained tenderness and the need for an adequate volume.

'I'm going to start by reading a poem that I know was close to Eleanor's heart. I introduced her to it, actually, and I know how much it spoke to her. I am sure that many of you will be familiar with it. It's "The Lake Isle of Innisfree" by William Butler Yeats.' She started reading in a loud lilting whisper.

I will arise and go now, and go to Innisfree,
And a small cabin build there, of clay and
wattles made;
Nine bean rows will I have there, a hive for
the honey bee,
And live alone in the bee-loud glade.

Whereas it was sophisticated enough to order nine oysters, thought Nicholas, there was something utterly absurd about nine bean rows. Oysters naturally came in dozens and half-dozens – for all he knew, they grew on the seabed in dozens and half-dozens – and so there was something understandably elegant about ordering nine of them. Beans, on the other hand, came in vague fields and profuse heaps, making the prissy precision of nine ridiculous. At the very least it conjured up a dissonant vision of an urban allotment in which there was hardly likely to be room for a clay and wattle cabin and a bee-loud glade. No doubt the Spiritual Tool Box thought that 'Innisfree' was the climax of Yeats' talent, and no doubt the Celtic Twilight, with its wilful innocence and its tawdry effects, was perfectly suited to Eleanor's other-worldly worldview, but in reality the Irish Bard had only emerged from an entirely forgettable mauve mist when he became the mouthpiece for the aristocratic ideal. '*Surely among a rich man's flowering lawns / Amid the rustle of his planted hills / Life overflows without ambitious pains / And rains down life until the basin fills.*' Those were the only lines of Yeats worth memorizing, which was just as well since they were the only ones he could remember. Those lines inaugurated a meditation on the 'bitter and violent' men who performed great deeds and built great houses, and of what happened to that greatness as it turned over time into mere privilege: '*And maybe the great-grandson of that house, / For all its bronze and marble, 's but a mouse.*' A risky line if it weren't for all the great mouse-infested houses one had known. That was why it was so essential, as Yeats was suggesting, to remain bitter and angry, in order to ward off the debilitating effects of inherited glory.

Annette's voice redoubled its excruciated gentleness for the second stanza.

And I shall have some peace there, for peace comes
dropping slow,
Dropping from the veils of the morning to where
the cricket sings;

There midnight's all a-glimmer, and noon a
purple glow,
And evening full of the linnet's wings.

Peace comes dropping slow, thought Henry, how beautiful. The lines lengthening with the growing tranquillity, and the deepening jet lag, and his head dropping slow, dropping slow onto his chest. He needed an espresso, or the veils of morning were going to shroud his mind entirely. He was here for Eleanor, Eleanor on the lake at Fairley, alone in a rowing boat, refusing to come back in, everybody standing on the shore shouting, 'Come back! Your mother's here! Your mother's arrived!' For a girl who was too shy to look you in the eye, she could be as stubborn as a mule.

Where the cricket sings, thought Patrick, is where you live with Seamus in my old home. He imagined the shrill grating coming from the grass and the gradual build-up, cicada by cicada, of pulsing waves of sound, like auditory heat shimmering over the dry land.

Mary was relieved that *plenty o' nuthin'* seemed to have gone down well with Patrick, and she felt that the make-believe simplicity of 'Innisfree' was a charming reminder of Eleanor's yearning to exclude the dark complexities of life at any price. What Mary couldn't relax about was the address she had asked Annette to make. And yet what could she do? There was no point in denying that side of Eleanor's life and Annette was better qualified than anyone else in the room to talk about it. At least it would give Patrick something to rant about for the next few days. She listened to Annette's singsong, cradle-rocking delivery of the final stanza of 'Innisfree' with growing dread.

I will arise and go now, for always night and day
I hear the lake water lapping with low sounds
by the shore;
While I stand on the roadway, or on the
pavements grey,
I hear it in the deep heart's core.

Annette closed her eyes and reached again for her amber necklace. '*Om namo Matta Meera*,' she murmured, re-empowering herself for the speech she was about to make.

'All of you will have known Eleanor in different ways, and many of you for much longer than me,' she began with an understanding smile. 'I can only talk about the Eleanor that I knew, and while I try to do justice to the wonderful woman that she was, I hope you will hold the Eleanor that you knew in what Yeats calls *the deep heart's core*. But at the same time, if I show you a side of her that you didn't know, all I would ask is that you let her in, let her in and let her join the Eleanor that each of you is holding in your heart.'

Oh, Jesus, thought Patrick, let me out of here. He imagined himself disappearing through the floor with a shovel and some bunk-bed slats, the theme music of *The Great Escape* humming in the air. He was crawling under the crematorium through fragile tunnels, when he felt himself being dragged backwards by Annette's maddening voice.

'I first met Eleanor when a group of us from the Dublin Women's Healing Drum Circle were invited down to Saint-Nazaire, her wonderful house in Provence, which I'm sure many of you are familiar with. As we were coming down the drive in our minibus, I caught my first glimpse of Eleanor sitting on the wall of the big pond, with her hands tucked under her thighs, for all the world like a lonely young child staring down at her dangling shoes. By the time we arrived in front of the pond she was literally greeting us with open arms, but I never lost that first impression of her, just as I think she never lost a connection to the child-like quality that made her believe so passionately that justice could be achieved, that consciousness could be transformed and that there was goodness to be found in every person and every situation, however hidden it might seem at first sight.'

Of course consciousness can be transformed, thought Erasmus, but what is it? If I pass an electric current through my body, or bury my nose in the soft petals of a rose, or impersonate Greta Garbo, I transform my consciousness; in fact it is impossible to stop transforming consciousness. What I can't do is describe what it is *in itself*: it's too close to see, too ubiquitous to grasp, and too transparent to point to.

'Eleanor was one of the most generous people it has been my privilege to know. You only had to hint that you needed something and if it was in her power to provide it, she would leap at the opportunity with an enthusiasm that made it look as if it was a relief to her rather than to the person who was asking.'

Patrick imagined the simple charm of the dialogue.

Seamus: I was thinking that it would be, eh, consciousness-raising, like, to own a private hamlet surrounded by vines and olive groves, somewhere sunny.

Eleanor: Oh, how amazing! I've got one of those. Would you like it?

Seamus: Oh, thank you very much, I'm sure. Sign here and here and here.

Eleanor: What a relief. Now I have nothing.

'Nothing,' said Annette, 'was too much trouble for her. Service to others was her life's purpose, and it was awe-inspiring to see the lengths she would go to in her quest to help people achieve their dreams. A torrent of grateful letters and postcards used to arrive at the Foundation from all over the world. A young Croatian scientist who was working on a "zero-energy fuel cell" – don't ask me what that is, but it's going to save the planet – is one example. A Peruvian archaeologist who had uncovered amazing evidence that the Incas were originally from Egypt and continued to communicate with the mother civilization through what he called "solar language". An old lady who had been working for forty years on a universal dictionary of sacred symbols and just needed a little extra help to bring this incredibly valuable book to completion. All of them had received a helping hand from Eleanor. But you mustn't think that Eleanor was only concerned with the higher echelons of science and spirituality, she was also a marvellously practical person who knew the value of a kitchen extension for a growing family, or a new car for a friend living in the depths of the country.'

What about a sister who was running out of cash? thought Nancy grumpily. First they had taken away her credit cards, and then they had taken away her chequebook, and now she had to go in person to the Morgan Guaranty in Fifth Avenue to collect her monthly pocket money. They said it was the only way to stop her running up debts, but the best way to stop her running up debts was to give her more money.

'There was a wonderful Jesuit gentleman,' Annette continued, 'well, he was an ex-Jesuit actually, although we still called him Father Tim. He had come to believe that Catholic dogma was too narrow and that we should embrace all the religious traditions of the world. He eventually became the first

Englishman to be accepted as an *ayahuascera* – a Brazilian shaman – among one of the most authentic tribes in Amazonia. Anyhow, Father Tim wrote to Eleanor, who had known him in his old Farm Street days, saying that his village needed a motor-boat to go down to the local trading post, and of course she responded with her usual impulsive generosity, and sent a cheque by return. I shall never forget the expression on her face when she received Father Tim's reply. Inside the envelope were three brightly coloured toucan feathers and an equally colourful note explaining that in recognition of her gift to the Ayoreo people, a ritual had been performed in Father Tim's far-away village inducting her into the tribe as a "Rainbow Warrior". He said that he had refrained from mentioning that she was a woman, since the Ayoreo took a "somewhat unreconstructed view of the gentler sex, not unreminiscent of that taken by old Mother Church", and that he would have "suffered the fate of St Sebastian" if he "admitted to his ruse". He said that he intended to confess on his deathbed, so as to help move the tribe forward into a new era of harmony between the male and female principles, so necessary to the salvation of the world. Anyhow,' sighed Annette, recognizing that she had drifted from her written text, but taking this to be a sign of inspiration, 'the effect on Eleanor was quite literally magical. She wore the toucan feathers around her neck until they sadly disintegrated, and for a few weeks she told all and sundry that she was an Ayoreo Rainbow Warrior. She was for all the world like the little girl who goes to a new school and comes home one day transformed because she has made a new best friend.'

Although arrested development was his stock in trade and he made a habit of shutting down his psychoanalytic ear when he was not working, Johnny could not help being struck by the ferocious tenacity of Eleanor's resistance to growing up. He was as guilty as anyone of over-quoting good old Eliot's 'Human kind cannot bear very much reality', but he felt that in this case the evasiveness had been uninterrupted. He could remember first meeting Eleanor when Patrick invited him to Saint-Nazaire for the school holidays. Even then she had a habit of lapsing into baby talk, very disconcerting for adolescents distancing themselves from childhood. The tragedy was that five or perhaps ten years of decent five-day-a-week analysis could have mitigated the problem significantly.

'That was the sort of breadth that Eleanor showed in her kindness to others,' said Annette, sensing that it would soon be time to draw her remarks to a conclusion. She put aside a couple of pages she had failed to read during her Amazonian improvisation, and looked down at the last page to remind herself what she had written. It struck her as a little formal now that she had entered into a more exploratory style, but there were one or two things embedded in the last paragraph that she must remember to say.

Oh, please get on with it, thought Patrick. Charles Bronson was having a panic attack in a collapsing tunnel, Alsatians were barking behind the barbed wire, searchlights were weaving over the breached ground, but soon he would be running through the woods, dressed as a German bank clerk and heading for the railway station with some identity papers forged at the expense of Donald Pleasance's eyesight. It would all be over soon, he just had to keep staring at his knees for a few minutes longer.

'I would like to read you a short passage from the *Rig Veda*,' said Annette. 'It quite literally leapt at me from the shelf when I was in the library at the Foundation, looking for a book that would evoke something of Eleanor's amazing spiritual depths.' She resumed her sing-song reading voice.

She follows to the goal of those who are passing on beyond, she is the first in the eternal succession of the dawns that are coming, – Usha widens bringing out that which lives, awakening someone who was dead . . . What is her scope when she harmonizes with the dawns that shone out before and those that now must shine? She desires the ancient mornings and fulfils their light; projecting forwards her illumination she enters into communion with the rest that are to come.

'Eleanor was a firm believer in reincarnation, and not only did she regard suffering as the refining fire that would burn away the impediments to a still higher spiritual evolution, but she was also privileged to have something very rare indeed: a specific vision of how and where she would be reincarnated. At the Foundation we have what we call an "Ah-ha Box" for those little epiphanies and moments of insight when we think, "Ah-ha!" We all have them, don't we? But the trouble is that they slip away during the course of a busy day and so Seamus, the Chief Facilitator of the Foundation, invented the "Ah-ha Box" so that we could write down our thoughts, pop them in the box and share them in the evening.'

Annette felt the lure of anecdote and digression, resisted for a few seconds, and then caved in. 'We used to have a trainee shaman with a shall I say "challenging" personality, and he was in the habit of having about a dozen Ah-ha moments a day. Many of them turned out to be covert, or not so covert, attacks on other people in the Foundation. Well, one evening when we had all waded through at least ten of his so-called epiphanies, Seamus said, in his incomparably humorous way, "You know, Dennis, one man's Ah-ha moment is another man's Ho-ho moment." And I remember Eleanor simply cracking up. I can still see her now. She covered her mouth because she thought it would be unkind to laugh too much, but she couldn't help herself. I don't think any portrait of Eleanor would be complete without that naughty giggle and that quick, trusting smile.

'Anyhow,' said Annette, recovering her sense of direction for a final assault, 'as I was saying: one day, after her first stroke but before she moved into the French nursing home, we found this amazing note from Eleanor in the Ah-ha Box. The note said that she had been on a vision quest and she had seen that she would be returning to Saint-Nazaire in her next lifetime. She would come back as a young shaman and Seamus and I would be very old by then, and we would hand the Foundation back to her as she had handed it to us in what she called a "seamless continuity". And I would like to end by asking you to hold that phrase, "seamless continuity", in your minds, while we sit here for a few moments in silence and pray for Eleanor's swift return.'

Standing behind the lectern, Annette lowered her head, exhaled solemnly and shut her eyes.

8

Mary thought that 'swift return' was going a bit far. She glanced nervously at the coffin, as if Eleanor might fling off the lid and hop out at any moment, throwing open her arms to embrace the world, with the awkward theatricality of the photograph on the order of service. Sensing Patrick's radiant embarrassment, she regretted asking Annette to make an address, but it was hard to think of anyone who could have spoken instead. Eleanor's slash and burn social life had destroyed continuity and deep friendship, especially after the lonely years of dementia and the fractured relationship with Seamus.

Mary had asked Johnny to read a poem and she had even been desperate enough to get Erasmus to read a passage. Nancy, the only alternative, had been hysterical with self-pity and unclear about when she was getting in from New York. The rather strained choice of readers was balanced (or made worse) by the familiarity of the passages she had chosen. Two great biblical staples were coming up next, and she now felt that it was intolerably boring of her to have picked them. On the other hand, nobody knew anything about death, except that it was unavoidable, and since everyone was terrified by that uncertain certainty, perhaps the opaque magnificence of the Bible, or even the vague Asiatic immensities that Annette obviously preferred, were better than a wilful show of novelty. Besides, Eleanor had been a Christian, amongst so many other things.

As soon as Annette sat down it would be Mary's turn to replace her at the front of the room. The truth was, she was feeling slightly mad. She got up with a reluctance that cunningly disguised itself as a feeling of unbearable urgency, squeezed past Patrick without looking him in the eye and made her way to the lectern. When she told people how nervous she was about any kind of public appearance, they said incredibly annoying things like, 'Don't forget to breathe.' Now she knew why. First she felt that she was going to faint and then, as she started to read the passage she had rehearsed a hundred times, she felt that she was choking as well.

Though I speak with the tongues of men and angels,
and have not love, I am become a sounding brass,
or a tinkling cymbal. And though I have the gift
of prophecy, and understand all mysteries and all
knowledge; and though I have all faith, so that I
could remove mountains, and have not love, I am
nothing. And though I bestow all my goods to feed
the poor, and though I give my body to be burned
and have not love, it profiteth me nothing.

Mary felt a scratching sensation in her throat, but she tried to persevere without coughing.

Love suffereth long, and is kind; love envieth not:
love vaunteth not itself, is not puffed up, doth not
behave itself unseemly, seeketh not her own, is not
easily provoked, thinketh no evil, rejoiceth not in
iniquity, but rejoiceth in the truth; beareth all things,
believeth all things, hopeth all things, endureth all
things. Love never faileth:

Mary cleared her throat and turned her head aside to cough. Now she had ruined everything. She couldn't help feeling that there was a psychological connection between this part of the passage and her coughing fit. When she had read it yet again this morning, it had struck her as the zenith of false modesty: love boasting about not boasting, love unbelievably pleased with itself for not being puffed up. Until then, it had seemed to be an expression of the highest ideals, but now she was so tired and nervous she couldn't quite shake off the feeling that it was one of the most pompous things ever written. Where was she? She looked at the page with a kind of swimming panic. Then she spotted where she had left off, and pressed forward, feeling that her voice did not quite belong to her.

but whether there be prophecies, they shall fail; whether there be tongues, they shall cease; whether there be knowledge, it shall vanish away. For we know in part, and we prophesy in part. But when that which is perfect is come, then that which is in part shall be done away.

When I was a child, I spake as a child, I understood as a child: but when I became a man, I put away childish things. For now we see through a glass, darkly; but then face to face: now I know in part; but then shall I know even as also I am known.

And now abideth faith, hope, love, these three; but the greatest of these is love.

Erasmus had not listened to Mary's reading of St Paul's Epistle to the Corinthians. Ever since Annette's address, he had been lost in speculation about the doctrine of reincarnation and whether it deserved to be called 'literally nonsensical'. It was a phrase that reminded him of Victor Eisen, the Melrose family's philosopher friend of the sixties and seventies. In philosophical discussions, after a series of vigorous proofs, 'literally nonsensical' used to rush out of him like salt from a cellar that suddenly loses its top. Although he was now a rather faded figure without any enduring work to his name, Eisen had been a fluent and conceited public intellectual during Erasmus's youth. In his eagerness to dismiss, which in the end may have secured his own dismissal, he would certainly have found reincarnation 'literally nonsensical': its evidence-free, memory-free, discarnate narrative failed to satisfy the Parfittian criteria of personal identity. Who is being reincarnated? That was the devastating question, unless the person who was asked happened to be a Buddhist. For him the answer was 'Nobody'. Nobody was reincarnated because nobody had been incarnated in the first place. Something much looser, like a stream of thought, had taken human form. Neither a soul nor a personal identity was needed to precipitate a human life, just a cluster of habits clinging to the hollow concept of independent existence, like a crowd of grasping passengers sinking the lifeboat they imagined would save them. In the background was the ever-present opportunity to slip away into the glittering ocean of a true nature that was not personal either. From this point of view, it was Parfitt and Eisen who were literally nonsensical. Still, Erasmus had no problem with a rejection of reincarnation on the grounds that there was no good reason to believe that it was true – as long as the implicit physicalism of such a rejection was also rejected! The correlation between brain activity and consciousness could be evidence, after all, that the brain was a receiver of consciousness, like a transistor, or a transceiver, and not the skull-bound generator of a private display. The . . .

Erasmus's thoughts were interrupted by the sensation of a hand resting on his shoulder and shaking him gently. His neighbour, after securing his attention, pointed to Mary, who stood in the aisle looking at him significantly. She gave him what he felt was a somewhat curt nod, reminding him that it was his turn to read. He rose with an apologetic smile and, crushing the toes of the woman who had shaken him on the shoulder, made his way towards the front of the room. The passage he had to read was from Revelations – or Obfuscations as he preferred to call them. Reading it over on the train from Cambridge, he had felt a strange desire to build a time machine so that he could take the author a copy of Kant's *Critique of Pure Reason.*

Erasmus put on his reading glasses, flattened the page against the slope of the lectern, and tried to master his longing to point out the unexamined assumptions that riddled the famous passage he was about to read. He might not be able to infuse his voice with the required feeling of awe and exaltation, but he could at least eliminate any signs of scepticism and indignation. With the inner sigh of a man who doesn't want to be blamed for what's coming next, Erasmus set about his task.

Then I saw a new heaven and a new earth, for the first heaven and the first earth had passed away, and the sea was no more.

Nancy was still furious with the clumsy oaf who had stepped on her toes and now, on top of that, he was proposing to take the sea away. No more sea meant no more seaside, no more Cap d'Antibes (although it had been completely ruined), no more Portofino (unbearable in the summer), no more Palm Beach (which was not what it used to be).

And I saw the holy city, new Jerusalem,

Oh, no, not another Jerusalem, thought Nancy. Isn't one enough?

coming down out of heaven from God, prepared as a bride adorned for her husband; and I heard a great voice from the throne saying, 'Behold, the dwelling of God is with men. He will dwell with them and they shall be his people, and God himself will be with them; he will wipe away every tear from their eyes, and death shall be no more, neither shall there be mourning nor crying nor pain any more, for the former things have passed away.'

All these readings from the Bible were getting on Nancy's nerves. She didn't want to think about death – it was depressing. At a proper funeral there were amazing choirs that didn't usually sing at private events, and tenors who were practically impossible to get hold of, and readings by famous actors or distinguished public figures. It made the whole thing fun and meant that one hardly ever thought about death, even when the readings were exactly the same, because one was struggling to remember when some tired-looking person had been chancellor of the exchequer, or what the name of their last movie was. That was the miracle of glamour. The more she thought about it, the more furious she felt about Eleanor's dreary funeral. Why, for instance, had she decided to be cremated? Fire was something one dreaded. Fire was something one insured against. The Egyptians had got it right with the pyramids. What could be cosier than something huge and permanent with all one's things tucked away inside (and other people's things as well! Lots and lots of things!) built by thousands of slaves who took the secret of the construction with them to unmarked graves. Nowadays one would have to make prohibitive social-security payments to teams of unionized construction workers. That was modern life for you. Nevertheless, some sort of big monument was infinitely preferable to an urn and a handful of dust.

And he who sat upon the throne said, 'Behold, I make all things new.' Also he said, 'Write this, for these words are trustworthy and true.' And he said to me, 'It is done. I am the Alpha and the Omega, the beginning and the end. To the thirsty I will give water without price from the fountain of the water of life. He who conquers shall have this heritage, and I will be his God and he will be my son.'

Johnny couldn't help being reminded by all these readings of a paper he had written in his opinionated youth, called *Omnipotence and denial: the lure of religious belief*. He had made the simple point that religion inverted everything that we dread about human existence: we're all going to die (we're all going to live for ever); life is terribly unfair (there will be absolute and perfect justice); it's horrible being downtrodden and powerless (the meek shall inherit the earth); and so on. The inversion had to be complete; it was no use saying that life was pretty unfair but not quite as unfair as it sometimes seemed. The pallor of Hades may have been its doom: after making the leap of believing that consciousness did not end with death, a realm of restless shadows pining for blood, muscle, battle and wine must have seemed a thin prize. Achilles said that it was preferable to be a slave on earth than king in the underworld. With that sort of endorsement an afterlife was headed for extinction. Only something perfectly counter-factual could secure global devotion. In his paper Johnny had drawn parallels between this spectacular denial of the depressing and frightening aspects of reality and the operation of the unconscious in the individual patient. He had gone on to make more detailed comparisons between various forms of mental illness and what he imagined to be their corresponding religious discourse, with the disadvantage of knowing nothing about the religious half of the comparison. Feeling that he might as well solve all the world's problems in twelve thousand words, he had tied in political repression with personal repression, and made all the usual points about social control. The underlying assumption of the paper was that authenticity was the only project that mattered and that religious belief necessarily stood in its way. He was now faintly embarrassed by the lack of subtlety and self-doubt in his twenty-nine-year-old self. Still in training, he hadn't yet had a patient, and was therefore much more certain about the operation of the human psyche than he was today.

Mary had asked him to read a long poem by Henry Vaughan that he had never come across before. She told him that it fitted perfectly with Eleanor's view that life was an exile from God, and death a homecoming. Other, more enjoyable poems had seemed conventional or irrelevant by contrast, and Mary had decided to stay loyal to Eleanor's metaphysical nostalgia. As far as Johnny was concerned, giving a religious status to these moods of longing was just another form of resistance. Wherever we came from and wherever we were going (and whether those ideas meant anything at all) it was the bit in between that counted. As Wittgenstein had said, 'Death is not an event in life: we do not live to experience death'.

Johnny smiled vaguely at Erasmus as they crossed paths in the aisle. He balanced his copy of *The Metaphysical Poets* on the ledge of the lectern and opened it on the page he had marked with a taxi receipt. His voice was strong and confident as he read.

Happy those early days, when I
Shined in my Angel-infancy!
Before I understood this place
Appointed for my second race,

Or taught my soul to fancy aught
But a white celestial thought;
When yet I had not walked above
A mile or two from my first Love,
And looking back at the short space
Could see a glimpse of His bright face;
When on some gilded cloud or flower
My gazing soul would dwell an hour,
And in those weaker glories spy
Some shadows of eternity;
Before I taught my tongue to wound
My conscience with a sinful sound,
Or had the black art to dispense
A several sin to every sense,
But felt through all this fleshy dress
Bright shoots of everlastingness.

Nicholas had started to feel that special sense of claustrophobia he associated with being trapped in chapel at school. Wave after wave of Christian sentiment without even the consolation of an overdue Latin translation tucked furtively in his hymnal. He cheered himself up with his own version of the Christian story: 'God sent his only begotten son to Earth in order to save the poor, and it was a complete washout, like all half-baked socialist projects; but then the Supreme Being came to his senses and sent Nicholas to save the rich, and it came to pass that it was an absolute *succès fou*.' No doubt with its deplorable history of torture, Inquisition, religious wars, crushing dogma, as well as its altogether more forgivable history of sexual impropriety and worldly self-indulgence, the Roman Catholic Church would look on this crucial development as a heresy; but a heresy was only the prelude to a new Protestant religious order. 'Nicholism' would sweep through what his ghastly American investment adviser called the 'high-net-worth community'. The great question, as always, was what to wear. As the Arch Plutocrat of the Church for the Redemption of Latter-Day Riches one had to cut a dash. Nicholas's imagination wandered back to the page's outfit he had worn as a ten-year-old boy at a very grand royal wedding – the silk breeches, the silver buttons, the buckled shoes . . . he had never felt quite as sure of his own importance since that day.

Johnny renewed his efforts at intonation for the final stanza.

O how I long to travel back,
And tread again that ancient track!
That I might once more reach that plain
Where first I left my glorious train;
From whence th'enlighten'd spirit sees
That shady City of palm trees!
But ah! My soul with too much stay
Is drunk and staggers in the way:–
Some men a forward motion love,
But I by backward steps would move,
And when this dust falls to the urn,
In that state I came, return.

Complete rubbish, thought Nicholas, to imply that one returned to the place from which one came. How could it be the same after one's immensely colourful contribution, and how could one's attitude to it be the same after passing through this Vale of Invitations and Sardonic Laughter? He glanced down at the order of service. It looked as if that poem by Vaughan was the last reading. At the bottom of the page there was a note inviting everyone to join the family at the Onslow Club for a drink after the ceremony. He would love to get out of it, but in a moment of reckless generosity he had promised Nancy that he would accompany her. He also had a four o'clock appointment to visit a dying friend at the Chelsea and Westminster Hospital and so it was in fact conveniently nearby. Thank goodness he had booked a car for the day; with distances of that kind (about six hundred yards) one always had to put up with the ill temper of cab drivers who were drifting around the Fulham Road dreaming of a fare to Gatwick or Penzance. He must keep a firm hold on his car; otherwise Nancy would commandeer it for her own purposes. He could easily totter out of the hospital, suffering from the 'compassion burn-out' he knew sometimes afflicted the most heroic nurses, only to find that his car was in Berkeley Square where Nancy was trying to bamboozle a Morgan Guaranty employee into giving her some cash. Her cousin Henry, who had unexpectedly turned up today, had once told him that when he and Nancy were children she had been known as 'the Kleptomaniac'. Little things used to disappear – special hairbrushes, childish jewellery, cherished piggy banks – and turn up in the magpie's nest of Nancy's bedroom. Parents and nannies explained, pedantically at first and then with growing anger, that stealing was wrong, but the temptation was too strong for Nancy and she was expelled from a series of boarding schools for theft and lying. Ever since Nicholas had known her, she had been locked into a state of covetousness, a sense of how much better she would have used, and how much more she deserved, the fabulous possessions belonging to her friends and family. She resisted envying things which belonged to people she didn't know at all, but only to distance herself from her maid, who filled the kitchen with prurient babble about the lives of soap-opera stars. Her recounting of their commonplace 'tragedies' was used to soothe what had been excited by earlier stories of unmerited rewards and ludicrous lifestyles.

Celebrities were all very well for the masses, but what counted for Nicholas was what he called 'the big world', namely the minuscule number of people whose background, looks, or talent to amuse made them worth having to dinner. Nancy belonged to the big world by birth and could not be exiled from that paradise by her perfectly ghastly personality. One had to be loyal to something, and since it offered more scope for treachery than anything except politics, Nicholas was loyal to the big world.

He watched Patrick with a predator's vigilance, hoping for a sign that the ceremony was finally over. Suddenly, the sound system swelled back to life with the brassy opening strains of 'Fly Me to the Moon'.

Fly me to the moon and let me play among the stars;
Let me see what spring is like on Jupiter and Mars

Here we go again, thought Nicholas, off to the bloody moon. Frank Sinatra's voice, oozing with effortless confidence, drove him to distraction. It reminded him of the kind of fun he had not been having in the fifties and sixties. No doubt Eleanor had imagined she was enjoying herself when she lowered the record needle onto a Frank Sinatra single, whizzing round at a giddy forty-five rpm, its discarded sleeve, among the lipstick-smeared glasses of gin and the overflowing ashtrays, displaying a photograph of that sly undistinguished face grinning from the upper reaches of a sky-blue suit.

He continued to stare at Patrick and Mary in the hope that they would leave. Then he saw, to his horror, that it was not Eleanor's son but her coffin that was on the move, sliding forward on steel rollers towards a pair of purple velvet curtains.

In other words: hold my hand
In other words: darling kiss me!

The coffin receded behind the closing curtains and disappeared. Mary got up at last and led the way down the aisle, followed closely by Patrick.

Fill my heart with song, and let me sing for ever more
You are all I long for, all I worship and adore!
In other words; please be true!
In other words: I love you.

Finding himself unexpectedly agitated by the sight of Eleanor's coffin being mechanically swallowed, Nicholas lurched hastily into the aisle, interposing himself between Mary and Patrick. He hobbled forwards, his walking stick reaching eagerly ahead of him, and burst through the doorway into the chill London spring.

9

Patrick stepped into the pallid light, relieved that his mother's funeral was over, but oppressed by the party that still lay ahead. He walked up to Mary and Johnny who stood under the barely blossoming branches of a cherry tree.

'I don't feel like talking to anyone for a while – except you, of course,' he added politely.

'You don't have to talk to us either,' said Johnny.

'Perfect,' said Patrick.

'Why don't you go ahead with Johnny?' asked Mary.

'Well, if that's all right. Can you . . .'

'Cope with everything,' suggested Mary.

'Exactly.'

They smiled at each other, amused by how typical they were both being.

As Patrick walked to Johnny's car, a plane roared and whistled overhead. He glanced back at the Italian-ate building he had just left. The campanile encasing the furnace chimney, the low arches of the brick cloister, the dormant rose garden, the weeping willow and the mossy benches, formed a masterpiece of decent neutrality.

'I think I'll get cremated here myself,' said Patrick.

'No need to rush,' said Johnny.

'I was going to wait until I died.'

'Good thinking.'

A second plane screeched above them, goading the two

men into the muffled interior of the car. Through the railings, beside the Thames, joggers and cyclists bobbed along, determined to stay alive.

'I think my mother's death is the best thing to happen to me since . . . well, since my father's death,' said Patrick.

'It can't be quite that simple,' said Johnny, 'or there would be merry bands of orphans skipping down the street.'

The two men fell silent. Patrick was not in the mood to banter. He felt the presence of a new vitality that could easily be nullified by habit, including the habit of seeming to be clever. Like everyone else, he lived in a world where the same patterns of emotion were projected again and again against the walls of an airless chamber, but just for the moment, he felt the absurdity of mistaking that flickering scene for life. What was the meaning of a feeling he had had forty years ago, let alone one he had refused to have? The crisis was not in the past but in clinging to the past; trapped in a decaying mansion on Sunset Boulevard, forced to watch home movies by a wounded narcissist. Just for the moment he could imagine tiptoeing away from Gloria Swanson, past her terrifying butler, and out into the roar of the contemporary streets; he could imagine the whole system breaking down, without knowing what would happen if it did.

At the little roundabout beyond the crematorium gates, Patrick saw a sign for the Townmead Road Re-Use and Recycling Centre. He couldn't help wondering if Eleanor was being recycled. Poor Eleanor was already muddled enough without being dragged through the dull lights and the dazzling lights and multicoloured mandalas of the Bardo, being challenged by crowds of wrathful deities and hungry ghosts to achieve the transcendence she had run away from while she was alive.

The road ran beside the hedge-filled railings of the Mortlake Cemetery, past the Hammersmith and Fulham Cemetery, across Chiswick bridge, and down to the Chiswick Cemetery on the other side. Acre upon acre of gravestones mocking the real-estate ambitions of riverside developers. Why should death, of all nothings, take up so much space? Better to burn in the hollow blue air than claim a plot on that sunless beach, packed side by side in the bony ground, relying on the clutching roots of trees and flowers for a vague resurrection. Perhaps those who had known good mothering were drawn to the Earth's absorbing womb, while the abandoned and betrayed longed to be dispersed into the heartless sky. Johnny might have a professional view. Repression was a different kind of burial, preserving trauma in the unconscious, like a statue buried in the desert sand, its sharp features protected from the weather of ordinary experience. Johnny might have views on that as well, but Patrick preferred to remain in silence. What was the unconscious anyway, as against any other form of memory, and why was it given the sovereignty of a definite article, turning it into a thing and a place when the rest of memory was a faculty and a process?

The car climbed the narrow, battered flyover that straddled the Hogarth roundabout. A temporary measure that just wouldn't go away, it had been crying out for replacement ever since Patrick could remember. Perhaps it was the transport equivalent of smoking: never quite the right day to give it up – there's going to be a rush hour tomorrow morning . . . the weekend is coming up . . . let's do this thing after the Olympics . . . 2020 is a lovely round number, a perfect time for a fresh start.

'This dodgy flyover,' said Patrick.

'I know,' said Johnny, 'I always think it's going to collapse.'

He hadn't meant to talk. An inner monologue had broken the surface. Better sink back down, better make a fresh start.

Making a fresh start was a stale start. There was nothing

to make and nothing to start, just a continuous breaking out of appearances from potential appearances, like speech from an inner monologue. To be on an equal plane with that articulation: that was freshness. He could feel it in his body, as if in every moment he might cease to be, or continue to be, and that by continuing he was renewed.

'I was just thinking about repression,' said Patrick, 'I don't think that trauma does get repressed, do you?'

'I think that's now the right view,' said Johnny. 'Trauma is too strong and intrusive to be forgotten. It leads to dis-association and splitting off.'

'So, what does get repressed?' asked Patrick.

'Whatever challenges the accommodations of the false self.'

'So there's still plenty of work for it to do.'

'Tons,' said Johnny.

'But there could be no repression at all, no secret burial; just life radiating through us.'

'Theoretically,' said Johnny.

Patrick saw the familiar concrete facade and aquarium-blue windows of the Cromwell Hospital.

'I remember spending a month in there with a slipped disc, just after my father died.'

'And I remember bringing you some extra painkillers.'

'I salute its ambitious wine list and its action-packed Arabic television channels,' said Patrick, waving majestically at the post-brutalist masterpiece.

The traffic flowed smoothly across the Gloucester Road and down towards the Natural History Museum. Patrick reminded himself to keep quiet. All his life, or at least since he could talk, he had been tempted to flood difficult situations with words. When Eleanor lost the power to speak and Thomas had not yet acquired it, Patrick discovered a core of inarticulacy in himself that refused to be flooded with words, and which he had tried to flood with alcohol instead. In silence he might see what it was he kept trying to obliterate with talk and drink. What was it that couldn't be said? He could only grope for clues in the darkness of the pre-verbal realm.

His body was a graveyard of buried emotion; its symptoms were clustered around the same fundamental terror, like that rash of cemeteries they had just passed, clustered around the Thames. The nervous bladder, the spastic colon, the lower-back pain, the labile blood pressure that leapt from normal to dangerously high in a few seconds, at the creak of a floorboard or the thought of a thought, and the imperious insomnia that ruled over them, all pointed to an anxiety deep enough to disrupt his instincts and take control of the automatic processes of his body. Behaviours could be changed, attitudes modified, mentalities transformed, but it was hard to have a dialogue with the somatic habits of infancy. How could an infant express himself before he had a self to express, or the words to express what he didn't yet have? Only the dumb language of injury and illness was abundantly available. There was screaming of course, if it was allowed.

He could remember, when he was three years old, standing beside the swimming pool in France looking at the water with apprehensive longing, wishing he knew how to swim. Suddenly he felt himself being hoisted off the ground and thrown high in the air. With the slowness of horror, when the density of impressions registered by the panic-stricken mind makes time thicken, he used all the incredulity and alarm that rushed into his thrashing body to distance himself from the lethal liquid he had been warned so often not to fall into by accident, but soon enough he plunged down into the drowning pool, kicking and beating the thin water until at last he broke the surface and sucked in some air before he sank back down again. He fought for his life in a chaos of jerks and gulps, sometimes taking in air and sometimes water, until finally he managed to graze his fingers on the rough stone edge of the pool and he gave in to sobbing as quietly as possible, swallowing his despair, knowing that if he made too much noise his father would do something really violent and unkind.

David sat in his dark glasses smoking a cigar, angled away from Patrick, a jaundiced cloud of pastis on the table in front of him, extolling his educational methods to Nicholas Pratt: the stimulation of an instinct to survive; the development of self-sufficiency; an antidote to maternal mollycoddling; in the end, the benefits were so self-evident that only the stupidity and sheepishness of the herd could explain why every three-year-old was not chucked into the deep end of a swimming pool before he knew how to swim.

Robert's curiosity about his grandfather had prompted Patrick to tell him the story of his first swimming lesson. He felt that it would be too burdensome to tell his son about David's beatings and sexual assaults, but at the same time wanted to give Robert a glimpse of his grandfather's harshness. Robert was completely shocked.

'That's so horrible,' he said. 'I mean a three-year-old would think he was dying. In fact, you could have died,' he added, giving Patrick a reassuring hug, as if he sensed that the threat was not completely over.

Robert's empathy overwhelmed Patrick with the reality of what he had taken to be a relatively innocuous anecdote. He could hardly sleep and when he did he was soon woken by his pounding heart. He was hungry all the time but could not digest anything he ate. He could not digest the fact that his father was a man who had wanted to kill him, who would rather have drowned him than taught him to swim, a man who boasted of shooting someone in the head because he had screamed too much, and might shoot Patrick in the head as well, if he made too much noise.

At three of course Patrick would have been able to speak, even if he was forbidden to say what was troubling him. Earlier than that, without the sustenance of narrative, his active memory disintegrated and disappeared. In these darker realms the only clues were lodged in his body, and in one or two stories his mother had told him about his very early life. Here again his father's intolerance of screaming was pivotal, exiling Patrick and his mother to the freezing attic of the Cornish house during the winter he was born.

He sank a little deeper into the passenger seat. As he recognized that he had gone on expecting to be suffocated or dropped, he felt the suffocation and vertigo of the expectations themselves, and if he asked himself whether infancy was destiny, he felt the suffocation and the vertigo of the question. He could feel the weight of his body and the weight on his body. It was like a restraining wall, buckled and sweating from the pressure of the hillside behind it; the only means of access, and at the same time a ferocious guard against the formless miseries of infancy. This was what Johnny might want to call a pre-Oedipal problem, but whatever name was given to a nameless unease, Patrick felt that his tentative new vitality depended on a preparedness to dig into that body of buried emotion and let it join the flow of contemporary feeling. He must pay more attention to the scant evidence that came his way. A strange and upsetting dream had woken him last night, but now it had slipped away and he couldn't get it back.

He understood intuitively that his mother's death was a crisis strong enough to shake his defences. The sudden absence of the woman who had brought him into the world was a fleeting opportunity to bring something slightly new into the world instead. It was important to be realistic: the present was the top layer of the past, not the extravaganza of novelty peddled by people like Seamus and Annette; but even something slightly new could be the layer underneath something slightly newer. He mustn't miss his chance, or his body would keep him living under its misguided heroic strain, like a Japanese soldier who has never been told the news of surrender and continues to booby-trap his patch of jungle, and prepare for the honour of a self-inflicted death.

Nauseating as it was to upgrade his father's cruelty to the 'front of the plane' in homicidal class, he felt an even greater reluctance to renounce his childhood view of his mother as the co-victim of David's tempestuous malice. The deeper truth that he had been a toy in the sadomasochistic relationship between his parents was not, until now, something he could bear to contemplate. He clung to the flimsy protection of thinking that his mother was a loving woman who had struggled to satisfy his needs, rather than acknowledging that she had used him as an extension of her lust for humiliation. How self-serving was the story of the freezing attic? It certainly reinforced the picture of Eleanor as a fellow refugee escaping with burns on her back and a baby in her arms from the incendiary bombs of David's rage and self-destruction. Even when Patrick found the courage to tell her that he had been raped by his father, she had rushed to say, 'Me too.' Falling over herself to be a victim, Eleanor seemed indifferent to the impact that her stories might be having at any other level. Suffocated, dropped, born of rape as well as born to be raped – what did it matter, as long as Patrick realized how difficult it had been for her and how far she was from having collaborated with their persecutor. When Patrick asked why she didn't leave, she had said she was afraid that David would kill her, but since he had already twice tried to kill her when they were living together, it was hard to see how living apart would have made it more likely. The truth, which made his blood pressure shoot up as he admitted it, was that she craved the extreme violence of David's presence, and that she threw her son into the bargain. Patrick wanted to stop the car and get out and walk; he wanted a shot of whisky, a shot of heroin, a revolver shot in the head – kill the screaming man, get it over with, be in charge. He let these impulses wash over him without paying them too much attention.

The car was turning into Queensbury Place, next to the Lycée Français de Londres, where Patrick had spent a year of bilingual delinquency when he was seven years old. At the prize-giving ceremony in the Royal Albert Hall, there was a copy of *La Chèvre de Monsieur Seguin* on his red plush seat. He soon became obsessed with the story of the doomed and heroic little goat, lured into the high mountains by the riot of Alpine flowers ('Je me languis, je me languis, je veux aller à la montagne'). Monsieur Seguin, who has already lost six goats to the wolf, is determined not to lose another and locks the hero in the woodshed, but the little goat climbs out through the window and escapes, spending a day of ecstasy on slopes dotted with red and blue and yellow and orange flowers. Then, as the sun begins to set, he suddenly notices among the lengthening shadows the silhouette of the lean and hungry wolf, sitting complacently in the tall grass, contemplating his prey. Knowing he is going to die, the goat nevertheless determines to fight until the dawn ('pourvu que je tienne jusqu'à l'aube'), lowers his head and charges at the wolf's chest. He fights all night, charging again and again, until finally, as the sun rises over the grey crags of the mountain opposite, he collapses on the ground and is destroyed. This story never failed to move Patrick to tears as he read it every night in his bedroom in Victoria Road.

That was it! Last night's strange dream: a hooded figure striding among a herd of goats, pulling their heads back and slitting their throats. Patrick had been one of the goats on the outer edge of the herd and with a sense of doom and defiance worthy of his childhood hero he reached up and tore out his own larynx so as not to give the assassin the satisfaction of hearing him scream. Here was another form of violent silence. If only he had time to work it all out. If only he could be alone, this knot of impressions and connections would untangle at his feet. His psyche was on the move; things that had wanted to be hidden now wanted to be revealed. Wallace Stevens was right: 'Freedom is like a man who kills himself / Each night, the incessant butcher, whose knife / Grows sharp in blood.' He was longing for the splendours of silence and solitude, but instead he was going to a party.

Johnny turned into Onslow Gardens and sped along the suddenly empty stretch of street.

'Here we are,' he said, slowing down to look for a parking space close to the club.

10

Kettle had explained to Mary her principled stand against attending Eleanor's funeral.

'It would be sheer hypocrisy,' she told her daughter. 'I despise disinheritance, and I think it's wrong to go to someone's funeral boiling with rage. The party's a different matter: it's about supporting you and Patrick. I'm not pretending it doesn't help that it's just round the corner.'

'In that case you could look after the boys,' said Mary. 'We feel exactly the same way about their coming to the cremation as you feel about going. Robert disconnected from Eleanor years ago and Thomas never really knew her, but we still want them to come to the party, to mark the occasion for them in a lighter way.'

'Oh, well, of course, I'd be delighted to help,' said Kettle, immediately determined to get her revenge for being burdened with an even more troublesome responsibility than the one she had been trying to evade.

As soon as Mary had dropped the boys off at her flat, Kettle got to work on Robert.

'Personally,' she said, 'I can't ever forgive your *other* grandmother for giving away your lovely house in France. You must miss it terribly; not being able to go there in the holidays. It was really more of a home than London, I suppose, being in the countryside and all that.'

Robert looked rather more upset than she had intended.

'How can you say that? That's a horrible thing to say,' said Robert.

'I was just trying to be sympathetic,' said Kettle.

Robert walked out of the kitchen and went to sit alone in the drawing room. He hated Kettle for making him think that he should still have Saint-Nazaire. He didn't cry about missing it any more, but he still remembered every detail. They could take away the place but they couldn't take away the images in his mind. Robert closed his eyes and thought about walking back home late one evening with his father through the Butterfly Wood in a high wind. The sound of creaking branches and calling birds was torn away and dissolved among the hissing pines. When they came out of the wood it was nearly night, but he could still make out the gleaming vine shoots snaking through the ploughed earth, and he saw his first shooting star incinerated on the edge of the clear black sky.

Kettle was right: it was more of a home than London. It was his first home and there could only ever be one, but he held it now in his imagination and it was even more beautiful than ever. He didn't want to go back and he didn't want to have it back, because it would be such a disappointment.

Robert had started to cry when Kettle came briskly into the drawing room with Thomas behind her.

'I asked Amparo to get a film for you. If you've got over your tantrum you could watch it with Thomas; she says her grandchildren absolutely love it.'

'Look, Bobby,' said Thomas, running over to show Robert the DVD case, 'it's a flying carpet.'

Robert was furious at the injustice of the word 'tantrum', but he quite wanted to see the film.

'We're not allowed to watch films in the morning,' he said.

'Well,' said Kettle, 'you'll just have to tell your father you were playing Scrabble, or something frightfully intellectual that he would approve of.'

'But it's not true,' said Thomas, 'because we're going to see the film.'

'Oh, dear, I can't get anything right, can I?' said Kettle. 'You'll be pleased to hear that silly old Granny is going out for a while. If you can face the treat I've gone to the trouble of organizing, just tell Amparo and she'll put it on for you. If not, there's a copy of the *Telegraph* in the kitchen – I'm sure you can get the crossword puzzle done by the time I'm back.'

With this triumphant sarcasm, Kettle left her flat, a martyr to her spoilt and oversensitive grandsons. She was going to the Pâtisserie Valerie to have coffee with the widow of our former ambassador to Rome. If the truth be told, Natasha was a frightful bore, always going on about what James would have said, and what James would have thought, as if that mattered any more. Still, it was important to stay in touch with old friends.

Transport by Ford limousine was all part of the Bunyon's Bronze Service package that Mary had selected for the funeral. Neither the four vintage Rolls-Royces of the Platinum Service, nor the four plumed black horses and glass-sided carriage of the High Victorian Service, offered any serious competition. There was room for three other people in the Ford limo. Nancy had been Mary's first dutiful choice but Nicholas Pratt had a car and driver of his own and had already offered Nancy a lift. In the end, Mary shared the car with Julia, Patrick's ex-lover, Erasmus, her own ex-lover, and Annette, Seamus' ex-lover. Nobody spoke until the car was turning, at a mournful pace, onto the main road.

'I hate bereavement,' said Julia, looking at the mirror in her small powder compact, 'it ruins your eyeliner.'

'Were you fond of Eleanor?' asked Mary, knowing that Julia had never bothered with her.

'Oh, it's nothing to do with her,' said Julia, as if stating the obvious. 'You know the way that tears spring on you, in a silly film, or at a funeral, or when you read something in the paper: not really brought on by the thing that triggers them, but from accumulated grief, I suppose, and life just being so generally maddening.'

'Of course,' said Mary, 'but sometimes the trigger and the grief are connected.'

She turned away, trying to distance herself from the routine frivolity of Julia's line on bereavement. She glimpsed the pink flowers of a magnolia protesting against the black-and-white half-timbered facade of a mock-Tudor side street. Why was the driver going by Kew Bridge? Was it considered more dignified to take the longer route?

'I didn't put on my eyeliner this morning,' said Erasmus, with the studied facetiousness of an academic.

'You can borrow mine if you like,' said Annette, joining in.

'Thank you for what you said about Eleanor,' said Mary, turning to Annette with a smile.

'I only hope I was able to do justice to a very special lady,' said Annette.

'God yes,' said Julia, reapplying her eyeliner meticulously. 'I do wish this car would stop moving.'

'She was certainly someone who wanted to be good,' said Mary, 'and that's rare enough.'

'Ah, intentionality,' said Erasmus, as if he were pointing out a famous waterfall that had just become visible through the car window.

'Paving the road to Hell,' said Julia, moving on to the other eye with her greasy black pencil.

'Aquinas says that love is "desiring another's good",' Erasmus began.

'Just desiring another is good enough for me,' interrupted Julia. 'Of course one doesn't want them to be run over or gunned down in the street – or not often, anyway. It seems to me that Aquinas is just stating the obvious. Everything is rooted in desire.'

'Except conformity, convention, compulsion, hidden motivation, necessity, confusion, perversion, principle.' Erasmus smiled sadly at the wealth of alternatives.

'But they just create other kinds of desire.'

'If you pack every meaning into a single word, you deprive it of any meaning at all,' said Erasmus.

'Well, even if you think Aquinas is a complete genius for saying that,' said Julia, 'I don't see how "desiring another's good" is the same as desiring others to think you're a goody-goody.'

'Eleanor didn't just want to be good, she was good,' said Annette. 'She wasn't just a dreamer like so many visionaries, she was a builder and a mover and shaker who made a practical difference to lots of lives.'

'She certainly made a practical difference to Patrick's life,' said Julia, snapping her compact closed.

Mary was driven mad by Julia's presumption that she was more loyal than anyone to Patrick's interests. Her fidelity to his infidelity was an act of aggression towards Mary that Julia wouldn't have allowed herself without Erasmus' presence and Patrick's absence. Mary decided to keep a cold silence. They were already in Hammersmith and she was easily furious enough to last until Chelsea.

When Nancy invited Henry to join her in Nicholas' car, he pointed out that he had a car of his own.

'Tell him to follow us,' said Nicholas.

And so Henry's empty car followed Nicholas' full car from the crematorium to the club.

'One knows so many more dead people than living ones,' said Nicholas, relaxing into an abundance of padded black leather while electronically reclining the passenger seat towards Nancy's knees so as to lecture his guests from a more convenient angle, 'although, in terms of sheer numbers, all the people who have ever existed cannot equal the verminous multitude currently clutching at the surface of our once beautiful planet.'

'That's one of the problems with reincarnation: who is being reincarnated if there are more people now than the sum of the people who have ever existed?' said Henry. 'It doesn't make any sense.'

'It only makes sense if lumps of raw humanity are raining down on us for their first round of civilization. That, I'm afraid, is all too plausible,' said Nicholas, arching his eyebrow at his driver and giving a warning glance to Henry. 'It's your first time here, isn't it, Miguel?'

'Yes, Sir Nicholas,' said Miguel, with the merry laugh of a man who is used to being exotically insulted by his employer several times a day.

'It's no use telling you that you were Queen Cleopatra in a previous lifetime, is it?'

'No, Sir Nicholas,' said Miguel, unable to control his mirth.

'What I don't understand about reincarnation is why we all forget,' complained Nancy. 'Wouldn't it have been more fun, when we first met, to have said, "How are you? I haven't seen you since that perfectly ghastly party Marie-Antoinette gave in the Petit Trianon!" Something like that, something fun. I mean, if it's true, reincarnation is like having Alzheimer's on a huge scale, with each lifetime as our little moment of vivid anxiety. I know that my sister believed in it, but by the time I wanted to ask her about why we forget, she *really* did have Alzheimer's, and so it would have been tactless, if you know what I'm saying.'

'Rebirth is just a sentimental rumour imported from the vegetable kingdom,' said Nicholas wisely. 'We're all impressed by the resurgence of the spring, but the tree never died.'

'You can get reborn in your own lifetime,' said Henry quietly. 'Die to something and go into a new phase.'

'Spare me the spring,' said Nicholas. 'Ever since I was a little boy, I've been in the high summer of being me, and I intend to go on chasing butterflies through the tall grass until the abrupt and painless end. On the other hand, I do see that some people, like Miguel, for instance, are crying out for a complete overhaul.'

Miguel chuckled and shook his head in disbelief.

'Oh, Miguel, isn't he awful?' said Nancy.

'Yes, madam.'

'You're not supposed to agree with her, you moron,' said Nicholas.

'I thought Eleanor was a Christian,' said Henry, who disliked Nicholas' servant-baiting. 'Where does all this Eastern stuff come from?'

'Oh, she was just generally religious,' said Nancy.

'Most people who are Christian at least have the merit of not being Hindu or Sufi,' said Nicholas, 'just as Sufis have the merit of not being Christian, but religiously speaking, Eleanor was like one of those amazing cocktails that make you wonder what motorway collision could have first combined gin, brandy, tomato juice, crème de menthe, and Cointreau into a single drink.'

'Well, she was always a nice kid,' said Henry stoutly, 'always concerned about other people.'

'That can be a good thing,' admitted Nicholas, 'depending on who the other people are, of course.'

Nancy rolled her eyeballs slightly at her cousin in the

back seat. She felt that families should be allowed to say horrible things to each other, but that outsiders should be more careful. Henry looked longingly back at his empty car. Even Nicholas needed to take a rest from himself. As his car sped past the Cromwell Hospital everyone fell silent by mutual consent and Nicholas closed his eyes, gathering his resources for the social ordeal that lay ahead.

After the film, Thomas sat on a cushion and pretended to be riding his own flying carpet. First of all he visited his mother and father, who were at his grandmother's funeral. He had seen photographs of his dead grandmother that made him think he could remember her, but then his mother had told him that he last saw her when he was two and she was living in France and so he realized that he had made up the memory from the photograph. Unless in fact he had a very dim memory of her and the photograph had blown on the tiny little ember of his connection with his granny, like a faint orange glow in a heap of soft grey ash, and for a moment he really could remember when he had sat on his granny's lap and smiled at her and patted her wrinkly old face – his mother said he smiled at her and she was really pleased.

The flying carpet shot on to Baghdad, where Thomas jumped off and kicked the evil sorcerer Jafar over the parapet and into the moat. The princess was so grateful that she gave him a pet leopard, a turban with a ruby in the middle, and a lamp with a very powerful and funny genie living in it. The genie was just expanding into the air above him when Thomas heard the front door opening and Kettle greeting Amparo in the hall.

'Have the boys been good?'

'Oh, yes, they love the film, just like my granddaughters.'

'Well, at least I've got that right,' sighed Kettle. 'We must hurry; I have a cab waiting outside. I was so exhausted by my friend's complaining that I had to hail a taxi the moment I got out of the patisserie.'

'Oh, dear, I'm so sorry,' said Amparo.

'It can't be helped,' said Kettle stoically.

Kettle found Thomas cross-legged on a cushion next to the big low table in the middle of the drawing room and Robert stretched on the sofa staring at the ceiling.

'I'm riding on a flying carpet,' said Thomas.

'In that case, you won't need the silly old taxi I've got for us to go to the party.'

'No,' said Thomas serenely, 'I'll find my own way.'

He leant forward and grabbed the front corners of the cushion, tilting sideways to go into a steep left turn.

'Let's get a move on,' said Kettle, clapping her hands together impatiently. 'It's costing me a fortune to keep this taxi waiting. What are you doing staring at the ceiling?' she snapped at Robert.

'Thinking.'

'Don't be ridiculous.'

The two boys followed Kettle into the frail old-fashioned cage of a lift that took them to the ground floor of her building. She seemed to calm down once she told the taxi driver to take them to the Onslow Club, but by then both Robert and Thomas felt too upset to talk. Sensing their reluctance, Kettle started to interrogate them about their schools. After dashing some dull questions against their proud silence, she gave in to the temptation of reminiscing about her own schooldays: Sister Bridget's irresistible charm towards the parents, especially the grander ones, and her high austerity towards the girls; the hilarious report in which Sister Anna had said that it would take 'divine intervention' to make Kettle into a mathematician.

Kettle carried on with her complacent self-deprecation as the taxi rumbled down the Fulham Road. The brothers withdrew into their private thoughts, only emerging when they stopped outside the club.

'Oh, look, there's Daddy,' said Robert, lunging out of the taxi ahead of his grandmother.

'Don't wait for me,' said Kettle archly.

'Okay,' said Thomas, following his brother into the street and running up to his father.

'Hello, Dada,' he said, jumping into Patrick's arms. 'Guess what I've been doing? I've been watching *Aladdin*! Not *Bin* Laden but *A*-laddin.' He chuckled mischievously, patting both Patrick's cheeks at once.

Patrick burst out laughing and kissed him on the forehead.

11

As he arrived at the entrance of the Onslow Club, with Thomas still in his arms and Robert walking by his side, Patrick heard the distant but distinct sound of Nicholas Pratt disgorging his opinions on the pavement behind him.

'A celebrity these days is somebody you've never heard of,' Nicholas boomed, 'just as "*j'arrive*" is what a French waiter says as he hurries away from you in a Paris cafe. Margot's fame belongs to a bygone era: one actually knows who she is! Nevertheless, to write five autobiographies is going too far. Life is life and writing is writing and if you write as Margot does, like a glass of water on a rainy day it can only dilute the effect of whatever it was you *used* to do well.'

'You are awful,' said Nancy's admiring voice.

Patrick turned around and saw Nancy, her arm locked in Nicholas', with a rather demoralized-looking Henry walking on her other side.

'Who is that funny man?' asked Thomas.

'He's called Nicholas Pratt,' said Patrick.

'He's like Toady in a *very* grumpy mood,' said Thomas.

Patrick and Robert both laughed as much as Nicholas' proximity allowed.

'She said to me,' Nicholas continued in his coy simpering voice, ' "I know it's my fifth book, but there always seems to be more to say." If one says nothing in the first place, there always *is* more to say: there's everything to say. Ah, Patrick,' Nicholas checked himself, 'how thrilling to be introduced, at my advanced age, to a new club.' He peered with exaggerated curiosity at the brass plaque on a white stucco pillar. 'The Onslow Club, I don't remember ever hearing it mentioned.'

He's the last one, thought Patrick, watching Nicholas' performance with cold detachment, the last of my parents' friends left alive, the last of the guests who used to visit Saint-Nazaire when I was a child. George Watford and Victor Eisen and Anne Eisen are dead, even Bridget, who was so much younger than Nicholas, is dead. I wish he would drop dead as well.

Patrick lazily retracted his murderous desire to get rid of Nicholas. Death was the kind of boisterous egomaniac that needed no encouragement. Besides, being free, whatever that might mean, couldn't depend on Nicholas' death, or even on Eleanor's.

Still, her death pointed to a post-parental world that Nicholas' presence was obstructing. His perfectly rehearsed contempt was a frayed cable connecting Patrick to the social atmosphere of his childhood. Patrick's one great ally during his troubled youth had always loathed Nicholas. Victor Eisen's wife, Anne, felt that the nimbus of insanity surrounding David Melrose's corruption had made it seem inevitable, whereas Nicholas' decadence was more like a stylistic choice.

Nicholas straightened up and took in the children.

'Are these your sons?'

'Robert and Thomas,' said Patrick, noticing a strong reluctance to put the increasingly burdensome Thomas down on the pavement next to his father's last living friend.

'What a pity David isn't here to enjoy his grandsons,' said Nicholas. 'He would have ensured at the very least that they didn't spend the whole day in front of the television. He was very worried about the tyranny of the cathode-ray tube. I remember vividly when we had seen some children who were practically giving birth to a television set, he said to me, "I dread to think what all that radiation is doing to their little genitals." '

Patrick was lost for words.

'Let's go inside,' said Henry firmly. He smiled at the two boys and led the party indoors.

'I'm your cousin Henry,' he said to Robert. 'You came to stay with me in Maine a few years back.'

'On that island,' said Robert. 'I remember. I loved it there.'

'You must come again.'

Patrick pressed ahead with Thomas, while Nicholas, like a lame pointer following a wounded bird, hobbled after him across the black-and-white tiles of the entrance hall. He could tell that he had unsettled Patrick and didn't want to lose the chance to consolidate his work.

'I can't help thinking how much your father would have enjoyed this occasion,' panted Nicholas. 'Whatever his drawbacks as a parent, you must admit that he never lost his sense of humour.'

'Easy not to lose what you never had,' said Patrick, too relieved that he could speak again to avoid the mistake of engaging with Nicholas.

'Oh, I disagree,' said Nicholas. 'He saw the funny side of *everything*.'

'He only saw the funny side of things that didn't have one,' said Patrick. 'That's not a sense of humour, just a form of cruelty.'

'Well, cruelty and laughter,' said Nicholas, struggling to take off his overcoat next to the row of brass hooks on the far side of the hall, 'have always been close neighbours.'

'Close without being incestuous,' said Patrick. 'In any

case, I have to deal with the people who have come to mourn my mother, however much you may miss my other amazing parent.'

Taking advantage of the tangle that had briefly turned Nicholas' overcoat into a straitjacket, Patrick doubled back to the entrance of the club.

'Ah, look, there's Mummy,' he said, at last releasing Thomas onto the chequerboard floor and following him as he ran towards Mary.

'I hate to sound like Greta Garbo, but "I want to be alone",' said Patrick in a ludicrous Swedish accent.

'Again!' said Mary. 'Why don't these feelings come over you when you *are* alone? That's when you phone up to complain that you don't get invited to parties any more.'

'That's true, but it's not my mother's after-funeral sandwiches that I have in mind. Listen, I'll just whizz around the block, as if I was having a cigarette, and then I promise I'll come back and be totally present.'

'Promises, promises,' said Mary, with an understanding smile.

Patrick saw Julia, Erasmus, and Annette coming in behind Mary and felt the stranglehold of social responsibility. He wanted to leave more than ever but at the same time realized that he wouldn't be able to. Annette spotted Nicholas across the hall.

'Poor Nick, he's got into a real muddle with his overcoat,' she said, rushing to his rescue.

'Let me help you with that.' She pulled at Nicholas' sleeve and released his twisted shoulder.

'Thank you,' said Nicholas. 'That fiend, Patrick, saw that I was trussed up like a turkey and simply walked away.'

'Oh, I'm sure he didn't mean to,' said Annette optimistically.

Having parked his car, Johnny arrived and added to the

weight of guests forcing Patrick back into the hall. As he was pushed inside by the collective pressure, Patrick saw a half-familiar grey-haired woman stepping into the club with an air of tremendous determination and asking the hall porter if there was a party for Eleanor Melrose's funeral.

He suddenly remembered where he had seen her before. She had been in the Priory at the same time as him. He met her when he was about to leave on his abortive visit to Becky. She had surged up to him at the front door, wearing a dark green sweater and a tweedy skirt, and started to talk in an urgent and over-familiar way, blocking his path to the exit.

'You leaving?' she asked, not pausing for an answer. 'I must say I don't envy you. I love it here. I come here for a month every year, does me the world of good, gets me away from home. The thing is, I absolutely loathe my children. They're monsters. Their father, whose guts I loathe, never disciplined them, so you can imagine the sort of horrors they've turned into. Of course I've had my part to play. I mean, I lay in bed for ten months not uttering a single syllable and then when I did start talking I couldn't stop because of all the things that had piled up during the ten months. I don't know what you're in here for officially, but I have a feeling. No, listen to me. If I have one word of advice it's "Amitriptyline". It's absolutely wonderful. The only time I was happy was when I was on it. I've been trying to get hold of it ever since, but the bastards won't give me any.'

'The thing is I'm trying to stop taking anything,' said Patrick.

'Don't be so stupid; it's the most marvellous drug.'

She followed him out onto the steps after his cab arrived. '*Amitriptyline*,' she shouted, as if he'd been the one to tell her about it, 'you lucky thing!'

He had not followed her fierce advice and taken up Amitriptyline; in fact in the next few months he had given up the oxazepam and the antidepressants and stopped drinking alcohol altogether.

'It's so weird,' said Patrick to Johnny as they climbed the staircase to the room designated for the party, 'a woman arrived just now who was in the Priory at the same time as me last year. She's a complete loony.'

'It's bound to happen in a place like that,' said Johnny.

'I wouldn't know, being completely normal,' said Patrick.

'Perhaps too normal,' said Johnny.

'Just too damn normal,' said Patrick, pounding his fist into his palm.

'Fortunately, we can help you with that,' said Johnny, in the voice of a wise paternalistic American doctor, 'thanks to Xywyz, a breakthrough medication that only employs the last four letters of the alphabet.'

'That's incredible!' said Patrick, wonder-struck.

Johnny dashed through a rapid disclaimer: 'Do not take Xywyz if you are using water or other hydrating agents. Possible side-effects include blindness, incontinence, aneurism, liver failure, dizziness, skin rash, depression, internal haemorrhaging, and sudden death.'

I don't care,' wailed Patrick, 'I want it anyway. I gotta have it.'

The two men fell silent. They had been improvising little sketches for decades, since the days when they smoked cigarettes and later joints on the fire escape during breaks at school.

'She was asking about this party,' said Patrick, as they reached the landing.

'Maybe she knew your mother.'

'Sometimes the simplest explanations are the best,' Patrick conceded, 'although she might be a funeral fanatic having a manic episode.'

The sound of uncorking bottles reminded Patrick that it was only a year since Gordon, the wise Scottish moderator, had interviewed him before he joined the Depression Group for daily sessions. Gordon drew his attention to 'the alcoholic behind the alcohol'.

'You can take the brandy out of the fruitcake,' he said, 'but you're still left with the fruitcake.'

Patrick, who had spent the night in a state of seething hallucination and cosmic unease, was not in the mood to agree with anything.

'I don't think you can take the brandy out of the fruitcake,' he said, 'or the eggs out of the soufflé, or the salt out of the sea.'

'It was only a metaphor,' said Gordon.

'*Only* a metaphor!' Patrick howled. 'Metaphor is the whole problem, the solvent of nightmares. At the molten heart of things everything resembles everything else: that's the horror.'

Gordon glanced down at Patrick's sheet to make sure he had taken his latest dose of oxazepam.

'What I'm really asking,' he persevered, 'is what have you been self-medicating for, at the end of the day, if not depression?'

'Borderline personality, narcissistic rage, schizoid tendencies . . .' Patrick suggested some plausible additions.

Gordon roared with therapeutic laughter. 'Excellent! You've come in with some self-knowledge under your belt.'

Patrick glanced down the stairwell to make sure the Amitriptyline woman wasn't nearby.

'I saw her twice,' he told Johnny, 'once at the beginning of my stay and once in the middle, when I was starting to get better. The first time she lectured me on the joys of Amitriptyline, but the second time we didn't even talk, I just saw her delivering the same speech to someone from my Depression Group.'

'So, she was a sort of Ancient Mariner of Amitriptyline.'

'Exactly.'

Patrick remembered his second sighting of her very clearly, because it had taken place on the pivotal day of his stay. A raw clarity had started to take over from the withdrawal and delirium of his first fortnight. He spent more and more time alone in the garden, not wanting to drown in the chatter of a group lunch, or spend any more time in his bedroom than he already did. One day he was sitting on the most secluded bench in the garden when he suddenly started to cry. There was nothing in the patch of pasty sky or the partial view of a tree that justified his feeling of aesthetic bliss; no wood pigeons thrummed on the branch, no distant opera music drifted across the lawn, no crocuses shivered at the foot of the tree. Something unseen and unprovoked had invaded his depressive gaze, and spread like a gold rush through the ruins of his tired brain. He had no control over the source of his reprieve. He had not reframed or distanced his depression; it had simply yielded to another way of being. He was crying with gratitude but also with frustration at not being able to secure a supply of this precious new commodity. He felt the depths of his own psychological materialism and saw dimly that it stood in his way, but the habit of grasping at anything that might alleviate his misery was too strong, and the sense of gratuitous beauty that had shimmered through him disappeared as he tried to work out how it could be captured and put to use.

And then the Amitriptyline woman appeared wearing the same green sweater and tweedy skirt that he had first seen her in. He remembered thinking that she must have come with a small suitcase.

'But the bastards won't give me any . . .' she was saying

to Jill, a tearful member of Patrick's Depression Group.

Jill had run sobbing out of that morning's session, after her suggestion that the group treat the word God as an acronym for Gift of Desperation had been greeted by the bitter and abrasive Terry with the words, 'Excuse me while I vomit.'

Anxious to avoid conversation with the two women, Patrick bolted behind the dark lateral branches of a cedar tree.

'You lucky thing . . .' The Amitriptyline speech continued on its inevitable course.

'But I haven't been given any,' Jill protested, clearly feeling the presence of God, as tears welled up in her eyes again.

'The last time I saw her, I got stuck behind a cedar tree for twenty minutes,' Patrick explained to Johnny, as they walked into a pale blue room with high French windows overlooking a placid communal garden. 'When I saw her coming, I dashed behind a tree while they took over the bench I'd been sitting on.'

'Serves you right for abandoning your depression buddy,' said Johnny.

'I was having an epiphany.'

'Oh, well . . .'

'It all seems so far away.'

'The epiphany or the Priory?'

'Both,' said Patrick, 'or at least they did until that woman turned up.'

'Maybe insight comes when you need to get out of the madhouse. The loony downstairs might be a catalyst.'

'Anything might be a catalyst,' said Patrick. 'Anything might be evidence, anything might be a clue. We can never afford to relax our vigilance.'

'Fortunately we can help with that,' Johnny slipped again

into his American doctor's voice, 'thanks to Vigilante. Fought over by fighter pilots, presiding over presidents, terrifying terrorists, the busy-ness behind the business of America. *Vigilante: "Keeping Our Leaders On The Job Around The Clock."*' Johnny's voice switched to a rapid murmur. 'Do not take Vigilante if you are suffering from high blood pressure, low blood pressure, or normal blood pressure. Consult your physician if you experience chest pains, swollen eyelids, elongated ears . . .'

Patrick tuned out of the disclaimer and looked around at the almost empty room. Nancy was already deep in a plate of sandwiches at the far end of a long table loaded with too much food for the small party of mourners. Henry was standing next to her, talking to Robert. Behind the table was an exceptionally pretty waitress, with a long neck and high cheekbones and short black hair. She gave Patrick a friendly open smile. She must be an aspiring actress between auditions. She was absurdly attractive. He wanted to leave with her straight away. Why did she seem so irresistible? Did the table of almost untouched food make her seem generous as well as lovely? What was the proper approach on such an occasion? My mother just died and I need cheering up? My mother never gave me enough to eat but you look as if you could do much better? Patrick let out a short bark of private laughter at the absurdity of these tyrannical impulses, the depth of his dependency, the fantasy of being saved, the fantasy of being nourished. There was just too much past weighing down on his attention, taking it below the waterline, flooding him with primitive, pre-verbal urges. He imagined himself shaking off his unconscious, like a dog just out of the sea. He walked over to the table, asked for a glass of sparkling water, and gave the waitress a simple smile with no future. He thanked her and turned away crisply. There was something hollow about the performance; he still found her utterly adorable, but he saw the attraction for what it was: his own hunger, with no interpersonal implications whatsoever.

He was reminded of Jill from his Depression Group, who had complained one day that she had 'a relationship problem – well, the problem is that the person I have a relationship with doesn't know that we have a relationship'. This confession had elicited peals of derisive laughter from Terry.

'No wonder you're in treatment for the ninth time,' said Terry.

Jill hurried from the room, sobbing.

'You're going to have to apologize for that,' said Gordon.

'But I meant it.'

'That's why you have to apologize.'

'But I wouldn't mean it if I apologized,' Terry argued.

'Fake it to make it, man,' said Gary, the American whose opportunistic tourist of a mother had created such a flurry during Patrick's first Group session.

Patrick wondered if he was faking it to make it – a phrase that had always filled him with disgust – by turning away so resolutely from a woman he would rather have seduced? No, it was the seduction that would have been faking it, the Casanova complex that would have forced him to disguise his infantile yearnings with the appearance of adult behaviour: courtesy, conversation, copulation, commentary; elaborate devices for distancing him from the impotent baby whose screams he could not bear to hear. The glory of his mother's death was that she could no longer get in the way of his own maternal instincts with her presumptive maternal presence and stop him from embracing the inconsolable wreck that she had given birth to.

12

As the room began to fill, Patrick was drawn out of his private thoughts and back into his role as host. Nicholas walked past him with haughty indifference to join Nancy at the far end of the room. Mary came over with the Amitriptyline woman in tow, followed closely by Thomas and Erasmus.

'Patrick,' said Mary, 'you should meet Fleur, she's an old friend of your mother's.'

Patrick shook hands with her politely, marvelling at her whimsical French name. Now that she had taken off her overcoat he could see the green sweater and tweed skirt he recognized from the Priory. Bright red lipstick in the shape of a mouth shadowed Fleur's own mouth, about half an inch to the right, giving the impression of a circus clown caught in the middle of removing her make-up.

'How did you know . . .' Patrick began.

'Dada!' said Thomas, too excited not to interrupt. 'Erasmus is a real philosopher!'

'Or at any rate a realist philosopher,' said Erasmus.

'I know, darling,' said Patrick, ruffling his son's hair. Thomas hadn't seen Erasmus for a year and a half, and clearly the category of philosopher had come into focus during that time.

'I mean,' said Thomas, looking very philosophical, 'I always think the trouble with God is: who created God? And,' he added, getting into the swing of it, 'who created whoever created God?'

'Ah, an infinite regress,' said Erasmus sadly.

'Okay, then,' said Thomas, 'who created infinite regress?' He looked up at his father to check that he was arguing philosophically.

Patrick gave him an encouraging smile.

'He's frightfully clever, isn't he?' said Fleur. 'Unlike my lot: they could hardly string a sentence together until they were well into their teens, and then it was only to insult me – and their father, who deserved it of course. Absolute monsters.'

Mary slipped away with Thomas and Erasmus, leaving Patrick stranded with Fleur.

'That's teenagers for you,' said Patrick, with resolute blandness. 'So, how did you know Eleanor?'

'I adored your mother. I think she was one of the very few good people I ever met. She saved my life really – I suppose it must have been thirty years ago – by giving me a job in one of the charity shops she used to run for the Save the Children Fund.'

'I remember those shops,' said Patrick, noticing that Fleur was gathering momentum and didn't want to be interrupted.

'I was thought by some people,' Fleur motored on, 'well, by everyone except your mother really, to be unemployable, because of my episodes, but I simply had to get out of the house and *do* something, so your mother was an absolute godsend. She had me packing up second-hand clothes in no time. We used to send them off to the shop we thought they'd do best in, keeping the really good ones for our shop in Launceston Place, just round the corner from your house.'

'Yes,' said Patrick quickly.

'We used to have such fun,' Fleur reminisced, 'we were like a couple of schoolgirls, holding up the clothes and saying, "Richmond, I think," or "*Very* Cheltenham." Sometimes we'd both shout, "Rochdale!" or, "Hemel Hempstead!" at exactly the same time. Oh, how we laughed. Eventually your mother trusted me enough to put me on the till and let me run the shop for the whole day, and that, I'm afraid, is when I had one of my episodes. We had a fur coat in that morning – it was the time when people started to get paint thrown at them if they wore one – an amazing sable coat – I think that's what tipped me over the edge. I was gripped by a need to do something really glamorous, so I shut up the shop and took all the money from the till and put on the sable coat – it wasn't very suitable at the height of June, but I had to wear it. Anyway, I went out and hailed a cab and said, "Take me to the Ritz!" '

Patrick looked around the room anxiously, wondering if he would ever get away.

'They tried to take my coat off me,' Fleur accelerated, 'but I wouldn't hear of it, and so I sat in the Palm Court in a heap of sable, drinking champagne cocktails and talking to anyone who would listen, until a frightfully pompous head waiter asked me to leave because I was being "a nuisance to the other guests"! Can you imagine the rudeness of it? Well, anyway, the money I'd taken from the till turned out not to be enough for the enormous bill and so the wretched hotel insisted on keeping the coat, which turned out to be very inconvenient because the lady who had given it to us came back and said she'd changed her mind . . .'

By now Fleur was falling over herself to keep up with her thoughts. Patrick tried to catch Mary's eye, but she seemed to be deliberately ignoring him.

'All I can say is that your mother was absolutely marvellous. She went and paid the bill and rescued the coat. She said she was used to it because she was always clearing her father's bar bills in grand places, and she didn't mind at all. She was an absolute saint and let me go on running the shop when she was away, saying that she was sure I wouldn't do it again – which I'm afraid to say I did, more than once.'

'Would you like a drink?' asked Patrick, turning back towards the waitress with renewed longing. Perhaps he should run away with her after all. He wanted to kiss the pulse in her long neck.

'I shouldn't really but I'll have a gin and tonic,' said Fleur, hardly pausing before she continued. 'You must be very proud of your mother. She did an enormous amount of practical good, the only sort of good there *is* really – touched on hundreds of lives, threw herself into those shops with tremendous energy – I firmly believe she could have been an entrepreneur, if she had needed the money – the way she used to set off to the Harrogate Trade Fair with a spring in her step.'

Patrick smiled at the waitress and then looked down at the tablecloth bashfully. When he looked up again she was smiling at him with sympathy and laughter in her eyes. She clearly understood everything. She was wonderfully intelligent as well as impossibly lovely. The more Fleur talked about Eleanor, the more he wanted to start a new life with the waitress. He took the gin and tonic from her tenderly and handed it on to the loquacious Fleur, who seemed to be saying, 'Well, do you?' for reasons he couldn't fathom.

'Do I what?' he asked.

'Feel proud of your mother?'

'I suppose so,' said Patrick.

'What do you mean, you "suppose so"? You're worse than my children. Absolute monsters.'

'Listen, it's been a great pleasure to meet you,' said Patrick, 'and I expect we'll talk again, but I probably ought to circulate.'

He moved away from Fleur unceremoniously and, wanting to look as if he had a firm intention, walked towards Julia, who stood alone by the window drinking a glass of white wine.

'Help!' said Patrick.

'Oh, hi,' said Julia, 'I was just staring out of the window vacantly, but not so vacantly that I didn't see you flirting with that pretty waitress.'

'Flirting? I didn't say a word.'

'You didn't have to, darling. A dog doesn't have to say a word when it sits next to us in the dining room making little whimpering sounds while strings of saliva dangle down to the carpet; we still know what it wants.'

'I admit that I was vaguely attracted to her, but it was only after that grey-haired lunatic started talking to me that she began to look like the last overhanging tree before the roar of the rapids.'

'How poetic. You're still trying to be saved.'

'Not at all; I'm trying not to want to be saved.'

'Progress.'

'Relentless forward motion,' said Patrick.

'So who is this lunatic who forced you to flirt with the waitress?'

'Oh, she used to work in my mother's charity shop years ago. Her experience of Eleanor was so different from mine, it made me realize that I'm not in charge of the meaning of my mother's life, and that I'm deluded to think that I can come to some magisterial conclusion about it.'

'Surely you could come to some conclusion about what it means to you.'

'I'm not even sure if that's true,' said Patrick. 'I've been noticing today how inconclusive I feel about both my parents. There isn't any final truth; it's more like being able to get off on different floors of the same building.'

'It sounds awfully tiring,' Julia complained. 'Wouldn't it be simpler to just loathe their guts?'

Patrick burst out laughing.

'I used to think that I was detached about my father. I thought that detachment was the great virtue, without the moral condescension built into forgiveness, but the truth is that I feel everything: contempt, rage, pity, terror, tenderness, and detachment.'

'Tenderness?'

'At the thought of how unhappy he was. When I had sons of my own and felt the strength of my instinct to protect them, I was freshly shocked that he had deliberately inflicted harm on his son, and then the hatred returned.'

'So you've pretty much abandoned detachment.'

'On the contrary, I just recognize how many things there are to be detached about. The incandescent hatred and the pure terror don't invalidate the detachment, they give it a chance to expand.'

'The StairMasters of detachment,' said Julia.

'Exactly.'

'I wonder if I'm allowed to smoke out here,' said Julia, opening the French windows and stepping outside. Patrick followed her onto the narrow balcony and sat on the edge of the white stucco balustrade. As she took out her packet of Camel Blue, his eyes traced the elegant profile he had often studied from a neighbouring pillow, now set against the restrained promise of the still-leafless trees. He watched Julia kiss the filter of her cigarette and suck the swaying flame of her lighter into the tightly packed tobacco. After the first immense drag, smoke flowed over her upper lip, only to be drawn back through her nose into her expanding lungs and eventually released, at first in a single thick stream and then in the little puffs and misshapen rings and drifting walls formed by her smoky words.

'So, have you been working out especially hard on your Inner StairMaster today?'

'I've felt a strange mixture of elation and free-fall. There's something cool and objective about death compared to the savage privacy of dying which my mother's illness forced me to imagine over the last four years. In a sense I can think about her clearly for the first time, away from the vortex of an empathy that was neither compassionate nor salutary, but a kind of understudy to her own horror.'

'Wouldn't it be even better not to think about her at all?' said Julia with a second languorous gulp of cigarette smoke.

'No, not today,' said Patrick, suddenly repelled by Julia's enamelled surface.

'Oh, of course, not today – of all days,' said Julia, sensing his defection. 'I just meant eventually.'

'The people who tell us to "get over it" and "get on with it" are the least able to have the direct experience that they berate navel-gazers for avoiding,' said Patrick, in the prosecuting style he adopted when defending himself. 'The "it" they're "getting on with" is a ghostly re-enactment of unreflecting habits. Not thinking about something is the surest way to remain under its influence.'

'It's a fair cop, guv,' said Julia, disconcerted by Patrick's sincerity.

'What would it mean to be spontaneous, to have an unconditioned response to things – to anything? Neither of us is in a position to know, but I don't want to die without finding out.'

'Hmm,' said Julia, clearly not tempted by Patrick's obscure project.

'Excuse me,' said a voice behind them.

Patrick looked round and saw the beautiful waitress. He had forgotten that he was in love with her, but now it all came back to him.

'Oh, hi,' he said.

She scarcely acknowledged him, but kept her eyes fixed on Julia.

'I'm sorry but you're not allowed to smoke out here,' she said.

'Oh, dear,' said Julia, taking a drag on her cigarette, 'I didn't know. It's funny, because it is outside.'

'Well, technically it's still part of the club and you can't smoke anywhere in the club.'

'I understand,' said Julia, continuing to smoke. 'Well, I'd better put it out then.' She took another long suck on her almost finished cigarette, dropped it on the balcony and ground it underfoot before stepping back indoors.

Patrick waited for the waitress to look at him with complicity and amusement, but she returned to her post behind the long table without glancing in his direction.

The waitress was useless. Julia was useless. Eleanor was useless. Even Mary in the end was useless and would not prevent him from returning to his bedsit alone and without any consolation whatever.

It was not the women who were at fault; it was his omnipotent delusion: the idea that they were there to be useful to him in the first place. He must make sure to remember that the next time one of the pointless bitches let him down. Patrick let out another bark of laughter. He was feeling a little bit mad. Casanova, the misogynist; Casanova, the hungry baby. The inadequacy at the rotten heart of exaggeration. He watched a modest veil of self-disgust settle on the subject of his relations with women, trying to prevent him from going deeper. Self-disgust was the easy way out, he must cut through it and allow himself to be unconsoled. He looked forward to the austere demands of that word, like a cool drink after the dry oasis of consolation. Back in his bedsit unconsoled, he could hardly wait.

It was getting cold on the balcony and Patrick wanted to

get back indoors, but he was prevented by his reluctance to join Kettle and Mary, who were standing just the other side of the French windows.

'I see that you and Thomas are still practically glued to each other,' said Kettle, casting an envious glance at her grandson draped comfortably around his mother's neck.

'Nobody can hope to ignore their children as completely as you did,' sighed Mary.

'What do you mean? We always . . . communicated.'

'Communicated! Do you remember what you said to me when you telephoned me at school to tell me that Daddy had died?'

'How awful it all was, I suppose.'

'I couldn't speak I was so upset, and you told me to *cheer up*. To *cheer up*! You never had any idea who I was and you still don't.'

Mary turned away with a growl of exasperation and walked towards the other end of the room. Kettle greeted the inevitable outcome of her spite with an expression of astonished incomprehension. Patrick hovered on the balcony waiting for her to move away, but watched instead as Annette came up to engage her in conversation.

'Hello, dear,' said Annette, 'how are you?'

'Well, I've just had my head bitten off by my daughter, and so just for the moment I'm in a state of shock.'

'Mothers and children,' said Annette wisely, 'maybe we should have a workshop on that dynamic and tempt you back to the Foundation.'

'A workshop on mothers and children would tempt me to stay away,' said Kettle. 'Not that I need much encouragement to stay away; I think I've finished with shamanism.'

'Bless you,' said Annette. 'I won't feel that I've finished until I'm totally connected to the source of unconditional love that inhabits every soul on this planet.'

'Well, I've set my sights rather lower,' said Kettle. 'I think I'm just relieved not to be shaking a rattle, with my eyes watering from all that wretched wood smoke.'

Annette let out a peal of tolerant laughter.

'Well, I know Seamus would love to see you again and that he thought you'd especially benefit from our "Walking with the Goddess" workshop, "stepping into the power of the feminine". I'm going to be participating myself.'

'How is Seamus? I suppose he's moved into the main house now.'

'Oh, yes, he's in Eleanor's old bedroom, lording it over all of us.'

'The bedroom Patrick and Mary used to be in, with the view of the olive groves?'

'Oh, that's a glorious view, isn't it? Mind you, I love my room, looking out on the chapel.'

'That's my room,' said Kettle. 'I always used to stay in that room.'

'Isn't it funny how we get attached to things?' laughed Annette. 'And yet, in the end, even our bodies aren't really our own; they belong to the Earth – to the Goddess.'

'Not yet,' said Kettle firmly.

'I tell you what,' said Annette, 'if you come to the Goddess workshop, you can have your old room back. I don't mind moving out; I'm happy anywhere. Anyway, Seamus is always talking about "moving from the property paradigm to the participation paradigm", and if the facilitators at the Foundation don't do it, we can't expect anyone else to.'

Patrick's primary objective was to get off the balcony without drawing attention to himself, and so he suppressed the desire to point out that Seamus had been moving in the opposite direction, from participating in Eleanor's charity to occupying her property.

Kettle was clearly confused by Annette's kind offer of her

old bedroom. Her loyalty to her bad mood was not easily shaken and yet it was hard to see what she could do except thank Annette.

'That's unusually kind of you,' she said dismissively.

Patrick seized his chance and bolted off the balcony, passing behind Kettle's back with such decisiveness that he knocked her into Annette's clattering cup of tea.

'Mind out,' snapped Kettle before she could see who had barged into her. 'Honestly, Patrick,' she added when she saw the culprit.

'Oh, dear, you're covered in tea,' said Annette.

Patrick did not pause and only called, 'Sorry,' over his shoulder as he crossed the room at a quick pace. He continued out onto the landing and, without knowing where he was going, cantered down the staircase with a light hand on the banister, like a man who had been called away on urgent business.

13

Mary smiled at Henry from across the room and started to move in his direction, but before she could reach his side Fleur surged up in front of her.

'I hope I haven't offended your husband,' she said. 'He walked away from me very abruptly and now he seems to have stormed out of the room altogether.'

'It's a difficult day for him,' said Mary, fascinated by Fleur's lipstick, which had been reapplied, mostly to the old lopsided track around her mouth but also to her front teeth.

'Has he had mental-health problems?' said Fleur. 'I only ask because – God knows! – I've had my fair share and I've grown rather good at telling when other people have a screw loose.'

'You seem quite well now,' said Mary, lying virtuously.

'It's funny you should say that,' said Fleur, 'because this morning I thought, "There's no point in taking your pills when you feel so well." I feel very, very well, you see.'

Mary recoiled instinctively. 'Oh, good,' she said.

'I feel as if something amazing is going to happen to me today,' Fleur went on. 'I don't think I've ever achieved my full potential – I feel as if I could do anything – as if I could raise the dead!'

'That's the last thing anyone would expect at this party,' said Mary, with a cheerful laugh. 'Do ask Patrick first if it's Eleanor you've got in mind.'

'Oh, I'd love to see Eleanor again,' said Fleur, as if endorsing Mary's candidate for resurrection and about to perform the necessary operation.

'Will you excuse me?' said Mary. 'I've got to go and talk to Patrick's cousin. He's come all the way from America and we didn't even know he was coming.'

'I'd love to go to America,' said Fleur, 'in fact, I might fly there later this afternoon.'

'In a plane?' said Mary.

'Yes, of course . . . Oh!' Fleur interrupted herself. 'I see what you mean.'

She stuck out her arms, thrust her head forwards and swayed from side to side, with an explosion of laughter so loud that Mary could sense everyone in the room looking in her direction.

She reached out and touched Fleur's outstretched arm, smiling at her to show how much she had enjoyed sharing their delightful joke, but turning away firmly to join Henry, who stood alone in the corner of the room.

'That woman's laugh packs quite a punch,' said Henry.

'Everything about her packs a punch, that's what I'm worried about,' said Mary. 'I feel she may do something very crazy before we all get home.'

'Who is she? She's kind of exotic.'

Mary noticed how distinct Henry's eyelashes were against the pale translucence of his eyes.

'None of us has ever met her. She just turned up unexpectedly.'

'Like me,' said Henry, with egalitarian gallantry.

'Except that we know who you are and we're very pleased to see you,' said Mary, 'especially since not a lot of people have turned up. Eleanor lost touch with people; her social life was very disintegrated. She had a few little pockets of friendship, each assuming that there was something more central, but in fact there was nothing in the middle. For the last two years, I was the only person who visited her.'

'And Patrick?'

'No, he didn't go. She became so unhappy when she saw him. There was something she was dying to say but couldn't. I don't just mean in the mechanical sense that she couldn't speak in the last two years. I mean that she never could have said what she wanted to tell him, even if she had been the most articulate person in the world, because she didn't know what it was, but when she became ill she could feel the pressure of it.'

'Just horrible,' said Henry. 'It's what we all dread.'

'That's why we must drop our defences while it's still a voluntary act,' said Mary, 'otherwise they'll be demolished and we'll be flooded with nameless horror.'

'Poor Eleanor, I feel so sorry for her,' said Henry.

They both fell silent for a while.

'At this point the English usually say, "Well, this is a cheerful subject!" to cover their embarrassment at being serious,' said Mary.

'Let's just stick with the sorrow,' said Henry with a kind smile.

'I'm really pleased you came,' she said. 'Your love for Eleanor was so uncomplicated, unlike everyone else's.'

'Cabbage,' said Nancy, grabbing Henry's arm, with the exaggerated eagerness of a shipwrecked passenger who discovers that she is not the only member of her family left alive, 'thank God! Save me from that dreadful woman in the green sweater! I can't believe my sister ever knew her – socially. I mean, this really is the most extraordinary gathering. I don't feel it's really a Jonson occasion at all. When I think of Mummy's funeral, or Aunt Edith's. Eight hundred people turned up at Mummy's, half the French cabinet, and the Aga Khan, and the Windsors; *everybody* was there.'

'Eleanor chose a different path,' said Henry.

'More like a goat track,' said Nancy, rolling her eyes.

'Personally, I don't give a damn who comes to my funeral,' said Henry.

'That's only because you know that it'll be solid with senators and glamorous people and sobbing women!' said Nancy. 'The trouble with funerals is that they're so last-minute. That's where memorials come in, of course, but they're not the same. There's something so dramatic about a funeral, although I can't abide those open caskets. Do you remember Uncle Vlad? I still have nightmares about him lying there in that gold and white uniform looking all *gaunt*. Oh, God, wagon formation,' cried Nancy, 'the green goblin is staring at me again!'

Fleur was feeling a sense of irrepressible pleasure and potency as she scanned the room for someone who had not yet had the benefit of her conversation. She could understand all the currents flowing through the room; she only had to glance at a person to see into the depths of their soul. Thanks to Patrick Melrose, who was distracting the waitress by getting her telephone number, Fleur had been able to mix her own drink, a glass full of gin with a splash of tonic, rather than the other way round. What did it matter? Mere alcohol could not degrade her luminous awareness. After taking a gulp from her lipstick-smudged tumbler, she walked up to Nicholas Pratt, determined to help him understand himself.

'Have you had mental-health problems?' she asked Nicholas, fixing him with an intrepid stare.

'Have we met?' said Nicholas, gazing icily at the stranger who stood in his path.

'I only ask because I have a feeling for these things,' Fleur went on.

Nicholas hesitated between the impulse to utterly destroy

this batty old woman in a moth-eaten sweater, and the temptation to boast about his robust mental health.

'Well, have you?' insisted Fleur.

Nicholas raised his walking stick briefly, as if about to nudge Fleur aside, only to replant it more firmly in the carpet and lean into its full support. He inhaled the frosty, invigorating air of contempt flooding in from the window smashed by Fleur's impertinent question; contempt that always made him, though he said it himself, even more articulate than usual.

'No, I have not had "mental-health problems",' he thundered. 'Even in this degenerate age of confession and complaint we have not managed to turn reality entirely on its head. When the vocabulary of Freudian mumbo-jumbo is emptied onto every conversation, like vinegar onto a newspaper full of sodden chips, some of us choose not to *tuck in*.' Nicholas craned his head forward as he spat out the homely phrase.

'The sophisticated cherish their "syndromes",' he continued, 'and even the most simple-minded fool feels entitled to a "complex". As if it weren't ludicrous enough for every child to be "gifted", they now have to be ill as well: a touch of Asperger's, a little autism; dyslexia stalks the playground; the poor little gifted things have been "bullied" at school; if they can't confess to being abused, they must confess to being abusive. Well, my dear woman,' Nicholas laughed threateningly, ' – I call you "my dear" from what is no doubt known as *Sincerity Deficit Disorder*, unless some ambitious quack, landing on the scalding, sarcastic beaches of the great continent of irony, has claimed the inversion of surface meaning as *Potter's Disease* or *Jones's Jaundice* – no, my *dear* woman, I have not suffered from the slightest taint of mental illness. The modern passion for pathology is a landslide that has been forced to come to a halt at some distance from my eminently sane feet. I have only to walk towards that heap of refuse for it to part, making way for the impossible man, the man who is entirely well; psychotherapists scatter in my presence, ashamed of their sham profession!'

'You're completely off your rocker,' said Fleur, discerningly. 'I thought as much. I've developed what I call "my little radar" over the years. Put me in a room full of people and I can tell straight away who has had *that* sort of problem.'

Nicholas experienced a moment of despair as he realized that his withering eloquence had made no impact, but like an expert tango dancer who turns abruptly on the very edge of the dance floor, he changed his approach and shouted, 'Bugger off!' at the top of his voice.

Fleur looked at him with deepening insight.

'A month in the Priory would get you back on your feet,' she concluded, 're-clothe you in your rightful mind, as the hymn says. Do you know it?' Fleur closed her eyes and started to sing rapturously, '"Dear Lord and Father of mankind / Forgive our foolish ways / Re-clothe us in our rightful minds . . ." Marvellous stuff. I'll have a word with Dr Pagazzi, he's quite the best. He can be rather severe at times, but only for one's own good. Look at me: I was mad as a hatter and now I'm on top of the world.'

She leant forward to whisper confidentially to Nicholas.

'I feel very, very well, you see.'

There were professional reasons for Johnny not to engage with Nicholas Pratt, whose daughter had been a patient of his, but the sight of that monstrous man bellowing at a dishevelled old woman pushed his restraint beyond the limits he had imposed on himself until now. He approached Fleur and, with his back turned to Nicholas, asked her quietly if she was all right.

'All right?' laughed Fleur. 'I'm extremely well, better than ever.' She struggled to express her sense of abundance. 'If there were such a thing as being too well, I'd be it. I was just trying to help this poor man who's had more than his fair share of mental-health problems.'

Reassured that she was unharmed, Johnny smiled at Fleur and started to withdraw tactfully, but Nicholas was by now too enraged to let such an opportunity pass.

'Ah,' he said, 'here he is! Like an exhibit in a courtroom drama, brought on at the perfect moment: a practising witch-doctor, a purveyor of psycho-*paralysis*, a guide to the catacombs, a guide to the sewers; he promises to turn your dreams into nightmares and he keeps his promises religiously,' snarled Nicholas, his face flushed and the corners of his mouth flecked with tired saliva. 'The ferryman of Hell's second river won't accept a simple coin, like his proletarian colleague on the Styx. You'll need a fat cheque to cross the Lethe into that forgotten underworld of dangerous gibberish where toothless infants rip the nipples from their mothers' milkless breasts.'

Nicholas seemed to be labouring for breath, as he unrolled his vituperative sentences.

'No fantasy that you invent,' he struggled on, 'could be as repulsive as the fantasy on which his sinister art is based, polluting the human imagination with murderous babies and incestuous children . . .'

Nicholas suddenly stopped speaking, his mouth working to take in enough air. He rocked sideways on his walking stick before staggering backwards a couple of steps and crashing down against the table and onto the floor. He caught the tablecloth as he fell and dragged half a dozen glasses after him. A bottle of red wine toppled sideways and its contents gurgled over the edge of the table and splashed onto his black suit. The waitress lunged forward and caught the bucket of half-melted ice that was sliding towards Nicholas' supine body.

'Oh, dear,' said Fleur, 'he got himself too worked up.

"Hoisted by his own petard", as the saying goes. This is what happens to people who won't ask for help,' she said, as if discussing the case with Dr Pagazzi.

Mary leant over to the waitress, her mobile phone already open.

'I'm going to call an ambulance,' she said.

'Thanks,' said the waitress. 'I'll go downstairs and warn reception.'

Everyone in the room gathered around the fallen figure and looked on with a mixture of curiosity and alarm.

Patrick knelt down beside Nicholas and started to loosen his tie. Long after it could have been helpful, he continued to loosen the knot until he had removed the tie altogether. Only then did he undo the top button of Nicholas' shirt. Nicholas tried to say something but winced from the effort and closed his eyes instead, disgusted by his own vulnerability.

Johnny acknowledged a feeling of satisfaction at having played no active part in Nicholas' collapse. And then he looked down at his fallen opponent, sprawled heavily on the carpet, and somehow the sight of his old neck, no longer festooned with an expensive black silk tie, but wrinkled and sagging and open at the throat, as if waiting for the final dagger thrust, filled him with pity and renewed his respect for the conservative powers of an ego that would rather kill its owner than allow him to change.

'Johnny?' said Robert.

'Yes,' said Johnny, seeing Robert and Thomas looking up at him with great interest.

'Why was that man so angry with you?'

'It's a long story,' said Johnny, 'and one that I'm not really allowed to tell.'

'Has he got psycho-paralysis?' said Thomas. 'Because paralysis means you can't move.'

Johnny couldn't help laughing, despite the solemn murmur surrounding Nicholas' collapse.

'Well, personally, I think that would be a brilliant diagnosis; but Nicholas Pratt invented that word in order to make fun of psychoanalysis, which is what I do for a job.'

'What's that?' said Thomas.

'It's a way of getting access to hidden truths about your feelings,' said Johnny.

'Like hide and seek?' said Thomas.

'Exactly,' said Johnny, 'but instead of hiding in cupboards and behind curtains and under beds, this kind of truth hides in symptoms and dreams and habits.'

'Can we play?' said Thomas.

'Can we stop playing?' said Johnny, more to himself than to Thomas and Robert.

Julia came up and interrupted Johnny's conversation with the children.

'Is this the end?' she said. 'It's enough to put one off having a temper tantrum. Oh, God, that religious fanatic is cradling his head. That would definitely finish me off.'

Annette was sitting on her heels next to Nicholas, with her hands cupped around his head, her eyes closed and her lips moving very slightly.

'Is she praying?' said Julia, flabbergasted.

'That's nice of her,' said Thomas.

'They say one should never speak ill of the dead,' said Julia, 'and so I'd better get a move on. I've always thought that Nicholas Pratt was perfectly ghastly. I'm not a particular friend of Amanda's, but he seems to have ruined his daughter's life. Of course you'd know more about that than I do.'

Johnny had no trouble staying silent.

'Why don't you stop being so horrible?' said Robert passionately. 'He's an old man who's really ill and he might hear what you're saying, and he can't even answer back.'

'Yes,' said Thomas, 'it's not fair because he can't answer back.'

Julia at first seemed more bewildered than annoyed, and when she finally spoke it was with a wounded sigh.

'Well, you know it's time to leave a party when the children start to mount a joint attack on your moral character.'

'Could you say goodbye to Patrick for me?' she said, kissing Johnny abruptly on both cheeks and ignoring the two boys. 'I can't quite face it after what's happened – to Nicholas, I mean.'

'I hope we didn't make her angry,' said Robert.

'She made herself angry, because it was easier for her than being upset,' said Johnny.

Only seconds after her departure, Julia was forced back into the room by the urgent arrival of the waitress, two ambulance men, and an array of equipment.

'Look!' said Thomas. 'An oxygen tank and a stretcher. I wish I could have a go!'

'He's over here,' said the waitress unnecessarily.

Nicholas felt his wrist being lifted. He knew his pulse was being taken. He knew it was too fast, too slow, too weak, too strong, everything wrong. A rip in his heart, a skewer through his chest. He must tell them he was not an organ donor, or they would steal his organs before he was dead. He must stop them! Call Withers! Tell them *to put a stop to it at once*. He couldn't speak. Not his tongue, they mustn't take his tongue. Without speech, thoughts plough on like a train without tracks, buckling, crashing, ripping everything apart. A man asks him to open his eyes. He opens his eyes. Show them he's still compos mentis, compost mentis, recycled parts. No! Not his brain, not his genitals, not his heart, not fit to transplant, still writhing with self in an alien body. They were shining a light in his eyes, no, not his eyes; please don't take his eyes. So much fear. Without a regiment of words, the barbarians, the burning roofs, the horses' hooves beating down on fragile skulls. He was not himself any more; he was under the hooves. He could not be helpless; he could not be humiliated; it was too late to become somebody he didn't know – the intimate horror of it.

'Don't worry, Nick, I'll be with you in the ambulance,' a voice whispered in his ear.

It was the Irish woman. With him in the ambulance! Gouging his eyes out, fishing around for his kidneys with her nimble fingers, taking a hacksaw out of her spiritual tool box. He wanted to be saved. He wanted his mother; not the one he had actually had, but the real one he had never met. He felt a pair of hands grip his feet and another pair of hands slip around his shoulders. Hung, drawn, and quartered: publicly executed for all his crimes. He deserved it. Lord have mercy on his soul. Lord have mercy.

The two ambulance men looked at each other and on a nod lifted both ends of Nicholas at once and placed him on the stretcher they had spread out beside him.

'I'm going with him in the ambulance,' said Annette.

'Thank you,' said Patrick. 'Will you call me from the hospital if there's any news?'

'Surely,' said Annette. 'Oh, it's a terrible shock for you,' she said, giving Patrick an unexpected hug. 'I'd better go.'

'Is that woman going with him?' asked Nancy.

'Yes, isn't it kind of her?'

'But she doesn't even know him. I've known Nicholas forever. First it's my sister and now it's practically my oldest friend. It's too impossible.'

'Why don't you follow her?' said Patrick.

'There is one thing I could do for him,' said Nancy, with a hint of indignation, as if it was a bit much to expect her to be the only person to show any real consideration. 'Miguel, his poor driver, is waiting outside without the least idea of what's happened. I'll go and break the news to him, and take the car on to the hospital, so it's there if Nicholas needs it.'

Nancy could think of at least three places she might stop on the way. The examination was bound to take ages, in fact Nicholas might already be dead, and it would help to take poor Miguel's mind off the dreadful situation if he drove her around all afternoon. She had no cash for taxis, and her swollen feet were already bulging out of the ruthlessly elegant inside edges of her two-thousand-dollar shoes. People said she was incorrigibly extravagant, but the shoes would have cost two thousand dollars *each*, if she hadn't bought them parsimoniously in a sale. She had no prospect of getting any cash for the rest of the month, punished by her beastly bankers for her 'credit history'. Her credit history, as far as she was concerned, was that Mummy had written a lousy will that allowed her evil stepfather to steal all of Nancy's money. Her heroic response had been to spend as if justice had been done, as if she were restoring the natural order of the world by cheating shopkeepers, landlords, decorators, florists, hairdressers, butchers, jewellers, and garage owners, by withholding tips from coatcheck girls, and by engineering rows with staff so that she could sack them without pay.

On her monthly trip to the Morgan Guaranty – where Mummy had opened an account for her on her twelfth birthday – she collected fifteen thousand dollars in cash. In her reduced circumstances, the walk to Sixty-Ninth Street was a Venus flytrap flushed with colour and shining with adhesive dew. She often arrived home with half her month's money spent; sometimes she counted out the entire sum and, seeming mystified by the missing two or three thousand, managed to walk away with a pink marble obelisk or a painting of a monkey in a velvet jacket, promising to come back that afternoon, marking another black spot in the complex maze of her debt, another detour on her city walks. She always gave her real telephone number, with one digit changed, her real address, one block uptown or downtown, and an entirely false name – obviously. Sometimes she called herself Edith Jonson, or Mary de Valençay, to remind herself that she had nothing to be ashamed of, that there had been a time when she could have bought a whole city block, never mind a bauble in one of its shops.

By the middle of the month she was invariably flat broke. At that point she fell back on the kindness of her friends. Some had her to stay, some let her add her lunches and her dinners to their tabs at Jimmy's or Le Jardin, and others simply wrote her a large cheque, reflecting that Nancy had barged to the front of the queue again and that the victims of floods, tsunamis, and earthquakes would simply have to wait another year. Sometimes she created a crisis that forced her trustees to release more capital in order to keep her out of prison, driving her income inexorably lower. For Eleanor's funeral, she was staying with her great friends the Tescos, in their divine apartment in Belgrave Square, a lateral conversion across five buildings on two floors. Harry Tesco had already paid for her air ticket – first class – but she was going to have to break down sobbing in Cynthia's little sitting room before going to the opera tonight, and tell her the terrible pressure she was under. The Tescos were as rich as God and it really made Nancy quite angry that she had to do anything so humiliating to get more money out of them.

'You couldn't drop me off on the way, could you?' Kettle asked Nancy.

'It's Nicholas' private car, dear, not a limo service,' said Nancy, appalled by the indecency of the suggestion. 'It's really too upsetting when he's so ill.'

Nancy kissed Patrick and Mary goodbye and hurried away.

'It's St Thomas' Hospital, by the way,' Patrick called after her. 'The ambulance man told me it's the best place for "clot-busters".'

'Has he had a stroke?' asked Nancy.

'Heart attack, they could tell from the cold nose – the extremities go cold.'

'Oh, don't,' said Nancy, 'I can't bear to think about it.'

She set off down the stairs with no time to waste: Cynthia had made her an appointment at the hairdresser's using the magic words, 'charge it to me'.

When Nancy had left, Henry offered the aggrieved Kettle a lift. After only a few minutes of complaint about the rudeness of Patrick's aunt, she accepted and said goodbye to Mary and the children. Henry promised to call Patrick the next day, and accompanied Kettle downstairs. To their surprise they found Nancy still standing on the pavement outside the club.

'Oh, Cabbage,' she said with a wail of childish frustration, 'Nicholas' car has gone.'

'You can come with us,' said Henry simply.

Kettle and Nancy sat in the back of the car in hostile silence. Up in front Henry told the driver to go to Princes Gate first, then on to St Thomas' Hospital and finally back to the hotel. Nancy suddenly realized what she had done by accepting a ride. She had forgotten about Nicholas altogether. Now she was going to have to borrow money from Henry to catch a taxi back to the hairdresser's from some god-forsaken hospital in the middle of nowhere. It was enough to make you scream.

Nicholas' fall, the commotion that followed, the arrival of the ambulance men, and the dispersal of some of the guests had all eluded Erasmus' attention. When Fleur had burst into song in the middle of her conversation with Nicholas, the words 're-clothe us in our rightful minds' sent a little shock through him, like a piercing dog whistle, inaudible to the others but pitched perfectly for his own preoccupations, it recalled him to his true master, insisting that he leave the muddy fields of inter-subjectivity and the intriguing traces of other minds for the cool ledge of the balcony where he might be allowed, for a few moments, to think about thinking. Social life had a tendency to press him up against his basic rejection of the proposition that an individual identity was defined by turning experience into an ever more patterned and coherent story. It was in reflection and not in narrative that he found authenticity. The pressure to render his past in anecdote, or indeed to imagine the future in terms of passionate aspirations, made him feel clumsy and false. He knew that his inability to be excited by the memory of his first day at school, or to project a cumulative and increasingly solid self that wanted to learn the harpsichord, or longed to live in the Chilterns, or hoped to see Christ's blood streaming in the firmament, made his personality seem unreal to other people, but it was precisely the unreality of the personality that was so clear to him. His authentic self was the attentive witness to a variety of inconstant impressions that could not, in themselves, enhance or detract from his sense of identity.

Not only did he have an ontological problem with the generally unquestioned narrative assumptions of ordinary social life but he also, at this particular party, found himself questioning the ethical assumption, shared by everyone except Annette (and not shared by Annette for reasons that were in themselves problematic), that Eleanor Melrose had been wrong to disinherit her son. Setting aside for a moment the difficulties of judging the usefulness of the Foundation she had endowed, there was an undeniable potential Utilitarian merit to the wider distribution of her resources. Mrs Melrose might at least count on John Stuart Mill and Jeremy Bentham and Peter Singer and R. M. Hare to look sympathetically on her case. If a thousand people, over the years, emerged from the Foundation having discovered, by whatever esoteric means, a sense of purpose that made them into more altruistic and conscientious citizens, would the benefit to society not outweigh the distress caused to a family of four people (with one barely conscious of the loss) who had expected to own a house and turned out not to? In the maelstrom of perspectives could a sound moral judgment be made from any other point of view but that of the strictest impartiality? Whether such a point of view could ever be established was another question to which the answer was almost certainly negative. Nevertheless, even if Utilitarian arithmetic, based on the notion of an unobtainable impartiality, were set aside on the grounds that motivation was desire-based, as Hume had argued, the autonomy of an individual's preferences for one kind of good over another still offered a strong ethical case for Eleanor's philanthropic choice.

There had been a widespread sense of relief when Fleur accompanied Nicholas' stretcher downstairs and appeared to have left the party, but ten minutes later she reappeared resolutely in the doorway. Seeing Erasmus leaning on the balustrade staring pensively down at the gravel path, she immediately expressed her alarm to Patrick.

'What's that man doing on the balcony?' she asked sharply, like a nanny who despairs of leaving the nursery for even a few minutes. 'Is he going to jump?'

'I don't think he was planning to,' said Patrick, 'but I'm sure you could persuade him.'

'The last thing we need is another death on our hands,' said Fleur.

'I'll go and check,' said Robert.

'Me too,' said Thomas, dashing through the French windows.

'You mustn't jump,' he explained, 'because the last thing we need is another death on our hands.'

'I wasn't thinking of jumping,' said Erasmus.

'What were you thinking about?' asked Robert.

'Whether doing some good to a lot of people is better than doing a lot of good to a few,' Erasmus replied.

'The needs of the many outweigh the needs of the few, or the one,' said Robert solemnly, making a strange gesture with his right hand.

Thomas, recognizing the allusion to the Vulcan logic of *Star Trek II*, made the same gesture with his hand.

'Live long and prosper,' he said, smiling uncontrollably at the thought of growing pointed ears.

Fleur strode onto the balcony and addressed Erasmus without any trivial preliminaries.

'Have you tried Amitriptyline?' she asked.

'I've never heard of him,' said Erasmus. 'What's he written?'

Fleur realized that Erasmus was much more confused than she had originally imagined.

'You'd better come inside,' she said coaxingly.

Glancing into the room Erasmus noticed that the majority of the guests had left and assumed that Fleur was hinting tactfully that he should be on his way.

'Yes, you're probably right,' said Erasmus.

Fleur reflected that she had a real talent for dealing with people in extreme mental states and that she should probably be put in charge of the depression wing of a psychiatric hospital, or indeed of a national policy unit.

As he went indoors, Erasmus decided not to get entangled in more incoherent social life, but simply to say goodbye to Mary and then leave immediately. As he leant over to kiss her, he wondered if a person of the predominantly narrative type would desire Mary because he had desired her in the past, and whether he would be imagining that fragment of the past being transported, as it were, in a time machine to the present moment. This fantasy reminded him of Wittgenstein's seminal remark that 'nothing is more important in teaching us to understand the concepts we have than constructing fictitious ones'. In his own case, his desire, such as it was, had the character of an inconsequential present-tense fact, like the scent of a flower.

'Thank you for coming,' said Mary.

'Not at all,' mumbled Erasmus, and after squeezing Mary's shoulder lightly, he left without saying goodbye to anyone else.

'Don't worry,' said Fleur to Patrick, 'I'll follow him at a discreet distance.'

'You're his guardian angel,' said Patrick, struggling to disguise his relief at getting rid of Fleur so easily.

Mary followed Fleur politely onto the landing.

'I haven't got time to chat,' said Fleur, 'that poor man's life is in danger.'

Mary knew better than to contradict a woman of Fleur's strong convictions. 'Well, it's been a pleasure to meet such an old friend of Eleanor's.'

'I'm sure she's guiding me,' said Fleur. 'I can feel the connection. She was a saint; she'll show me how to help him.'

'Oh, good,' said Mary.

'God bless you,' Fleur called out as she set off down the stairs at a cracking pace, determined not to lose track of Erasmus' suicidal progress through the streets of London.

'What a woman!' said Johnny, watching through the doorway as Fleur left. 'I can't help feeling that somebody should be following her rather than the other way round.'

'Count me out,' said Patrick, 'I've had an overdose of

Fleur. It's a wonder she was ever allowed out of the Priory.'

'She looks to me as if she's just at the beginning of a manic episode,' said Johnny. 'I imagine she was enjoying it too much and decided not to take her pills.'

'Well, let's hope she changes her mind before she "saves" Erasmus,' said Patrick. 'He might not survive if she rugby tackles him on a bridge, or leaps on him while he's trying to cross the road.'

'God!' said Mary, laughing with relief and amazement. 'I wasn't sure she was ever going to leave. I hope Erasmus made it round the corner before she got outside.'

'I'm going to have to leave myself,' said Johnny. 'I've got a patient at four o'clock.'

He said goodbye to everyone, kissing Mary, hugging the boys, and promising to call Patrick later.

Suddenly the family was alone, apart from the waitress, who was clearing up the glasses and putting the unopened bottles back into a cardboard box in the corner.

Patrick felt a familiar combination of intimacy and desolation, being together and knowing they were about to part.

'Are you coming back with us?' asked Thomas.

'No,' said Patrick, 'I have to go and work.'

'Please,' said Thomas, 'I want you to tell me a story like you used to.'

'I'll see you at the weekend,' said Patrick.

Robert stood by, knowing more than his brother but not enough to understand.

'You can come and have dinner with us if you like,' said Mary.

Patrick wanted to accept and wanted to refuse, wanted to be alone and wanted company, wanted to be close to Mary and to get away from her, wanted the lovely waitress to think that he led an independent life and wanted his children to feel that they were part of a harmonious family.

'I think I'll just . . . crash out,' he said, buried under the debris of contradictions and doomed to regret any choice he made. 'It's been a long day.'

'Don't worry if you change your mind,' said Mary.

'In fact,' said Thomas, 'you should change your mind, because that's what it's for!'

14

As he laboured up to his bedsit, a miniature roof conversion with sloping walls on the fifth floor of a narrow Victorian building in Kensington, Patrick seemed to regress through evolutionary history, growing more stooped with each flight, until he was resting his knuckles on the carpet of the top landing, like an early hominid that has not yet learned to stand upright on the grasslands of Africa and only makes rare and nervous expeditions down from the safety of the trees.

'Fuck,' he muttered, as he got his breath back and raised himself to the level of the keyhole.

It was out of the question to invite that adorable waitress back to his hovel, although her telephone number was nestling in his pocket, next to his disturbingly thumping heart. She was too young to have to squeeze herself out from under the corpse of a middle-aged man who had died in the midst of trying to justify her wearisome climb to his inadequate flat. Patrick collapsed onto the bed and embraced a pillow, imagining its tired feathers and yellowing pillowcase transformed into her smooth warm neck. The anxious aphrodisiac of a recent death; the long gallery of substitutes substituting for substitutes; the tantalizing thirst for consolation: it was all so familiar, but he reminded himself grimly that he had come back to his non-home, now that he was alone at last, in order to be unconsoled. This flat, the bachelor pad of a non-bachelor, the student digs of a non-student, was as good a place as he could wish for to practise being unconsoled. The lifelong tension between dependency and independence, between home and adventure, could only be resolved by being at home everywhere, by learning to cast an equal gaze on the raging self-importance of each mood and incident. He had some way to go. He only had to run out of his favourite bath oil to feel like taking a sledgehammer to the bath and begging a doctor for a Valium script.

Nevertheless, he lay on the bed and thought about how determined he was: a Tomahawk whistling through the woods and thudding into its target, a flash of nuclear light dissolving a circle of cloud for miles around. With a groan he rolled slowly off the bed and sank into the black armchair next to the fireplace. Through the window on the other side of the flat he could see slate roofs sloping down the hill, the spinning metal chimney vents glinting in the late-afternoon sun and, in the distance, the trees in Holland Park, their leaves still too tight-fisted to make their branches green. Before he rang the waitress – he took out the note and found that she was called Helene – before he rang Mary, before he went out for a long sedative dinner and tried to read a serious book, under the dim lighting and over the maddening music, before he pretended that he thought it was important to keep up with current affairs and switched on the news, before he rented a violent movie, or jerked off in the bath because he couldn't face ringing Helene after all, he was going to sit in this chair for a while and show a little respect for the pressures and intimations of the day.

What exactly had he been mourning? Not his mother's death – that was mainly a relief. Not her life, he had mourned her suffering and frustration years ago when she started her decline into dementia. Nor was it his relationship with her, which he had long regarded as an effect on his personality rather than a transaction with another person. The pressure he had felt today was something like the presence of infancy, something far deeper and more helpless than his murderous relationship with his father. Although his father had been there with his rages and his scalpels, and his mother had been there with her exhaustion and her gin, this experience could not be described as a narrative or a set of relationships, but existed as a deep core of inarticulacy. For a man who had tried to talk his way out of everything he had thought and felt, it was shocking to find that there was something huge that he had failed to mention at all. Perhaps this was what he really had in common with his mother, a core of inarticulacy, magnified in her case by illness, but in his case hidden until he heard the news of her death. It was like a collision in the dark in a strange room; he was groping his way round something he couldn't remember being there when the lights went out. Mourning was not the word for this experience. He felt frightened but also excited. In the post-parental realm perhaps he could understand his conditioning as a single fact, without any further interest in its genealogy, not because the historical perspective was untrue, but because it had been renounced. Someone else might achieve this kind of truce before their parents died, but his own parents had been such enormous obstructions that he had to be rid of them in the most literal sense before he could imagine his personality becoming the transparent medium he longed for it to be.

The idea of a voluntary life had always struck him as extravagant. Everything was conditioned by what had gone before; even his fanatical desire for some margin of freedom was conditioned by the drastic absence of freedom in his early life. Perhaps only a kind of bastard freedom was available: in the acceptance of the inevitable unfolding of cause and effect there was at least a freedom from delusion. The truth was that he didn't really know. In any case he had to start by recognizing the degree of his unfreedom, anchored in this inarticulate core that he was now at last embracing, and look on it with a kind of charitable horror. Most of his time had been spent in reaction to his conditioning, leaving little room to respond to the rest of life. What would it be like to react to nothing and respond to everything? He might at least inch in that direction. As he had been trying to tell an unreceptive Julia, he was less persuaded than ever by final judgements or conclusions. He had long suffered from Negative Incapability, the opposite of that famous Keatsian virtue of being in mysteries, uncertainties and doubts without reaching out for facts and explanations – or whatever the exact phrase was – but now he was ready to stay open to questions that could not necessarily be answered, rather than rush to answers that he refused to question. Maybe he could only respond to everything if he experienced the world as a question, and perhaps he continually reacted to it because he thought that its nature was fixed.

The phone on the little table next to him started to ring and Patrick, dragged out of his thoughts, stared at it for a while as if he had never seen one before. He hesitated and then finally picked it up just before his answerphone message cut in.

'Hello,' he said wearily.

'It's me, Annette.'

'Oh, hi. How are you? How's Nicholas?'

'I'm afraid I've got terrible news,' said Annette. 'Nicholas didn't make it. I'm so sorry, Patrick, I know he was an old family friend. He actually stopped breathing in the ambulance. They tried to revive him when we got to the hospital, but they couldn't get him back. I think all those electrodes and adrenalin are so frightening. When a soul is ready to go, we should let it go gently.'

'It's difficult to find a legal formulation for that approach,' said Patrick. 'Doctors have to pretend that they think more life is always worth having.'

'I suppose you're right, legally,' sighed Annette. 'Anyway, it must be overwhelming for you, and on the day of your mother's funeral.'

'I hadn't seen Nicholas for years,' said Patrick. 'I suppose I was lucky to get a last glimpse of him when he was on top form.'

'Oh, he was an amazing man,' said Annette. 'I've never met anyone quite like him.'

'He was unique,' said Patrick, 'at least I hope so. It would be rather terrifying to find a village full of Nicholas Pratts. Anyhow, Annette,' Patrick went on, realizing that his tone was not quite right for the occasion, 'it was very good of you to go with him. He was lucky to be with someone spontaneously kind at the time of his death.'

'Oh, now you're making me cry,' said Annette.

'And thank you for what you said at the funeral. You reminded me that Eleanor was a good person as well as an imperfect mother. It's very helpful to see her from other points of view than the one I've been trapped in.'

'You're welcome. You know that I loved her.'

'I do. Thank you,' said Patrick again.

They ended the conversation with the improbable promise to talk soon. Annette was flying back to France the next day and Patrick was certainly not going to call her in Saint-Nazaire. Nevertheless he said goodbye with a strange fondness. Did he really think that Eleanor was a good person? He felt that she had made the question of what it meant to be good central – and for that he was grateful.

Patrick took in the news that Nicholas was dead. He pictured him, back in the sixties, in a Mr Fish shirt, making venomous conversation under the plane trees in Saint-Nazaire. He imagined himself as the little boy he had been at that time, shattered and mad at heart, but with a ferocious heroic persona, which had eventually stopped his father's abuses with a single determined refusal. He knew that if he was going to understand the chaos that was invading him, he would have to renounce the protection of that fragile hero, just as he had to renounce the illusion of his mother's protection by acknowledging that his parents had been collaborators as well as antagonists.

Patrick sank deeper into the armchair, wondering how much of all this he could stand. Just how unconsoled was he prepared to be? He covered his stomach with a cushion as if he expected to get hit. He wanted to leave, to drink, to dive out of the window into a pool made of his own blood, to cease to feel anything for ever straight away, but he mastered his panic enough to sit back up and let the cushion drop to the floor.

Perhaps whatever he thought he couldn't stand was made up partly or entirely of the thought that he couldn't stand it. He didn't really know, but he had to find out, and so he opened himself up to the feeling of utter helplessness and incoherence that he supposed he had spent his life trying to avoid, and waited for it to dismember him. What happened was not what he had expected. Instead of feeling the helplessness, he felt the helplessness and compassion for the helplessness at the same time. One followed the other swiftly, just as a hand reaches out instinctively to rub a hit shin, or relieve an aching shoulder. He was after all not an infant, but a man experiencing the chaos of infancy welling up in his conscious mind. As the compassion expanded he saw himself on equal terms with his supposed persecutors, saw his parents, who appeared to be the cause of his suffering, as unhappy children with parents who appeared to be the cause of their suffering: there was no one to blame and everyone to help, and those who appeared to deserve the most blame needed the most help. For a while he stayed level with the pure inevitability of things being as they were, the ground zero of events on which skyscrapers of psychological experience were built, and as he imagined not taking his life so personally, the heavy impenetrable darkness of the inarticulacy turned into a silence that was perfectly transparent, and he saw that there was a margin of freedom, a suspension of reaction, in that clarity.

Patrick slid back down in his chair and sprawled in front of the view. He noticed how his tears cooled as they ran down his cheeks. Washed eyes and a tired and empty feeling. Was that what people meant by peaceful? There must be more to it than that, but he didn't claim to be an expert. He suddenly wanted to see his children, real children, not the ghosts of their ancestors' childhoods, real children with a reasonable chance of enjoying their lives. He picked up the phone and dialled Mary's number. He was going to change his mind. After all, that's what Thomas said it was for.